Praise for A Willow Tree Becomes a Forest

"Chinese have been immigrating to the United States since the 1800's. They built the railroads, Chinatowns, and farmlands, infusing their culture into their adopted country. Yet, their history is not known to most Americans.

This story bears witness to this history. The book has many valuable archives, documents, photos, and materials related to the experiences of a single Chinese American family. Using these primary sources, this multigenerational story takes us back to a laundry in Salem, Oregon, in the 1800s, a nearby hop farm, and into the lives of young men going off to defend their country in WWII.

This novel tells an important story that fosters our understanding of a significant chapter in Chinese American history. It is a personal story about who we are and how we got to where we are today, told with great imagination and passion. I thoroughly enjoyed reading this fascinating novel, and I am sure you will too."

Li-Rong Cheng, PhD
Professor, Historian, Linguist,
Inductee into the Women's Museum Hall of Fame
Founder of the SDSU Chinese American Cultural Center

CHINESE CULTURAL
CENTER

"This novel is a joy to read. The characters had me immediately invested in them. Being familiar with the Snake River area, I was there with them as they traveled up the river to the massacre site. The Nez Perce had a stone monument installed at the site around ten years ago, as a memorial for the men who were murdered. It is in Nez Perce, English and Cantonese. I did help with the language carved into the monument. Judging by his photo, Hop Lee could've passed for a Nez Perce. In those days, Nez Perce were not treated well by most of society, and I imagine Asian people suffered the same. Working on a Chinese-owned farm was less tense than working on a White-owned farm. I also know love for fish was most likely a commonality the Nez Perce and Chinese shared".

Thomas Gregory/ tátlo
Nez Perce Language Team Leader
Nez Perce Language Program
Nez Perce Tribe

Chinese Massacre Cove Memorial in English, Cantonese, and the Nez Perce languages.

"Dive into Russ Low's captivating novel, 'A Willow Tree Becomes a Forest,' where the journey of Low Sun Fook unfolds as he arrives in the US and Oregon in 1877, embarking on a voyage into the unknown with unyielding courage. As he navigates this unfamiliar terrain, Low Sun Fook's resilience, resourcefulness, and intelligence shine, shaping a remarkable new life for himself.

Unveiling the tender humanity of the protagonist is a rare gem in this narrative, infusing it with warmth and empathy. In a landscape where stories of Chinese men often remain distant, the portrayal of Low Sun Fook's interactions with his children radiates a truly extraordinary quality. This tale deviates from the norm, presenting a father who not only shares emotions but also fosters profound bonds with his children. A departure from the reticent grandfather stereotype often found in immigrant chronicles, here it's the father who exchanges love and emotion with his offspring, creating a poignant and heartwarming dynamic.

In this book, trials and triumphs intertwine, but it's the tapestry of joy, affection, and sorrow woven by this Chinese immigrant that resonates long after the final page. Low Sun Fook, known as Hop, becomes an individual you'd yearn to encounter, and through Russ Low's artful storytelling, you can now embark on this encounter. With anticipation building, readers can't help but wonder what marvels await in Low's next literary creation."

Sue Lee
Executive Director
Chinese Historical Society of America 2004-2017

"An amazing missing piece of Salem's history. The author deftly weaves family stories, heirlooms, and primary documents together to bring the history of Hop Lee and family to life. What an honor to be able to read Low Sun Fook's family journey through history and the Salem community. The narrative format provides a unique and personal view of their experiences. The Low family story is an important one that has been missing from our local museums and bookshelves for too long. It is an amazing celebration of small moments of joy, big dreams and heartaches all while weaving in lessons in our community history."

Kylie Pine
Curator and Collections Manater
Willamette Heritage Center

Connecting generations by gathering, preserving and sharing the Mid-Willamette Valley history

A Willow Tree Becomes a Forest

The Story of Hop Lee

Russell N. Low

Gum Saan Journeys Publications

Cover Background Photography by Bonnie Moreland
"Winter Sunset on Farmland in the Willamette Valley"

978-1-7344937-6-4 – Paperback

Library of Congress Control Number: 2023907164

For more information about this book
contact threecoins1@yahoo.com

DEDICATIONS

This is work is dedicated to the memory of Candace Tom and Christopher Sun Fook Low, who shared my fascination with and passion for preserving the life of our grandfather, Low Sun Fook, aka Hop Lee.

To Loren Low, aka Gwunde, my father, and the irrepressible fourth son of Hop Lee, whose stories kept the memories of Duke and Barney and the hop farm alive for future generations.

And to the millions of immigrants whose independent spirit and diligence built and enriched our nation.

Loo Dak Ming 4th Generation out of 22 Loo Family generations recorded in the Jiapu.

Contents

Prologue - Visiting Father – 1938

G wunde quietly stepped down off the Little House's porch, careful not to wake his mother and sis sleeping in the front room. It was well past midnight, his favorite time to visit Father. The bright moonlight cleared his path across the bottomlands as he navigated his way through the endless rows of hop vines. Frankly, he could have done it in pitch black as he knew the way by heart.

The locals called the six hundred acres hop farm by its American name, Fir Grove Farm. Gwunde, however, preferred the Chinese name his father had given the place, Fook Chong Ranch, when he purchased the original Alvis Smith Homestead in 1914 for a small fortune.

Gwunde stopped to take in a deep breath of the cool Keizer night air. Keizer was six miles north of Salem, Oregon, where he had spent his childhood. Across the fields, he heard the neighing of Queen, Pat, and King, Percheron draft horses, coming from the barn near the pasture.

Gwunde quietly set off across the hop fields heading for the highlands on the Northern edge of the farm. The ground was soft, having been recently tilled.

After a few minutes, Gwunde froze when the snap of a twig pierced the silent night air. "Crack!"

Crouching down behind a hop vine, Gwunde could hear his heart beating. Motionless, he waited. After what seemed like an eternity, a deep voice broke the silence, "Get up, boy. I know you are there."

Standing, Gwunde let out a relieved sigh, "Yellow Fox! What are you doing out in the hop fields at this hour?"

"What am I doing out here? I live out here, boy. Where are you going, and why are you so noisy?"

"I didn't think anyone else was out here."

"That's the idea of being silent, so no one else will know, Gwunde. I taught you better. And I know where you're going, to see your father."

Yellow Fox had been on the farm for decades. The locals knew him as Jim Yee, the Chinese hop man. The Chinese called him Jing Gai. For a long time, Gwunde had known that Jim Yee was a Nez Perce whose name was tilípeʔ maqsmáqs. [1]

He didn't say much, but he watched out for Hop Lee's son. When he and Hop met as young men, Yellow Fox had been a fugitive without a home. Hop had taken Yellow Fox in and given him a new life and identity. He had even come to like Cantonese food and could speak passable Cantonese.

"Come on, boy. We will go together to visit the spirits."

The two crossed the moonlit fields and entered the fir grove, passing through a grouping of ten willow trees at the edge of the property. They came upon a six-foot fence, which the two men scaled quickly, silently dropping down into the edge of Claggett Cemetery.

"He's over here, Jim."

"I know where Hop's body lies. I follow you here every night."

Gwunde looked at the Nez Perce, wondering how he could have missed someone so large. Yellow Fox stood six feet in his moccasins.

"But his spirit is not here, Gwunde. Hop's spirit is free to roam the earth and the heavens. He is at peace."

Gwunde sat down next to his father's grave and thought of the man he had known so briefly. The Chinese characters on the stone were a mystery to Gwunde. But the boldly carved letters "FATHER" told of the man he came to visit every night. Yellow Fox squatted next to his young friend, keeping him company.

Breaking the silence, Yellow Fox offered, "Someday, I will tell you the story of how

---

1. tilípeʔ maqsmáqs is Nez Perce for Yellow Fox.

we met. It is a good story. Hop's life is a good story, and you, his son, will continue his journey." [2]

Low Sun Fook Gravestone - Claggett Cemetery, Keizer, Oregon

2. Some of the earliest graves in the Salem area are in Claggett Cemetery, with the first being that of a four-month-old daughter of Alvis and Sally Pugh Smith, who settled on the 643-acre homestead. The Smith log house and farm buildings were located in the same grove where the Fir Grove Farm buildings were located.

Chapter One

Loo Sun Fook Arrives in Albany, Oregon – 1877

L oo Sun Fook looked away from his journal's blank pages and saw the lush Oregon countryside passing by as the 'City of Salem' steamboat made its way down the Willamette River towards Albany.

Ha Chun Chong Village with rice fields. Low Family Collection

The endless green pastures and fir trees looked nothing like his home in Southern China. He imagined Haiyan on the coast of Toishan with its rice fields, mountains, and beaches along the Pearl River Delta. The months he had been traveling seemed like years.

His daydreaming was rudely interrupted by a sharp jab in the side. Looking to his left, he saw his ever-smiling cousin, Loo Sai Yee.

"When are you going to write something in that journal? You have been staring at it for hours. Just make an entry so you can start this great novel!" laughed Sai Yee.

"It's not that easy, cousin. We have already come so far, but the words are stuck in my pen," explained Sun Fook.

The boys were on their way to Albany, Oregon, to work on the railroad. Both boys were dressed in identical blue cotton Chinese jackets with five buttons and loops and loose blue pants called *dai dong foo*. The boys laughed at that word and its meaning, "Big Crotch Trousers."

"It's easy. Just write the end of the story first! But start in the front like an American book, not on the last page like a Chinese book. You always say you want to learn the White customs. And use a brush," chided Sai Yee.

Sun Fook looked down at his little journal, turned to the first page, and let the words flow as his life in Gum Saan began in earnest.

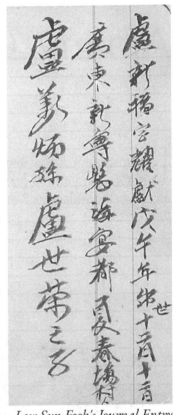

Low Sun Fook's Journal Entry 1877. Low Family Collection

"I am Loo Sun Fook, born in the Chinese year 4556 or 1858 Guangdong Province, Toishan Hoiyin, in the village of Ha Chun Chong. I am Loo Sai Wing's son and Loo Man Bing's grandson."

As the steamboat slowed, he hurriedly added the last line to his first entry, "I wish to be an American."

Willamette River at Albany, Oregon. Public Domain. California Historical Society and University of Southern California Libraries.

The Willamette steamboat came to a stop at the dock. The boys grabbed their few belongings and headed down the aisle for the exit. Holding on to the handrail Sai Yee ran down the gangplank onto the wooden docks, ready to start this new adventure.

"Hurry up, cousin! They are going to build the railroad without us if you don't get moving!"

Loo Sun Fook [1] took his time stepping off the boat, watching all the White people around him hurrying along their way. As he stepped onto the dock, he looked around for Sai Yee, but his cousin was already off exploring. Each boy had tucked his queue inside his Mandarin hat to be less conspicuous.

It is hard to be inconspicuous traveling with Cousin Sai Yee.

---

1. Low Sun Fook was his given name. His married name is Loo Yao Hing. To the people of Salem, he was "Hop Lee."

Occident Stern-wheel paddle steamer at Albany 1875. Wikimedia Commons.

Sun Fook smelled the delicious aroma of *cha siu bao*.[2] It was early morning, and the boys had not eaten since yesterday morning. He knew the Chinese merchants were preparing food in their outdoor ovens. So, he headed in the direction of the smell, assuming that Albany's Chinese quarter was nearby.

As he walked along the platform past the seagulls looking for a free meal, Loo Sun Fook spotted something on the ground up ahead. As he approached, it looked like a small brown leather wallet stuffed with American paper money. He had seen people using these odd papers in Portland stores where their ship had docked last week.

Sun Fook bent down to pick up the wallet, looking around for its owner. It was heavy and bulging from its contents. Suddenly he spotted a tall man in a black coat up ahead, frantically searching his pockets. Sun Fook ran up to the man and tugged on his sleeve.

"*Sin saan* [3], is this what you are looking for?"

---

2. cha siu bao is a Cantonese barbecue-pork-filled bun

3. Sin Saan – Cantonese for Mister

The man turned around, revealing a friendly bearded face and a bright gold star on his jacket. "Yes! Thank you, son. Where did you find it? I have a month's wages in that pouch. You just saved me from a very long walk home!"

Examining the wallet, he continued, "My name is Thomas Reynolds. I am the Sheriff of Marion County. Here, let me reward you," said Sheriff Reynolds as he pulled out a bill from the wallet.

Loo Sun Fook looked at the man with a puzzled expression. "No, I cannot take your money. My father taught us to be honest and to remember the family name."

Thomas smiled at the boy and wondered how long he would last before someone took advantage of him. "Well, then, what is your name, son?"

"I am Loo Sun Fook and the son of Loo Sai Wing from Guangdong, China!" he proclaimed proudly.

"Well, that is quite a mouthful, and I will never remember all that. You need an American name. I will call you Jim after my father. You can be called Jim Loo."

Sun Fook beamed at his new American name but corrected, "In Chinese, we put our family name first. I will be Loo Jim!"

Thomas extended his hand, and Loo Jim happily shook the hand of his first White

First Street Albany, Oregon. Public Domain.

friend in Gum Saan. Their chance encounter would grow into a friendship, lasting for over 40 years.

Loo Sun Fook finally caught up with his cousin heading east on 1st Avenue towards the smells of breakfast in the Chinese quarter of Albany at 2nd and Lyon Streets. Sai Yee's sense of smell, fueled by his empty stomach, was as keen as his own! The two boys arrived at Quing Sing's store, their family friend, whom they called Uncle.

Sing was famous in these parts. Two years earlier, Sing had lit off Chinese rockets for the New Year's celebration in Albany. The locals had never seen such a spectacle, making Quing Sing an instant celebrity. This year he supplied the rockets and fireworks for the American July 4th celebration. Business was good.

Entering the store, Loo Sun Fook spotted Uncle Sing high on a ladder, restocking his shelves.

"Greetings, Uncle! My parents send their respects and this humble gift." Sun Fook handed Uncle the gift from the family village in Hoiyan.

"Well, hello, boys!" exclaimed Quing Sing from the top of the ladder. "I have been expecting you! But you are much taller than the little boys I last saw in the village!"

The boys had not seen Uncle since they were children but remembered his fun sense of humor. Even back then, he liked to explode rockets for the village boys.

"*Saig Fahn Mah*? (Have you eaten)

"You must be hungry!"

Both boys nodded in unison as the smells from the kitchen were almost too much to bear.

"Come sit down. I will prepare a little feast for my traveling nephews!"

Sun Fook and Sai Yee did not have to be asked twice. They scampered into the kitchen and sat at the table as Uncle set it, bringing trays from the steamer filled with dim sum, rice porridge, and Sun Fook's favorite, sticky rice wrapped in banana leaves.

The boy's eyes grew wide with anticipation, and their empty stomachs were growling loudly.

Ha Chun Chong Village with Pond. Low Family Collection

"Eat! Eat!" instructed Uncle. "No time to lose. We have people to meet before you join the railroad crew!"

The breakfast was delicious. Loo Sun Fook couldn't help but think of his mother and the family breakfast in their ancestral home in Hoiyin. His parents and his two brothers now seemed so very far away.

That evening, Sun Fook was frantically rummaging through his bag.

"Where is it? I can't lose it! My father paid a lot of money to that fortune teller, and he made me promise to protect it with my life."

"What are you talking about?" Sai Yee asked.

"You know. The fortune-teller scroll that shows my life's journey. Ahah! Here it is," he announced, pulling the folded-up paper from the bottom of the bag.

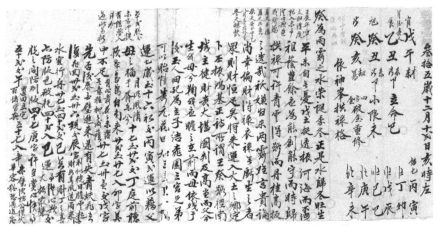

Fortune teller scroll for Low Sun Fook. Low Family Collection.

Four dates are in the upper right-hand corner of Hop Lee's fortune. Low Family Collection.

"What's it all mean?"

"Every important date and event in my life is shown on this fortune."

"Yeah, sure. Let me see that paper."

"See, right here, it says I was a "happy-go-lucky" child. And over here, it says I was born in winter during a time of great waters. But it's everything else, coming down the road is such a great mystery.

"Look at these dates at the top. Only the first one, 1858, makes any sense. That was the year I was born," Sun Fook continued. "After that, I have no idea what the other three dates mean."

Sai Yee inspected the paper, "We can't worry about your life 50 years from now, cousin. That's crazy."

"I guess you're right."

"Well, you better see what it says about your working on the railroad because we have an early start tomorrow."

"Yes, and I know how you hate getting up early." Sun Fook smiled and returned the fortune to the bottom of his bag.

Fortune Teller Scroll describes a happy-go-lucky childhood. Low Family Collection

Chinese Fortune Teller 1879. Wikimedia Commons.

Chapter Two

"zhuī zhú" Hungry Chinese Chase Sun Fook Down the Tracks! – 1877

The Oregon and California Railroad had come to Albany in December 1871, bringing the promise of economic and industrial growth. Local businessmen raised $50,000 to ensure the rails would not bypass Albany. The five hundred Chinese men brought in to build the railway settled in Albany, forming the Chinatown at Second and Lyon Streets. [1]

The desire to extend the rail lines was inevitable. The Willamette Valley & Coast Railroad was the brainchild of Colonel T. Egenton Hogg, who dreamed of connecting Corvallis and Albany, Oregon, with Yaquina Bay on the Pacific coast. Hogg planned on running the railroad from Yaquina Bay Eastward through Oregon and into Idaho. He brought hundreds of Chinese workers to build the railroad to Yaquina Bay. After many false starts, the WV&C finally broke ground on May 17, 1877.

The boys had risen early to enjoy Uncle's breakfast before heading to the train depot to meet the Willamette Valley & Coast Railroad gang boss.

---

1. zhuī zhú Cantones words meaning "to chase"

"*Fai di laa*! Eat faster, boys!" encouraged Uncle as the boys finished their rice porridge.

"You don't want Colonel Hogg to leave without you!"

Uncle knew everyone in Albany. So as soon as he heard that they were hiring Chinese to build the railroad to Yaquina Bay, he immediately went to the Kwong Mow & Co. on Ferry Street and signed up his nephews. "Don't keep the Colonel waiting for you. Stand up straight! I may have told him you are a little bigger and stronger than you look."

The boys stood up from the table and wiped the last of the breakfast from their mouths. Uncle handed each boy a red envelope.

"Here is a little something to keep you going."

"Uncle Sing, you are too generous," Sun Fook replied as he tried to refuse Uncle's gift.

"Nonsense! I must take care of my nephews. You are far from Ha Chun Chong Village, and I am your only family in Gum Saan. So, take this and make your old Uncle happy."

"Thank you, Uncle," both boys said in near unison as they received Uncle Sing's gift and placed the red envelopes in their tunics.

"Now hurry, boys, and don't forget to write me to send word about how you are doing on this railroad."

With that, the two cousins headed down Lyon Street towards the depot and their next adventure in America. Arriving at the depot, Sai Yee spotted the men from the WV&C in a tent sitting behind a table surrounded by a small group of Chinese.

"That must be the place to sign up!"

"I hope they have our names from Uncle Sing. He said everything was set," replied Sun Fook.

When they finally reached the front of the line, the man looked up from his ledger with a pen in hand. "What are your names?"

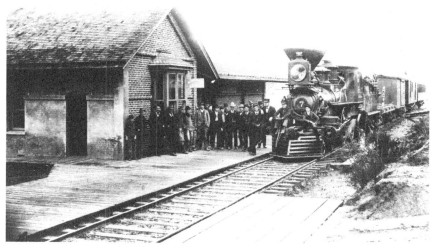

Willamette Valley & Coast Railroad.

"I am Loo Sun Fook from Hoiyin in Kwangtung China. You can call me Loo Jim."

"And I am his cousin, Loo Sai Wing, also from Hoiyin. The village's name is Ha Chun Chong."

"Alright, you can be Loo Jim, and we will call you Sai. Now, what do you know how to do? You are a lot smaller than your Uncle told us."

"I am stronger than I look, and I can learn any job you show me," proclaimed Sai Wing proudly, trying to stand up straight.

"And what do you know how to do, Loo Jim? You look a little bigger than Sai. Do you know how to swing a sledgehammer?"

Loo Jim quickly looked around and spotted some empty cooking pots and utensils scattered about behind the tent.

"I know how to cook! That's right! I am a cook! I will feed the men and keep them fat and happy so they can work hard for you!"

Sai Yee stared at his cousin in amazement but said nothing.

Willamette Valley & Coast Railroad

"OK, Loo Jim, we need a cook for this crew, and you fit the bill. So both of you go to that tent and pick up your provisions and tools. And Loo Jim, pick up those pots, and get your kitchen set up."

As the boys left the tent, Sai Wing had a pick and shovel, and Sun Fook carried his pots, pans, and utensils.

"When did you learn how to cook, cousin?" Sai Wing hissed.

"As soon as he started talking about sledgehammers! I'll figure it out. It can't be that hard to cook. Our mothers did it every day, and I ate plenty of their cooking!"

Sai Yee rolled his eyes, "I hope you figure it out quickly. These Chinese look hungry and a little grumpy!"

"You can put your supplies on that car. We will be taking you all to the end of the line," the White gang boss ordered as he herded the Chinese toward the waiting train.

Loo Jim and Sai Yee followed the other Chinese men as they climbed onto the flatbed rail car. Loo Jim had his hands full with all the pots and cooking gear, but with Sai Yee's help, they managed to get everything loaded just as the train began to pull away from the Albany Station.

"Look at the view, cousin!" exclaimed Sai Yee. "Smell the clean air!"

"It smells like smoke to me!" Loo Jim replied as the black smoke from the wood-burning locomotive briefly enveloped the rail cars.

The train rumbled along through the flatlands west of Albany, eventually reaching the town of Corvallis. As the train continued, they passed through small towns named Philomath and Wren. The rolling hills turned into forests of green fir trees. The air was now cooler as the train climbed into the low foothills. The train finally came to a stop. There were two rickety wooden buildings at the end of the track.

"They call this place Burnt Woods. We are about 30 miles from Albany. This is where the tracks end. You get off here and walk the rest of the way," ordered the gang boss.

"You can set up camp over by that stand of trees."

The Chinese climbed off the flat car and made their way to the fir grove clearing. They quickly set about putting up tents and making camp. The tents were up before long. Loo Jim and Sing Yee started a fire, and soon a big kettle of water was boiling to make tea for the men.

Loo Jim was rummaging through the food supplies.

"Where is the tea?"

He pulled out baskets full of dried seafood. Next came bags of dried oysters, shrimp, cuttlefish, and dried vegetables. Next, there were huge bags of rice. Fortunately, the railroad men knew what the Chinese liked to eat and had well-stocked provisions for the crew. Finally, at the bottom of a burlap sack, Loo Jim found large tins full of black tea leaves!

"Gotcha!"

Opening a tin, he scooped out a handful of the tea leaves and then looked around for the pot of boiling water.

He whispered to Sai Wing, "Cousin, should I put these tea leaves in the pot or each cup?"

Sai Yee groaned, "This is going to be trouble for you, Sun Fook! Put them in the pot."

Sai Yee in Gum Saan

Loo Jim threw the tea leaves into the pot and stirred them around for good measure before replacing the lid. "This isn't so hard!"

Pouring the tea into cups, he served the Chinese men, who had all washed up before dinner.

"Here you are, my friends. Enjoy some hot tea!"

The men drank the tea appreciatively and then started a game of Mahjong to pass the time before dinner.

In the kitchen, Loo Jim puzzled over the ingredients at his disposal.

"Sai Yee, what would you like for dinner?"

"You are the cook, cousin! But you had better get moving because that game of Mah Jong won't keep them busy for long."

"OK! We can have rice and stir fry with oysters and vegetables! How does that sound?"

Loo Jim set about putting the dried oysters and vegetables into pots of water to soften them up.

I wonder how much food to make. There are ten men plus Sai Yee and myself.

He scooped two large mounds of oysters and loads of dried vegetables into the pots of water.

Well, that looks about right!

"Sai Yee, how do I make the rice? Should I just put it in the wok with the oysters and vegetables? Yes! That sounds good!"

"No! You have to wash it and then boil it in water until it is cooked just right!"

"How much water?"

"You are impossible! Didn't you ever help your mother cook?"

"No, that's women's work!"

"Well, a woman might be more useful right now! Cover the rice with enough water so that the water is one knuckle above the rice! Bring it to a boil on the campfire and let it cook slowly. Not too fast, or you will burn it!"

"OK! Thanks, cousin."

Loo Jim set about washing the rice and then added just enough water measuring with his knuckle as Sai Yee had instructed. He then placed the pot over the campfire before turning his attention to the wok to begin his stir-fry creation.

He added the now-plump oysters, vegetables, and bean sprouts to the wok, added some sesame seed oil, and quickly began to stir his creation over the fire. The sizzling aromas were intoxicating.

"Look, cousin! It is magnificent!"

1860s cooking pot over campfire.

"Not bad, Sun Fook! Here, put some of this Hoisin sauce into it for good Chinese flavor."

Adding the thick brown sauce to the mixture, Loo Jim beamed at his creation. "Mother would be proud!"

"The rice! It's boiling over into the fire! I told you to cook it slowly!"

Loo Jim gasped as he saw his huge rice pot sputtering foamy water into the campfire. The smell of burnt rice filled the camp. "Quickly, pull it off the fire!"

The boys tried to remove the pot of rice from the fire, but it was too hot and burned their hands when they grabbed it. The water was now gone, and the smell of burnt rice was growing stronger.

"Aiyaah! What are we going to do, Sai Yee?"

"Here, you grab the other end of these two sticks, and we will lift the pot off the fire."

The boys carefully positioned the sticks under the pot's lip and gently lifted it off the fire.

"Careful! Don't let it tip over!"

Placing the pot on the ground, the boys looked at one another expectantly.

"You take the lid off, Sai Yee!"

"No way! This is your doing, Sun Fook! You take it off."

Loo Jim slowly removed the lid stuck to the top of the pot. The rice was cooked but looked brown and smelled burnt.

"Let me stir it around. It might not be so bad on the bottom," Loo Jim offered hopefully.

He scooped off the top layer of rice, revealing the brown crusty, burnt mess underneath.

"Oh no! Now, what can I do? Let me make another pot of rice."

"Too late, cousin," groaned Sai Yee. "The men have finished their game and are coming over with their plates! You better give them the stir fry and try to hide the rice."

As the ten Chinese gathered around Loo Jim served them his stir-fry creation to appreciative quips. "Not bad, kid! You can cook like a woman!"

"Leave the kid alone! He did alright!"

"Well, we need some rice now, kid."

Loo Jim froze, not knowing whether to admit his failure or to try to fake it. He decided to fake it.

Scooping out the least burnt part of the rice, he explained, "This is a special rice dish with some added flavoring to make it more woodsy!"

Sai Yee rolled his eyes and waited as the men tried the rice.

"You burned the rice!"

"No Chinese cook burns the rice! How do you expect us to eat this?"

The men threw their rice at Loo Jim and glared at him angrily.

"It is not so bad, really! He will get better with a little practice," offered Sai Wing.

"He's no cook!"

"They pay him more to cook for us, and this is what he serves us!"

"We should run him off before he kills us with his cooking!"

The men rose and started to come across the camp. Loo Jim needed no further encouragement. He grabbed his gear and ran out of camp. The angry Chinese gave chase with their picks and shovels in hand, but Loo Jim was younger and quicker as he ran off toward Albany.

Looking over his shoulder, Loo Jim called out, "Cousin take care and come find me at Uncle's store when you get back to Albany!"

"So long, cousin!" Sai Yee couldn't help but laugh as Loo Jim ran down the tracks ahead of the angry and hungry Chinese mob. He seemed to be pulling away as he went over the first hill into the evening sky.

Yakima Railroad at Blodgett, Oregon.

Chapter Three

Low Sun Fook the Albany Laundryman

It took two days to walk back to Albany. Loo Jim was nervous about revealing the ignominious end to his brief stint as a railroad cook. But he needn't have worried. As Loo Jim told the story of the angry Chinese men chasing him down the tracks, Uncle's concerned expression evaporated, and he burst out laughing.

"Ha! Ha! You must have been a real sight! Too bad your mother didn't teach you how to cook! Or too bad your Uncle didn't teach you how to tell a fib! But at least you can run fast. Wait till your father hears this one."

Uncle was clearly enjoying hearing about Loo Jim's adventure and predicament. Changing the subject, Loo Jim handed Uncle the red envelope he had given him just yesterday. "Sorry, Uncle. Here is the money back."

"Nonsense, nephew! It was worth every penny just to hear your story! Keep it. You will need money to get yourself set up here in Albany."

"Thank you, Uncle. I don't deserve this gift."

"How would you like to work in a Chinese laundry? I have a friend who is opening a second laundry and could use a smart young man to work for him. You aren't afraid of some honest work, are you? There is no cooking involved! I promise!" Grinning widely, Uncle slapped Loo Jim on the back.

That afternoon Uncle Sing took Loo Jim over to the Chun Wah Laundry on Main Street.

"*Neih hou*, Ah Chun," Uncle called out as they entered the laundry. "This is my nephew Sun Fook. He wants to be called Loo Jim! Crazy boy. But he is a hard worker!

"*Neih hou*, Loo Jim," beamed Ah Chun. "Your Uncle tells me you want to learn to be a laundryman. Well, this is the place to learn! I have two Chinese laundries in Albany and have most of the laundry business in town. It is the American way to become rich if you work hard!"

Loo Jim perked up at the mention of making money and the American way. Making his fortune was why he had come to Gum Saan in the first place. To make a fortune the American way! This little Chinese laundryman had his full attention.

"Teach me everything, please, Ah Chun. I want to be successful just like you!"

"Well, Sing. This young boy has the right attitude. I can see that he wants to be a lot more than a laundry worker! Before long, he will be driving me out of business!"

"Don't worry. We can send him to Salem to expand your business up North."

"First things first. Let's start with the boiler room. Follow me."

A counter with shelves underneath dominated the front room of the laundry. Behind the counter were rows upon rows of wooden shelves stuffed with neatly stacked packages wrapped in brown paper. Each package of clean laundry was neatly wrapped and tied with a string. Chinese characters on each package identified the owner. Ah Chun lifted a hinged section of the counter, allowing them to pass into the laundry's inner sanctum.

Next came the drying and folding room, where the men hung clean clothes from wires strung across the room. A wood-burning stove, dominating the chamber's center, kept the place heated and the flat irons leaning up against its side warm. As the men used the flat irons to press clothes, they quickly cooled off and had to be exchanged for a new hot flat iron.

"The next room is where the real work is done," explained Ah Chun.

The back room was humid and hot. The air smelled of soap, sweat, and food. The clothes were washed by hand in wooden troughs and then boiled in big pots on top of a wood-burning stove. It wasn't elegant, but it was effective.

Chinese laundry in Philadelphia 1876.

The men ate, slept, and gambled in the middle room of the laundry. Loo Jim spotted no less than six men working in the various rooms.

"OK, Loo Jim! Your job is to keep the stoves burning while stirring the boiling water vats to clean the clothes. Once the clothes in the pots are clean, you will wring out the water and then take them to the drying room. Any questions?"

"I would like to learn to iron the clothes," Loo Jim offered.

"First, you learn how to do the dirty work in the back room. If you are still here in a week, I will show you how to iron. Deal?"

"Don't you worry. I am not going anywhere!" promised Loo Jim.

One week later, Loo Jim was tired and dirty. His hands were raw, and his back ached, but to everyone else's surprise, he was indeed still there. He slept and ate in the laundry. He got up every day at 6 am and worked until late in the evening, only stopping long enough for a quick lunch and a very late supper. By the time supper was over, he was so tired all he could do was crawl into bed, where he immediately fell asleep.

Low Sun Fook in Albany, Oregon Crawford Paxton Photography

"OK, Uncle Chan. I am ready for my ironing lesson," Loo Jim reminded him.

"Well, you are still here, Loo! I guess we didn't work you hard enough! Ha! Ha!" When he saw that Loo Jim wasn't smiling, he quickly added, "Alright, today we teach you the finer points of spray ironing!"

Loo Jim followed Uncle Chan to the front room, happy to get a break from the drudgery of the washing and boiling room in the back.

As they walked into the drying room, recently washed clothes hung heavy on their wires. A potbellied stove stood in the middle of the floor with flat irons leaned up against its side. The men used hot flat irons to press out the wrinkles in the clean clothes.

But first, each Chinese ironer bent over an enamel bowl filled with water, sucking into his mouth just the right amount of water to spray out over the clean clothes with an explosive "Phhht!" Warm steam filled the room as the workers pressed the clothes on the padded ironing tables.

"OK, Loo! You try it! Here, bend down over the bowel like this! And then suck the water up through this metal pipe."

Loo Jim sucked up a mouthful of water and then waited. Now what?

"Alright, Loo, now spray the water out over this shirt. Make it a nice and even spray pattern like this. Phhht!"

Loo Jim spit the water out weakly, not covering even half the shirt.

"No! No! Use more humph and spray the water over the whole shirt. Now try it again. Suck and spray! Easy!"

Loo sucked up the water through the silver pipe and then was determined to get it right this time. 'Phhht!' The water sprayed out over the shirt in a magnificent waterworks display.

"Perfect Loo! You are a born ironing man!"

Loo Jim beamed as he looked at the moist shirt.

"Now grab that hot flat iron and press out all the wrinkles!"

The shirt steamed as it came into contact with the heated flat iron. The wrinkles magically disappeared as Loo slid the warmed iron over the shirt.

A Chinese laundry in San Francisco - "The Coming Man Washing, Drying, Sprinkling and Ironing Clothes: From Leslie's Illustrated Newspaper 14 May 1870. Public Domain

"OK, Loo. Now you need to practice so you can keep up with the pace. You have to move quickly. Spray and press! That's the stuff!"

Loo Jim spent the rest of the afternoon practicing and perfecting his technique for spraying and ironing. It was a skill he would teach to dozens of Chinese men in Salem in the years to come. For the first time, he felt he had learned a skill that could keep him employed here in Gum Saan.

After dinner, Hop pulled out his fortune and examined the predictions for his life, smiling as he began to fill in the blanks of his life's journey.

"Uncle Chan, look at the fortune teller's prediction for my life."

"You still have a long road to travel. How is he doing so far?"

"Well, the first prediction is pretty easy. I did have a happy childhood. I guess my lucky bird in the second prediction was my trip to Gum Saan when I was 19 years old. The third prediction is too weird. Something didn't work out, but something else comes into my life. What could that be?"

Uncle Chan laughed and explained, "That's your short career as a gourmet railroad chef turned Chinese laundryman!"

"Whoa! I guess I better hang on to this fortune. It's three for three so far!"

Predictions for Loo Sun Fook's Life

- 7 - 16 years has good fortunes from both mother and father
  Had a happy childhood

- From 17 – 22 years old this person will hear news from the lucky bird
  Came to America in 1877 when 19 years old

- 23 - 27 years something that he wants to do but it doesn't happen, but something else will come into his life. 1881 – 1885
  Career as a railroad cook ends abruptly, but learning Chinese laundry business opens new opportunities

Loo Sun Fook's fortune teller scroll - Prediction for his life. Low Family Collection

Chapter Four

Loo Jim Loses His Britches to a Scoundrel

Loo Jim had been working in Uncle Chan's laundry for almost a year. He knew it was time to strike out on his own, but he liked Albany and did not want to compete with Uncle Chan's business. Most of the White citizens of Albany had taken to the young, hard-working Chinese boy. But there were a few who took exception to anyone different. And for as much as Loo wanted to be a successful American businessman, he looked and dressed like a Chinese, which made him different.

Sunday was Loo Jim's one day to relax. It was also the only day he had time to do his own laundry. So, he took off his everyday clothes and proceeded to wash them in the tub in the back room of the laundry. He scrubbed his loose blue pants. Even now, the name *dai dong foo* or big crotch trousers made him laugh. They sure were comfortable. It was a sunny day, so Loo went out back and hung the pants from the clothesline running from the woodshed to the laundry. The warm spring sun felt good on his face. The air was clean and smelled of lilacs. He liked Oregon because the weather was much cooler here than back home in Toishan. He remembered those sweltering summers, working in the rice fields back home. Green rice fields and ponds covered the Hoiyin landscape. Oregon was green as well, from the seemingly endless meadows. Personally, he preferred the green meadows and fir trees here in Oregon.

Oregon Wildflowers and meadows. Tom McCall Nature Preserve. Oregon. Bonnie Moreland. Public Domain

Today would be a good day to go for a walk in the meadows surrounding Albany, Loo mused.

Loo spent the day exploring the countryside with Uncle Sing. Uncle had lived here for over ten years and knew every creek, meadow, and footpath for miles around. It was a relaxing day that made Loo forget the laundry business but not about his dream to make it rich here in America.

"Tell me, Uncle, how will I ever have my own business here in America? I'm already 24 years old! I have to make a name for myself, and I worry that I will never do that while working for Uncle Chan as his ironing boy," Loo lamented.

"Don't worry so much, nephew! You are still young and have your whole life to make your name and fortune here in Oregon. Just relax! It will happen when the time is right."

Loo Jim heard his Uncle but was still impatient for his life in America to take hold. "Yes, of course, you're right, Uncle Sing."

That afternoon when he got back from his walk with Uncle Sing, Loo went out back to bring in his laundry. He found the clothesline, but his pants were missing. Thinking the wind might have blown them off the line, he searched around the backyard. No pants! Just as he turned to go back into the laundry, he spotted Joel Manly from Schmeer's Livery dancing around the street. He was wearing Loo Jim's Chinese pants! Joel was the town prankster and was used to making everyone laugh at his antics.

"Hey, look at me! I am a Chinaman! Loo's baggy pants fit me like a charm! All I need now is a pigtail!"

The townspeople roared with laughter. "Joel, say something in Chinese!"

"I am a Ching Chong Chinaman!" Joel called out as he danced around Main Street. "I hope Loo appreciates how good I look in his pants!"

Loo Jim ran up to Manly, "Give me my pants back! You have no right to take my property!"

"Ah, don't get your feathers ruffled, Loo. I was just having a little fun."

"I want those pants now! Give them to me, or I will call the Sheriff to arrest you for stealing!"

"OK. OK. Just relax, Loo. I can't very well take them off here in the middle of Main Street. I'll go home and change and will put your precious pants back on the clothesline where I found them."

Loo looked at Manly skeptically, "Alright, but do it now, and I will charge you to have them cleaned!"

Later that afternoon, Loo Jim looked out the laundry's back door and found his pants were on the line as promised with a little something extra courtesy of Joel Manly. His pants were coated in coal tar and axle grease and were covered with white chicken feathers!

Loo was livid. He ran down to Sheriff Reynold's office and demanded justice.

"Look at these pants! They are ruined!"

Thomas Reynolds had not forgotten the kindness Loo Jim had shown him by returning his wallet. Besides, he was responsible for naming Loo Jim.

"They're a mess, Jim. Manly is a jokester, but this is going too far!"

"You should arrest him!"

"Well, I could throw him in jail, but then you would have an enemy here in Albany. The townsfolk would not like you, and you still would not have your pants back."

Loo stopped and thought about it and saw the wisdom of the Sheriff's words.

"I have another idea, Jim. Let's go and pay Mr. Manly a visit and see if we can find a better way to work this out."

They found Joel working at Schmeer's Livery wearing his own pants and an embarrassed expression when he saw Loo Jim and Sheriff Reynolds approaching.

"I understand you have been having some fun at Loo's expense."

"No harm intended, Sheriff. I was just horsing around!"

"Destroying another man's property isn't amusing, Joel. I can take you in and have you locked up for this prank!"

Joel was now looking more concerned as he thought about his options.

"However, Jim does not want to cause you any trouble. He asked me to be lenient. So, here's my decision, Joel. You can pay Jim the $1.50 for the pants, or you can be arrested right here, and I will take you back to the jail to spend some time behind bars at the taxpayer's expense. Personally, I would love to have some company back at the jail. It's your choice, Joel. What's it going to be?"

Joel hesitated for several seconds, looking at the Sheriff and then at Jim, searching for a way out of his predicament. He was cornered but did not want to give up his money so easily.

Growing impatient, the Sheriff pulled out his handcuffs and spun Manly around, slapping the cuffs on his wrists.

"Never mind. I'm taking you in!"

"Sheriff Reynolds, please don't throw Mr. Manly in jail. I know he has a family to feed," Loo Jim said just as he had rehearsed with the Sherriff.

It did not take Manly more than a second to see the wisdom of paying up for his fun. He freed up his hands, reached into his pants, and pulled out a wad of money.

"Here's the $1.50 Sheriff."

"It's not for me, and you owe Jim an apology."

Manly turned to Loo Jim. "Here's the money for your pants, Jim. I am, ahh, am sorry for causing you trouble and ruining your pants."

Loo Jim took the money with a smile.

It was clear to Joel and the townsfolk that Sheriff Reynolds was all too eager to have him behind bars. It was only thanks to the generosity of Loo Jim that Manly had gotten off easy. Loo became something of a celebrity around Albany as the Chinese who had kept Joel out of the pokey.

For Loo Jim, this day had been a life lesson in the value of public opinion and goodwill. Sheriff Reynolds helped him to see the wisdom of taking the higher road. From that day forward, Joel Manly was Jim's friend and loyal customer. Loo also kept a closer watch on his laundry.

He Wore The Breeches.

The other evening one of the employes in Schmeer's Livery stable was struck with a mad desire to dress himself up in Oriental costume and consequently purloined a pair of Hop Lee's Sunday breeches from the line in the next lot. They fit him like a charm, and for several hours said employe exhibited himself in Hop Lee's immaculate apparel much to the amusement of the passers by. His curiosity being then satisfied, he profusely illustrated them with coal tar and axle greese and hung them on Hop Lee's back fence. Hop failed to appreciate the joke in the manner that it was intended, and yesterday morning the knight of the curry comb was informed that he could either take the breeches and pay for them or be arrested. He paid his $1 50 like a little man, but whether or not he intends to wear the breeches in the future remains to be seen.

"He Wore the Breeches" Morning Daily Herald (Albany)

Chapter Five

Loo Jim Arrives in Salem – 1884

L oo said his goodbyes to his friends and customers in Albany when suddenly Uncle Sing came out of his store with his bag packed

"Well, let's go, Nephew! No time to waste."

"Uncle, where are you going?"

"I am going with you to Salem, of course. Someone has to keep an eye on you, so those big city folks don't take advantage of you."

"Thank you, Uncle, but I can take care of myself."

"Enough said. I am coming, and Sai Lee will watch after my store while I help you set up your laundry business in Salem. Here, take your bag. I packed your things and lunch."

Loo Jim knew it was no use to argue with Uncle Sing once his mind was made up. Besides, he could use the company in the big city. Salem had over 3,000 people and 300 Chinese. He would miss little Albany, his home for seven years, but it was time to move on.

Just then, the Wells Fargo Overland Stage Coach pulled up. It was magnificent! Its bright yellow wheels slowly came to a stop with a cloud of Oregon dust surrounding the dark red coach.

"Hi, Jim! Are you going with us to Salem?"

Loo Jim looked up at the driver of the stagecoach. It was Sheriff Reynolds! He had given up his lawman's star for a job managing the Wells Fargo Express Office in Salem.

"I thought you might like to have a friend with you on your trip up to Salem, so I talked the regular driver into giving me this route today."

Jim smiled and remembered how Thomas Reynolds was the first White friend he had made in Albany.

"Thanks, Sherriff!"

"Not the Sheriff anymore. I gave up that star, and I am now an ordinary citizen of Salem."

Loo and Uncle Sing hopped on board and climbed up on top of the stagecoach. Mr. Reynolds sat ramrod straight in the front holding the reins in one hand and a whip in the other. Inside, the coach was a bit crowded with nine passengers sitting three abreast in three rows. Two seats on the ends were facing fore and aft, and the third seat was in the middle. It was a tight squeeze with only 15 inches for each passenger. The passengers hardly noticed the fine leather padding lining the seats and coach interior.

Reynolds turned around as Loo and Uncle found their spot on top between the luggage and freight.

"Isn't she a beauty, Jim? This Concord stagecoach can hold 4,000 pounds."

Two bearded men came out of the Wells Fargo Express Office and loaded a green locked strongbox, straining to hoist the box up to the driver's seat. An armed guard rode shotgun to protect the valuables. He held his double-barreled, 10-gauge shotgun across his lap, ever-watchful of the crowd gathering around the stagecoach.

Reynolds hopped down and finished his last-minute inspection, walking slowly around the coach, checking the six sleek chestnut bay horses' running gear and harnesses. The hostler held the reins of the two lead horses while Reynolds completed his inspection. Finally, satisfied that all was in order, he climbed back aboard and took up the reins and whip.

"All aboard!" He nodded to the hostler, who let loose the reins of the lead horses and stepped aside. Reynolds gently pulled up the reins, then suddenly loosening them and releasing the brake, he shouted, "G-long! H-up, there!"

Oregon California Wells Fargo Stage Coach

The six horses lurched forward, traces snapped tautly, and the stage leaped into motion. Loo Jim felt the coach rock backward and then roll forward as the coach trundled along. They were on their way! The horses picked up speed as they entered into a smooth gait, with all six horses in perfect synch, their front legs hitting the ground simultaneously.

From his perch on top of the stage, the beauty of six horses moving as one entranced the young Jim.

"Aren't they gorgeous, Uncle," Jim exclaimed, pointing at the six bay horses. As the coach picked up speed, his queue flew behind him, blowing freely in the wind.

"Is this your first time on a stagecoach, Jim?" Reynolds shouted over his shoulder above the noise of the rolling wheels.

"Yes, Sherriff Reynolds," Loo replied.

"Call me Thomas. I am not the Sherriff. Today, I am your Wells Fargo Express driver. Frankly, Jim, it's a lot more fun!"

The trip from Albany to Salem was 26 miles and took most of the day to complete, with the 2500-pound coach averaging just over five mph. They stopped midway for a change of horses, which took about 30 minutes.

As the stagecoach pulled into the Salem Overland Stagecoach Station behind the Chemeketa Hotel, a reporter from the Oregon Statesman came out to interview the passengers. [1]

Loo hopped off the stagecoach first, followed by Uncle Sing. Mr. Reynolds was busy helping to unload the strongbox while the guard stood by with his shotgun in hand.

"Well, young man, why are you coming here to Salem?"

Loo looked at the reporter, wondering what he wanted. Before he could form a word, Uncle Sing replied, "This is the new owner of the Hop Lee Wash on Commercial Street!"

"Well, Hop Lee, welcome to Salem. Now step aside so these White passengers can get out of the coach."

All nine passengers looked tired and stiff as they squeezed out of the coach.

"I am glad we sat on top, Uncle. Why did he call me Hop Lee?

"Me too. The view and company were better, and our tickets were cheaper! You should get used to the name Hop Lee. You never know; it just might stick!" Uncle Sing laughed.

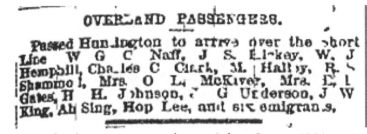

Overland passengers arrival notice Salem, Oregon. 1884

---

1. The Overland Stagecoach station was a barn like building located immediately behind the Chemeketa Hotel on Commercial Street. The Hop Lee and Hop Sing Laundry was directly across the street.

2

—ele—

---

2. In 1880 the Chinese population in Oregon had tripled in a decade to over
   9,500 Chinese, comprising 5.5% of the state's population. In 1880, 25% of
   the population of Portland and 36% of Astoria's population were comprised
   of Chinese immigrants.

Chapter Six

Raging Fire Destroys Hop Lee Laundry – June 3, 1885

S alem's Chinese Quarter was located on State Street between Liberty and High Streets. Over 300 Chinese men lived and worked in this part of the city where few Whites ventured. The buildings were dilapidated, and the conditions were unsanitary and crowded. Exposés in the local paper had described the unsavory conditions in great detail. For Loo Jim, his new business on Commercial Street was a dream come true. Uncle Sing helped him buy the business from Ah Fong, who had found some success as a Chinese laundryman but now wanted to retire with his money and go back to China.

"I have had enough of those endless days working from sunrise to after sunset. And the lonely nights are the worst. It is all yours now, Loo. Good luck!"

Ah Fong waved at Loo Jim as he handed him the key and hurried out the rickety wooden door.

Loo Jim stood and watched Fong scurry down Commercial Street, stirring up a small cloud of dust. The dirty glass window at the front of the laundry proclaimed in bold red letters, "Hop Lee Laundry." The letters were backward, but Loo knew the letters by heart forward or backward. This laundry was his home, his business, and his future in America. Finally, he was on his way! Loo Jim took out his journal and entered the name of his new American business, Hop Lee Laundry. The four Chinese characters spelled out his future in his adopted country.

Uncle Sing was right. The name Hop Lee stuck like glue. Once the people of Salem read the notice in the Oregon Statesman and met the young Chinese man at his business, there was no turning back. He was Hop Lee forevermore. Loo tried to correct them, but it was no use.

"Don't worry about the name," Uncle Sing reassured him. "It is a good thing that they have a name they can remember. Whites have a short memory for Chinese names. To them, Hop Lee sounds Chinese!"

"I guess you are right, Uncle. I just liked being Loo Sun Fook and then Loo Jim. Now I am Hop Lee. It doesn't sound too American to me."

"No, but they like you, and that is more important for business, nephew!"

The tinkling bell at the front door announced Hop's first guest, a White man in a dark suit with a graying beard and hair and piercing dark eyes. He stuck out his hand. "Mr. Lee, I am Ed Hirsch your new landlord. Welcome to the old Rector Building." [1]

Hop shook his hand and sized up the man behind the beard. Hop's first words surprised Hirsch.

"I will have your rent the first of every month, and I'll do your laundry for free."

"And you might as well call me Hop. The name seems to have stuck."

Edward Hirsch. Kay Low's album

---

1. Marion County pioneer William H. Rector (1806-1890) erected this two-story, wood-frame building that housed commercial and governmental organizations. Located on the west side of Commercial Street, between Trade Street and Ferry Street, this pioneer building served as Salem's first city hall and, after a fire destroyed the OR State Capitol #1 in 1855, accommodated temporarily the state legislature, as well. The Rector Building was at least on the same block and may be the same spot as the rebuilt Hop Lee laundry on S. Commercial Street.

"Well, Hop. You and I will get along just fine. Are you going to hire help?"

"I need to work as much as possible to save up my money to make investments. For now, I'll invest in my own sweat."

"I may be able to help you out with your taxes and money matters. When I'm not collecting rent, I am the State Treasurer."

Hop eyes lit up. *Here's someone who understands money.*

This old two-story wooden building was Salem's first City Hall and briefly was home to the State Legislature. She's old, but has good bones."

"It's my first business," Hop replied proudly.

"Welcome to Salem, Hop. Good luck with your business plans."

It was true that the people of Salem took an immediate liking to Hop Lee. The hard-working and industrious young Chinese was more helpful and considerate than many of the White merchants. Hop Lee also took part in the town's community events and fundraising. This year he was the first to donate to the July 4th fundraising campaign. Hop gave $1.00, which was a considerable part of his day's earnings. If all worked out, Uncle Sing would sell the Salem town council the Independence Day fireworks.

"Hi, Hop!" Mr. R.J. Hendricks, the Oregon Statesman publisher, called out from the newspaper's office on Commercial Street.

"Hi, Mr. Hendricks. Nice day today. How is your business?" Hop asked in his best English.

Hop took every opportunity to practice his English. If he was to be an American, he had to speak and act like one.

"Hop, you can call me Bob. I'm younger than you."

Low Sun Fook, aka Hop Lee 1894.Provenance Trover. Low Family Collection

"Sure thing, Mr. Hendricks. How's your new newspaper?"

"Business is good, Hop. You should come by and talk to me about taking out an advertisement in the paper. It is the surefire way to build your laundry business."

Hop had never considered advertising, but if his friend Mr. Hendricks said it was good, then he was going for it.

"Thanks, Mr. Hendricks. I will come by this week."

"We're upstairs in this Griswold-Murphy building. See you soon, Hop!"

Robert Jackson Hendricks

Hop waved at his new friend and neighbor. He was happy to have such an important new friend here in Salem.

**NEW WASH HOUSE
HOP LEE**
South of Hop Sing, on Commercial St., South of Post Office, in the building owned by Ed Hirsch.
WASHING AND IRONING
Prices cheaper than any other place and better work. Three of his men are just from California and understand the science of washing as it is taught. He delivers washing.

Hop Lee's first laundry business advertisement in Orgon Statesman.

It was Wednesday evening, June 3rd, and Hop had finished another long day washing and ironing the shirts, pants, dresses, and underwear for the good people of Salem. Business was booming thanks to the advertisements in the paper. It was more than he could manage on his own. Hop hired three Chinese washermen from *Dai Fow* to help him with the work so he could attend to growing his business. Hong You and Hong Chan were brothers. You was 27 years old, and Chan was 20 years old. Both were experienced laundrymen. He hired his cousin, Loo Hop, as the cook.

Hop finished his simple meal of rice and fish and bok choi. His trusty wok was put away but not washed, and he went upstairs to sleep before beginning the whole process again in a few hours. The men slept downstairs in the back room.

Hop had been asleep for less than an hour when he was startled by someone shouting,

"Fire! Fire!"

Hop jumped out of bed and ran downstairs in his nightclothes. Smoke and flames engulfed the laundry. He covered his face, but the smoke and heat were too intense. He couldn't breathe.

"Loo! Hong! Get out! Fire! *Fai di lah!* Hurry!" Hop called out but couldn't see through the thick smoke. Where are they?

Blinded by the smoke, Hop bumped into the washtubs in the darkness. The fire was everywhere! All the walls were burning. The old wooden structure was going up in flames like tinder in a campfire.

Hop heard Loo's muffled voice and the men pounding on a door to the right.

"Help! We're trapped!"

Hop stumbled towards the voice. A huge washtub that had fallen from its shelf in the blaze blocked the room's door. Shoving the tub aside, he pulled open the door revealing three panicked Chinese men.

"Hurry! Grab the equipment and get out! The whole place is going up in flames!"

Chan and You picked up the basins and tubs while Loo grabbed his wok as they followed Hop out of the back room.

"Where is the door?"

Hop stumbled and tripped over something. He felt around the floor, found a flat iron, and realized he was in the front room. Grabbing the hot irons, he stood up and ran forward through the smoke and flames, bumping into the counter.

Humph! It knocked the wind out of him, but now he knew where he was! His eyes were burning, but in the darkness, he wouldn't be able to see anyway. He felt under the counter for the door to the secret compartment. Rescuing the cash box, Hop grabbed the counter and lifted it, revealing their escape route. Stumbling forward, he crashed into a wall. Reaching up, he felt the glass window. It was hot.

"The door is to the right!"

Bursting through the front door, Hop stumbled out onto Commercial Street.

The Hong brothers and Loo Hop were right behind him, loaded down with laundry equipment and cooking gear. The cool Salem night air engulfed them as they collapsed to the ground, coughing and gasping for air.

"Hop! How did you manage to get out of there!"

Hop looked up at RJ Hendricks, who was wearing a fireman's billed hat and pointing at his laundry building.

"The whole building is going up in flames! We thought you were burned alive for certain."

Rector Building on Commercial Street. Salem, Oregon.

Salem Fire Brigade 1885. Courtesy of Willamette Heritage Center.

Hop turned around and understood Hendricks's amazement. The entire barn-like Rector Building was engulfed in flames, destroying Hop's beloved laundry.

"Oh no! All the laundry has burned! How will I ever replace the shirts and underwear of your staff?" Hop groaned.

"Don't worry about those clothes. They aren't important, Hop. They can be replaced. I am just glad you got out alive!"

The Salem fire brigade had arrived on the scene with the first alarm accompanied by three firefighters teams. The Tigers came in for the first water, with the Capitals a very close second and Salem Engine Company No. 3, following right behind.

It was evident at once that the fire was a hot one, as it had a considerable headway. The horse-drawn steamer was stationed at the Chemeketa cistern, and within minutes four streams of water were playing on the flames from the engine. For 15 minutes, it looked as if the adjacent post office block would go as sparks and coals flew into adjoining buildings. The roof of the barn behind the Chemeketa Hotel across the street caught from a spark or coal but was immediately discovered and put out.

Tiger Fire Company No. 2 on Commercial Street in Salem, Oregon 1886. Courtesy of Willamette Heritage Center.

The embers from the blaze ignited The Chemeketa House roof four times that evening. Each time, Ah Toy, a wiry Chinese, dangled over the hotel's cornice by his wrist, quenching the fire with a wet broom.

The Rector Building burned to the ground, destroying the Hop Lee Laundry. It was a total loss. As the laundrymen later reported, a stovepipe going through the washhouse ceiling probably started the fire.

The Ladies Coffee Club was out in full force that night, offering hot coffee and assistance to Salem's firemen and citizens.

"Hello, Hop! We're so sorry to see your new business burn. Would you care for some coffee? My name is Mrs. Hundsaker and my helper this evening is Miss Lenta Stolz."

"Thank you, ma'am. We saved most of our equipment, but I am afraid the clothes we were washing burned up with the building."

"Pleasure to meet you, Miss Stolz," Hop hurriedly added, glancing at the teenager pouring the coffee.

Lenta smiled and moved on to the next group of firemen and spectators.

Marion Hotel Commercial Street Salem, Oregon. Ben Maxwell, Post Card. Low Family Collection.

"Don't worry about the burned-up shirts and underwear, Hop. Will you reopen your Hop Lee Wash?" Mrs. Hundsaker asked.

"Yes, but we will need to look at another location. Perhaps just up Commercial Street closer to the Post Office. We will have a reopening sale with discounts for all my American friends in Salem.

Hendricks, who had been listening to Hop's plans, spoke up, "Let me introduce you to my friend Nes. People call him A.N. Bush. His Father, Asahel Bush, owns Ladd & Bush Bank."

"Nes, this is Mr. Hop Lee, the proud owner of what once was the Hop Lee Laundry."

"Hop, this is Nes Bush, a fine photographer, and an honest banker."

"Hello, Mr. Bush," Hop greeted his new American friend.

"Come by the Ladd & Bush Bank anytime, Mr. Hop Lee. I hear good things about you."

A.N. Bush

"Just call me Hop like everyone else in Salem."

Hendricks interrupted, "I have to get back on the fire line and man the hoses. I joined the Tigers last March and this is the biggest blaze I've been called to fight. You should volunteer, Hop!"

"Sure thing, Mr. Hendricks, I mean R.J.," Hop waved as Hendricks raced back towards the fire.

The smell of smoke and wet smoldering embers was thick in the night air, but the chance meeting of these three young men that evening set a course that continued for four decades.

Hop considered his losses. It could have been much worse. No one was hurt. Later that night, he took out his journal and made another entry:

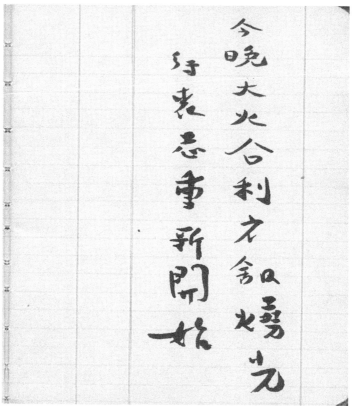

Hop Lee's journal entry 1885. Big fire tonight. Hop Lee Wash is a total loss. But do not despair. Tonight will be a new beginning, and I will become a successful American businessman.

Deep in thought, Hop planned out his next advertisement in the Capital Journal.

QUICK ORDERS—Promptly filled,
Increased facilities. Good work
and promptly delivered. Call on
the old reliable laundry. Hop Lee,
Commercial street.   10 3 3t*

Hop Lee's latest laundry advertisement. Daily Capital Journal.

Chapter Seven

Bust the Trust – 1887

Not only did Hop rebuild his laundry as promised, but with his advertising and keen business sense, he soon dominated the Salem laundry business. The Hop Lee Laundry moved into another wooden building on the same block at 191 South Commercial, just south of the Smith Brick Building on the southwest corner of Commercial and Ferry Streets. The Capital Journal soon occupied the same building, which was fortunate for Hop, who now included Ernst and Andy Hofer as friends in the newspaper business.

Smith Building SW corner of Commercial & Ferry Streets
with Post Office adjacent to Capital Journal.

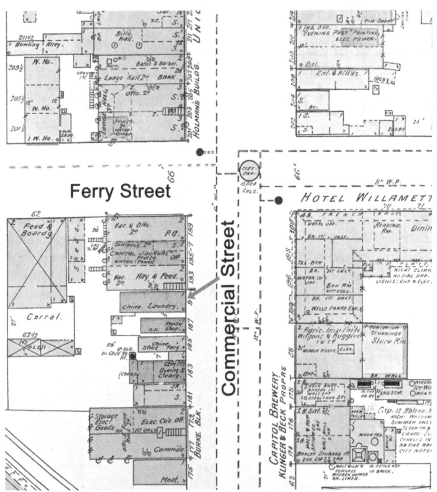

1895 Sanborn Fire Insurance Map Shows Hop Lee Laundry (arrow) at 191 S Commercial Street just south of the Smith Brick Building, which houses the Post Office and the Capital Journal office. Note the Willamette Hotel and Wells Fargo Express Office across Commercial street. Library of Congress.

Mr. Ernst Hofer and Mr. Andreas Hofer publishers of the Capital Journal located next door to the Hop Lee Laundry on S. Commercial Street in Salem, Oregon.

The Chinese had a monopoly on the soiled linen line in Capital City, making them a target of White businessmen and civic leaders who resented the "unfair" success of the Chinese. In September 1888, the Salem Chinese laundrymen banded together, forming a combine, and demanded higher prices for their services. The resulting anti-Chinese laundry fervor rose to cries of "Bust the Trust!" encouraging Salem's citizens to give their support to American laundries.

In November, workmen were busy remodeling the South Salem brick store's interior for the new steam laundry owned by D.T. Williams. The articles in the Weekly Oregon Statesman proclaimed that the new steam laundry would "bust the blasted Chinese wash-house trust" as soon as the machinery arrives from the East. The 10-horse power Kriebel engine, the steam washer, and the steam-heated ironing machine finally arrived on December 21, 1888. The steam laundry opened on Monday, January 14, 1889. D.T. Williams was out of business within the year. But the way of the future was clear, and it was steam. In 1891 Col J. Olmsted opened the Salem Steam Laundry at 230 Liberty Street in the building, formerly Salem's First Methodist Church, advertising that White labor performed all the work.

Salem Steam Laundry.

In Albany, the Chinese responded to a steam laundry business in Pendleton by reducing the price to $2 a month or 50 cents for family washings, which no White laundry could match.

Unable to compete on price, the advertising continued to grow uglier as the Salem Steam Laundry fought for market share.

Personals in Daily Capital Journal October 13, 1893:

> *Don't patronize a Chinaman when you can give your business to a White man. Take your laundry to the Salem Steam Laundry. Only White help employed.*

Three days later, on October 16, 1893, a follow-up entry in the Capital Journal fanned the growing Anti-Chinese fires.

Pride. Have you any pride in the prosperity of your city? If so, patron-ize the Salem steam laundry in preference to the Chinese washhouses. It is a permanent institution and employs only White help, all of whom contribute to the support of the place.

By January 1894, Olmsted was employing 25 White men at the Salem Steam Laundry. The Salem Steam Laundry continued in business for over 40 years. In 1921, it was sold to E.L. and C.H. Weider, the Albany-Magnolia Steam Laundries' joint owners. They later moved to High Street, becoming the Salem Laundry.

Fortunately, Hop had a following of loyal Salem customers. Even with Olmsted's Steam Laundry's competition, business was good for the man they called the Chinese laundry magnate. Even though Hop was the most popular Chinese amongst Salem's citizens, he worried about whether he could keep up the business with a promise of lower prices for his quality hand washing and ironing.

Hop was deep in thought when the bell on the front door of the laundry rang. Cling! Cling!

"Hello, Mrs. Hundsaker! How are you today?"

"Good morning, Hop! I was in the neighborhood, so I thought I would pick up my laundry and save you and that old horse of yours a delivery trip."

Once a day, Hop took out the horse-drawn wagon, delivering to his customers across the city the bundles of clean laundry wrapped in brown paper.

"Thank you, Mrs. Hundsaker, Bessie is getting some new horseshoes made at Herman Pohle's blacksmith shop on State Street so I'll be a little late today. But I am always happy to deliver your clean laundry to your home. It is part of my service to keep my customers happy."

"No need, Hop! I am here, and I will always be your customer. That old Colonel Olmsted, with his fancy steam machines, doesn't know a thing about quality hand laundry. Have you ever seen his work on collars? Pitiful!"

Pohle & Scriber's blacksmith carriage shop in on State Street between Commercial and Front Streets, Salem, Oregon, 1880's. Herman Pohle with wagon wheel. Ben Maxwell. SPL. Herman's daughter, Alma, sent flowers to Hop's family in 1925. The Pohle's lived on Court Street, two blocks from the Hop Lee's home at 125 N 13th Street.

"I am afraid he is already driving some of the other Chinese washhouses out of business. I just took over another Chinese laundry near the covered bridge from Wing Lee. He couldn't make a go of it with Olmsted siphoning off work for his steam machines."

"Why do you want another laundry, Hop?"

"Wing owed me money but had none to pay, so I had to take over his business. It's not worth much. He has more unhappy and unpaid employees than customers."

The front door to Hop's laundry flew open, followed by a bat-wielding Chinese!

"Lee! What do you want? I told you that Wing Lee owes you your wages!"

"I worked for that lying Chinese for three months, and he never paid me! Now you owe me my money! You took over his laundry, so pay up!"

"I have no money for you! Go and find Wing Lee!" Hop watched the livid Lee Young closely. There was no telling what he would do. "Now, go away! Your money is not my problem."

Lee Young's eyes bugged out, and the veins in his neck looked like they were about to explode. He clenched the bat tightly in his fist as he glared at Hop.

Hop was trying to push Lee towards the front door when Lee exploded and ran into the laundry's backroom with the bat raised over his head. He swung the bat down, smashing Hop's wash kettle over and over until it was a dented and mangled mess on the floor.

Lee was panting from the exertion. He looked up at Hop and immediately wished he were anywhere else. Lee ran out the door, bat in hand, leaving Hop with the pummeled wash kettle and Mrs. Hundsaker with her mouth agape.

Hop immediately went before Recorder Conn at City Hall and swore out a warrant for Lee Young's arrest, charging him with unlawful destruction of property. He later agreed to dismiss the case and pay costs, and Lee Young agreed to pay Hop Lee the price of the kettle, amounting to $17.

Western Electric Crank Phone.

While at City Hall, Hop observed first-hand the newly installed telephone at the police headquarters. The telephone company had been stringing their wires throughout Salem for weeks, but Hop had never seen their new-fangled device close up. The strange wooden box with two brass bells and black pieces fascinated Hop. It looked thoroughly modern. Immediately, he knew that he had to learn about this new American invention.

On the way back from the City Hall, Hop passed the store run by his good friend, George Sun. In Salem's Chinese quarter, George's first store had been at State and High Street. His current dry goods store was at Ferry and High Street. George sold coffee, tea, candy, and tobacco. George had come to Salem in 1868 when he was 16 years old. George was a leader amongst the Chinese in Salem and was known as the 'Mayor of Chinatown

"Hi, George! How is business?" Hop greeted his old friend with a smile.

"Can't complain, Hop. Now that I brought my wife, Leong Shee, over from China, life is better. Our children You, Woo, and Lai Yee are growing up here in America. They are Americans, just like you always said we should be someday."

"Yes, the children just wake up one day, and they are American! You and I have to work at it every day, and we may never get the chance, George. But I won't give up."

"Hop, I want to vote like an American. I have been here for 22 years, and I still can't vote! This is some kind of mistake. Others come over to this country and stay not very long three or four years. They can vote. Why I be here 22 years and cannot vote? I ought to be a citizen too. They must make a mistake. Something is wrong!" George fumed.

"You are right, George. But You, Woo, and Lai Yee will vote and are American children because of you. That is good. We will keep working at it. Someday I want to be a Statesman. I cannot be a laundryman my whole life. Besides, that Colonel Olmsted and his Steam Laundry are trying to steal the Chinese business."

"You need to think about the future, Hop. Maybe it is time for you to go back to China and find a wife so you can have American children like me! How old are you anyway?"

"I am 33 years old, George. You are right. A wife and children would be a comfort, but I need an American wife."

"You're crazy, Hop! Where will you find an American Chinese girl?"

"There are a few Chinese families with American-born children in Dai Fow. I will be patient. One of my laundry workers, Hong You, has a cousin who married a young girl in Dai Fow last year. Who knows? But enough idle talk. Let me help you load up your delivery wagon."

George Sun's other business was growing vegetables on land he leased at the McNary-Stoltz farm in Mission Bottom near Keizer. They grew radishes, beets, carrots, and green onions and sold them three bunches for 10 cents to local grocers who resold them for five cents a bunch. They washed the vegetables in Claggett Creek and bunched them in preparation for the two-hour ride over gravel roads into Salem.

"Thanks, Hop. I have to get back out to Mission Bottom to pick up tomorrow's delivery to the market. They need the vegetables by 6 a.m., so my day starts at 3 a.m. No sleep tonight! I can't wait for the boys to grow up so they can help."

"Where do you keep your horse, George? I'm thinking of getting a wagon and horse to deliver my clean bundles of laundry."

"At R.H.Westacott's livery on Ferry just west of the Post Office. It's really near your laundry, Hop."

"I'll check it out. Hope it's not too expensive."

"Good luck, Hop."

George hopped up on the wagon's front seat and took up the reins, but the old horses knew the way even without any encouragement from George. They started down Ferry Street, turning north on Commercial Street. The trip to the McNary Ranch was about six miles along the old River Road following the Willamette River towards Keizer.

"So long, George! Don't give up hope on the vote, my Chinese friend!"

George turned and waved at Hop as the horses and wagon disappeared in a cloud of Salem dust.

—— *ele* ——

Chapter Eight

Massacre at Deep Creek – May 1887

F or the Chinese in Gum Saan, trouble was brewing. Almost 400 miles east of Salem, along the Snake River at Hells Canyon, as many as thirty-four Chinese gold miners were ambushed and murdered by a gang of horse thieves and schoolboys from Wallowa County. The massacre site was adjacent to the Nez Perce Indian reservation.

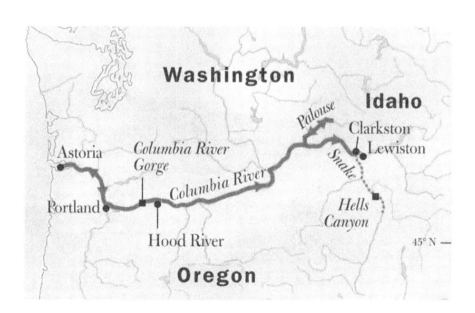

The crime was discovered when some of the bodies, thrown by the killers into the Snake River, were spotted near Lewiston, Idaho Territory, sixty-five miles to the north. News accounts reported that the bodies showed evidence of torture. The first accounts of the killings at Deep Creek said that ten men had been murdered. Eventually, the number of murdered Chinese would grow to become the worst murder in Oregon's history. The first accounts of the massacre appeared in the Lewiston Teller on June 16th, with the news reaching Salem soon thereafter.

As the OCN steamboat made its way along the Columbia River Gorge, Hop was deep in worry, hardly noticing the spectacular canyon scenery

"Aiyaah! I told him not to go, but Sai Yee wouldn't listen. I told him he was no miner. Ever since he finished working on that blasted railroad, he has been itching for another adventure. Being a clerk for uncle wasn't good enough for him. He went up this river to mine gold, and now he's missing," Hop lamented.

Columbia River. Bonnie Moreland. Public Domain. Mark 1.0

"Don't worry, Hop. We'll find your cousin. I remember when you boys arrived in Albany a decade ago. Sai Yee was wiry and tough. He's probably hiding out in the mountains," Thomas Reynolds tried to reassure his friend.

"They found those bodies of the murdered Chinese miners in Lewiston. Something bad has happened, and Sai Yee is in the middle of it all. I have to find him and bring him home. I promised his mother I would watch out for cousin."

"When was the last time you heard from him?"

"It's been over three months. There's been nothing but silence. Sai Yee is never silent. You can't keep him quiet, ever."

"Alright, Hop. I'm glad I'm going with you so I can keep you out of trouble. Eastern Oregon around Hells Canyon is pretty rugged, and the people out there are rough and lawless. I don't wear mystar any longer, but I am packing my Colt Peacemaker just in case, and I am prepared to use it."

The six-day trip up the Columbia and Snake Rivers followed the western half of the Lewis and Clark Expedition. It took them past Stevenson and The Dalles with the deepening canyons marking the start of the spectacular Columbia River

OCN Steamship on the Columbia River. Public Domain. California Historical Center and University of Southern California Libraries.

Gorge. Hop hardly noticed the waterfalls. Before reaching Richland, the paddle-wheeler turned northeast, heading upstream along the Snake River. Near the Idaho border at Clarkston, Washington, they switched to a smaller boat and continued the journey up the Snake River in route to Hells Canyon, the deepest gorge in North America.

Hop spent most of the trip at the bow of the ship wrapped in a blue wool coat, gazing ahead as if he hoped to spot his cousin along the shore.

I know you're here, Sai Yee. Just give me a sign, so I know you're alive.

There was no sign, and near the end of the journey, Hop was despondent and silent.

"I know he is dead, Thomas, and it's all my fault."

"We don't know that, Hop, and Sai Yee is a grown man who made up his own mind. Don't give up on him, Hop. Sometimes hope is all we have to go on."

The steamboat traveled through the deep gorge for another day. The scenery that engrossed the other passengers passed Hop by as if he were lost in a trance.

Hells Canyon, Oregon. Bonnie Moreland. Public Domain Mark 1.0

At Lewiston, Hop and Thomas disembarked and headed for the Sherriff's office. Located at the Snake and Clearwater Rivers' confluence, Lewiston, founded in 1861 in the Idaho Territory, served as a supply center for the mines. Hundreds of thousands of dollars passed through Lewiston each year from the gold mines along the Salmon and Clearwater Rivers. Lewiston was home to gold miners, outlaws, horse thieves, gamblers, and loose men and women of all descriptions.

"What was Sai Yee thinking coming out here?" Hop exclaimed. "Now, all I can do is find his body and take him home to his mother."

"Come on, Hop. Let's go see the Sherriff," Thomas offered, opening the creaking wooden door to the office.

Alfred William "Fred" Kroutinger 1859-1939. Sherriff Lewiston, Idaho. Public Domain.

Inside they found the Sherriff sitting with his boots propped on the wooden desk. He was a young man with dark brown hair and a bushy mustache.

"I'm Sherriff Fred Kroutinger. What can I do for you boys?

"I am Thomas Reynolds, former Sherriff in Marion County in Oregon. We are here looking for a friend who's missing in these parts."

"Your friend got a name?"

"His name is Loo Sai Yee. He is my cousin. He came up here to mine gold and has been missing for three months."

"We don't keep track of you Chinese! You all look the same, and we can't say your names anyway. Sorry, I can't help you," the Sherriff said as he stood, showing Hop and Thomas to the door.

"What's your rush, Sherriff? You got something to hide?"

"Look, you said you were a lawman, so you know I'm just trying to keep the peace around here. Your Chinese friend coming around stirring up trouble is not what we need."

"No trouble, Sherriff. I just want to find my cousin."

"Alright. Where was he mining?

"His last letter said they had a camp on the Snake River at a place he called Robinson Gulch."

The Sherriff visibly winced. "You don't say. Well, there are lots of you Chinese camped out along the river mining for gold. Not everyone likes the Chinese taking the gold out of these waters, but I can't say what happened to your friend."

"Look, Sherriff. It's been a long trip upriver from Portland, and we aren't leaving until we get some answers."

"Suit yourself but stay out of trouble, or you'll end up in my jail cell. That's a promise!"

"Come on, Hop. Let's go find the local undertaker. If anyone knows about bodies washing ashore along the Snake River, he is surely the one.

Lewiston, Idaho. 1800s Public Domain

Hop and Thomas made their way along Main Street's wooden sidewalks, passing saloons and hurdy-gurdy houses. In the 1880's Lewiston had two ferries, three hotels, nine saloons, a brewery, a sawmill, two bakeries, seven mercantile stores, seven lawyers, and three doctors. Finally, at the edge of town, they arrived at the funeral home. Its white wooden sign proclaimed in dark bold letters Furniture Maker - Undertaker & Embalmer.

Thomas and Hop entered and found the local undertaker, John Menomy. Except for a white shirt, Menomy was dressed entirely in black; pants, vest, jacket, and bow tie. His handlebar mustache and gold wire-rimmed glasses gave him a distinguished look, although his countenance seemed irritated as he looked up from a heated discussion with a miner.

"You'll have to wait your turn! I'm busy now."

"No problem. We'll just look around here for some action," Thomas replied with a smile.

Turning back to the miner, "You know I can't show you the bodies without written permission from next of kin. And since there is no kin, you're out of luck. Who are you, anyway?"

"I'm Joseph Vincent. People call me Joe," he replied, extending his hand. "I was mining along the Snake River near Deep Creek when I ran into some Chinese. They were working at Robinson Gulch. Anyway, I was short on supplies and food, so those Chinese fellas did me a good turn. They fed me and gave me some provisions to see me through. That Chinese grub isn't so bad once you get the taste of it."

"What's any of that have to do with why you're here?"

"Well, I owed them a favor, so I agreed to take a letter and send it back to their hometown in China. They also gave me gold dust to send home and lots of it too! When I heard of this trouble, I wanted to see if the dead men are the Chinese whose gold I'm carrying. 'Cause if they're dead, they won't be needing this gold anymore, if you catch my drift."

"Sorry, Mr. Vincent. I still need next of kin permission."

"Maybe we can help," Thomas interjected. "Hop Lee here is looking for his cousin who was mining at Robinson Gulch. That would make him next of kin."

Menomy eyed Hop suspiciously. "What's your cousin look like?"

"He is about my height and has black hair pulled back into a queue, and he's kind of skinny."

"That describes every Chinese around these parts! But if you say he's your cousin, then that makes you next of kin. So, I guess you are in luck, Mr. Vincent. You can all follow me.

Menomy led them into the back room of the funeral home. Hop gave a shiver as Chinese don't much like dead people, and these men he was looking for were good and dead.

"The bodies began washing up along the Snake River near Lime Point and Log Cabin Island a couple of weeks ago. So far, we have seven bodies, and I heard another three bodies were found in their ransacked camp."

"Can we see the bodies? Hop here needs to see the faces to identify his missing cousin."

"As you wish, but it's pretty gruesome," Menomy warned as he pulled back the white sheet from the first victim.

As Sherriff, Thomas Reynolds had seen his share of corpses, but this was truly ghastly. The Chinese face was unmistakable, and the long-braided queue was still intact. But the body had been mutilated with an ax. It was sliced and gouged until it was a mess of misshapen flesh. It looked like an animal that had been savagely butchered. For some reason, the face was intact."

"Not him," Hop gasped, looking away.

"Where are the bullet holes? Thomas asked.

Menomy turned the body over, "Here."

There were four penetrating wounds spaced randomly over his back.

"Someone shot this poor fella in the back while he was running away, and then they mutilated his body with an ax and dumped the body in the river. He must have been floating in the water for some time. But the cold water preserved the body."

Vincent, who had been quietly observing, reached out and pulled the sheets from the next victims. They all had been shot in the back and mutilated to varying degrees with an ax.

"Is your cousin here, Mr. Hop?"

Hop, with tears streaming down his face, was overwhelmed by grief for his coun-trymen. They had come to Gum Saan in peace only to die a violent and gruesome death.

"No," was the only word Hop could utter as he sobbed for these men he would never know.

Outside in the sunlight and fresh Idaho air, Hop took a deep breath and exhaled slowly. "I'm glad that cousin Sai Yee was not among the dead, but I am afraid there will be more bodies found."

"Thank you for your help, Mr. Hop. Is there anything I can do for you and your friend?"

"You can start by telling us what you're really up to, Mr. Vincent. You're certainly not a miner."

Joseph Vincent stood silently for a moment. "How did you know?"

"Your hands are a dead giveaway. They have never seen a day of hard labor. You spend your days behind a desk or in a shop, Joseph."

Vincent smiled, "You're right, Mr. Lee. I am a Justice of the Peace from the next county. The Sam Yup Company hired me in San Francisco to investigate these murders."

"Why the miner impersonation?" Thomas asked.

"Well, people around these parts don't like anyone snooping into their dirty laundry if you know what I mean. In truth, they might make a man disappear if they thought he was going to expose their dirty deeds."

"So, you thought that by impersonating a miner carrying a letter and some Chinese gold dust that you could get closer to the crime."

"Exactly! Someone needs to inspect the evidence before the locals make the whole mess go away."

"Do they know who is responsible for these murders?"

"No, but even if they did, they would never arrest them or hold them accountable. I am afraid that out here, the standards of law and order are not the same for

Whites and Chinese."

"The law is the law. This is America; even if those Chinese were not citizens, surely, they must have rights that need to be protected. Otherwise, you are all just savages."

"You don't have to convince me, Mr. Lee. I am a justice of the court, sworn to uphold the law for all men who set foot in my courtroom."

"What's next for you, Mr. Vincent?"

"Call me Joseph. Remember, out here, I'm a miner."

"Alright, Joseph. Where are you headed next?"

"I need to inspect the Chinese camp before someone destroys the evidence. But it's 65 miles from here, and it's all upriver."

"We'll ask around Lewiston to see if anyone will take us up the Snake River," Thomas offered.

"We're going with you, Joseph."

"Suit yourself, Mr. Lee, but it's not going to be easy. The current is swift, and the river is full of rapids. We'll spend more time pulling the boat upstream than paddling."

They scoured the town looking for anyone willing to take them upriver. The spring runoff from the melting snow had slowed, but the current was still swift enough to make the trip upriver long and arduous. Just as they were about to give up their idea, Hop spotted a scow pulling up to the shore.

"You fellas want to take us upriver?"

The men looked at Hop like he was a lunatic. "No way! We just finished this trip from Rogersburg. We want to unload and then head for the nearest watering hole."

Thomas was inspecting their flat-bottomed boat, "What are you going to do with this thing?"

"You mean this ugly old scow? We're going to tear it apart and sell the lumber."

"We'll save you the trouble. How much you want for this boat as she sits?"

Flat bottomed scow on the Snake River.

"We'd get $100 for the lumber and ..."

"You won't have to break the boat down if you sell it to us, and you'll get to your drinking that much sooner," Thomas offered. "How about $50?'

They eventually settled on $75, and Joseph, Thomas, and Hop stood on the shore admiring their new flat-bottomed scow.

"You know what to do with this thing?" Joseph asked, looking first at Hop and then at Thomas Reynolds.

As Hop shook his head, Thomas interrupted, "Sure, I grew up around these parts. Paddling on the river was how we got around back then. You just do what I say, and at the end of the trip, we'll be tired, but we'll make it."

The trip began with a gentle paddle upstream in the slowly flowing wide section of the river just south of Lewiston. The provisions they had purchased were tied down in waterproof canvas sacks.

"This isn't so bad, Thomas. It's just like paddling through the Pearl River Delta back home in China."

Thomas smiled at Hop but didn't say a word. After two hours, the river narrowed, and the current picked up speed. Hop, Thomas, and Joseph strained against their oars, pulling them through the swift waters with beads of sweat dripping from their brow.

"Head over to the side. The current's slower there," Thomas instructed. "We can use the poles over here in the shallows."

Each man took a wooden pole pushing the scow through the water a few feet with each push. After another hour, Hop's arms were aching.

"My arms are going to fall off, Thomas. Let's take a break."

"Ok, head for that little inlet on the right. We can tie her up to that tree and rest a spell."

Thomas jumped off the scow into the shallow waters, clambered ashore, and tied the rope around a boulder. "Ok, follow me."

Hop and Joseph made it ashore, all too glad to be on solid ground.

"How far do you think we've gone, Thomas?"

"Not nearly far enough. Here, let's have some lunch."

The men sat on the boulders feasting on sourdough bread, cheese, and venison jerky. "Nothing like a little manual labor to make a meal taste like it's fit for a king," Thomas laughed.

"I hope we brought enough food," Joseph added, looking at the pile of provisions in the middle of their boat

"Well, I planned for a two-week trip upriver, two or three days to inspect the camp, and a shorter float back to Lewiston. We'll have to do some fishing and hunting to supplement our food supply."

"The river will widen a bit up ahead, and the going will be easier for a spell. Enjoy it while you can because the first little rapids are upstream a few miles."

"How are we going to get through the rapids?" Joseph asked with a furrowed brow.

"You'll see. Don't worry about it just yet. Just enjoy the rest of your lunch and get us some river water to wash it down."

The clear cold water of the Snake River was delicious. "Just like a cold brew! That hits the spot. Now let's get back on the river. We have a few more hours of daylight left before we camp for the night."

As Thomas had predicted, the stream widened after a bit, and they were able to make good progress rowing upstream. The scenery along the Snake River was rugged, sparse, and beautiful. There were few trees. The canyon wall seemed to go straight up to touch the sky. In truth, the men were so preoccupied with the task of rowing that they barely noticed the scenery or the eyes watching them from the ridge top.

Hop looked ahead and spotted the white water of the first little rapids. "I think we have trouble ahead, Thomas."

"Just keep rowing until we get closer, and then we'll head for the shore on the right in that narrow section."

Hop and Joseph followed Thomas's directions. As they approached the shore, Thomas instructed, "OK, boys, this is where we earn our keep. We have to pull this scow through the rapids. You two take this rope and head up along the shore. Tie her up to that rock, and whatever you do, don't let go of the rope, or it's going to be a long walk back to Lewiston!"

Thomas grabbed the other rope, tried it around his waist, and jumped into the slowly flowing stream. He waded and then struck out for the opposite shore, swimming strongly into the current. Hop and Joseph watched in horror as the current swept Thomas downstream.

"Thomas, are you crazy? What are you doing?" Hop screamed after his friend.

Thomas swam with sure strong strokes, making it across the river just as the rope grew taught. He grabbed a bush and hauled himself out of the river. Standing on the shore dripping and cold, Thomas waved at his relieved companions.

"No sweat, boys. Now grab ahold of your rope, and let's head upstream towards those rapids.

Thomas's plan became apparent as the men pulled the scow through the water. The footing was solid, and pulling the scow was easier than rowing. Thomas was bigger and stronger than Hop and Joseph, so their combined efforts kept the boat

Snake River at Hells Canyon. Public Domain. Wikimedia Commons

centered in the river. As they approached the rapids, the going got tougher.

"Tie her up to a boulder so we can take a break," Thomas called out.

After a few minutes break, Thomas picked up his rope and motioned for Joseph and Hop to do the same. "This one's not too long. We can pull it upstream and then find another rock to tie her up so we can rest. It will take a few stops, but we'll make it through."

Once they reached the little rapids section, the real test began. Straining on the ropes, the men pulled the scow upstream a few feet at a time.

"Put your whole body into it, boys!" Thomas grunted.

Hop felt like his body was going to explode. His arms burned, and his legs felt like mush, but they kept straining on the rope, making slow, steady, and painful progress.

"Tie her up on the next big boulder. We need a rest," Thomas gasped.

Hop and Joseph, happy to oblige, secured their rope around a man-sized boulder and then collapsed to the ground, gasping for air.

"We're more than halfway through this section, Hop. You boys are doing terrific."

"I don't know, Thomas. This is crazy," Hop answered.

"Don't you quit on me now. It's all in your head. Just think, I can make it! No sweat!"

"My head does hurt, but it's my arms, back, and legs that are screaming, STOP!"

"No complaining, Hop. We're out here looking for your cousin," Thomas reminded his friend.

Thomas was correct. With a little more effort, they made it through the second half of the rapids and were rewarded with a broad and slow section of the river upstream.

"I think that's enough for our first day. Let's find a spot to camp for the night."

"We still have another hour of daylight left. Let's keep going," Joseph implored.

"We don't want to get stuck on the river at night. Men have died out here trying to push too hard. Flat spots along the river don't come up too often. We need to find a place to stop soon."

Thomas was right. The light was fading as they pulled into a little cove along the shore. Hop looked up just in time to see the sun's last orange glow disappearing behind the mountains.

"They call that the aspen glow, Hop. Pretty, isn't it?"

Thomas started a campfire while Hop and Joseph prepared their first dinner in the wilderness. This meal was even more of a feast as the three friends sat around the campfire devouring a meal of cornbread, dried beef, and beans.

The men prepared their camp. They agreed they were too tired to pitch a tent. The clear sky, filled with more stars than they had ever seen, did not portend any rain.

"Let's sleep under the stars tonight, boys."

The three men placed their bedrolls on the ground around the campfire, still orange from the glowing embers.

"Good night, Thomas. Good night, Joseph."

"Sleep well, Hop. We have another big day ahead of us tomorrow."

As Hop settled into his bedroll for the night, he thought that he had never been so tired or so far from his home in Salem. After a few moments, even the loud snoring of the other two men couldn't keep Hop awake a moment longer as he drifted off into a deep slumber.

The next morning Hop climbed out of his bedroll, started a campfire, and began to prepare breakfast. Leftover sourdough bread, oatmeal, and cowboy coffee hit the spot. The roar of the nearby flowing river was surprisingly loud.

"I can't believe we slept through the whole night with all that noise," Thomas marveled.

"Well, we were dead tired, and I, for one, was glad for the river noise. It drowned out your snoring!" Hop laughed.

"I don't snore!"

"Neither do I," Thomas and Joseph objected in unison.

"Whatever you say, boys. Why don't you two start to clean up the kitchen? I need to take a walk in the woods if you catch my drift."

"Don't stray too far, Hop," Thomas warned. 'Walk in a straight line and walk back in the same direction. It's easy to lose your bearings out here."

"No problem. I'll be right back."

Hop followed a deer path upstream and then, ignoring Thomas's instructions, headed uphill away from the water. He was a few hundred feet from the camp when he found the perfect spot. He looked around for a big stick to turn over a rock, revealing a small hole perfect for his purposes. Hop was bending over, perfecting the latrine, when he heard a noise, a branch breaking. He froze, quickly looking around for a grizzly bear. There was nothing but trees and boulders.

Stop it, Hop. You're imagining things and scaring yourself. There's nothing out here but you and your latrine!

He was standing, pulling up his *dai dong foo* pants, when he heard the noise again. Quickly tying his pants, Hop whirled around desperately, trying to locate the bear. His breathing quickened, and his heart was pounding.

"Come out where I can see you!"

Hearing another noise behind him, Hop spun around. His right shoe slipped into a hole between rocks pinning his foot as his body continued to turn around. The pain was excruciating as he collapsed onto all fours with his right foot still pinned between the rocks.

"Aiyaah!" Hop screamed.

He slowly extracted his right foot and was bending over, rubbing the swollen and bruised ankle. *Maybe it's not broken, but how am I going to walk on this thing?*

Hop limped a few feet and sat down in a little clearing rubbing his ankle gingerly. *Stupid......*

Before he could finish the thought, a dark, naked shape flew at him from across the clearing, knocking him to the ground. Hop's head hit a rock. He struggled to sit up, but the weight on his chest had him pinned down.

Looking up, he saw the dark form with his arm raised high above his head, about to swing the ax forward to crush Hop's life. His chest was bare, and his tensed, rippling muscles made his intentions clear.

"Stop!" a voice called out from behind Hop's head. "Don't hurt him!"

The man paused and looked up. His silhouetted head looked huge, with two long braids of black hair framing his face and the single feather reaching for the sky.

Hop rolled to his right as the native stood, looking at the source of the voice. Hop followed his gaze, and with his head half-turned, he spotted a Chinese in big crotch trousers.

"Cousin! What are you doing here? I thought you were dead!"

"Well, I should be dead, Sun Fook, but this Nez Perce found me and kept me alive."

Chinese mining camp 1885.

"Why are you out here, Sai Yee? You must know about all the trouble along the Snake River. Some horse thieves killed a group of Chinese miners. The bodies have been washing up for weeks. I was sure you were one of the dead."

"Know about it? I was there when it happened!"

"What do you mean, cousin? Why are you still alive?" Hop asked in amazement.

"I hooked up with Chea Po's group at Dead Creek a few weeks ago. He had ten clansmen working that bar."

Sai Ying's voice grew soft as he looked away, remembering his friends.

"Chea-Po was the headman. I remember all of their faces. Sun, Yow, Shun, Cheong, and Ling was only a boy," Sai sobbed.

"The others were Chow..." Sai choked, unable to continue with tears streaming down his face.

"That's enough, cousin," Hop replied, embracing Sai as he recalled the Chinese in the Lewiston morgue.

"Because I was alone, they let me join them, but I had to work apart from them upstream about a quarter-mile. That's what saved me.

Chinese gold miners. Artist and date are unknown.

"What happened?"

"We had just finished our morning meal, and I was heading to my little spot upstream. I had been working it for a few days with a sluice box and was having some good luck finding a few gold specks and gold flour."

"What about the trouble?" Hop reminded his cousin impatiently.

"I had just gone around the bend along the river when I heard the shooting. I climbed to the top of a boulder and crouched down so I wouldn't be seen."

Sai paused and took a deep breath before continuing. "I saw White men on horseback on the ridge above the camp, firing long rifles at Chea Po's men. Another group of White men with rifles was down by the river. The Chinese tried to flee, but they didn't stand a chance. They were shot in the back. It was cold-blooded murder, cousin. I saw the bloodied corpses littering the camp."

"How long did this go on?"

"The killing went on for over half an hour. At first, I could hear the Chinese yelling and screaming, but then there was just silence and the sound of the river. What they did next was hard to watch."

"Tell me, cousin," Hop said quietly.

"They started to chop up the bodies with their axes. Then they threw the Chinese into the river like garbage." Sai Yee sobbed with tears streaming down his face. "They butchered my friends like they were animals."

"How did you manage to stay hidden?"

"I knew the location of a small cave that's well hidden and impossible to spot. I think it's a bear den in the winter. I stayed there for several days until the White men had been gone for some time. When I finally came out, I was starving and weak. I wandered back to the camp, but the stench of death was heavy, and the sadness was unbearable. I found a little food and struck out along the river."

"You walked back this whole way?"

"Actually, by about the third day, I was starving and almost dead. Yellow Fox found me and gave me food and shelter. He is Nez Perce but calls himself a Niimíipuu. Yellow Fox was a scout for the army, so he speaks pretty good English. The soldiers were escorting the Nez Perce from Oklahoma back to a reservation in Idaho, but Yellow Fox escaped and has evaded capture for two years."

Hop looked at Yellow Fox now sitting quietly on a rock near his white spotted horse. "He almost killed me."

"I know. Yellow Fox thought you and those two White men were sent to hunt us down."

"Why doesn't he go home to the reservation in the Idaho Territory?"

"Yellow Fox doesn't trust the lies of the White man. He wants to be free to hunt and fish all of the lands of the Niimíipuu."

"We were on a mission to find you and to check out the Chinese mining camp."

"Well, you found me, and now there is no reason to go on to that death camp. I've told you much more than you could ever figure out on your own. You're not much of a detective anyway, cousin. Just take my word for it. It was horrible. I don't ever want to go back there." Sai Yee added softly.

Yellow Fox placed Hop Lee with his still throbbing ankle on his white spotted horse, and the trio made their way back to Thomas' campsite along the river. Thomas and Joseph sat quietly while Sai Yee and Hop retold the story of the murders and Sai Yee's escape from certain death.

"If it weren't for Yellow Fox, I would still be wandering around in the wilderness," said Sai Yee as he finished his story.

"What's going to happen to him?" Thomas asked, looking in the direction of the Nez Perce who was attending to his Appaloosa horse.

"Not sure," Sai Yee confided. "It's amazing he's avoided capture for this long."

"He is a man on the run with no home and no friends," Joseph said.

"Maybe we can hide him and take him with us," Hop offered tentatively.

"He's a fugitive, Hop. If they catch you helping him, they'll throw you both in jail," Thomas warned his friend.

"Well, we can't leave him out here. This place is going to be crawling with White men looking for answers to those Chinese murders," Joseph added.

"I wouldn't be so sure. I doubt if anyone other than the embalmer cares much about a few dead Chinese miners," Thomas replied.

"Well, we should try to help him. If it weren't for Yellow Fox, I would be another dead Cantonese miner," Sai Yee replied.

"Enough said. Let's see if we can convince him to trust us. We can take him back to Salem. He can live with us on one of the Chinese hop farms. He looks like a Cantonese. I think he'll blend right in and look like one of the farmhands," Hop offered hopefully.

As crazy as Hop's plan sounded, there was a possibility it just might work. The Nez Perce did look like a close cousin of Hop Lee. With Sai Yee's help, they explained their plan and offered to help him start a new life as a Chinese hop man.

Yellow Fox looked first at Sai Yee and then at Hop Lee. Without saying a word, he took their hands in his and said, "Nayàz," the Nez Perce word for "my brothers."

Tipya-la-lwilpilp Nez Perce – Frank La Roche 1899. Public Domain. Wikimedia Commons.

By the time they floated the boat back down the river to Lewiston, they had dressed Yellow Fox in a Chinese blue tunic, *dai dong foo* pants, and a broad-brimmed black felt hat. Hop braided Yellow Fox's long black hair into a queue and then stood back to view the transformation.

"Not too bad. You could pass for a Chinese with any White man. Now we need to give you a proper Chinese name," Hop added.

Hop thought pensively for a moment, and then his face brightened, "I know! We'll call you Jim Yee after Loo Jim and Sai Yee!"

Jim Yee became part of Hop's extended family, living and working on the hop farms around Keizer, north of Salem. He learned enough Cantonese to pass for a countryman, and Hop learned some of the Nez Perce language in return. When Hop eventually became a serious hop farmer, Jim Yee was his right-hand man. Jim came and went over the years. Hop never knew where he went, and he never asked. Like clockwork, Jim always reappeared just before planting season. He eventually gave up his Cantonese disguise, but for many years the Nez Perce lived as Jim Yee, the Chinese hop man.

Parlor of the Hop Lee home. Hop's son, Loren, described the painting of Yellow Fox, the Nez Perce warrior on his Appaloosa horse on the left.

Chapter Nine

Noodles and Stagehands – September 1891

After Hop's adventure on the Snake River with Thomas, life quickly returned to normal for the Chinese laundry magnate. The bell over the door at the Hop Lee Wash on Commercial Street had been tinkling nonstop all afternoon. Business was good.

Maybe a little too good. Hop sighed and wrapped up the last package of clean laundry with brown paper, carefully writing in Chinese, the name of the shirt's owner. He added it to the mountain of packages to be delivered in the morning.

"Tinkle! Tinkle!"

Hop looked up, expecting to see yet another customer.

"Hop! Put down your dirty shirts. You work too hard. You need to relax a bit, my friend," George Sun admonished with a smile.

"These are clean shirts, George!"

Well, forget about collars and spray ironing for a while. Let's get something to eat at Lem's place."

Hop hadn't stopped to eat all day, and his growling stomach was protesting at the mention of Wah Hong's noodles.

"Ok. I'll finish up here."

"Good. Because I'm starving, and you aren't much of a cook."

The three-block stroll to Wah Hong's Noodles at 170 N. Liberty was brisk in the chilly nighttime Salem air.

"Come on, Hop. Let's run. We have to get there before the play ends, or the place will be mobbed."

Wah Hong's Noodles was directly across the street from the Reed Opera House and was a favorite hangout for the stagehands who came for Lem's noodles after every performance.

As George and Hop entered the small noodle shop, it was obvious; they were too late. The place was packed, which didn't take too many hungry patrons, as Wah Hong's Noodle shop was tiny.

Hop spotted Lem in the back wearing his lucky red shirt. At that moment, Lem looked up with his ever-present smile.

"Hop! George! *Nei hou*, my old friends. Come in and sit down."

"Sorry, we are late, Lem. You look really busy. How long of a wait for some of your noodles, Lem? Maybe we should come back later."

"Nonsense!" Lem protested as he handed two steaming bowls of noodles to his friends.

"You should serve your young customers first," Hop protested, looking around the room at the stagehands and young people waiting for a cheap meal after the play.

"Come, sit in the kitchen with me. There is plenty of room, and after you're finished eating, maybe I'll put you to work." Lem laughed.

Hop and George devoured the savory noodles mixed with pork and Chinese greens. Lem made the noodles himself, grinding wheat into flour and kneading the dough with a bamboo pole contraption out back.

"You make the best jook-sing noodles in Oregon, Lem."

"The trick is to knead the dough with my special bamboo pole. My father was a master noodle chef in Ho Sun City in Canton."

"Well, the young people of Salem have your father to thank for these delicious noodles."

"I have been making noodles like this in Gum Saan since I arrived in 1877. That's a lot of noodles!" Lem laughed.

"For my noodles, I need lots of duck eggs to mix with the wheat flour. Maybe you should go into the poultry business, Hop. You could be my egg supplier."

With chopsticks in hand, Hop looked up at his friend, "That's a terrific idea, Lem."

"Hop, how are my cousins, Hong You and Hong Chan, doing at your laundry? They better work hard so they don't embarrass me."

"No worries at all, Lem. They are hard workers and rarely complain. They also told me about another of your Hong cousins in Dai Fow, Hong Lai Wah, who a couple of years ago married a young girl from the Jesus House."

"Yes, Lai Wah was a crazy railroad worker. His brother Jick Wah also worked on the long railroad through the mountains. Jick lost his right eye in a blasting accident. He's lucky to be alive. I think he lives in Montana now, and his brother Lai Wah rolls cigars in Dai Fow."

"Your cousin, Lai Wah, found a Chinese girl in Gum Saan?" George asked in surprise.

"Yes, but it wasn't easy. There are a lot of stories about how they met. Something about a kidnapping. It sounds crazy to me. But now they live in Dai Fow and are starting a family."

"OK. Are you finished eating? Then take these noodles to the young boys out front. They look hungry."

Hop and George became waiters at the noodle shop. In truth, they both liked talking to the young boys who worked at the Reed Theater.

"Here's your noodles, boys."

"Thanks, Hop."

"How was the play tonight?"

"Really good. It was called 'The Galley Slave.' The Belmour-Gray Dramatic

Reed's Opera House 1893. Public Domain

Company from Portland put it on tonight. They were first class all the way."

"The audience really got into the play. It was a drama, but there was this comedian who kept everyone laughing."

"I bet you boys work hard to pull off the performance," Hop admired.

"Well, the actors deserve the credit, but we do what we can tomake sure it all runs smoothly."

"I bet they pay a lot," Hop added seriously.

The boys all laughed, "No, Hop. We get paid in bowls of noodles, and we're happy to get it."

"It's probably better work than being a laundryman, but I do pay a little better," Hop smiled at his young friends.

"We are all going to the State Fair tomorrow."

"Shouldn't you be in school?" George asked.

"No, they closed the schools in Salem for ten days so we can all go to the Fair."

"Yes, I have seen the steady stream of people coming into town for the Fair," Hop added.

"They say the attendance this year will be immense! Usually, only half is from Salem, so there are going to be a lot of visitors."

"There is so much to see," George added, looking up from his newspaper. "There will be several horse races every day. You boys had better not place any bets unless they will take a bowl of noodles!"

"I want to see the Salem Second Regiment Band in the Grand Pavilion. They have daily concerts," one of the boys said.

"And the Fruit Palace will be a fruit lovers' masterpiece. The whole wooden building is covered with real fruit from top to bottom!" his friend added.

George looked up from his paper, "Hey, Hop. Will you look at this? The State Poultry Association is having a meeting for anyone who wants to breed thoroughbred chickens. The meeting is on Wednesday evening during Fair Week. This is perfect for your new venture with Lem as his duck egg supplier!"

"Let me see that," Hop mused. "Well, I just may go to that meeting. Just think, I will be the only Chinese poultry man in Salem."

"You two keep working," Lem called out to George and Hop. "I have to go out to feed Shep and Jerry. They're good dogs, but Shep will start howling if I don't feed them soon. Hate to bother the neighbors."

Wah Hong had two dogs, a black shepherd he called Shep and a pink-eyed bull terrier named Jerry. Shep howled several times a day with a delightful staccato, almost musical, barking and howling when the whistles blew for eight o'clock and eleven. Jerry, however, maintained a dignified silence.

The next week, early Fall rains put a damper on the high spirits following the State Fair. The air was heavy and wet, and the air put a chill in the bones of the heartiest of Salem residents.

Hoping for some of Lem's streaming jook-sing noodles to warm them up, George and Hop arrived expectantly at Wah Hong's Noodle Shop.

"The place looks closed, Hop. I wonder where Lem is. I hope everything is alright," George said, peering through the dirty window.

"I'm sure he's fine. Lem likes to go out for walks in the rain. Seems foolish to me, but he says that he likes to smell the rain."

Hop and George huddled under the awning of the shop, trying to get out of the drizzle.

"This is pretty miserable, George. Maybe we should go."

George was about to reply when they both spotted Lem across Liberty Street talking to a child.

"I wonder what he's doing. And what's that kid doing out in the rain?" Hop wondered.

George smiled, "Just watch. I've seen Lem do this before, lots of times. He can't help himself."

Puzzled but curious, Hop watched the scene across the street unfold and strained to hear Lem's words.

"What's your name, son?"

"Joey."

"What are you doing out here, and where are your shoes?"

The child was not more than seven years old. His threadbare clothes had holes in both knees.

"My Pa's out looking for work, and my shoes are, ahh, at home."

"Where do you live?"

Growing uneasy, Joey started to fidget as he looked around for an escape. "None of your business, mister."

"You can call me, Lem. Are you hungry? I make noodles in that shop across the street."

He had Joey's attention.

"Before you have the noodles, you have to do me a favor."

"What?" Joey asked, growing suspicious.

"Just follow me if you want the noodles."

Lem started walking down Liberty towards Commercial. He turned around and saw Joey hanging back.

"Come on, if you're hungry. I'm not going to hurt you."

Joey followed ten paces behind Lem in case he had to run.

At Commercial Street, Lem stopped in front of the Myer's Mercantile store.

"Come inside, Joey. My friend will help us."

"Tinkle! Tinkle"

Lem entered the store with Joey right behind. The warm, dry air felt good.

"Mildred, can you help my friend, Joey?"

Mildred came out from behind the counter.

"How can I help you, Lem?"

"Not me. Joey needs some shoes."

"You paying again, Lem? You can't pay with noodles," Mildred laughed.

"Yeah, I have a little money," Lem replied, reaching into his pocket and pulling out two dollars and a few coins.

"OK, Lem, but this is the third time this month you've bought some poor child shoes. Are you made of money or what?"

Lem smiled, "Just fit Joey with some shoes to keep his feet dry,"

Mildred obliged, bringing out several pairs of brown leather shoes.

"Let's try these on, Joey."

"He needs some socks too, Mildred."

"Whatever you say, Lem. It's your hard-earned money."

Joey's eyes lit up as he tried on the shoes.

"Thanks, Mister Lem. I never had shoes like these without holes."

Lem paid three dollars for the shoes and socks, and the two walked back to Wah Hong's Noodles.

"Ok, Joey. Let's get you something to eat."

Spotting his friends still waiting under the awning, Lem called out, "Hey, George and Hop! How long you been waiting here?"

"Long enough to see you spend your noodle money on this young man," Hop laughed. "And we are plenty cold and wet."

"Come in. It's free noodles for my friends tonight."

Lem went into the back and busily prepared Wah Hong's House Specialty Noodles.

He reappeared a few minutes later, carrying four large bowls.

"Here you go. My house specialty needles have a little bit of everything. Pork, shrimp, clams, greens, and water chestnuts for a little added crunch!"

The four sat around a small round table admiring their bowls of Lem's creation.

"Let's eat!" Lem encouraged his friends, looking directly at Joey.

Joey's wide-eyed expression of joy was all the thanks that Lem needed. Wah Hong's noodles were a feast on any day. But tonight, basking in the glow of their friendship and Lem's kind-hearted generosity, the House Specialty noodles was a meal fit for royalty.

REED'S OPERA HOUSE.

Fair Week, 1891.

The Belmour-Gray Dramatic Company
will appear during the week
in a choice repertoire of

POPULAR PLAYS.

Opening MONDAY September 14th with

"THE GALLEY SLAVE."

And presenting change of play each
evening.
☞ Reserved seats at Patton's.

Daily Capital Journal. September 14, 1891

Chapter Ten

Hop's First Foray into American Cuisine at Strong's Restaurant – 1892

T he tinkling bell over the front door announced the next customer at the Hop Lee Laundry.

Looking up from his ledger, Hop smiled at the young woman. "Hello, Miss Lenta Stolz. Are you serving coffee and donuts today?"

"Not today. I married the year after your big laundry fire, so now, I'm Mrs. W.G. Westacott, but you can call me Lenta, Mr. Lee."

"OK, Lenta, as long as you call me Hop. Did you bring your laundry for me to clean? We do the best handwashing and ironing in all of Willamette Valley."

"Maybe next time, Hop. I noticed you frequent Lem's Noodle House quite often."

"Yes. Lem makes the best jook-sing noodles outside of Hong Kong."

"Well, I would like to invite you to our Strong's Restaurant for dinner. It's the best food in Salem, and you can get a five-course dinner for two bits." Lenta pulled

STRONG'S RESTAURANT

REGULAR DINNER 25 cts.
DINNER FROM 11 A. M. UNTIL 2 P. M.
MENU

Soups	Clam Chowder.	Green Turtle.
Fish	Baked Salmon.	
Boiled	Ham.	
Entree	Minced Turkey, Oyster Patties, Lamb Chops Breaded and French Peas, Orange Fritters.	
Roast	Beef, Mutton, Veal, Pork Chicken with Dressing,	
Vegetables	Green Peas Sugar Corn. Mashed Potatoes.	
Pastry	Cranberry Pie.	
Deserts	Strawberry Meringue.	
Fruit	Candy, Nuts.	
Tea,	Coffee,	Milk.

Strong's Restaurant Menu 1893.

out the latest advertisement for Strong's Restaurant. "See. We serve dinner from 11 A.M. until 2 P.M."

Perusing the menu, Hop wondered how he would manage to eat without chopsticks.

"I may have to bring my own eating utensils."

Lenta smile, "Of course. You can give me lessons with chopsticks, and I will demonstrate a knife and fork."

"It's a deal."

"Come by around noon, and you can meet Mr. Westacott and Mr. Irwin, who manage the place. We're at 271 N. Commercial across from the Statesman."

Hop arrived right on time and stood outside, admiring the sign and the multi-

Strong's Restaurant - Pioneer Bakery and Candy Manufactory.
Oregon Statesman January 1, 1892.

colored striped awning and the bold sign, announcing "Strong's Restaurant – Pioneer Bakery and Candy Manufactory."

As he passed through the doors, Hop entered the Pioneer Confectionery and Bakery. The sweet smells filling the room and the visual treats of the candy shop were unlike anything Hop had ever encountered. Shelves holding rows of glass jars, displaying colorful candies lined the walls, while the baked goods called out to him from their glass display cases. Looking up at the magnificent glass chandelier, Hop bumped into a stool on the left. Finally, he spotted a gold-colored sign over the door at the end of the room, announcing "Restaurant."

Lenta, serving as hostess, warmly greeted Hop.

"Hop! I am so glad you made it to dinner. Let me seat you here so everyone can see our special guest."

"No need to make a fuss, Lenta. I'm just plain old Hop."

"Well, Hop, have a look at the menu and let me know what you fancy."

It was the same Strong's Restaurant menu he'd seen in the Oregon Statesman.

1892. Pioneer Bakery and Confectionary Store leading to Strong's Restaurant. W.G Westacott (taller man on the left) and William Irwin on the right) are co-owners in the business located at 271 Commercial Street.

Preparing for his first American meal, Hop had studied the newspaper's menu intently. Gazing at the sea of White patrons crowding the room, Hop felt a bit conspicuous. However, looking more closely, Hop recognized many of Salem's politicians, bankers, and businessmen who were regulars at Strong's Restaurant.

When Lenta returned, Hop rattled off, "I'll have the Green Turtle Soup, Minced Turkey, Vegetables and Sugar Corn, and Cranberry Pie."

"Hop, I am impressed. You ordered your dinner like a regular. But no one has ever ordered the turtle soup. That was our Chinese cook, Toy Sam's, idea, but it hasn't caught on."

"Turtle soup is a delicacy back home."

Well, the cook will be pleased, but he may have to go and catch a turtle for your dinner," Lenta replied, smiling. "What would you like to drink?"

"Green Tea to go with my Green turtle soup," Hop laughed.

"We don't have Green Tea. How about coffee or beer?"

"Hot water, please."

"Would you like a glass of ice water? We make our own ice.

"Oh no. Chinese never have cold drinks. It's bad for the chi. Hot water is perfect."

Lenta returned in 15 minutes with two plates of food. She served Hop and smiled, asking, "Do you mind if I join you?"

"Please. I am ready for my lesson with the American knife and fork. I did bring chopsticks for you," Hop laughed, pulling out a pair of ivory chopsticks.

"Perfect. Let me show you the knife and fork first. Take the knife in your right hand and the fork in your left hand......."

The lesson went better than expected.

"OK. Now it is your turn," Hop noted smiling as he placed a special rubber band around the two ivory chopsticks separated by a folded-up piece of paper. [1]

---

1. Stephen Perry invented the rubber band on March 17, 1845.

Lenta took Hop's modified chopstick contraption.

"How does this work?"

"Well, the rubber band keeps the chopsticks aligned and gives them spring action. You can't miss with these chopsticks. Try them out. You squeeze the back and grasp food and release it to hold on to the food."

Lenta gave it a try, using Hop's new-fangled chopsticks as directed. As she released the pressure the sticks closed on a carrot, securely grabbing the morsel.

"It works!" Lenta exclaimed.

"Works every time," Hop laughed. "Now, try this pea for a real test!"

Lenta tentatively approached the pea and easily picked it up with the chopsticks, placing it into her mouth.

"I love this new way of eating!"

"Once you get the hang of it, I'll teach you to use them without a rubber band."

Returning to his knife and fork, Hop practiced cutting the turkey, spearing it with the fork and placing the morsel into his mouth.

"We call American food *Fon Gwei Low*. It's pretty good," Hop said, cutting into the minced turkey. "In Chinese cooking, we cut up all the food into small pieces, so you don't need a knife."

"Well, American men like big thick, juicy steaks that require a sharp steak knife to eat."

Hop took a bite of the cranberry pie and frowned, "It's ahh very sweet."

"Isn't it delicious?"

"Chinese don't eat food this sweet, but I may grow to like it."

Wait until you try our ice cream and confections. Mr. Irwin has a dairy farm north of Salem so that we have all the dairy products we need."

Hop smiled and went back to the Green Turtle Soup. "This turtle soup hits the spot, Lenta."

"Well, you are the only person to try the chef's turtle soap so far. We may need you to recommend it. Here, let me get you some of our house specialty New York ice cream."

When Lenta returned, Hop, who had reverted to his chopsticks, picked up some of the creamy yellow ice cream and gently placed it into his mouth.

The rich, creamy texture and the explosion of sweet lemony flavor were intoxicating.

"This is wonderful! Ice cream is the best American food ever!"

A deep voice boomed from across the room, "Well, you can't live on ice cream, but we're glad you like it!"

"Hop, meet my husband, W.G. Westacott. He's the co-owner and manager of Strong's Restaurant."

"I'm also in charge of making the ice cream and confections," W.G. laughed. "I'm glad you approve. We can deliver ice cream to your house if you like."

"Your ice cream creation should draw in a lot of customers."

"A lot more than our turtle soup experiment. Don't get me wrong. Toy Sam is a terrific chef. We stole him from the Chemeketa House where he ran the kitchen for eight years," W.G. replied.

"The turtle soup is good too, but I'll tell you what. I will gladly send all of my laundry customers to Strong's just to try your ice cream."

"Now, that's a promise I hope you'll keep, Mr. Lee."

"Just plain old Hop is fine with me, Mr. Westacott. By the way, do you own the Westacott livery on Ferry where I keep my horse?"

"Almost. That's my brother, R.H. We call him Dick."

The two men shook hands while a smiling Lenta looked on, recalling the night she met Hop outside his laundry business, going up in flames.

It looks like things have changed for both of us since then.

As Hop was walking out of the restaurant, he heard his name being called out.

"Hi, Hop!"

Hop turned to his right and spotted his friend R.J. Hendricks. "Hello, Mr. Hendricks. How's the newspaper business?"

Otto J. Wilson Sr. 1868-1942 started the Salem Cyclery in the1890's.
Courtesy of the Family of Otto J. Wilson, Sr.

"Just fine, Hop. Let me introduce you to my friends. This is our mayor, C.P. Bishop, and the new owner of the Salem Woolen Mill Store. You remember Nes Bush. These youngsters are Jos Albert, another banker from the Capital National Bank, and Otto Wilson. Otto is a proponent of bicycles and bowling."

"Gentlemen, this is Hop Lee, the proprietor of the Hop Lee Laundry and Poultry Store near the Post Office."

Hop nodded, greeting the men as he shook hands the American way.

"Otto will sign you up for his new bicycle club and will have you peddling through Salem's streets in no time," Hendricks laughed.

"Actually, I have my eye on those new horseless carriages. The gas-powered automobile is the wave of the future," Otto exclaimed. "Four wheels is better than two!"

"Mr. Lee, stop by my store at 299 Commercial and I'll outfit you in a fine American wool suit," C.P offered.

"Well, I am partial to my *dai dong foo* Chinese pants and tunic, but I do like those Derby hats," Hop laughed.

Hop did not give up Lem's jook-sing noodles, but from that day forward, he made regular appearances at Strong's Restaurant, where he became friends with many of Salem's business and political elite. Hop also became a regular customer at C.P. Bishop's Woolen Mill Store, developing a life-long affinity for Derby hats and American suits. [2]

---

2. In 1889, Charles Pleasant Bishop, his father-in-law, Thomas Lister Kay, and Squire Farrar, founded the Thomas Kay Woolen Mill. The mill began operations In March 1890. The following year, C.P. Bishop bought the Salem Woolen Mill Store on Commercial Street, which sold woolen goods, men's clothing, fabric, and blankets. C.P. Bishop served as Salem's mayor for three consecutive terms (1889-1905), followed by two terms in the Oregon legislature. As ardent Republicans and Presbyterians, he with his wife, Fannie, were active in local affairs.

The Avenue Tennis Club founded in 1889 by Jos Albert in the first row on left. Otto J Wilson is also in the first row, reclining on the right.

Chapter Eleven

Busted for Stud Poker & Resisting Dog License Act – 1893

"**H**ello, Hop! We saved you a seat over here," George Sun waved to Hop from across the room, pointing to the empty seat next to his three sons.

Hop made his way across the room crowded with Salem Chinese and sat next to Wu Sun, George's third son. Wu was three years old and as bright as a shiny American penny. His older brother, You, was six years old. You had been sick for some time with the wheezing disease, but tonight he seemed happy and excited. Another brother, four-year-old Lai Yee, was fidgeting and playing with his brother's queue. All three boys were dressed in their finest Chinese clothes with silk gowns and lavender caps.

"Hi boys! Are you ready to hear some real Chinese music?" Hop asked, smiling at the young boys.

The two older boys nodded in unison. Their younger brother was playing with his cap. Hop smiled and felt a deep longing, wondering if he would ever have sons.

The hall was above the Quong Yuen Company Store on Ferry Street. It served as a meeting hall for the Chinese and a sometimes gambling joint. Tonight, it was a concert hall for the visiting musical troupe led by Lee You and Sing One.

The eight-member Cantonese orchestra was traveling the Northwest and had just arrived from Portland. George spotted the instruments neatly aligned at the front

George Sun and Family 1891 Oregon Historical Society. Public Domain.

of the room. "Come on, boys. Let's go and see the musicians' instruments."

Hop followed his friend and the three boys, tripping over the feet of Lee Young sitting next to him.

"Looks like you need some new shoes, Lee. Too bad you had to pay for my wash kettle!"

Lee looked straight ahead and scowled but didn't say a word to Hop.

George was already at the front of the hall, pointing at each instrument in turn.

"This is the *Erhu* or horsehead fiddle. And this is a *Jong Wu*. It's like the *Erhu*, but its sound is a little lower. And this is a Cantonese dulcimer or *Yanquin*. We call it a butterfly lute."

"This is my favorite, the *Ruan* or Moon Guitar! It makes deep bass noises," added Hop. "Boom!" Boom!"

"And these are flutes called *Dizi*, and we call these wind instruments *Sor Lap*."

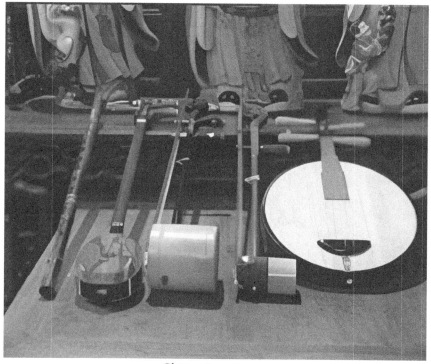

Chinese instruments

"You boys can play these percussion instruments," added Hop, pointing to the cymbals, gongs, bells, and clappers."

Arriving late, Chongyen Huie took the last seat next to Hop. "Hello, C.Y." How's business at your new store?"

"We're still stocking the shelves with all our imported exotic oriental goods," C.Y. replied.

"What are you going to call the place?"

"Huie Wing Sang Co. It's on Court Street near the Opera House and Lem Wah's Noodle Shop. Import business is where the money is, Hop."

"Tonight, we forget about business and listen to music from the old country," Hop replied, closing his eyes with his hands folded on his belly, waiting for the performance.

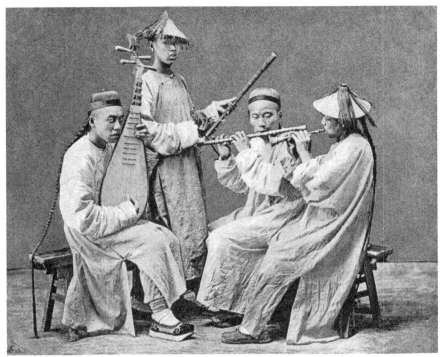

Chinese musicians. Shanghai. Wikimedia Commons. Public Domain.

At that moment, the eight Cantonese musicians entered the room from behind a curtain framing the makeshift stage. They smiled at the three boys and motioned for everyone to take their seats. The instruments, which the boys had just seen, took on a life of their own that night. The *Erhu* started it out but was quickly joined by the *Jong Wu*, the butterfly lute, and the Moon guitar with its deep bass sound. Once the cymbals, gongs, and bells got into the act, the boys were hooked.

For the next two hours, the men of Salem's Chinese quarter were transported back to the homeland, each remembering the sounds of his youth. Hop and George had their eyes closed. The boys watched in wide-eyed amazement at the onslaught of new sounds coming from the instruments.

A reporter from the Weekly Oregon Statesman had cotton balls stuffed in his ears as he took notes for the morning paper.

A MONGOLIAN MUSICALE —Last night at their ball over Quong Yuen Co's store the Chinese band gave an exhibition of its proficiency in handling its curious instruments, before a few invited guests The band is under the leadership of Lee You and Sing One, and the music, though rather harsh to the unaccustomed ear, is no doubt very good from a Chinese standpoint.

The Salem Chinese concert at the Quong Yuen Store on Thursday February 23, 1893

Four months later, on the evening of June 29, 1893, the Quong Yuen meeting hall was heavily guarded. The music hall had undergone a transformation into a Chinese gambling den. This was stud poker night for the Chinese in Salem, and the Quong Yuen hall was their favorite locale. The men were on edge as the Salem police had raided a Chinese lottery being run out of the same hall just a few nights earlier. Tonight, Loo Jim was the dealer. He decided to revert to his old name since a friend visiting Charlie Mon was also named Hop Lee. The other stud poker players that evening included Jim Toy, Ham Joe, Charlie Mon, Ah Kee, Hop Lee, and Ah Foon.

Jim Toy Salem 1890. Willamette Heritage Center

Two kerosene lanterns gave off a yellow glow, and the dimly lit room was filled with smoke from the Chinese cigars. Salem had electric lights powered by Mill Creek, but electricity had not made its way into the Chinese quarter.

"Hit me, Hop! I mean Loo Jim!" Charlie Mon motioned to Hop to deal him two more cards.

Hop obliged and then looked around the table at the other players. Ham Joe was losing big time and looked a bit desperate. Ah Kee, as usual, wore his best poker face and was hard to read. The other men sat with their cards fanned out in their hands as each calculated his chances for a winning hand.

The visiting Hop Lee motioned for three cards and then briefly smiled as he picked up the dealt cards and added them to his hand. His smile, although brief, was an obvious "tell" that all the men had seen. Hop was reaching for his coins to increase his bet when the door to the room flew open.

Ah Chan came running in, shouting, "Get out now! The cops are pounding on the door! *Fai Di Lah!* [1] Go out the windows onto the roof and then jump!"

Loo Jim was the first through the window when he felt someone pulling him back.

---

1. Fai di lah – hurry in Cantonese

Hop looked down onto Ferry Street and saw the ring of police waiting for them below. They were trapped!

"Give it up, Hop! We have you this time. The place is surrounded!" Chief Minto called out.

"Hop, come this way," Charlie Mon yelled, pulling him back through the window.

"Quickly, go down the stairs into the basement."

Charlie led the way with a kerosene lantern leading the way down the rickety stairs, creaking under the weight of seven men.

The basement was dank and filled with the sounds of rats scurrying away into the dark corners.

"Why did we come down here? We're trapped," Loo Jim exclaimed.

"Give me a hand. Move this cabinet aside. There's a door out of here," Charlie explained.

The men grunted and huffed as they pushed the heavy wood cabinet aside, revealing a rusting steel door.

"See. I told you," Charlie said, turning the handle and pulling the door open.

A blast of cool damp air greeted the men as the lantern light revealed a tunnel leading into the darkness.

"Where does this go?" Hop asked

"Away from Chief Minto, I hope," Charlie replied. "Let's go!"

The seven men stumbled through the dark passageway, bumping into one another and scraping against the narrow walls of the tunnel.

"Stop shoving!"

"Move your fat butt!"

"There's an exit over here!" Charlie called out.

"Let's get out of here. This place gives me the creeps."

"How far do these tunnels go, Charlie?" Hop asked.

"There's a maze of passages down here. You could easily get lost."

Charlie opened the door. A shaft of sunlight was a welcome sight as the men exited the maze of tunnels under Salem's Chinatown.

"Hey! We're on Ferry Street behind George Sun's store!"

The men were dusting themselves off, feeling smug with their crafty escape, when Chief Minto came around the corner with three other officers of Salem's finest.

Harry P. Minto

"Looks like you have a losing hand tonight, Hop! Ha! Ha! You should have stuck to washing laundry!" Minto laughed. "Cuff him and take him to the City Jail!"

The other Chinese gamblers were unceremoniously handcuffed, and all seven men were loaded onto the waiting horse-drawn police wagon and taken to the City Jail on the east side of Liberty just south of State Street. It was a short but embarrassing ride for Hop as his customers watched the scene unfolding in Salem.

At the station, they were booked for gambling and assigned a bail of $50. Charlie Mon and Ah Foon paid the bail. The other five Chinese men, including Loo Jim, spent an uncomfortable night in the city jail. Their hearing with Police Judge Edes was set for 11 a.m. the next day. The men were found guilty of gambling, and each paid the $100 fine. [2]

---

2. In Multnomah the local Police were paid $12 per month by each Chinese lottery or $6 per week for the privilege of conducting the game. Money was paid to one Chinese agent who turned it over to Lee Git. The amount of protection money paid each month in this manner was between $1000 and $1100.

As they were walking back to the Chinese quarter, Ah Kee grumbled, "Next time, we should remember to pay off the Chinatown police. A little money to grease the wheels will be a lot cheaper than all these fines!"

Hop saw George coming down Commercial Street long before he entered the Hop Lee Laundry.

"Good morning, Hop. I heard you had a rough night sleeping at the jail."

"I've had better," Hop grumbled, not wanting to look at his friend.

"If you are going to gamble, at least don't get caught. These people in Salem like you, Hop, but they won't give you their business if they see you being taken to the City Jail in the police wagon!"

Hop knew his friend was right, so he remained silent, waiting for George to continue.

"Do you remember when I was arrested with Lee Ho and George Hong for gambling in 1888? The charges were dropped when they found out some Chinese had turned us in falsely, but still, the Salem customers stayed away for months. Public opinion is fickle, Hop."

"OK, I get your message, George," Hop replied glumly.

"Well, there are more important issues for the Chinese these days. We have until May 5th to decide if we are going to register."

"You mean to decide if we will submit to being licensed like a dog!" Hop growled.

"The Chinese Six Companies have instructed the Chinese not to register for the Geary Act," George explained. [3]

Growing more upset, Hop replied, "I know of no Chinese in Salem who will register. Besides, the photograph is too expensive. It costs between 75 cents and $1.25 for two photos."

"A lot of Chinese are superstitious about having their photograph taken. If you

---

3. The Geary Act was a United States law that extended the Chinese Exclusion At of 1882 by adding the onerous requirement that the Chinese residents of the United States carry a resident permit.

Hop Lee by Provenance Trover. Low Family Collection

get a bad one and it fades in few years, it could mean bad luck for you!"

"Well, George, they took away your right to vote and to be a citizen, and now they want you to register like a dog!"

"We must stand up against their threats of sending us back to China or a year of hard labor," George agreed.

The Salem Chinese were true to their word. Ross E. Chamberlain, the deputy collector for the internal revenue service, was at the Willamette Hotel on April 20 to register the Chinese according to the provisions of the Geary Act. After spending the day in more or less anxious expectation, he went to Albany without having registered a single Chinese.

On May 26, 1893, the local Salem paper reported tongue-in-cheek that even George Sun's new infant daughter was resisting and would not register for the Geary Act.

In September 1893, the Chinese went out on strike in Los Angeles to protest the Geary Act. Laundrymen, Chinese vegetable dealers, and cooks struck. Not one vegetable wagon was seen on the streets. The hotel keeps were forced to send wagons into the country to get vegetables. Laundries were shorthanded, and patrons were notified that no more work would be taken. Over 300 applications for warrants were made, but the jail was so crowded with Chinese that they had to suspend issuing any new warrants.

The registration deadline was extended. By the following January 17, 1894, the Chinese were registering slowly. In the whole country, 500 had so far registered, and in Portland, forty Chinese had complied. F.C. Greer, the special deputy internal revenue collector, arrived from Albany on the Overland in the morning. He spent a day at Sheriff Noland's office until Saturday night to receive Chinese registrations. In Albany, sixty registered, but in Salem, the resistance to the Geary Act continued in full force as only four Chinese showed up to register.

On March 20, 1894, in a sudden reversal, the Chinese Six Companies ordered all Chinese to comply. The Chinese consul just returned from Washington, and the Six Companies issued the new order to register at once. The Chinese suspected they had been sold out in some secret deal.

May 4, 1894, was the last day on which the Chinese could register under the extended Geary Act. Few appeared in Collector Mize's office. The collector thought his clerks would be kept busy from the beginning of office hours until late in the evening registering eager Chinese, but he was disappointed. It was believed that there were 800 to 1000 unregistered Chinese in the city and vicinity who would be liable to deportation if the law were strictly enforced. Protests continued in Salem and across the country as the Chinese stood up for the rights they believed they deserved. Their objection to the "Dog Tag Law" sparked perhaps the largest organized act of civil disobedience in the United States as thousands of Chinese refused to register.

Ultimately, the case made it all the way to the Supreme Court. In 1893, the Supreme Court upheld the resident permits in Fong Yue Ting vs. the United States. In 1902 the Chinese Exclusion Act was made permanent. It was finally repealed by Franklin D. Roosevelt in December 1943, 61 years after it was passed.

George Sun was the leader of the Salem Chinese. But that April, his heart and his mind were elsewhere. On Monday, April 16, 1894, Sun You, the eldest child of George Sun and Leong Shee, died suddenly from asthma. You was seven years old.

Chapter Twelve

The Rise of the Chinese Hop Growers

I t was the fall of 1894. The passing of George's oldest son, You, left a yawning emptiness in the heart of Salem's Chinese quarter. There were still only a handful of children in the colony. The Sun boys, with their quick and eager smiles, were favorites of their 300 bachelor uncles. Every day the old Chinese men burned incense for You in the temple.

But life in Salem would not pause for their mourning. Times were changing quickly, and George knew he had to adapt to survive.

"Hop, we need to branch out in our business ventures. I can't just sell goods in my store and a few vegetables at the market. And you, my friend, are famous for your Chinese laundry, but it will not be enough in a few years. The Steam Laundry is driving the Chinese out of the laundry business. Sung Lung is thinking about closing his wash house and going back to China."

"You're right, George. I feel the competition coming. It is like a big weight on my head!"

George Sun's Children. Sun Yu, Sun Wu, and Sun Lai Yee. Tover.

"Well, Hop, I think there is money in growing hops. Every week I take my delivery wagon out to the McNary farm to pick up my vegetables. I drive past acres and acres of hops. There are more hops in Mission Bottom and South Bottom than you can imagine. I asked the farmhands how the hops business pays. They said the owners are rolling in beer money!"

"We can't buy the land to grow anything, George. They won't sell land to Chinese."

"I am not so sure that is true, but anyway, we don't have to buy. We can lease the land just like I do for my vegetable patch. We would just need a whole lot more land to grow hops."

In truth, the Chinese had been growing hops in Marion County since before 1889. K. Young, Sim Yuen, Kam Sing, Jo Wing, Sam Gee, and Chin Hang secured a five-year lease of 30 acres of land from F. Levi on the old Townsend place three miles southeast of Salem. These six Chinese put out a hop yard and cultivated it in the first-class style, expecting a yield of 30 tons in hops in 1889. They hired eight to ten Chinese, including Hop's friend Jim Yee to tend the hops year-round and employed the latest cultivation methods. Their hops commanded the greatest attention and price from buyers.

Willamette Valley Hop Picking 1890s. Post Card. Low Family Collection.

In fact, all of the Chinese hop growers had uncanny success wherever they chose to cultivate their crops, making them the envy of White growers.

By September 4, 1894, George Sun was leasing land near Keizer north of Salem from Mr. W.H. Holmes to grow his hops. George's hops were the finest for miles around, far exceeding in quantity and quality of the surrounding White growers' crops. All the pickers cast an envious eye towards the Chinaman's hops, but George could not employ them all. By December 1896, George had a hop contract for 25,000 pounds. This was just the beginning of the Chinese hop yards that were to become a fixture in the fertile Willamette Valley.

In 1897, Hop Lee leased 60 acres from Ed Dove in Eola Polk County, five miles west of Salem along the Willamette River. He planted his first crop of hops. Loo Jim, who learned the lessons of hop growing from George Sun, put Jim Yee in charge of his hop yard. Their efforts paid off with a fine field of hops that had been cultivated to perfection. At the end of August, Hop was ready for his first harvest, advertising for 100 pickers. Interested pickers should apply at the Hop Lee wash at 187 Commercial Street in Salem. Transportation out and back from the farm was provided. August 25th was the big day.

The work of hop-pickers consisted of pulling all the hops off the vines and placing them into barrels. It took three common sugar barrels to make one nine-bushel box for which the workers were paid 30 cents. The price per box had steadily

Willamette Valley Hop Picking 1890s. Post Card. Low Family Collection.

declined from 50 cents in 1893. Times were hard, so no one complained. Growers eventually switched to paying by the pound to counter the pickers who liked to fluff up the hops in filling the boxes. The hop vines were hard on the skin, so the workers all wore long-sleeved shirts and hop picking gloves, which sold for 25 cents a pair.

The pickers lived comfortably in tents with cookstoves and tables on the ground to cook their provisions. Most were simple tents. Others were quite elegant with all the amenities of home life. The whole community waited with great anticipation for the start of the picking season. This was a festive time for families to work, live, and play together. Hop picking was, indeed, a family affair, and the extra money from picking hops helped many a family make it through the long winters.

The Willamette Valley was the self-proclaimed "Hops Capital of the World," and for a glorious three weeks, the hop yards were a melting pot of cultures and generations. The local families were joined every season by the itinerant Native American and Chinese workers, who showed up like clockwork at the end of August. Some growers paid the non-White workers less per pound of picked hops. Knowing that inequity was a sure recipe for disaster, at Loo Jim's hop yards, all were welcome, and all were paid equally for a hard day's work.

Hop stood gazing at his 55 acres of beautiful Willamette hops, recalling all the work of planting and cultivating the hops. In the morning, the picking would finally commence.

That afternoon he wrote in his journal, "Tomorrow I become an American hop farmer. This is just the beginning."

Later that afternoon, Hop was deep in thought, looking out the laundry's front window, when the light in his mind started flashing.

Hop laughed out loud, exclaiming, "There's my hop's market! It's right across the street. The Capital Brewery! Mr. Beck definitely needs my fine Willamette hops to brew his beer."

Hop ran across the street as Seraphin Beck was coming out of his Capital Brewery.

Capital Brewery

"Mr. Beck!" Hop called out. "I have a deal for you! I grow the finest hops in the Willamette Valley at the Ed Dove ranch. I will save you some of the first crop."

"Hello there, Hop. I didn't know you were branching out from the Hop Lee Wash House."

"Yes. I am a hop grower now," Hop replied proudly. Sensing that Seraphin Beck was skeptical of his Chinese hops, he changed tactics. "Tell you what. I'll trade you some free hops for a couple of barrels of your best beer. Mr. Dove says I have to throw an end-of-the-season party for the pickers."

"Sure, Hop. You got a deal. And if I like your hops, we can be a regular customer."

That evening Hop pulled out his fortune paper and searched for the characters meaning land. "Aha! There it is. Hmmm. It says I will buy farmland and build a house. There must be some mistake because Chinese can't buy land in Gum Saan. Well, I guess the fortune teller can't be right about everything."

To Buy

Field – Farm Land

To build

House

Loo Fortune Teller Scroll. Low Family Collection.

Chapter Thirteen

A New Century in America Brings a Bank Failure & Turtle Soup – 1900

By 1900, Hop Lee had been in America for 23 years and had accumulated more wealth than he ever could have imagined as a young boy in Ha Chun Chong Village. His laundries and hop growing farm brought in more money than he could safely keep at his business. The security of the American banking system was the obvious answer. Hop opened an account at the Gilbert Brothers' Bank. Like many Salem citizens, the offer of 5%- 6% on his savings was hard to resist. It seemed like free money and too good to be true.

In January 1900, the banks introduced the Salem public school savings system with a flattering reception. Several schools placed their deposits in the Gilbert Brothers' Bank in the amount of $25 on the program's first Monday.

For Hop and the other citizens of Salem, the bank's promise of interest payments was indeed too good to be true. On April 23, 1901, Gilbert Brothers Bank at 207 Commercial Street closed its doors with only $1000 in cash in the safe. The best estimate was that the aggregate deposits in the bank were $125,000. Many unfortunate Salem citizens were "in the soup." The brunt of the loss was born by the working class of Salem. The recently widowed Mrs. Ida Muthis had entrusted $1,213 to the bank for safekeeping. The Public-School Savings Depositors

1890s Run on a Bank

included 255 children holding accounts of $1,116.78. It seemed that everyone in Salem was affected by the bank's closure.

Walking down Commercial Street to his laundry Hop was deep in thought about the Gilbert Bank. As was his custom, he was walking head down, staring at the ground, unaware of the world around him. News of the Gilbert Brothers' bank failure had spread like wildfire throughout Salem. All of his savings were in that bank. A Daily Capital Journal reporter, looking for investors to interview, rudely interrupted Hop's worries.

"Hop! I hear you had some money in the Gilbert Brothers' bank. What does the bank failure mean to you?"

Hop looked up just in time to avoid walking into the reporter, notepad in hand.

"I was making arrangements to go back to China to visit my home and family in Hoiyin. Now, I will have to postpone the trip. My parents are old and may not be alive when I save enough money to go home."

"How much money did you have in the bank?"

"$1,000. It was everything I saved last year from the laundry and hops."

"What is your opinion of the Gilbert Brothers' bank, Hop?"

Hop paused and then decided to let it flow.

"The injustice of your banking system that allows favored private parties, who are on the inside, to get in and swipe the assets, would be met with capital punishment in China!"

"You mean you would advocate executing the bankers?" the astonished reporter asked.

"You heard me, and you can quote me! The good people of Salem put their hard-earned savings in this bank, and they deserve better treatment!" Hop fumed.

Public sympathy for the loss of the Salem school children ran high. In December 1902, John H. Albert, president of the Capital National Bank, announced that he would pay the face value of the public-school children's deposits in the suspended Gilbert Brothers' Bank. For everyone else in Salem, the loss of their hard-earned money was a bitter pill to swallow.

For Hop, this was just another reason to think up his next scheme to make money. He needed something more than dirty laundry and growing hops. The challenge was to find a new way to make money without having any money to invest.

ℓℓℓ

Hop was walking south on Commercial Street, deep in thought. Looking at the ground, he was oblivious to the world around him, as he pondered his next move here in Salem. Life was like a game of mahjong. You never know what the next tile will bring.

Hop had just crossed over a branch of the Willamette Slough when he spotted something up ahead. At first, it looked like a large dark green rock in the middle of the street, but then he thought he saw it move! As Hop approached, the rock transformed into a turtle slowly crawling down Commercial Street, its short legs moving its shell forward one step at a time. It must have been a good six inches across. Hop bent down and picked up the turtle, which immediately retracted its head and legs into its protective shell.

"Hi, there, little fella! What are you doing all the way out here?"

Hop tucked the turtle into his pocket and was walking back towards the slough when the light came on. For Hop, the light in his mind often flashed, but this one was really brilliant!

Hop ran back to his laundry with the turtle bouncing up and down inside his tunic. He burst through the doors and went immediately to the back room.

"Loo Hop! Do you know how to make turtle soup?" Hop placed his newly found turtle onto the washroom table.

His cousin came out of the makeshift kitchen looking at his half-crazed boss.

"Sure, I can make you a turtle soup."

The cook spotted Hop's new turtle slowly crawling across the table. He was about to pick it up to put it into the pot when Hop grabbed his hand.

"No, not with this one! This little fella we keep and call him Myrtle. He is part of my plan for true turtle wealth."

Hop took the turtle from his cousin and placed him in a box.

"But Hop, that turtle is a real delicacy. It will make a delicious soup!"

"I don't want the turtle soup. Myrtle is my ticket to the turtle soup business! We are going to supply turtles to all the Chinese cooks in Portland! Now I just need to find an army of turtle hunters here in Salem."

At that moment, the bell at the front door to the laundry rang. Ting! Ting!

Hop went to the front to attend to his customer still thinking about his turtle. It was Mr. Wautensaugh, whose wife was a regular customer. Thomas Wautensaugh was an unbelievably tall man with a long white beard.

"Hello, Thomas! What brings you to my washhouse? I usually expect to see Mrs. Wautensaugh."

She is down with the croup. So, I am doing the laundry today."

Hop realized that he was still carrying the box housing his turtle.

"Thomas, do you know where to catch these turtles?

"Sure, Hop. They're all over the slough. Those turtles are a real nuisance."

"Are there a few hundred turtles down there?"

"Hundreds? You mean thousands of turtles! Those Willamette turtles are everywhere! At least they are if you know where to look for them, which I do. We used to catch these turtles for fun when I was a boy here in Salem."

The light in Hop's mind was flashing nonstop. "Bring them to me! I will pay you by the dozen. How about $2 for every dozen turtles?"

"You want to pay me for turtles? You must be kidding! What are you going to do with dozens of turtles?"

"Never mind. Just bring them to me, alive. All the turtles you can find!"

With those words, Hop's turtle business was hatched. He rushed next door to the Capital Journal office and took out an ad for more Salem turtle hunters.

Thomas Wautensaugh was true to his word. Within the week, he brought in his first haul of 53 turtles for Hop's inspection.

Dropping the three burlap sacks onto the table, "Here you are, Mr. Lee! Turtles just like I promised!"

"Not Mr. Lee, Thomas. Just call me Hop like everyone else. Now let's take a look."

Hop emptied the first sack onto the table. There must have been 20 Willamette turtles of various sizes, all squirming around and crawling over one another.

"Thomas, these are perfect! They will make a fine turtle soup."

Hop proceeded to empty the other two sacks and counted the turtles one by one as he placed them into a barrel.

"Fifty-three turtles, Thomas! I will pay you $1.80 per dozen turtles. Larger ones will fetch a better price. Say $2.50 per dozen."

Hop pulled out $6 from his pocket and handed it over to Thomas who eagerly accepted his payment.

"Can you find more turtles?"

"Mr. Hop, I can get you as many as you want!"

"Where is the best place to find so many turtles?"

"I'd rather not say."

"OK, just keep bringing them in, and I'll have your money waiting for you."

SHIPMENT OF TURTLES—
Agent Thomas H. Reynolds, of the local office of the Wells, Fargo Express Company, yesterday received a shipment to be forwarded to Portland, that stands unique as an express shipment from this city. The consignment consisted of three sacks filled with fresh water turtles, caught in the vicinity of Salem and forwarded by Hop Lee, the local Chinese laundry man, to a countryman of his in Portland.

Oregon Statesman August 1, 1902.

Thomas Wautensaugh stuffed the cash into his coat pocket and hurried out the door and on down Commercial Street into town. Hop wondered if he was going to tell his wife about their newly formed business arrangement. No matter. Hop's turtle business was underway.

The next morning Hop stopped by the Wells Fargo Express office behind the hotel.

"Hello, Hop! How's the laundry business?" Thomas Reynolds called out as Hop entered the office.

"Business is good, Thomas, but I have a new venture that needs your services."

"What are you getting into now, Hop?"

"Turtles, Thomas, and hopefully lots of them!"

Reynolds's curious expression was skeptical. "Well, Hop. You certainly know how to squeeze a penny from a rock, so how can I help you?"

"I need you to deliver a load of turtles to the Chinese market in Portland. They have to arrive alive and in good condition. Can you do this?"

"Sure, Hop. How many turtles are you talking about?"

Portland's Chinatown 1890s.

"Several hundred turtles with more to come."

"OK! Wells Fargo will be the "Turtle Express Company!""

"Ha! Ha! Thomas, we want you to go fast like the Pony Express, not slow like a turtle!"

Wautensaugh had Hop's turtle business to himself for a few weeks. Before long, a reporter for the Weekly Oregon Statesman got wind of Hop's new enterprise and ran stories in the paper marveling at Hop Lee's ability to make money from the lowly pesky turtles that inhabited the creeks and sloughs around Salem. Paying $2 for a dozen turtles seemed like folly, but it was a madness that every young boy in Salem wanted to be a part of.

Soon the slough was crawling with turtle hunters, each with a unique turtle catching technique. Hop's turtle barrel was filled to the brim, and the local Chinese restaurants eagerly anticipated the weekly shipments of turtles to the Chinese in Portland. How much profit Hop made on these turtles was never revealed, but Hop never gave another thought to the Gilbert Brothers' Bank fiasco. Why worry about water under the bridge when you could find real cash in the Salem sloughs!

Oregon Western Pond Turtle. Creative Commons Attribution-Share Alike 2.0 Generic

That evening Hop consulted the fortune teller scroll and checked off another life event. *I wonder if that tai soeng lou* [1] *knew about my turtle business.*

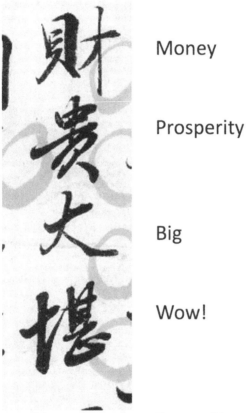

Money

Prosperity

Big

Wow!

Detail form Loo Family Scroll - You will have the opportunity to make lots of money. Low Family Collection.

---

1. tai soeng lou - fortune teller in Cantonese.

TURTLES SENT TO PORTLAND

An Industry that has Recently Developed in This City

HOP LEE, THE CHINESE LAUNDRY MAN, MAKES REGULAR SHIPMENTS — PAYS A GOOD PRICE FOR THEM—ONE MAN SUPPLIES THE MARKET IN SALEM.

The Statesman of yesterday contained a brief item on the shipment of turtles from this city to Portland. This was only one shipment of many. The turtle business has been conducted here for some time. The shipment mentioned, on Thursday morning, was of three sacks, weighing 154 pounds. There were 128 turtles in the shipment.

The turtles are bought and shipped by Hop Lee, who owns the Chinese laundry opposite the Willamette Hotel. He has for a long time been making shipments of chickens, ducks, geese, etc., to a Portland Chinese firm. He commenced the shipment of turtles to this firm some months ago, and has kept it up since.

He pays from $1.50 to $2.50 per dozen for the turtles here, owing to size and quality. What prices are realized in Portland he does not know. The turtles enter into the turtle soup consumed by the Chinese residents of Portland, and this is a dish much sought after by the people of that nationality. The French and the Americans, too, are very fond of turtle soup; but it is not known that they use turtles of the kind found here in Oregon.

Mr. Wautenspaugh, a very tall man with a long white beard, has been furnishing most of the turtles for the demand supplied by Hop Lee. He brought in forty-three fine specimens on Thursday evening, and Hop had them in a barrel behind his place of business yesterday, waiting for enough additional specimens to make a good sized shipment, when they will go forward by Wells, Fargo & Co. express. The turtles are shipped alive. In fact, they are very hard to kill. About a year ago one of the specimens dropped through the floor, and Hop Lee found him only a few days ago, alive. There is no other animal that is more tenacious of life. Even after the head of one of them is cut off, life will not be extinct for a long time.

For the forty-three turtles Mr. Wautenspaugh brought in on Thursday evening he was paid $1.80 per dozen, so he had over $6 for his day's work. Hop says he does not know how Mr. Wautenspaugh gets his turtles, or where, but he thinks he uses a barrel with which to trap them, in the creeks and sloughs.

A Salem man who came from Indiana says when he was a boy he used to have to catch the turtles and kill them, in order to protect the young ducks. He says he used to put hot coals on their backs to see them stick out their heads. He avers that is used to be said that a turtle has twelve kinds of meat. He did not mention the kinds, or whether beef steak, pork chop, mutton chop and chicken were included.

Now that the turtle business is a public matter, it is safe to predict that Mr. Wautenspaugh will no longer have a monopoly of it. He will not be a trust or a merger all by himself any more. Seeing that turtles have a commercial value here of $1.50 to $2.50 per dozen, there will be plenty of small boys to engage in their capture, and the turtles of this section would better harden their shells and pull their heads further into their holes.

Statesman Journal. Salem Oregon. August 2, 1902.

Chapter Fourteen

Hop Lee Brings Home Bride – 1903

"**W**ell, George, my friend, it's time. I have been a lonely bachelor here in Salem for 25 years. I am 45 years old, and I'm not getting any younger! I have money, and I have friends, but I do not have a family. I am like a lonely blade of grass that will die and vanish as if it never existed! I have no roots in this country."

"I have been telling you this for over a decade, Hop! But you have been too busy making money washing other people's clothes and making turtle soup! Are you still insisting on finding an American-born Chinese bride?"

"Yes, and my fortune says that a little happy bird from the south will bring me good fortune, singing, dancing, and double happiness. See it's right here," Hop insisted pointing at the well-worn fortune.

George inspected Hop's fortune, nodding in agreement. "You need to take better care of this paper, Hop. It's falling apart. I still don't know where you can find a Chinese girl born in Gum Saan."

"Well, Y.C. Huie married Daisy who was born in California and now they have two daughters and a son!" Hop exclaimed. [1]

---

1. Yongshen Y.C. Huie married Daisy in 1897. Anna, Eunice, and Fred Huie were born in 1898, 1900, and 1902. They would eventually have five sons and four daughters born in Salem between 1898 and 1915.

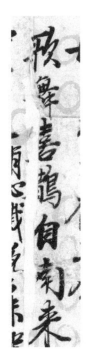 Little Happy Bird from South Bring Good Fortune

Singing

Dancing

Double Happiness

Coming from South

Little happy bird from the South will bring good fortune, singing, dancing, and double happiness.

"Yes, and his import business, Huie Wing Sang Co. will keep those children busy!" George laughed. "Maybe your plan will work."

"I have been in contact with Fong Shee, a matchmaker in Dai Fow. She found a suitable bride for me who was born in San Francisco. But I must hurry because this girl is like a rare jewel. There are almost no available Chinese women in Gum Saan and almost none who is American-born. If I don't leave immediately for San Francisco, she will be gone, given away to some other unworthy Chinese suitor!"

"Then get going, my friend. I will watch after your business while you are away. Now go!"

Hop reviewed the timetables as he planned his trip to San Francisco. The Southern Pacific ran the California Express train for the Oregon and California Railroad between Portland and San Francisco, covering the 495 miles in just ten hours. The daily express train left at 9:45 pm arriving in San Francisco the next morning at 7:45 am. The return train left San Francisco at 8:05 pm and arrived in Portland at 6:30 am. To get to Portland, he would need to take the Overland

Stagecoach.[2]

Several days later, George came back to Hop's store and laundry with a neatly wrapped package.

"You can't arrive empty-handed, Hop," George smiled as he placed his gift on the growing pile at Hop Lee's store on Commercial Street. "Besides, we want her family to know that we are not country bumpkins just because we don't live in the big city."

Hop's trip to Dai Fow to find a bride created gossip that spread throughout Salem like wildfire. Everyone in Salem knew Hop, and all his friends and customers stopped by to hear the news firsthand.

"Thanks, George. And thank Leong Shee for the nice wrapping and bows."

Hop picked up his bag and the boxes of gifts for his new bride's family. He would have to purchase more bride gifts in Dai Fow, but his friends here in Salem had loaded him down with presents and candies for his new bride.

Crossing Commercial Street, Hop went behind the Willamette Hotel to the Wells Fargo Express Office.

"Hello, Thomas!" Hop called out to his longtime friend as he entered the office.

"Hello, Loo Jim! Are you ready to take one last ride on the stagecoach?"

"Yes. Do you remember when you brought me to Salem 20 years ago with Uncle?"

"Of course. Those were the glory days for the Overland Express Stage. I am afraid our days are now numbered with the railroad and the iron horse spreading everywhere. You realize, Jim, that you could catch the train at the Southern Pacific station on 12th Street."

"Yes, but I like your stagecoach. Today you and your six horses can take me to the train station in Portland. I will send a telegraph from San Francisco so that you will know when I am returning with my new bride. I want her to arrive in Salem the same way I did. Those were the days, Thomas."

---

2. The Oregon Electric Train would not connect Salem to Portland until 1908, so the Overland Stage still ran this route.

Wells Fargo Stagecoach.

"Whatever you say, Jim. Now let's load up the stage with your luggage and boxes. What is all this stuff?"

"Gifts from the people of Salem for my new bride and her family in San Francisco," Hop replied with a sigh.

"Well, Jim, you need to come with me to check out the load of crates that I picked up for you in Portland. What is all this stuff?"

Hop inspected the crates in the storeroom and pulled out the formal list of goods. "Yes, it looks like it's all here."

"Don't keep me in suspense, Loo Jim."

Hop looked up and smiled sheepishly, "These are gifts for my new bride that I ordered from China."

"But you don't have a bride yet, Jim. Aren't you getting ahead of yourself?"

"If I find the little happy bird in San Francisco, I don't want to take any chances. I may only get one chance at making a good impression on her family. Her parents aren't going to give their daughter to a laundryman."

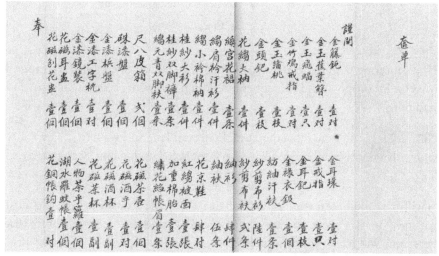

1903 Gifts for the bride. Low Family Collection.

"OK. I get it. What's in the boxes?"

Hop unfolded the red paper and began to read aloud the contents and finished by adding, "I may have gotten carried away. These gifts cost me a small fortune."

Thomas whistled, "She had better be one special girl."

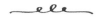

The ten-hour train trip from Portland to Dai Fow was a blur. Hop spent most of the time worrying that he might be too late to marry this young Chinese girl. She was from the Hung family, just like the two brothers, who, after all these years, still worked for him at his laundry.

Hop mused, *what if I am too late? What if she does not like me? I have money, but I am so much older. These young girls want romance. What do I know of such things? She will probably reject me!*

With all of Hop's worrying, he hardly noticed the Oregon and California countryside zipping past. Hop had been to Dai Fow as a young man but had spent most of his adult life in little Albany and Salem in Oregon's Willamette Valley. He felt a bit like a country cousin coming to the big city.

—e ℓ ℓ—

Hop's meeting with the matchmaker Fong Shee helped to establish the ground rules for his proposal and subsequent wedding if all went according to plan and traditions.

"It's very easy. Just remember the Three Letters and the Six Etiquettes," Fong Shee said with a flourish of her aged hands as if she were waving him away to married life.

"I will make it simple for you and will take care of all the details, but first, you must pay me. I do have to eat, you know. My fee is $300, and there is no guarantee that her family will accept your proposal!"

Hop handed the old woman the money enclosed in a red envelope.

"I know the three letters. The Betrothal Letter, Gift Letter, and the Wedding Letter, but what are these six etiquettes?"

Fong Shee looked more than a bit exasperated.

"Where have you been living? In a barn? The Six Etiquettes are the basis for your proposal, gift exchange, and wedding. Without these formalities, they will see you as a heathen or a country bumpkin!"

Hop decided to hold his tongue with this pompous matchmaker. He needed her assistance. Although she would not guarantee results, she was the most highly regarded of all the Dai Fow matchmakers. He would tolerate her sharp tongue for a bit longer.

Not waiting for his reply, Fong Shee continued, "These are the Six Etiquettes. Try to pay attention, Mr. Loo!

- The Proposal. I will communicate your interest in Ah Kay to her parents through the Betrothal Letter.

- Birthday Matching. I will check your birthdays and birth hours to see if you are compatible.

- Present the betrothal gifts.

- Present the wedding gifts. These include tea, lotus seeds, longan, red beans, green beans, red dates, nutmeg, oranges, pomegranate, lily, bridal cakes, coconuts, wine, red hair braid, and a money box.

- Picking the wedding date. I will consult the stars to select the most favorable date for the ceremony.

- Finally, there is The Wedding Ceremony. But that is getting way ahead of ourselves!"

Hop listened intently, head tilted in concentration, but he could not keep the annoyance off his face at the matchmaker's condescending tone.

"You will have to pay for the ceremony, your bride's gowns, all the gifts, and the assorted decorations and details. I assure you it is not cheap! I hope you brought a lot of money with you. Her family is not well off, so they will need you to provide for her portion of the wedding," Fong Shee warned, looking at Hop warily, trying to assess the size of his pocketbook.

"Don't worry about the money! You just take care of your part of the proposal and ceremony. I will handle the finances!" Hop replied indignantly.

Traditional Chinese Wedding ceremony. Detail of scroll about Suzhou made on the order of Emperor Qianlong Wikimedia Commons.

"Good! Now that we have that settled, I will write the Proposal Letter and deliver it to the girl's parents. They live on Sacramento Street at the corner with Stockton."

He had tried to tell her about his businesses in Salem, but she dismissed him like a schoolboy.

"You men all say the same things! I am not impressed with your laundry and turtles, Mr. Loo."

All Hop could do now was wait for the matchmaker to work her magic. He went to his cousin's store on Commercial Street to await word from the matchmaker. At least he wasn't too late. That would have been a disaster to have traveled all the way from Portland only to find out that the girl had married some other Chinese! As he walked along Dupont Street, Hop stopped to examine some dried cuttlefish and shark's fin a rare delicacy to bring his cousin for dinner.

Wilhelm Hester San Francisco Chinatown 1890s.

The next day Fong Shee was at the front door of his cousin's apartment.

"Open up, Mr. Loo! Hurry up! We have no time to waste!"

Hop opened the door and found the obnoxious little matchmaker fuming impatiently.

Not waiting for his greeting, she blurted out, "They want to meet you. This request is highly irregular, but they have another suitor from a different matchmaker! It is a seller's market these days. There are so few of these Chinese girls available. Put on something nice. We need you to make a good impression."

Hop hurriedly put on his best coat, combed his queue, and put on his Derby hat.

"What kind of a silly hat is that?" Fong Shee demanded. "You look like a Chinese in a White man's hat!"

Hop had had enough of this woman. "This is my best hat. If you don't like it, you can give me back my $300, and I will find another matchmaker!"

"Settle down, Mr. Loo. Your hat is all right. It is just a bit unusual for a Chinese man to wear one like that here in Dai Fow."

"Well, in Salem, these Derby hats are quite fashionable."

"Ok, let's get going before that other matchmaker steals away this bride."

Hop in his black Derby hat, and Fong Shee the matchmaker were an odd sight walking through Chinatown. Hop ignored the stares. He was becoming self-conscious about his hat, but in truth, the Chinese merchants were staring because he was a stranger coming to take away one of their daughters.

Walking downhill on Dupont Gai, they turned right on Sacramento and headed up the hill. Little Fong Shee led the way as Hop struggled to keep up with the matchmaker, who was used to the hills of Dai Fow. They finally came to a stop at the corner of Stockton and Sacramento Streets, where she entered the apartment building.

Hop noted the number on the building 820 Sacramento. They walked up to the second floor, where Fong Shee rapped on the apartment door. The door opened a crack, and a little boy peered out.

"What do you want?"

Wilhelm Hester. San Francisco Chinatown 1890s.

"I am Fong Shee, the matchmaker. I am here to see your parents."

Ed Toon looked skeptically at the old woman, "Who is he?"

Fong Shee looked exasperated and was about to demand that the boy open the door when Hop stepped forward.

"I am Loo Sun Fook, but you can call me Loo Jim or Hop Lee," Hop smiled and patted Ed Toon on the head. "Are your parents at home?"

Just then, the door opened a bit wider, and two more boys peered out at Hop.

"I am Bing, and this is my brother Kim. Where are you from, Mister Hop?"

"Salem, Oregon is my home, boys."

"Is that near Montana? Do you have any Indians in Salem, Oregon? How far is that from here?" asked a wide-eyed Bing.

Hop smiled at the three boys. "Yes, we have lots of Indians in Oregon, and Montana is not too far away by train."

Now it was Kim's turn. "Have you ever ridden on the Great Northern train? Have you seen those locomotives with the 12-foot drive wheels? I want to be an engineer someday!"

"Yes, I have been on the Great Northern train out of Seattle. Those locomotives are something to see pulling their long trains over the Cascade Mountains."

Feeling left out, Ed Toon interjected, "Mister Hop, I like your hat!"

Hop smiled and placed his favorite felt Derby on Ed Toon's head. "In Salem, it is the American fashion to wear a Derby Hat ."

Just then, the boys' parents entered the front room. The man was tall and a bit older than Hop. The woman was small but stood straight and looked Hop in the eye, sizing him up.

"Please sit. Boys, where are your manners?" Ah Ying scolded her three sons as she ushered Fong Shee and Hop into the small dining room.

"I am Tom Shee, and this is my husband, Hung Lai Wah. Everyone calls me Ah Ying."

Hop and Fong Shee took a seat at the table.

"Ed Toon, give Mr. Loo his hat."

"It is all right if the boy likes to wear my Derby. It was getting a lot of stares from the merchants along Dupont Gai."

"Actually, they were staring at you because they know why you are here. You see, those men took care of me when I was growing up. They are all my uncles, my family, and they know you are coming to take away my daughter Ah Kay. You can't blame them for being a bit protective. Most of them are bachelors. These children are their family."

Lai Wah finally spoke up, "We all want to be certain that you are worthy of our first-born child."

"Yes, we want to know that you can support her and will treat her with kindness," Ah Ying added, looking at Hop directly. "We have seen too many Chinese men whose intentions are not honorable. They marry girls and then force them into a life of slavery."

Hop hadn't expected this grilling from the girl's parents. They were both staring at him intently, waiting for his reply. Not sure of how to respond, he decided to go with the truth.

"I have been alone in Gum Saan, far away from my family in Kwangtung, for almost 30 years. I have been very successful in business, but it is all worthless to me without a family. Your daughter, Ah Kay, is more precious than a jewel, and if she accepts me, she will have my devotion and a life of luxury. I will protect her and provide all the material wealth that she desires," Hop replied earnestly. "I will make her my partner in my business and our marriage," he added.

Ah Ying stared silently at the Chinese man, trying to size him up. He was smaller than her Gee Sung. His hands were soft, unlike the Chinese laborers that filled the streets in Chinatown. Perhaps he was a successful merchant, as he claimed. And his words seemed earnest, even a bit desperate.

Suddenly, she smiled, "Well, Mr. Loo, I have a good feeling about you. What do you think, Gee Sung?"

"I think that if Mr. Loo does not keep his word, there is no place on earth he could hide from me and the Bing Kong Tong!" Lai Wah glared at his guest.

Hop was taken aback by the intensity of Lai Wah's words but did not miss a beat.

"I am a man of my word. I will teach our children to keep their word just as I will honor my promise to you. Ah Kay will always be treated with kindness and respect. That is my word."

Ah Ying had made up her mind.

"Thank you, Mr. Loo. We will give our answer to Fong Shee." She then smiled and added, "We like you."

With those simple words, the meeting was concluded. Fong Shee and Hop descended the stairwell and exited the building onto Sacramento Street. Hop had not dared to be this hopeful, but now it seemed that he might find a bride and an American-born bride at that!

Remembering a critical detail, Hop stopped dead in his tracks, "I must have proof that Ah Kay was born in America. It is essential."

"Chinese do not have birth certificates, Mr. Loo. Why do you need this? Your extra demand may undermine all of my hard work!" Fong Shee sniffed.

"I need this birth certificate, and it needs to be notarized. I will pay to have it made for Ah Kay and her sister as well."

"Alright. It's your money. I will ask her parents to obtain the birth certificate. I just hope you are not screwing up this marriage proposal."

Ah Ying and Lai Wah understood Hop's requirement for Ah Kay to have a certificate confirming her American birth. Such a document made her even more valuable. Having a birth certificate for her sister Chun Ngo would help the family when it became time for her to marry. They agreed to obtain the birth certificates as long as Mr. Loo agreed to pay the fees, which would not be trivial for such a formal document. Loo also suggested that they have a family portrait taken to mark the special occasion.

Fong Shee grumbled, but she arranged for the girls' notarized birth certificates and had the Hong family assembled in front of a three-story stone building at 8 Montgomery Street opposite the Palace and Grand Hotels.

"Well, Mr. Loo, I hope you have a lot of money. You chose the most expensive photographer in San Francisco for this portrait!"

"Only the best for my new wife's family. Besides, I have my reasons," Hop replied mysteriously.

Ah Ying looked at the sign with a puzzled expression, "Hibernia Bank." Why are we going to a bank? Didn't you bring enough money for the portrait?"

"No! No! No!" Fong Shee fumed. "It's up there," she exclaimed, pointing her long bony finger at the second floor.

"Where are Ah Kay and Lai Wah?" Hop puzzled.

"They will be along shortly. It would be bad luck for Kay to see you before the wedding, Mr. Loo," Ah Ying explained.

Fong Shee led Ah Ying, her four children, and Hop up the stairs to the second floor, where they stopped in front of the large glass and wooden door with gold-trimmed letters proclaiming, "I.W. Taber Photographic Gallery."

8 Montgomery Street in San Francisco. The I.W. Taber Gallery is on the 2nd floor.

Before she could reach for the knob, the door opened wide, revealing the proprietor with his ever-ready smile and an unmistakable bushy handlebar mustache.

"Mr. Taber!" Ah Ying laughed. "I never expected to see you again."

"When I heard your first-born daughter was getting married and that this Fong Shee woman was looking for a photographer, I insisted that you come to my studio."

Isaiah West Taber. Public Domain.

"Mr. Taber, you took that photograph of the Mission Home family at the church. You took two portraits that day, as I recall. And then you took our family photograph at the Midwinter Exposition in Golden Gate Park!"

"True and true again, Ah Ying. But I took an earlier photograph of a young Chinese girl on the landing docks, looking very lost and homesick. I am certain it was you, Ah Ying. Here let me show you that image."

Taber rummaged around in his files for a bit. "Here it is!"

He presented the photograph for the family to inspect. "See, the girl in the foreground standing on a wooden crate," Taber explained, pointing.

"That is me!" Ah Ying exclaimed. "And that woman next to me is that evil woman who sold me to that horrible family on Jackson Street!"

"How did you know that was me after all these years?"

"Well, you made quite an impression. You looked like you were about to run away. You jumped off the crate, turned around, and bolted for the Street, almost running over me and my tripod!"

"I was so scared and alone, and I wanted to be anywhere but on that dock with that woman,"

"Well, Ah Ying, hopefully, our paths will continue to cross. Now, let's get your family set up for this special portrait. But where is your daughter and Gee Sung?"

"They're coming," Ah Ying explained.

"Mr. Loo, you hide in this back room and don't come out! You can peek through this little window if you must see. But don't make a peep, or you will bring bad luck to your marriage!" Fong Shee demanded. "This request is highly irregular!"

The San Francisco landing docks 1880. Isaiah West Taber. Public Domain.

Just as Fong Shee sequestered Hop in his hiding place, Lai Wah and Ah Kay entered through the gallery front door.

"Here, Gee Sung, you sit in the middle, and Ah Ying, you sit on his right. Now, the two girls sit on the left, the little boy in the middle between his parents, and that leaves you, two boys, on the right."

The family quickly took their positions as Mr. Taber had instructed.

"Well, we need some props. Here, you boys hold these scrolls to symbolize learning. And the girls hold these fans."

"What do I get?" inquired tiny Ed Toon feeling a bit left out.

Taber looked into his box of photographic props. "Hmm, no more scrolls. Here, just hold this fan."

"That's for girls!" Ed Toon protested. "I want a scroll-like Bing and Kim!"

"Just take the fan and try not to look so glum," Ah Ying said to her youngest.

Ed Toon took the fan but thrust it into his Father's lap. No one will think Dad's a girl, Toon mused.

"Alright, everyone. Hold still and look happy. One, two, and three!"

The bright flash was blinding, and the smoke's smell was strong indoors, but they held still, and the Hong Family Portrait, taken on September 12, 1903, was preserved for all time. Little did they know that this was the last time the family would be together.

—ele—

1903 Hong Family Portrait. Low Family Collection.

The next day, the early morning light filtered through the curtains as Ah Ying skillfully worked the Singer sewing machine's foot treadle. She had been up all night and finished the red veil for Ah Kay's wedding dress. Mr. Loo had generously offered to buy a delicate Chinese gown, but she had refused his offer. No one could make a finer dress for her first-born daughter. She was the best seamstress in Dai Fow. She had let Mr. Loo purchase the red silk brocade cloth. This fine material from China was beyond their means, but she had sewn the dress herself with the love of a mother missing her daughter.

"Ah Kay! Hold still! I am almost finished, but if you keep squirming around, the dress will not fit!"

"Sorry, Mama," Kay replied, still unable to hold still. "Why can't I see him before we are married?"

"That would be very bad luck and disastrous for your marriage," Ah Ying replied, looking up from her work.

"But you and Papa met long before you were married, and you fell in love first! It is not fair that I have to marry a stranger!"

"Shush! I am sorry I told you those silly stories," Ah Ying replied, no longer looking at her daughter. She smiled as she remembered her Gee Sung and felt a deep sadness for her Kay, who would have to find love another way.

"They are not silly at all! Chun Ngo and I want to marry for love, not money! Why did you get to find love and not me?" Kay sniffed as she stood perfectly still in her red wedding gown.

"Because we can no longer feed the family, Kay. Your Father cannot work full time, and there is no money left after we

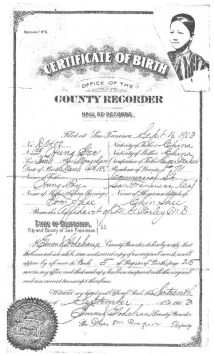

Birth certificate of Kay Hung September 1903. Low Family Collection

pay the rent. My sewing does not bring in enough extra money," Ah Ying replied softly with a sadness in her heart that she would never fully show her daughter.

"I can get a job, Mama."

"Your job is to marry and be a good wife. He is very well off and will provide for you and will treat you kindly. I am sure of this, and your father will see to it that he keeps his word."

Ah Ying rose from the Singer. Standing behind her daughter, she placed the red veil over Kay's head as the two looked at their reflections in the cracked mirror.

Ah Ying stood a bit taller than her daughter. Her face was beginning to show the years that had passed. She was no longer the young mui tsai, who had fallen in love with Gee Sung.

"You look beautiful, Kay. You will be the perfect bride."

"What if he does not like me, Mama?"

"How could any man not fall in love with you, Kay? He told me that you are a rare jewel. Wait until he sees you in this dress."

With those words, she reached into her pocket and pulled out three coins, handing them to her daughter. "These are for good luck. Chinese call them *mixiqian* or Chinese marriage coins. Study them later so you will know what to expect on your wedding night."

Ah Kay began to inspect the coins when Ah Ying interrupted. "No, later. Take the dress off. We have to prepare the front room for the wedding ceremony. By Chinese custom, you should be married at the home of Low Sun Fook's parents, but we will have to make due since his family is in Hoiyin, China."

"Who will be my good luck woman for the hair combing ceremony, Mama?"

"I have asked Chin Shee to be your good luck woman. She was at my marriage, so now she can comb your hair as well. And since she has four children, she will bring you good fortune."

Chapter Fifteen

Wedding Day –
September 13, 1903

A h Kay had always dreamed of arriving at her wedding in a decorated sedan chair. Those were the stories of marriages in the old country she had always heard. She had even enlisted Bing, Kim, and Toon's support to help carry her sedan chair to the wedding. But those were dreams of the old days. This was America, and traditional customs had to change. There would be no sedan chair today. She and Ah Ying had decorated the front room with fresh flowers, red ribbons, and good luck papers. They tidied up the family altar, preparing new sticks of incense and fragrant sandalwood.

Ah Ying inspected the room. Everything was perfect. "Come, Ah Kay. It is time to get dressed in the bedroom. Mr. Loo must not see you when he arrives."

Ah Kay followed mama into the bedroom and changed into the red wedding dress her mother had sewn. The two-piece outfit was elegant and classic, constructed from silk brocade with expert weaving handiwork to make the flowers & vines woven into the fabric. Made with a mother's love, a delicate red frog (pankou) button and loop fasteners secured the dress and collar. Matching handmade shoes and an organic headpiece completed the wedding outfit.

As fine as the dress was, it could not hide Kay's growing apprehension about marrying this man she had never met.

"Mama, what if I don't like him? Can I come home?"

Photographs of Kay's 1903 wedding dress, shoes, and headpiece are courtesy of Catherine Low Doo.

"Shush, Ah Kay," Ah Ying softly replied as she buttoned up the back of the wedding dress. "He is a nice man. Your father and I talked to him, and we chose him for you. You will come to like him, and he will take care of you."

There was a knock at the door, causing a commotion as Toon ran to see who had arrived for the wedding.

Photographs of Kay's 1903 wedding dress, shoes, and headpiece are courtesy of Catherine Low Doo.

"Hello, Toon!" Chin Shee greeted her nephew.

"Hello, Auntie. Mama and Ah Kay are waiting for you in there!" exclaimed Toon pointing to the closed bedroom door. "Why do you get to go in? They won't let me in to see Ah Kay!"

"Today, I am your sister's good fortune woman," explained Chin Shee as she quietly entered the bedroom, closing the door behind her.

"Hello, my dear Ah Ying!" Chin Shee greeted her old friend.

"*Jou sahn*, Sing Yee," Ah Ying smiled. "Do you remember when you were my good fortune woman?"

"What I remember is how you had me sneak you out of the Mission Home to steal visits with your Gee Sung!" laughed Sing Yee.

"Shush, don't tell such stories to the children!"

"We were mere children ourselves when we first met on that wretched ship, and so much has happened since then. Where have the years gone, my friend?"

"Enough old memories! Did you bring the wedding comb?" Ah Ying asked, brushing a tear from her eye.

"Of course. Now, where is the bride?" Chin Shee asked, turning to Ah Kay, who was sitting quietly in the corner.

Kay had a panicked look on her face. "Mama, I don't want to do this!"

Before Ah Ying could reply, Chin Shee took Ah Kay by the hand and gently led her to the seat by the window.

"Quiet, my little one. Everything will be fine. Today is a blessed day. You will have a happy marriage with many children," Chin Shee softly cooed as she stood behind Kay, running the comb through her hair.

"Your mother and I and all the other Chinese women share this hair combing ceremony. It is a tradition that binds us together and to our husbands," Chin Shee continued. "It will bring your marriage good fortune."

"Now listen carefully to my words. These are blessings for you and Low Sun Fook." With each stroke of the comb, Chin Shee repeated the blessings that she and Ah Ying knew so well.

'Continuous from beginning to end, may you be together all of your lives'

'May you have closeness and harmony in your marriage for a hundred years, till a ripe old age'

'May you fill your home with children and grandchildren'

'May you enjoy a long life together, until your hair and even eyebrows are white.

Ah Ying reached into her pocket and pulled out a golden hair clip shaped like a butterfly. For months she had been saving a little from her sewing money each week so she could buy this gift for her daughter. Placing the hair clip into Ah Kay's hand, she murmured, "Do not forget your family."

Ah Kay inspected the golden butterfly adorned with jade. "*Doh Jeh*, Mama. I will remember you and Papa and Bing, Kim, Chung Ngo, and little Toon."

Ah Ying took the clip and placed it in Ah Kay's freshly brushed hair.

Wedding Butterfly Hair piece worn by Kay's sister, Chun Ngo, on her wedding day in 1910. Courtesy of Dorothy H. Yim. Translation of Chinese characters on the pin, "The wife is Respectful of the husband and the husband is polite to the wife."

Reaching into the inseam of her jacket Ah Ying next pulled out a small packet wrapped in cloth. Slowly opening the cloth, she handed its contents to her daughter.

"I have been saving these earrings for you. They are from my mother. She hid them in the lining of the jacket I wore the day I was kidnapped. I kept them hidden for all these years and have never shown them to anyone."

Ah Kay's eyes widened as her mother's treasure came into view. "Mama, they are beautiful!"

The perfectly matched jade earrings were set in a row of tiny black pearls and trimmed with gold. "They are too much. You must keep them for yourself."

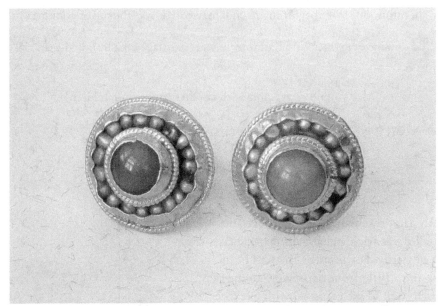

Earrings – Gold, jade, and pearls courtesy of Laurel Low Depolo.

"No. I want you to have these earrings to wear on your wedding day, my Ah Kay. I hid them from the slave owners and the Mission ladies, and even your father. Each time I sewed a new jacket, I made the secret pocket to hide the earrings. Now they are yours, so you will always remember your mother's love."

"Now, where is the veil and headpiece?" Ah Ying asked, changing the subject as she wiped a tear from her eye.

"First drink this sweet soup with white and pink rice balls symbolizing your sweet marriage together," instructed Chin Shee.

Ah Kay drank the sweet wedding soup as the three women sat quietly, each lost in her thoughts. Ah Ying smiled, remembering her first day with her Gee Sung in their tiny apartment on Dupont Gai after running away from the Mission Home.

"I was so young," she murmured. Looking up at her daughter, she continued, "I thought my life was complete after I ran away from the Mission Home and could finally be with your father. But life is so much more than romance. Be good to your husband, and he will take care of you always. If you are lucky, he will become your friend, as your father is mine."

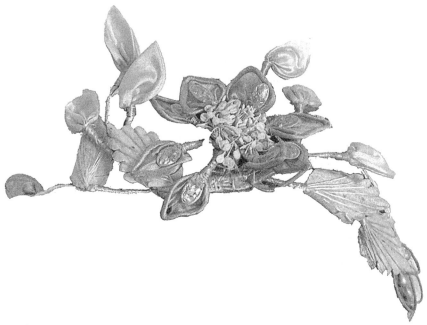

Kay's 1903 Wedding headpiece. Organic and floral forms are in keeping the Art Nouveaux style popular from 1890 – 1910. Courtesy of Catherine Low Doo.

Ah Kay was not convinced but was quietly listening to the sounds coming from the front room. "I think he has arrived, Mama. I hear another voice."

Ah Ying stood, taking her daughter's hand. Chin Shee placed the red veil over Ah Kay's face and then reached for the doorknob. "Are you ready, Kay?"

Before Ah Kay could answer, Chin Shee slowly opened the door to the front room. Through the wedding veil, the entire room was red and out of focus. Her father, Kim, Bing, Toon, and sister Chun Ngo gathered around the family altar near the front window. As soon as the door opened, all eyes were upon Ah Kay. Ah Ying took Kay's hand and led her to the altar.

Kay scanned the room, wishing she could remove the veil so she could get a better look. Then Papa took a step forward to greet his daughter, revealing the face of her new husband standing behind him. He was smiling and looking directly at her. Ah Kay felt her face flush but couldn't stop looking at him. Her knees shook slightly as the three women walked into the room and approached the altar.

Photographs of Kay's 1903 wedding dress, shoes, and headpiece. Courtesy of Catherine Low Doo.

"Stand next to Mr. Loo," Ah Ying instructed her daughter.

When Ah Kay didn't budge, she shoved her daughter forward until she was standing on the right side of her new husband.

Kay had a death grip on her mother's hand as Ah Ying tried to pull away to stand behind her daughter. Finally, losing grip on her mother's hand, Ah Kay was alone in front of the family altar with this stranger. She refused to look at him but instead looked frantically around the room for another friendly face. Her empty hands were shaking, and she felt beads of sweat forming on her brow. Just when she thought she might pass out, she felt a gentle touch on her left shoulder.

Looking to her left, Ah Kay saw Mr. Loo's face come into focus.

"I am nervous too, Ah Kay. Maybe you can help me, and I will help you. We will do this together. I think we just have to breathe," he took a deep breath and slowly exhaled. "Now you try it. Breathe slowly in and out."

Kay took in a small breath and exhaled as the red veil fluttered in front of her face.

"Good! Now, don't you feel better? Would you like some tea?"

Ah Kay replied meekly, "No, thank you." She did feel better and was surprised by her husband's kind voice.

The rest of the ceremony was a blur as Ah Kay and Loo Sun Fook did as they were instructed, reciting blessings to Heaven and Earth, and the family ancestors. Ah Kay and Loo Sun Fook next bowed three times and were married by the Chinese custom. The two served tea to Ah Ying's family with red dates, peanuts, and lotus seeds. Loo Jim thought briefly of his parents in Toishan, wishing that they could be with him on this joyous day.

The wedding feast was held at Hang Far Low restaurant on Dupont Gai. Uncle Chan came out of retirement to make a twenty-course feast for his favorite, Ah Ying, and her newlywed daughter.

"My little Ah Ying! Where have all the years gone?" Uncle Chan whispered as he instructed the waiters to serve the honored guests.

"Uncle Chan! I have missed you so! Do you remember...."

"Of course, I remember when you came to this same restaurant as a mere child, a mui tsai. Those cruel owners of yours on Jackson Street made you haul their

Hop Lee's wedding jacket. 1903. Courtesy of Laurel Low Depolo.

meals up the street twice a day. The stack of bamboo steamers was taller than you were!" laughed Uncle Chan.

"I was skinny as a rail and always hungry. It was lucky for me that I had you as my friend and a secret Chinese cook. Your bowls of noodles kept me alive and gave me hope and something to look forward to. Thank you, Uncle Chan," she said softly.

"You and Sue Lee were my favorites, Ah Ying! Speaking of your friend, I have a surprise for you," Uncle Chan grinned as he stepped aside, revealing Sue Lee, who had been hiding behind him.

"Sue Lee!" Ah Ying gasped as she jumped up out of her seat, hugging her long-lost best friend.

"My Ah Ying! *Nei hou ma*? And where is little Chun Ngo? Remember when I carried your baby girl while you and Gee Sung, Kay, and Bing went on that horrible Firth Wheel ride at the Midwinter Fair?"

"Yes, of course, I remember, Sue Lee. But the children are almost grown. Bing is already 11 years old and ready to take on the world," Ah Ying smiled.

"But today, your Ah Kay is leaving home to join her husband in Salem, Oregon! She is so young, Ah Ying!" exclaimed Sue Lee.

Ah Ying looked deeply into her best friend's eyes before she replied, "She is too young. But what are we to do? There isn't any work for Gee Sung, and there never seems to be enough to feed the children."

"So today we will celebrate her wedding and her new life," Sue Lee replied.

"Yes, Loo Sun Fook is a good man and is a wealthy merchant. He will be a good husband and father. I will keep an eye on him just in case to make sure he takes good care of my little girl!"

The wedding feast that Uncle Chan prepared for the 100 guests was the talk of Chinatown for days. There hadn't been a culinary celebration like this for some time.

At the end of the evening, Ah Ying approached Ah Kay and her new husband at the head table.

"Thank you for the wedding banquet, Loo. You have been very generous," Ah Ying smiled at her new son-in-law.

"*Ngoihmóu*,[1] I am honored to be a part of your family and to offer this humble dinner to help us celebrate the wedding tonight. Your Ah Kay is a precious jewel, and I will treasure her always. I have waited for decades to marry and to start a family in Gum Saan."

Ah Ying smiled silently and then gave her daughter a small hug. Before she could say a word, Ah Ying turned and walked away with a small tear trickling down her cheek.

———*ele*———

1. Ngoihmóu Cantonese for mother-in-law

Wedding Shoes 1903 courtesy of Catherine Low Doo. Art Nouveau ornamental style flourished between 1890 and 1910.

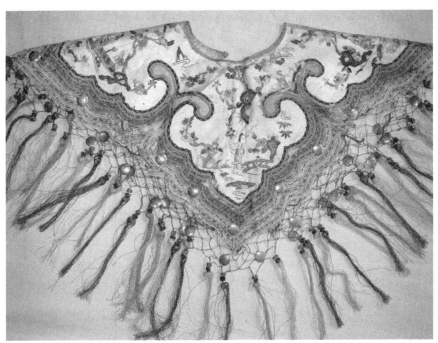

Wedding shawl gift from Hop Lee to his new bride in September 1903.

Chapter Sixteen

New Life in Salem, Oregon – 1903

H op put down his pen and sighed. Looking at the words on the pages of his journal, he marveled at how his dream had come true.

He smiled as he recalled their trip from Dai Fow back to Salem.

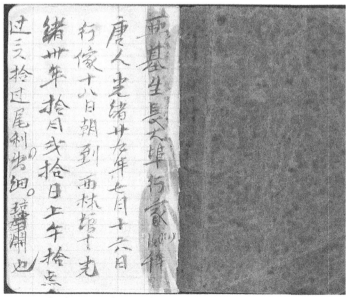

Married Ah Kay, who was born and raised in San Francisco. We arrived in Salem on September 16, 1903. Low Family Collection

The 10-hour trip on the Southern Pacific train from San Francisco to Portland began right on time, with the train departing at 8:05 pm from the 3rd Street Depot. Wearing her red wedding dress, Ah Kay sat quietly across from Loo Jim, hardly speaking a word. She tried looking out the window, but it soon became pitch black outside as the train headed north through California and then on into Oregon.

Hop tried to engage his young wife, but his attempts at conversation while attentive were met with silence or a brief nod.

"Ah, Kay, are you comfortable? Would you like something to eat or a blanket to stay warm?"

Ah Kay looked at him and shook her head but did not utter a word.

Poor girl. She must be frightened and lonely, Hop mused.

He patted her arm, trying to reassure her, "We can become friends when you are ready. I will be patient, Ah Kay."

After an hour, Ah Kay looked up at her husband and smiled shyly, "What should I call you? Hop, Loo Jim, or Sun Fook? You have a lot of names like my father."

"You can call me Hop like everyone else in Salem, or you can call me *jeuhngfu*, which means......."

"It means husband," Ah Kay interrupted, "But I want to call you 'Hubby.' It sounds more modern."

"Yes, Ah Kay. I will be your Hubby if you like. We do need to be modern like Salem's White men and women. We will teach our children to be American."

Ah Kay finally closed her eyes as they passed the state border and slept with her head resting on the window.

Hop gently placed a blanket over Ah Kay and found a soft pillow for her head to rest upon. He smiled. *She really is a precious jewel.*

7193. Union Depot, Portland, Oregon.

Union Station Portland Oregon Postcard. Low Family Collection

Early the next morning, the red Wells Fargo Express Stagecoach pulled up to the Portland Union train station with its yellow wheels rolling to a stop. The station built in 1896 along the Willamette River was right next to Portland's Chinatown. It was well known for its 150-foot clock tower visible throughout the city.

A smiling Thomas Reynolds jumped down from the driver's seat, calling out, "Hi Hop! Welcome home. We've all been waiting to meet your misses."

After the long journey, it was good to see a familiar and friendly face.

"Hi, Thomas. This is Ah Kay, Salem's newest citizen."

"Welcome, Ah Kay. You know, Hop was only a little older than you when we first met. I could tell you some stories," Thomas added with a smile.

Thomas opened the door and helped Ah Kay and Loo Jim up into the coach. Hop briefly inspected the empty compartment, "No other passengers today, Thomas?"

"No. Today is a special run of the Wells Fargo Express for you and your new bride. Well, I did bring along someone to keep me company."

Removing the lid from a small wooden box, "Have a look! Here is my friend and good luck charm!"

Peeking into the box Ah Kay and Loo Jim laughed at the site of Myrtle the Willamette Turtle straining its neck to greet Loo Jim and Ah Kay.

Thomas Reynolds jumped into the driver's seat and took up the reins. "G-long! H-up, there!"

The six horses lurched forward, the traces snapped taut, and the stage leaped into motion carrying Ah Kay to her new home in Salem.

Years later, Kay told her grand-daughters how she rode into Salem in a Wells Fargo stagecoach wearing her red wedding dress.

As the stagecoach pulled into the Red Front Livery in Salem, a vehicle of an entirely different form of horsepower came barreling down Commercial Street.

"Watch out, Hop! I'm still learning how to steer this thing!" Otto Wilson called out from his new Oldsmobile horseless carriage.

"How long have you been driving that contraption, Otto?" Thomas called out.

"I took delivery in April. This is the first automobile in our state outside of Portland. It's the future."

Thomas Reynolds shook his head, "I guess that pretty much puts the final nail in the Wells Fargo Express coffin."

"Well, Thomas, we will always remember our final trip," Hop replied

Ernst Hoffer of the Capital Journal got wind of Hop's arrival with his new bride and was the first to scoop the story of Salem's newest resident.

On April 16, 1903 Otto J Wilson received his $650 1903 Oldsmobile with curved dash and tiller steering and single piston engine. CC0 1.0 Universal Wikimedia Commons. Dr. Bernd Gross.

The next morning a soft rapping on the door startled Ah Kay. Their apartment was just above the Hop Lee Laundry on Commercial Street but had its own entrance on the building's side at the end of a flight of rickety wooden steps. Hop, who had risen early, was nowhere to be seen. Unsure, Kay took two steps towards the door, waited, and listened.

Rap! Rap! Rap! "Ah Kay, are you in there?" a woman's voice called out.

Ah Kay reached for the door handle and slowly opened the door, squinting into the early Salem morning sunlight. She encountered a woman with white hair and a smiling face. Ah Kay waited silently with the door halfway open.

"Hello, Ah Kay. I am Beatrice Hundsaker. Hop, I mean Loo Jim asked me to check in on you and to see how you are doing."

As she finished her introduction, Beatrice looked closely at the young girl,

---

Hop Lee Married.

It is not generally known, but Lou Jim, proprietor of the Hop Lee launddry, in The Journal office block, about a month ago went to California and took to himself a wife, and his lady has become a resident of the city. Lou Jim is best known as Hop Lee, having succeeded to the name along with the business. His many friends have been congratulating him, and he is one of the best known and most popular Chinamen in the Capital City.

Daily Capital Journal Thursday October 8, 1903.

"My dear! You are just a child! Well, no matter. Hop wants me to help you adjust to your new life in Salem, so let's get to work."

"First things first. Do you know how to cook? No? Well, how about cleaning? Can you sew?"

Growing exasperated with the woman's questioning Ah Kay blurted out, "Of course I can sew! My mother was the finest seamstress in Dai Fow!"

"Where is Die Foul?"

"Dai Fow is the first City. San Francisco to you."

"OK. So, you are a Big City girl. But you will need to learn to cook and keep house if you want to live here in Salem as Sun Fook's wife. And I am just the person to teach you!"

"Let's begin with lesson number one: making a pot of rice. This dish is something of a specialty for Loo Jim! You should ask him about the time he was a cook on the Albany Railroad. His rice was so bad the Chinese workers ran him out of camp and chased him down the rails!" Beatrice laughed.

"My mother showed me how to make rice. First, you wash it and then cover it with clean water so that the water is one knuckle above the rice."

"Very good, Ah Kay. And then what do you do with the pot?"

"You place it over the fire and slowly let it come to a boil until it foams."

"Excellent, my dear Kay. Any young wife who can make a good pot of Chinese rice is well on her way to becoming a proper housewife and cook."

The rest of the morning was a blur of cutting, chopping, stirring, and tasting the delicious meal that Beatrice Hundsaker prepared. Ah Kay tried to absorb it all, but it became clear that she had a lot to learn about everything.

"Alright, Ah Kay. That's enough for today. Tomorrow we can start with the house cleaning lessons."

"*Doh jeh*, Beatrice."

"No thanks are necessary, Ah Kay. Just be sure to feed Hop the meal we prepared for his supper. And tell him you made it all by yourself," Beatrice added with a wink.

Both women surveyed the kitchen admiring the morning's creation, the pot of perfect white rice, a delicious pot roast, biscuits, an upside-down pineapple cake, and freshly picked and steamed mixed vegetables from Beatrice's garden. It was magnificent! A mountain of dirty pots, pans, dishes, and utensils lay scattered about the kitchen in the background.

"Don't worry, Kay. We can have this kitchen spick and span in no time."

Kay and Beatrice set about the task of rinsing, cleaning, and scrubbing and quickly had the kitchen back in order.

Beatrice smiled as she observed Ah Kay scrubbing tenaciously at a stubborn stain on the last pot. She was humming a song from her childhood. *This one is fastidious and does not give up easily.*

"What is that song you are humming, Kay?"

"It is just a song my mother used to sing to us when we went to sleep each night. She told us it is a Cantonese song from her village in Toishan. Her sister Chun Fah used to sing to the other girls in the Home."

The moon is bright, the wind is quiet,

The tree leaves hang over the window,

My little baby, go to sleep quickly,

Sleep, dreaming sweet dreams

Beatrice Hundsaker quickly became Ah Kay's indispensable teacher and best friend. Their friendship would last for decades.

———ele———

That evening, Kay, beaming, proudly served Loo Jim the meal she and Beatrice had prepared.

"Kay, you are a marvel!" Hop exclaimed as he admired the feast laid out on the small wooden table.

"Well, I did have some help from Mrs. Hundsaker," Kay confessed softly.

"Beatrice stopped by the laundry and reported that you are a quick and eager learner," Hop confided as he tasted the pot roast and biscuits with gravy.

"Here, you must have rice with your meal, and I made you some tea."

Hop smiled as he enjoyed the meal and company of his new wife and friend.

Kay stood up and walked over to the small kitchen, returning with her special dessert. "Loo Jim, this cake will become my specialty," she beamed, revealing the upside-down pineapple cake.

Kay's pineapple upside down cake. Kimberly Vardeman CCA 2.0

"Kay, that cake is my favorite!"

"Well, my hubby, now you can have it anytime you wish," Kay exclaimed with a proud smile.

"My precious jewel, all I will ever need is your smile," said Hop as he picked up a bite of the pineapple cake with his chopsticks.

The next morning Kay responded quickly to the soft rapping, opening the door for her new and only friend in Salem.

"*Jousahn*, I mean, good morning, Beatrice."

"A good morning to you, Ah Kay," Mrs. Hundsaker replied, handing Kay a pair of white gloves.

Kay's puzzled expression amused Beatrice.

"Don't worry, Ah Kay. You'll understand the purpose of these fine white gloves in just a bit," Beatrice laughed.

Entering the apartment, Beatrice placed a white glove on her right hand, motioning for Kay to do the same.

As Kay slipped the glove onto her hand, Beatrice looked around the apartment.

"Today, we will clean your home from top to bottom."

"But I cleaned it yesterday after you left. It is spotless."

"We will see about that," Beatrice smiled as she took her gloved hand and ran fingers along the top of the cupboard in the kitchen.

Kay gasped when Beatrice turned her hand over for her young friend to inspect. "*Aiyaah*! I worked all afternoon cleaning!

"Don't worry. I will show you how to clean properly, but the white glove test is the key."

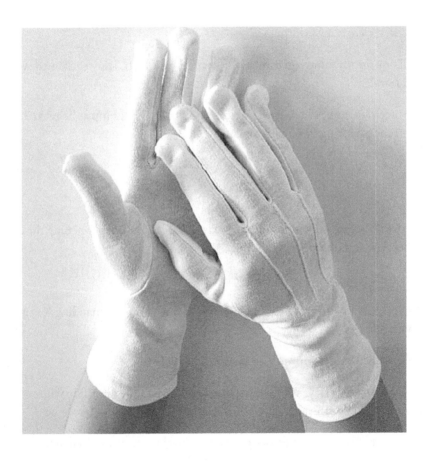

As Beatrice had promised, the two spent the rest of the morning cleaning and scrubbing every inch of the home from top to bottom. When they finished, Beatrice handed Kay the clean left-hand white glove.

"Now, you check our work."

Kay ran her white-gloved left hand over the floor and turned it over for Beatrice to inspect.

"Now you have a clean home," Beatrice declared.

Kay kept that white glove as a reminder of cleaning lessons from her friend in Salem. She became renowned as a fastidious house cleaner, and in the years to come, all of her daughters-in-law came to dread the moment during Popo Kay's visits when she pulled out the white glove from her delicate pearl-studded purse.

"Now, let's cook Hop another fine supper," Beatrice proclaimed, heading for the sparkling kitchen. "And afterward, I will take you for a walk to show you the sights along Salem's Commercial Street.

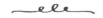

Chapter Seventeen

Ah Kay Becomes a Hop Farmer – March 1904

Hop looked at his young wife across the kitchen table, "Today, my precious jewel, you will join me as my business partner and become a hop farmer."

Kay wrinkled her nose, "I don't know anything about hop farming."

"Well, Kay, you will learn. But first, we must go down to the County Clerk's Office to record a deed for a hop farm we are purchasing."

"Alright, Hop, but can we see this farm? I am a city girl, you know. Will we have any cows?"

"No," Hop laughed. "But we will have over 122 acres of prime bottomland to grow our crops and maybe a few peach trees if you like."

Later that morning, Hop pulled the horse-drawn wagon up in front of the laundry on Commercial Street. Kay was waiting inside, peering out through the window with its red letters in reverse proclaiming, "Hop Lee Laundry." She saw her husband motion for her to come out and join him.

Hop jumped down from the wagon and helped Kay climb up onto the front seat next to him. She was wearing a blue dress with a long skirt that almost touched the ground. Mrs. Hundsaker had helped Kay sew the dress. It was her first American clothing. She was more comfortable in the Chinese au foo, but Hop had insisted that they needed to dress like their White neighbors in Salem. There had been so many changes in her life in the six months since she left her parents in San Francisco. But Hop was patient and kind with his young wife.

The horses headed North on Commercial Street and then up along the Old River Road towards Keizer.

"When I was a young boy, I passed by here on the steamboat on the way to Albany. Cousin Sai Yee and I were so young," Hop reminisced.

"Where is your cousin now?"

"Sai Yee is still in Albany. He took over Uncle's store and is doing good business. But I don't think that Sai Yee was made to be a shop keeper. He has too much energy. On the steamboat, he couldn't sit still for five minutes!"

After an hour on the dusty River Road, they passed the McNary farm and turned left. "That's the old Claggett cemetery. I have my eye on that piece of land next door, but it's too much money. I heard they want to sell the land to Dr. Mark Skiff; I don't know why a dentist wants to own a hop farm."

After another mile, Hop slowed the wagon as they approached a man standing in the road.

"Hi there, Hop!"

"Good morning, Mr. Fedit! I brought Mrs. Hop Lee to see the property you are selling us!"

"Good morning, ma'am, I mean Mrs. Hop Lee."

"In Chinese, it is our custom for the wife to keep her maiden name, so Kay's married name will be Hung Hop Lee."

"Well, Mrs. Hung Hop Lee, it is a pleasure to meet you. Hop is everyone's favorite Chinese around these parts. Most of us use his laundry and poultry store. There isn't a man, woman, or child for miles around that doesn't know and like your husband."

Kay smiled shyly, "Do you have any cows, Mr. Fedit?"

William Fedit laughed, "No cows, but there is plenty of room and lots of green grass if you are thinking about starting a dairy farm."

Mr. Fedit led them around the property. He was right. Kay saw more green grass and hops than she could ever have imagined growing up in Dai Fow.

"Look, there is a little river!" said Kay pointing at a babbling brook winding its way across the farm.

Hop smiled, "Yes, and it has a bridge, and we haven't even seen the peach orchard."

"I think we should build a house by the stream and live here," Kay exclaimed, "It's perfect!"

"Well, my Ah Kay, we can visit here anytime you like, but someone has to run the laundry and poultry store back in Salem."

"Maybe someday we can have our house in the country," said Kay hopefully.

"OK, and I will get you your cow!" Hop laughed.

The old horse knew the way back to Salem, so Hop gave Ah Kay the reins and let her drive the wagon south along the old River Road. For Kay, this new-found freedom was glorious. Her life in Salem was a million miles from San Francisco's Chinatown.

Hop took over the reins as they entered Salem and stopped in front of Marion County Courthouse on High Street. Inside, he and Kay went to the Marion County Clerk's Office.

"We have to record the deed to our new farm, Kay," Hop explained as Kay marveled at the ornate brick French Renaissance building with its 51-foot cupola and clock tower. [1]

---

1. The 1873 Courthouse, built by Wilbur F. Boothby and associates, blended exuberant Victorian styles, reflecting 19th century community pride in public buildings. Marion County paid W.W. Piper $4,500 as supervising architect for his elaborate French Renaissance design. Final costs for the permanent Courthouse were between $110,000 and $115,000. WHC.

Marion County Courthouse.

The clerk opened the window. "Hello, Hop. Are you still trying to buy property for your hop farm? You know I cannot record a land sale to a Chinese."

"Yes, Mildred, but I am not the buyer. My wife is," Hop proclaimed as he handed the clerk a copy of Kay's American birth certificate.

"She is an American citizen!"

"Well, Hop, I see that your wife was born in San Francisco. What is her full name?"

Make the deed of the property in the name of Mrs. Hung Hop Lee!" Hop proclaimed proudly, "She is my new wife and business partner."

The clerk disappeared. After a few minutes, she returned with the recorded deed, and little Ah Kay was officially the youngest landowner in Marion County in the State of Oregon.

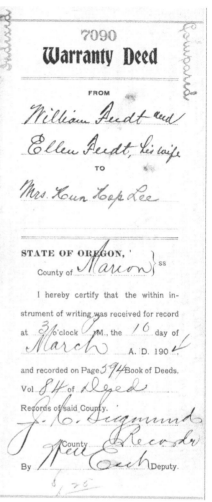

Low Family Collection

Chapter Eighteen

Hop Lee Marries His Wife – October 8, 1904

It was only seven months later that Hop and Ah Kay found themselves back at the Marion County Clerk's Office for an entirely different purpose.

"Hop, what brings you back to our office," a smiling Mildred inquired. "Did your young wife buy another hop farm?"

"We need a marriage license," Hop explained.

"What? I thought you already married Ah Kay in San Francisco over a year ago."

"Well, yes, it's true that we were married by the Chinese Custom last September at her parent's home. But we need to be certain that the White laws recognize our marriage. There can be no doubt that we are married and that our children are American citizens," Hop explained, patting Ah Kay's round belly.

"Alright, but you will need a witness, Hop."

Hop stepped aside, revealing his long-time friend George Sun. "George will be my witness."

"Well, we certainly all know George Sun, the unofficial mayor of Salem's China-town."

Mildred filled out the license, which Hop proudly signed *Low Sun Fook*. Ah Kay made her mark with a shaking hand, and George witnessed their signatures.

As Hop and Kay admired the official-looking document, Mildred offered, "Judge Judah is free and can marry you right now in his chambers."

"No. We want to be married at the Hop Lee Laundry tomorrow so my friends can attend the wedding," Hop explained. "Can Judge Judah perform the ceremony tomorrow morning?"

"I will have the Judge at your business on Commercial Street tomorrow at 10:30 am. Any other requests, Hop?"

"No, thank you, Mildred. Just tell the Judge to bring his laundry. We will give it the special hand-washed and ironed treatment. It's on the house!"

Ah Kay and Mrs. Hundsaker decorated the laundry's front room with white garlands and pink roses in a flurry of activity. They covered the counter and tables with white sheets and placed dozens of candles around the room.

Kay admired their handiwork. "*Do jeh*, Beatrice. It is perfect and so romantic."

"Anything for you, my young friend."

Kay wore the earrings her mother had given her and a new gold chain necklace, a gift from her husband."

"Here, Ah Kay. I also have a present for you," Beatrice smiled. She handed her friend a white box tied with a yellow ribbon. "Go ahead and open it now before the guests arrive."

Kay gently removed the ribbon and opened the box, revealing a sparkling crystal pitcher with a gold leaf trim.

"It is so elegant and beautiful, Beatrice! Thank you, but it is too much."

"Nonsense, Kay. Hop always calls you his precious jewel. This crystal pitcher is perfect for your new home," Beatrice smiled.

"Thank you, Beatrice. You were my first friend in Salem. I don't know what I would have done without you."

Kay looked up as the front door bell tinkled, announcing a recent arrival. "Mr. Reynolds! Hello."

"Good morning, ma'am, I mean Mrs. Hop Lee," Thomas offered.

"Did you bring your stagecoach, Mr. Reynolds? You should call me Kay."

"Not today, Kay. That's business. Today is a special day for an old friend and his wife."

With another jingle of the front doorbell, the next guests, George Sun and Hop's cousins Lee Tong and Sai Yee, arrived, crowding into the shrinking front room of the laundry.

Hop entered from the back room, smiling at his guests. "Well, we will need a bigger laundry very soon to hold all our friends!"

Sai Yee slapped Hop on the back, "Congratulations, cousin. I hear you have officially retired from the rice-making business!"

"Yes, cousin. Don't worry. Kay and Mrs. Hundsaker don't let me anywhere near the kitchen."

"Where is the judge?" Hop asked, looking around the room.

At that moment, a horse-drawn carriage came to a stop in front of the laundry. A distinguished man about Hop's age in a long dark coat and top hat climbed down from the rig and approached the Hop Lee Laundry.

"Hello, Judge Judah," Hop called out to his friend. [1]

"Good morning to you, Mr. Hop Lee,"

"Not mister, please, just plain old Hop. Did you bring your laundry, Judge?"

A sheepish Judge Judah brought out his sack of dirty clothes, "I appreciate your kind offer, Hop."

---

1. Judge Neely Johnson was born in California and was married to Ella Henrietta Sloper. In Salem he was the City Recorder referred to as "Judge Judah." He later lived in Astoria, Oregon and Mendocino, California. NJ Judah also was a journalist, newspaper man and Customs House Inspector.

Judge Neely Johnson "NJ" Judah 1856-1925. Photograph in Astoria 1914.

"Of course, Judge. It is my honor to have you as my distinguished customer and friend!"

The civil ceremony was brief and official. It was all a blur for Ah Kay, whose swollen belly and ankles made it difficult to stand for long.

"By the power invested in me by the State of Oregon, I pronounce you Mr. and Mrs. Hop Lee."

"Hop, you may kiss your bride."

Hop proceeded to give Ah Kay an affectionate kiss as she smiled shyly, standing in front of a laundry-room full of their guests.

Later that evening, after the excitement of the day had passed, Kay whispered, "Hop, today we were truly married. Last year, I was so nervous and scared, and my parents chose you for me. Today, we chose each other. You chose me, and I chose you. I am happy," Kay sighed.

Hop pulled his young wife close, "My precious jewel, you have made my life complete."

Even after the candle burned out, the glow in their home at 191 Commercial Street continued long into the night.

HOP LEE MARRIES HIS WIFE

Prominent Laundry Man and Hong Kee Enjoy Christian Wedding

A wedding took place this morning about 10:30 o'clock at 191 Commercial street, connected with which are probably the most peculiar circumstances of any other like occasion that ever occurred in Salem. Hop Lee, everybody's friend, who is a cleanser of soiled linen, was this morning married to the same woman with whom he was joined in wedlock 14 months ago in San Francisco.

Hop, who has been a resident of this state for 10 years, grew lonely about a year and a half ago, and decided to take unto himself a wife. Going to San Francisco he wooed and won pretty little Hong Kee, and they were married by the Chinese rites at that time, but Hop, during his years of labor, has managed to accumulate considerable worldly wealth, and wishing to become a good citizen of the United States, and have his descendants full citizens, he decided that it would be necessary for a Christian marriage, and so this morning, for the second time, he led the blushing Hong to the altar.

Hop was born in China, but Mrs. Lee has never set foot on the native soil, she being born in San Francisco.

Judge Judah married the happy couple, the witnesses being Thomas H. Reynolds and Low Lee Tong.

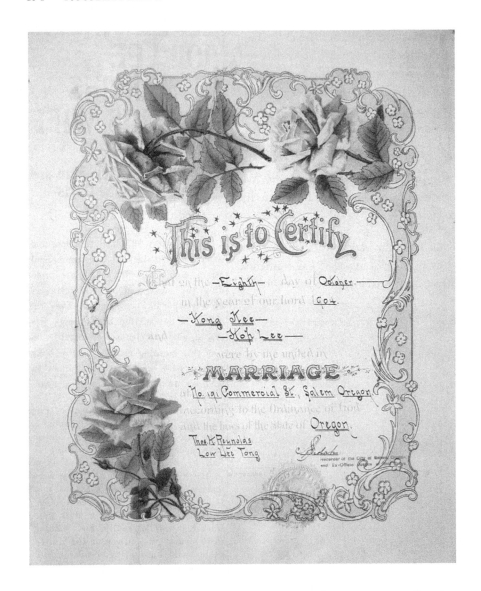

Marriage Certificate for Hong Kee and Hop Lee October 8, 1904. Low Family Collection.

Chapter Nineteen

Salem's Newest Resident – December 5, 1904

H op was frantically searching the kitchen. All the cabinet doors were opened, the drawers pulled out, and the pantry door was wide open. It was chaos at 191 Commercial Street. The Hop Lees were about to christen their firstborn, and Hop's head was spinning.

"Ah Kay! Where is the red egg? I set the special egg aside for the baby's christening, and now I can't find it anywhere! I must be going crazy!"

"Hop, what's so special about this egg? We have dozens of chickens at your poultry store. Just use another egg."

"No, this is my special double-yolk egg. I found it candling the eggs. It is rare and will bring good luck to our baby!"

Ah Kay sat on the couch and felt a lump under the seat cushion. Reaching under the cushion, she felt the smooth oval-shaped egg and smiled. "Hop dear, here is your egg," Kay laughed as she held out the prized egg. "You're lucky I didn't squash it."

Hop's eyes lit up, as he jumped up to retrieve the red egg, which he gently placed in his tunic pocket. "Thank you, Ah Kay. You saved our baby and me from a lifetime of bad fortune."

Red eggs and ginger for the infant's one-month ceremony by Paulo Leong. CCA 4.0

"You know, Hop. Our baby is only three weeks old. The Moon Yut party with red eggs and ginger and hair cutting ceremony is supposed to happen at one month."

"Do you want to continue the sitting month for another week?"

"Not on your life. My mother warned me about the one month of sitting around and doing nothing. It drove her crazy. She called it the 'baby prison!'"

"Not even more of the ginger pig's feet in sweet black bean sauce can entice you to sit another week, Ah Kay?" Hop asked with a smile.

"No, let's get on with the christening and haircutting."

The front door tinkled, announcing Beatrice Hundsaker's arrival downstairs.

Hop hurried downstairs to greet their friend. "Hello, Mrs. Hundsaker."

"*Nei hou*, Hop!" Beatrice returned his greeting. "Ah Kay has been teaching me Cantonese," she explained. "She says I have a knack for Chinese intonations."

"Yes, Beatrice. You have a good ear for our language."

Beatrice followed Hop upstairs. "Do you have the chickens dressed and ready for me to boil?" Beatrice asked, looking around the kitchen.

"The two dozen chickens were dressed at my poultry store on Ferry Street and were delivered this morning."

"Well then, show me the way. I will start my pots of boiling water for those chickens."

"We also have to make six-dozen red-dyed boiled eggs."

"No problem, Hop. I have it all under control."

"That's a lot of work, Beatrice. Do you want some help?"

"No, Hop. You just clear out, and let me take care of the cooking."

Hop was relieved not to have to set foot in the kitchen. *I have to find my razor and get the altar set up with incense.*

The front doorbell tinkled downstairs in the laundry as George Sun arrived carrying a large box. Hop came downstairs to greet the latest arrival.

"Hi, George. What's in the box, my friend?"

"*Nei hou*, Hop," George replied, setting the box on the counter. "These are the sticky rice cakes filled with delicious sweet mung bean paste. Lenora and the boys helped me shape each one like a tortoise!" George replied proudly, showing Hop his delicious creations.

"They're perfect, George!"

"The boys were happy you had a new baby girl, so we shaped the rice cakes into little turtles."

Hop laughed, "Your little turtle rice cakes celebrate our new baby girl and my booming turtle soup business!"

"Can I see the baby, Hop?"

"Sure. Ah Kay is bathing her upstairs. Come on up."

Kay and baby Elsie 1904. Low Family Collection

The two friends went up the wooden stairs entering the apartment. Hop led the way into the bathroom, where Kay and the nurse were washing the baby in a white porcelain basin filled with warm water infused with pomelo leaves.

"Hop, she is so small and perfect," George whispered.

"I am glad she looks like her mother and not like me."

"Actually, Hop, I think she has your Loo forehead."

Hop looked at his daughter, inspecting her forehead, "I think you're right, George. Well, my father, Sai Wing, would be proud."

Elsie Hop Lee 1904. Low Family Collection.

"Now we must dress the baby in a fine Chinese outfit," the nurse proclaimed, drying off the tiny infant.

"No! Our baby is American!" Hop exclaimed. "She will wear American baby clothes."

"Whatever you say, Mr. Lee."

"But she can wear this Chinese cap after the head-shaving ceremony," Hop offered, holding up a baby's mandarin cap richly trimmed with silk tassels and tiny sparkling mirrors.

A tinkle of the laundry's front door announced the final guests to arrive, Uncle Sing and a reporter from the Oregon Statesman office.

Hop carried his baby daughter downstairs, cradled gently in his arms. He took each step cautiously, trying not to upset his precious cargo.

Mrs. Hundsaker had prepared the laundry's front room with an elegant feast table covered with white table clothes upon which she set the two-dozen boiled chickens, six dozen red eggs, and George Sun's turtle-shaped sticky rice cakes.

The nurse gently took the baby from Hop Lee's arms and carried her to the altar set up in the front of the room. While everyone gathered around, she held the baby while Hop proceeded to shave the baby's head leaving only a lock of hair untouched at the crown. He then reached into the pocket of his blue coat, pulling out his lucky red egg. Hop gently rolled the red egg over his infant's forehead.

The nurse then placed the baby into Hop's outstretched arms. Hop held the baby up in front of the altar and bowed three times, reciting a Chinese incantation.

Hop opened his eyes, looked at the reporter, and explained, "This is like saying grace before a meal."

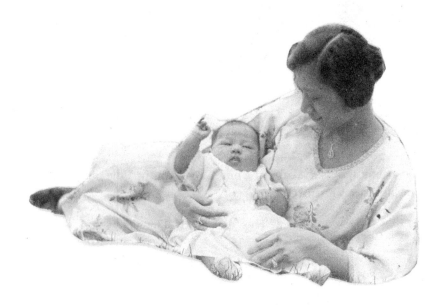

Kay and Baby Elsie 1904. Low Family Collection.

The reporter was watching and furiously scribbling, trying not to miss any part of the unusual Chinese one-month ritual.

The nurse then took the baby from Hop and placed her into Ah Kay's waiting arms. Kay rocked the baby and stroked her infant's head, gently humming the song that her mother sang when she was a young girl.

"When will your parents send the baby's name?" Hop inquired.

"Very soon, I hope," Kay replied softly, still gazing lovingly at her daughter's face.

Hop turned to his friend, "George, can you and your boys help us to deliver the boiled chickens and red-dyed eggs to our friends and neighbors?"

"Sure, Hop. The boys and I would be happy to help. They can load up their old red wagon with chickens and red eggs and make the rounds of Chinatown. Your friends will enjoy this Moon Yut feast."

"Make sure we also share with those of our community who are less fortunate."

"Of course, Hop," George smiled.

Hop Lee's kindness and concern for the well-being of all the citizens of Salem, Whites and Chinese alike, had engendered a great fondness of the man.

The next morning a telegram arrived from the Western Telegraph Office:

> Overjoyed at the news of our first granddaughter. Stop. Her milk name is Fung Wah, and her Chinese name is King Siu. Stop. Signed: Lai Wah and Ah Ying.

The gifts, which had been arriving for the past three weeks, did not slow down. The apartment was overflowing with gold bracelets, jade jewelry, caps with solid gold ornaments, and clothing of every imaginable type, both Chinese and American. Ah Kay's favorite gift was a pair of tiger shoes from her mother's favorite, Uncle Chan, who still worked at Hang Far Low restaurant on Dupont Gai in San Francisco's Chinatown. Enclosed was a mysterious note, "For baby King Siu to protect you on your life's journey and to bless you with feet as fast as those of your grandmother, Ah Ying."

Kay placed the cute tiger shoes on King Siu's tiny feet.

"What does the message mean about fast feet?" Hop asked, looking over his wife's shoulder.

"You will have to ask my mother about her adventures with the tong highbinders when she was a young girl."

Even more puzzled, Hop thought, There must be more to my mother-in-law than meets the eye.

That evening Hop sat down with his journal, picked up his pen, and proudly made an entry for his firstborn American child. Hop later corrected his mistaken entry for Elsie's date of birth:

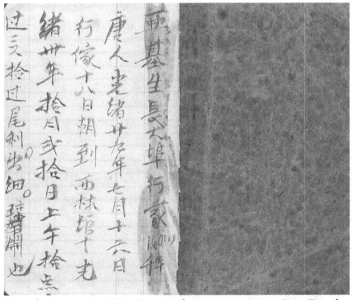

October 20, 1905, King Siu was born at 10:19 am. Low Family Collection.

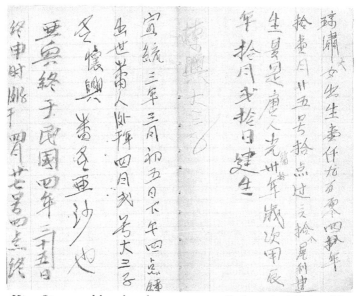

King Siu, our oldest daughter, was actually born in 1904 on November 25 at 10:10 am. Low Family Collection.

CHINESE BABY IS CHRISTENED

The home of Hop Lee, the well-known laundryman, two doors south of The Journal office, has been the scene of much celebrating and feasting during the past three weeks, by the birth of a little daughter to the family.

Thursday, December 15th was the day set apart for christening the little one, and the preparations were elaborate in the extreme. A magnificent feast was prepared, but, instead of inviting the relatives and friends to the home to partake of it, a bountiful portion was sent to the homes of the favored ones who were overjoyed to have this share in celebrating upon such a notable occasion. The only guests of the happy parents was an uncle of Hop Lee one American woman, besides the nurse, who is an American woman. Before christening the babe's head was shaved, and it was robed in American garments, except upon its head was placed a Chinese cap, richly trimmed with silk tassels and tiny mirrors. It was then laid in the father's arms, who bowed the proper number of times, and knelt before the feast table, then prayed in his native tongue, which, he explained, was the same as an American grace before eating. He then handed the baby to the nurse, who, in turn, gave it into the arms of its mother.

The food was next removed from the table, none of it having been eaten, and the christening was completed, though the name for the little one was not received from his grandparents in San Francisco until the next morning. It being the custom for the parents of the mother to send a name for the new babe.

Presents, more or less valuable, have been pouring in in great numbers ever since the arrival of little ''Fung Wa Lee'' was made public, consisting of gold bracelets, caps with solid gold ornaments, and clothing of every sort, both American and Chinese style.

Hop Lee is proud of this addition to the family, and proudly shows his little girl to his interested friends who call.

December 17, 1904. Daily Capital Journal

Two weeks later, the Christmas dinner table was prepared with place settings for ten guests with flickering candles, holly wreaths, and Kay's best porcelain China from the treasure trove of Hop's wedding gifts. A Christmas goose and a roasted pig enticed the guests with delicious aromas, emanating from the back of the laundry. Mrs. Hundsaker prepared the meal with the efficiency of a culinary drill sergeant.

"Where is Hop and his roasted pig?" Beatrice demanded. "We have a laundry room full of hungry guests and this goose will not be nearly enough for all of them!"

"Hop will be here," Kay reassured her friend. "He's been preparing for his big moment for days. Hop picked out the fattest young pig and started digging his pit yesterday. He made his cousins haul those big rocks from the creek to line the pit. Then he lit a huge fire early this morning to make the coals. I thought we were going to have to call in the Tiger Company to put out the flames!"

"Whoever heard of burying a pig in the ground to roast it!" Beatrice complained in exasperation.

"Hop says that's how they did it in the village."

"Village, smillage! I am a city girl and we do our cooking in the kitchen! What happens to all the dirt? I don't want to serve our guests Salem Soil in their Christmas dinner!"

Just then they heard shouting from the backyard behind the laundry. "Kay! Come quickly! Now!"

Kay and Beatrice rushed out the back door, encountering a most unexpected sight.

Hop was desperately shoveling the coals out of the pit. "*Fai Di La*! Quick! Help me unbury my pig! I think I overdid it! Fire too big! She's going to be burnt to a crisp!"

Cousin Sai was already shoveling coals off Hop's culinary creation. "She's perfect, Hop! Looks like you lucked in to the perfect pig, cousin!"

Hop pulled back the banana leaves, revealing a golden brown

Hop's glorious roast pig. Courtesy of cousin Xiong Guang Ming.

roasted pig. The aroma was intoxicating. "Well, I'll be a son of a Chinese chef!"

"Looks, like you've been taking cooking lessons since you burnt the rice and got chased out of camp, cousin!" Sai laughed slapping Hop on the back

"No sweat!" Hop proclaimed. "Now we just have to light the incense and say a prayer to the ancestors before we serve our guests my Christmas roasted pig!"

Hop and cousin Sai proudly carried the roast pig inside, gently placing the wooden tray on the table as their guests gathered around to admire the fruits of Hop's culinary skills.

"She weighs a ton, Hop," Sai complained, panting from the exertion.

Hop's roast pig 1904. Low Family Collection.

"Oops! We forgot to remove the rocks," Hop confessed. "I wanted to make sure she cooked thoroughly so we filled her up with hot rocks."

"Well, she's a beauty, Hop!" R.J. Hendricks admired. "I'm so glad you invited me to Christmas dinner! Wait till I tell our readers about this pit-roasted pig."

Nes Bush raised his glass of ale in a toast to their hosts, "Here's a toast to Hop and his beautiful family and especially to our guests of honor, little baby King Siu and her mother, Kay!"

Blushing from all the attention, Kay handed baby King Siu to Hop who raised his infant daughter into the air, proclaiming, "May Baby King Siu be the first of many American-born babies in the Hop Lee family." Pausing, while looking directly at Mrs. Bush Hop added, "Baby King Siu needs an American name. We will call her *Lulu*."

"Hear! Hear!' Thomas and Martha Reynolds, proclaimed with their glasses raised to the roof.

After a round of good cheer, the guests took their seats around the large wooden table, Mrs. Hundsaker served the guests the fruits of their labors, juicy roast suckling pig, roast goose with cranberry sauce, fresh garden salad, sun ripened tomatoes, sweet apple compote with cinnamon and freshly whipped cream, and

Kay's special dessert, pineapple upside down cake adorned with Salem's Bing cherries. It was the perfect ending to this first Christmas dinner for Salem's latest All-American family.

Chinese Will Celebrate.

The Chinese 400 will celebrate Christmas "allee samee Melican man, and among the many prominent events that will occur will be the Christmas dinner given by Mr. and Mrs. Hop Lee in honor of their little daughter.

The intimate friends of Mr. and Mrs. Hop Lee have been invited and the affair promises to be the swellest of the year.

Sunday December 25, 1904 Oregon Statesman.

Chapter Twenty

The Day the Ground Shook – 1906

K ay sat bolt upright in bed. It was still dark outside, and the Hop Lee laundry on Commercial Street was silent. Something was wrong.

"Hop, wake up."

Hop rolled to his side, pulling the covers with him, leaving Kay sitting in Salem's cold morning chill.

Kay pushed her husband, "Wake up!"

Hop groaned without moving and mumbled. "It's still dark. Let me sleep,"

"Something's wrong, Hop. Go check the baby."

Hop rubbed his eyes, "What's wrong, Kay."

I don't know, but I feel it."

"What do you mean? Did you hear something?"

"No. I feel it. It's bad. Please go check the baby."

Hop stumbled out of bed, bumping into the dresser in the darkness. In the next room, he found King Siu, sleeping soundly in her bed.

Retracing his steps to their bedroom, he found Kay still sitting up in bed with the covers piled up next to her. "She's fine, Kay. What's wrong? Are you sick?"

"No…"

"Then try to go back to sleep. It's still too early," Hop squinted at his pocket watch in the semi-darkness. "It's just after 5 a.m., Kay. I need to sleep some more. Busy day ahead."

But Kay did not sleep. She lay in the darkness with a deep foreboding that something was wrong. It would not be the last time that Kay's premonitions haunted her.

The news of the devastation in San Francisco began to trickle in slowly, starting early that morning. By midday, the trickle became a flood of destruction.

Mr. Hendricks, the publisher of the Oregon Statesman, quietly entered the Hop Lee Laundry. "Hop, I need to share this with you before we run the story. I know that Kay's family is in San Francisco." He opened the special edition of the paper and gently handed it to his long-time friend. "You need to read this, Hop."

The newspaper headline confirmed Kay's fears.

Hop read the headlines again and again without uttering a word.

"I am so sorry, Hop. We don't have any more information yet, but I wanted you to hear about this horrible news from me."

Hop numbly mumbled, "How did she know?"

Daily Oregon Statesman. April 19, 1906 Earthquake and Fires
San Francisco

The account of the destruction in the next day's Daily Capital Journal obliterated any hope for a reprieve from the nightmare by the bay.

> "At 6 o'clock this morning, San Francisco is a mass of ruins, and the flames continue the work of destruction, obliterating the few remaining inhabitants. All night the heavens were lighted by the vast conflagration. The morning clouds of smoke mark the continuance of destruction amid a scene of unspeakable horror. The water has absolutely failed, and nothing can save the city. Fire is spreading west, north, and south throughout the residence districts, and all are helpless and hopeless." – Thursday, April 19, 1906

It soon became apparent that San Francisco's Chinatown was wholly destroyed. The newspapers spared no details as they painted an appalling picture of grim death for the densely populated Chinese Quarter residents, caught like rats in a trap. Seeking a story, the local reporters circled the Hop Lees like buzzards.

By Friday, the relief effort was underway in full swing as Salem's citizens opened their hearts and pocketbooks to support their brethren in the City by the Bay. Everyone was aware that Hop's wife's family was missing, and all of Salem was praying for their deliverance from the horrors of the earthquake and fires.

The tinkle of the bell announced the visitor to the Hop Lee Laundry. Hop looked up in time to greet Mrs. Hundsaker, who entered with a logbook in hand.

"Good morning, Hop. I am collecting subscriptions for the Earthquake and Fire Relief Fund."

"Hello, Beatrice."

"Have you heard any news from your wife's family?"

"No, and Kay is a wreck. I keep telling her to keep the faith, but it is so hard for her not knowing."

"Poor thing. I must come by to console her. She mustn't give up hope."

"I am glad she got to see her parents and brothers at King Siu's christening. Her father, Lai Wah, passed away last December."

1906 Earthquake and Fires SF

"But you came to collect donations for the Earthquake Fund. Here is my one-dollar contribution, and here are fifty cents for baby Hop Lee."

"Thank you, Hop. I will record your one-dollar donation and 50 cents for baby King Siu. Now, where are your employees hiding out?"

"They are working in the back room. Follow me, Beatrice."

Hop's cousins Low Ma, Low Tong, and Low Gow each donated one dollar to the fund, as did his other employees, Ah Go and Ah Gong. Hop's old friend Thomas Reynolds contributed five dollars to the fund across the street at the Wells Fargo Express Office. Hop's old landlord, Postmaster Ed Hirsch donated $25 and Dr. J. N. Smith, the superintendent of the State Institution for Feeble-Minded, donated $100.

To relieve the suffering of those in need in San Francisco, all of Salem's citizens contributed generously and gladly. A Southern Pacific train pulling boxcars filled with foodstuffs and supplies was soon heading south from Salem to the Bay Area.

Kay waited on pins and needles for days, expecting to hear the good news of her mother, younger brother, and sister in San Francisco. She hoped for the best, but deep down, her worst fears tormented her night and day. It had been one week, and there had been no word from her mother. It could only mean one thing. They had perished along with the thousands of other residents of the Chinese Quarter. The words of the newspaper article Hop read to her haunted Kay's every waking moment, "Caught Like Rats in a Trap."

Hop gazed across the semi-darkened room at his young wife sitting motionless on a chair staring out the window. It was too early to be up, but he knew that Kay had been in that position for hours. Hop rose from their bed and draped a shawl over his wife's shoulders. She hardly moved as a single tear trickled down her young face.

"I will go," Hop offered.

"Go where? It is too early to wake your cousins at the laundry."

"No. I will go to Tong Yan Gai to find your family."

"How can you do this, Hop? The trains aren't running yet. There is no water, and the whole city is in ruins."

1906 Earthquake Chinatown

"I know all of this, Kay. But I know my mother-in-law. She is tough and a fighter. That woman would never give up. What's that thing she whispered to you every night?"

"*To never ever give up hope*. It was like her mantra. I think those words kept her alive in the worst of times when she was just a child alone in Dai Fow."

"She is alive, Kay. I know it, and I will find her and your brother and sister!"

Hop's promise quickly materialized into a plan of action. He took the Southern Pacific train from Salem as far south as it would run. The line ended in San Rafael, where he found a horse and wagon to complete his journey. Frankly, he had no idea where to start his search. But he figured that by going back to Dai Fow, he might find someone who had news about Ah Ying. He had heard about the refugee camps lining the bay. He figured that was the place to begin his searching, but Providence intervened in San Anselmo.

As Hop was driving his horse-drawn wagon through Ross Valley towards San Anselmo, he encountered two castles on the rolling green hills and heard the sweet voices of dozens of girls singing praise to the Lord Jesus. As he crested the rise, Hop came across a most incredible and heavenly vision Three dozen Chinese maidens in their native dress stood on a grassy knoll overlooking the bay singing to the Heavens the words of "Have You Any Room for Jesus" and "Savior, More than Life to Me."

Hop stopped the white dapple mare short of the magnificent spectacle and sat quietly watching and listening to this unexpected visual and auditory treat.

A dark-haired matron in a long blue dress approached the wagon.

"Are you here to sing praise to our Lord and Savior?"

"No, ma'am, but I do know the words to those songs. My wife, Kay, sings them to our baby daughter. Her mother, Ah Ying, taught them to her. She says she learned the songs at the Jesus House in Dai Fow."

San Francisco Theological Seminary, San Anselmo 1892.

The woman's face lit up with a glow that outshone the fog-shrouded bay sun.

"My name is Donaldina Cameron. I am the director of this Jesus House you mentioned. At least, I was the director until the fires destroyed our beloved home. But Praise the Lord, all of our family is safe and sound, and thanks to our friends, we have a new temporary home at this monastery."

"But who is this mysterious Ah Ying you mentioned?" she continued. Surely you don't mean our sewing teacher, Ah Ying! My predecessor used to call her "Runaway, Ah Gew."

"Yes! Yes! Ah Ying is my mother-in-law and a fabulous seamstress! What news do you have of her?"

"Well, mister......." Donaldina began.

"My apologies, Miss Cameron. My name is Low Sun Fook, but most people call me Hop Lee."

"Well, Mr. Lee. I do indeed have news for you. Ah Ying and her two children and her friend Sing Yee and her two children joined our Mission Home family as we all fled the fires in San Francisco this past April 18th."

"What happened to them?" Hop asked

Donaldina Cameron. Public Domain.

"We parted ways the next morning, but she and the children and Sing Yee were all safe at that time. We headed for the Ferry docks, and they were headed west towards the Presidio."

Donaldina paused, recalling the events of that day etched into her memory, "I have no idea what happened to them, but knowing Ah Ying, I am certain she survived and is probably across the Bay in Oakland by now."

"Oakland! Did she say she was going there?"

Escaping the fires in San Francisco on April 20, 1906.

"Yes, she mentioned Oakland. Most of the Chinese from San Francisco headed that way."

By now, many of the girls had gathered around Hop's wagon. A few were feeding the horse slices of apples and carrots.

"Girls, this is Mr. Lee. He is searching for your sewing teacher, Miss Ah Ying!"

"Mr. Lee, we love Ah Ying! She is the best with a needle and thread!"

"We also like her to tell us the stories about the highbinders and how a boy named Billy helped her to escape on the cable car!"

Hop laughed, "Yes, I have heard those stories from my wife, her daughter, but I wasn't sure how much to believe."

"Oh, we believe the stories, Mr. Lee. Miss Ah Ying is one of our sisters. She would never tell us a lie," the girls protested.

"Alright, girls, but how can I go about finding runaway Ah Ying in Oakland?"

Donaldina interrupted, "It is getting to be too late to make the journey today.

You must spend the night with us at the monastery and get an early start in the morning. Our accommodations are a bit rustic as we are staying in the barn, but the girls have made it our home, and you are most welcome to spend the night with us."

"Do you know any stories, Mr. Lee?" the girls asked hopefully.

"No girls, I can't compete with my mother-in-law! Besides, I am just a laundry-man and hop rancher from Salem, Oregon."

"Well, Mr. Lee, I'd advise you to think up a good story because these girls won't stop pestering you until you provide them with some entertainment this evening," Donaldina Cameron laughed.

"Well, who could say no to such an enchanting group of young women?"

After a modest but highly satisfying dinner of freshly picked vegetables and meatloaf, the girls escorted Hop to the next room. They seated Hop in front of a wood-burning stove as they gathered around sitting on the floor.

Hop's mind was scrambling to come up with a story to entertain these young women who were eagerly awaiting his tale. The silence was deafening, and their expectant stares were making him more nervous.

Finally, he had it! "well, girls, let me tell you a story about how I lost my pants to a scoundrel but ended up making a new friend."

The girls smiled and giggled, waiting for Hop's story.

"And that is the end of my true story. I figured I could never get those pants clean, so I gave them to Joel Manly as a reminder of how not to treat strangers."

"Another story, please, Mr. Hop," pleaded the girls.

"Girls, it's time to let Mr. Lee get some rest. He has a very long journey tomorrow to Oakland to find your sister, Ah Ying, and her family.

The girls groaned in unison, but each thanked Hop for his entertaining story.

⁓ℓℓ⁓

The next morning Hop bid farewell to Donaldina and the 30 girls who had risen early to give Hop a proper send-off.

"What's the best way to get to Oakland, Miss Cameron?"

"You could take your wagon up North around San Pablo Bay, but that is a long and unnecessary journey."

"What do you recommend? I don't think this old horse would last that trip."

"We took the ferry from San Francisco to Sausalito. They may have a ferry going directly to Oakland. It's probably easier to head to the Tiburon ferry on the peninsula. That would spare you and that old horse a long trip."

"Thank you for your hospitality, Miss Cameron," Hop called out as he turned and waved to his new young friends, "Goodbye, girls!"

"Goodbye, Mr. Lee! Please say hello to our sister, Ah Ying."

The trip to Tiburon was only 11 miles, but it took most of the morning to navigate the dirt roads. Along the way, Hop admired the scenery, with Mount

Mount Tamalpais and Mill Valley in Marin County. 1910

Tamalpais looming off to the right. He passed through the towns of Ross and Corte Madera and saw the road heading West into Mill Valley. On his left, the tranquil Richardson Bay with hundreds of birds lining its shore belied the devastation that had occurred just one week before. In Tiburon, he headed to the waterfront and found the ferry building that was actually just a wooden shack.

Donaldina was correct about the ferry service. The Southern Pacific and the California Northwestern had established ferry services between Sausalito, Tiburon, and Oakland.

The trip to Oakland was uneventful. Hop was enamored with the wind-swept, billowing fog banks blowing in from the Golden Gate that enshrouded the landscape. But his thoughts soon returned to the task at hand.

How will I ever find my mother-in-law, Ah Ying? There will be tens of thousands of Chinese camped out in Oakland.

His thoughts were interrupted by a passenger seated next to him, "You're lucky you weren't trying to take the ferry right after the quake."

Hop looked at the stranger but remained silent.

Richardson Bay.

"I was on a ferry trying to flee San Francisco the morning after the quake. It was chaos, mister. People were fighting to get on board the boats. Women were trampled underfoot in the panic. One thousand souls were packed in like sardines, and the boat was so overloaded that the ferry was listing to the side. I thought we were going to sink!"

"Guess I'm lucky I'm a bit late to the party."

"Believe me; it was no party. Because of the danger, they suspended ferry service for a while. Things are returning to normal, at least for the ferry service. They even have night runs now. Around here, nothing happens without these ferry boats."

Hop looked away, returning to his worries about finding Ah Ying in the sea of Chinese refugees.

ell

On the docks in Oakland, Hop's worst fears were confirmed. There were Chinese everywhere, camped out in any available space. He stopped the first friendly looking person he saw, asking for directions.

"I am searching for my mother-in-law and her two children. Where should I begin?

The stranger looked at Hop like he was from another planet, "Look around you, mister. We are all over this city or at least the Chinese Quarter. Some Chinese found empty buildings for shelter, but most are camped out in vacant lots or any unoccupied space. Seeing an opportunity for profit, some locals have rented out their mansions. The city is trying to round up the Chinese to take us to a refugee camp at Lake Merritt, a half-mile northeast of here. "

Hop looked around. The stranger was not exaggerating. It was chaos, and the smell was horrific.

"Thanks," he muttered.

"Go north on Broadway. You'll find a lot of Chinese camped out on 7th street. Lake Merritt is a bit further north and to the east. Good luck."

Chinese refugees from San Francisco's earthquake & fires April 1906.

Hop followed Broadway north, turning right on 14th street running into Lake Merritt's shores in a few minutes. The pristine dark blue lake was a welcome relief from the chaos of Oakland's overrun Chinatown. The Chinese were camped out under the willow trees on the southern shore of Lake Merritt. The mansions of the rich and elite of Oakland served as a striking backdrop to the Chinese refugee tent city. The White refugees were housed in a separate encampment at Adams Point at the lake's north end.

Hop wandered into the tent city with its row upon row of sizeable house-shaped canvas tents set up under the weeping willow trees on the lakeshore. He waited patiently, but there was an uncanny silence in the camp.

Finally, growing impatient, he stuck his head into the first tent, calling out, "*Nei hou.*"

The reply was immediate and a surprise, "Mr. Hop! Where's your funny hat?"

Hop laughed when he spotted little Ed Toon, jumping up from his cot to greet him like a long-lost friend.

Camp Willow for Chinese refugees at Lake Merritt in Oakland

"Toon! I have been searching for you and Ah Ying for days!"

"No, you haven't. You just got here! Where is your hat?"

"I didn't bring my Derby hat on this trip, Toon. When you come with me to Salem, I will buy you your own hat," Hop laughed.

Just then, Ah Ying and her daughter Chun Ngo entered from the opposite side of the tent.

"Mr. Loo! What on earth are you doing here"?"

"I came to find you, Ah Ying. We hadn't heard a word from you, and Ah Kay has been worried sick for days. She was sure you were all dead, killed in the earthquake and fires."

"We could not get word to you in Salem. The telegraph was down, and we don't have the money for a telegram, anyway. But as you can see, we are fine."

Chun Ngo looking worried, asked, "Why are you here?"

"I am going take you back to Salem as soon as I can arrange passage on the next train north."

"I don't want to go!" Chun Ngo shouted more loudly than she meant to.

"Hop was confused, "You can't stay here. Why.."

"There's a boy," Ah Ying explained, interrupting Hop.

"We have lots of boys in Salem. You can have your pick!"

"Thank you for traveling all this way to find us, Mr. Loo. But I am afraid that our life is here now. My friend Sing Yee and her children are part of our refugee family. We can't leave them, and as you can see, Chun Ngo is lovestruck."

"Bring the boy, then. There is always room for one more."

"Ah Ying smiled, "It's not that simple, Mr. Loo. My life and my heart are here in this place. Your Oregon is like a strange wilderness to us. Sing Yee would never leave here, and we cannot separate the children until this puppy love thing runs its course. "

Hop let out a sigh. "I don't know what I am going to tell Ah Kay."

"Tell her that we are fine here in Oakland. We are safe and have a home with food and shelter. For now, that is more than enough, and she can relax knowing that we are safe."

Hop knew when he was beaten. No amount of negotiating was going to change Ah Ying's mind. "As you wish, *Ngoihmóu*," Hop said, using the Cantonese title for mother-in-law.

Stay with us long as you like. It will give me a chance to get to know you better, so we are not strangers when I come to visit you, Kay, and my grandchild in Salem."

"Actually, Ah Ying, your second grandchild will be arriving this summer, just in time for your visit," Hop added with a smile.

—*ele*—

Chinese at refugee camp at Lake Merritt in Oakland 1906.

Hop stayed with Ah Ying, Ed Toon, and Chung Ngo for several days, regaling them with stories of Nez Perce Indians, Chinese gamblers, hop farming, and of course, the latest news of Ah Ying's granddaughter, King Siu.

That evening by candlelight Hop picked up his brush, opened his journal and made an entry in Chinese calligraphy.

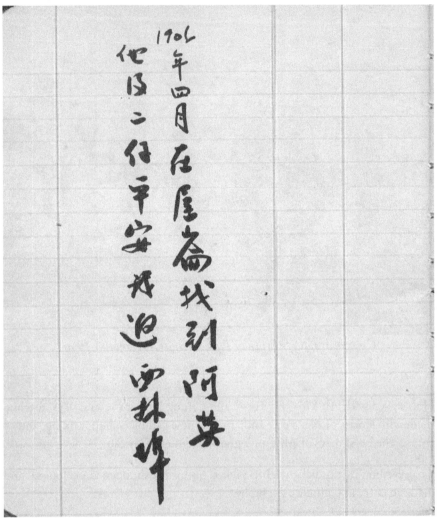

I have found Ah Ying and her two children in Oakland. They are safe and wish to stay. I miss my family and will return to Salem. – April 1906.

Chapter Twenty-One

A Willow Tree Becomes a Willow Forest

T he Hop Lee family did its best to maintain the dwindling Salem Chinese population. Ella, the second daughter, was born in 1906, and their first-born son, Willie, arrived in September 1908. Mary M. Staples, MD, delivered all of the children. There would be no midwives bringing Hop's family into the world.

BORN.

HOP LEE—To Mr. and Mrs. Hop Lee, a son.

.The boy has been christened Willie Hop Lee. The parents now have a family of three, two girl and one boy. The father is a laundryman in Chinatown.

Statesman Journal September 3, 1908.

Hop Lee dutifully recorded each birth in the little journal he started on the steamboat with cousin Sai Yee in 1877. All of the children had Chinese names, of course, but Hop was insistent that they were Americans. Each child was given both an American and a Chinese name. King Siu was Elsie, and King Sin was Ella, and Wy Fay was known as Willie. The people of Salem only knew the children's American names. Except for a few staged photos with Chinese costumes, the children were always immaculately dressed in the finest American clothing.

Early on, Hop hired a German seamstress who came to the home twice a year to make new outfits for each child and Kay. Hop Lee had accumulated wealth beyond his wildest dreams, and he spared no expense to take care of his growing family.

Hop's desire that his children become American in every way had some unexpected consequences. The family had moved from the Hop Lee Laundry on Commercial Street to their first real home at 296 Church Street. Hop heard that American children drink cow's milk, a foreign and strange concept for Chinese children. Nevertheless, the ever-accommodating Hop found a Guernsey cow, purchased the beast, and was walking the cow down the middle of Church Street when he ran into Officer Williams.

"Hop! Where are you going with that thing?"

"Good day, Officer Williams. I am taking my cow home."

"Well, I don't think I can let you walk down the streets of Salem with a farm animal. Don't you remember when I had to arrest you for bringing your laundry cart onto the sidewalk on Commercial Street?"

"I'm not on the sidewalk. The cow and I are in the street. Besides, that was some ridiculous hand-cart ordinance, not a cow ordinance," Hop added, pleading his case.

Unsure of his legal ground, but pretty confident that he had never seen a cow walking down any Salem streets, Officer Williams paused, considering his next move.

Sensing an opening, Hop continued, "I'll have her home and off the street in no time. Our home is on the next block. My children need milk, and this Guernsey is a guaranteed milk producer. If you let me continue, I will do your laundry for free for the next month."

Free laundry service was too good an offer to pass up. "OK, but have you discussed this with your misses? A cow in the front yard is going to be mighty smelly."

"No problem. Kay and the children will help me milk the cow every morning, and we will have plenty of free fertilizer to sell!"

Shaking his head but unable to argue with Hop's business plan, Officer Williams waved Hop and his cow along as the two continued on their way down State Street.

Kay was a city girl and was afraid of the cow, but the children loved having a pet cow and grew to enjoy the milk every morning. They named her Gretta. Learning to milk the cow was another matter entirely.

Hop got Thomas Wautensaugh to stop by after he dropped off his latest turtle catch at the laundry. Thomas had grown up in the country and promised to show Hop his best milking techniques.

"Here, Hop. You just sit on this stool next to the cow and gently pull on the udder. See, just like this. Pull and squirt. Pull and squirt. See, she likes it!"

Hop took his place on the milking stool and gazed at the cow's udders. "Which one should I pull, Thomas."

"It doesn't matter. They all squirt, Hop. Give it a try."

Hop gently grabbed the nearest udder and yanked down on it but jumped back when the Gretta let out a protesting "Mooo."

"Not so hard, Hop. Gently squeeze and pull down. Now try it again," Thomas encouraged.

Greta rewarded Hop's next gentler attempt with a drop of milk.

"I think I am getting the hang of this," Hop proclaimed.

"OK. Keep practicing, but I think we better milk Greta a bit faster. She looks pretty full."

Hop was milking the cow within half an hour with a less than an expert but effective touch. Thomas took over and finished up the job to the relief of Gretta, the cow.

"Maybe we should get you some help to milk Greta every morning, Hop," Thomas suggested.

> **WANTED—A GIRL FOR GENERAL**
> housework. One that can milk a
> cow and is a good clean cook. Phone
> 218 ,or 191 South Commercial street.

Oregon Statesman July 17, 1908

"We can get a house cleaner, cook, and cow milker all in one," Hop suggested.

"Girls, look this way and smile."

"We need a pillow to prop up Willie."

"Here, try this cushion," offered Kay.

Hop picked up Willie while Kay placed the cushion on the back of the chair.

"OK, now let's try again. Come along, girls. Stand next to your brother and smile."

"Willie is going to fall over," said Kay.

"It's OK. Just take the photo."

"No. Willie's head is crooked," Kay protested.

"He's perfect for a boy. Besides, the Chinese headdress is probably too heavy."

"Look this way, hold very still, and smile! One, two, and three!"

The bright flash startled Elsie and Ella, who jumped back. Willie fell to the side and was caught by Hop just before he slid off the chair.

"Perfect!" exclaimed Mr. Burns. "Now, that's one for the family album."

For this one photograph, Hop allowed his American family to look very Chinese.

Elsie, Bill, and Ella Hop Lee 1910. Kay kept this treasured photograph in her album for the next seven decades. Low Family Collection.

That evening, Hop sat down with his journal, pen in hand determined to bring his book up to date. Let's see, I have to make entries for second daughter, King Sin and our firstborn son, Wy Fay.

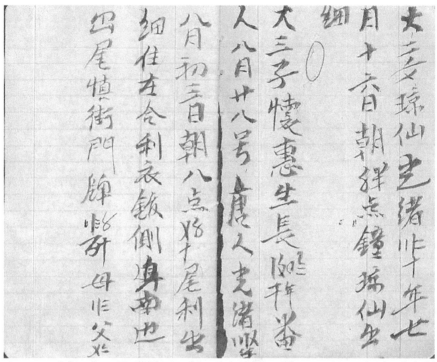

Our second daughter King Sin was born at 5:30 am July 16, 1907. The third child and first-born son, Wy Fay, was born at 8:45 am on American date August 28, 1908, at the Hop Lee Laundry 225 S. Commercial Street. His mother is 23 years old, and I am 42 years old. Low Family Collection.

Chapter Twenty-Two

Kim Departs Kalispell, Montana – 1910

K im gazed out the window as the black smoke and steam blew by, partially obscuring his view of the passing mountain scenery. The rhythmic noise and rumble of the train wheels rolling over the miles upon miles of iron track were somehow soothing.

This is the life. Maybe I can still be an engineer.

He imagined being upfront in the giant locomotive, wearing a cap and blue and white bandana, as he guided this monstrous beast with its twelve six-foot drive wheels through the mountain passes of the Cascade Range. But fate seemed to have other things in store for his life.

Kim sighed, remembering how he and his older brother Bing had taken this very same Great Northern train from Seattle to Kalispell just six years ago. The trip from Dai Fow to Montana had been the biggest adventure of their young lives. Now, it seemed like an eternity had passed.

He laughed, remembering how Mother had dressed them in their finest Chinese Mandarin robes and skull caps to make the journey and had given them those three Chinese coins to throw into the bay. Today he was dressed in an American suit tailored by Uncle Jick's seamstress in Spokane, who usually made the frilly lingerie he sold to the ladies of the night. Kim long ago cut off his queue. That was another story worth remembering.

"Kuikuriku! Kukuriku!"

Bing groaned, "Shut that stupid rooster up! What time is it anyway?"

Kim, who had bounded out of bed at the first wakeup call, replied, "6 a.m., of course. Roosters have circadian rhythms and can anticipate daylight for about one hour. According to my Farmer's Almanac, sunrise today, September 16th, is at 7 a.m."

"Be quiet, Professor Kim," Bing mumbled, pulling the blanket over his head. "Let me go back to sleep."

"Get up, Bing. We have chores to do before school."

"You go feed the chickens and wake me up when you're done. I was dreaming about wild Indians and hunting buffalo when that blasted rooster interrupted my dream."

1903 photograph cropped. Bing Qong Hong and Kim Seung Hong. Low Family Collection

Grumbling but resigned, Bing got out of bed and dressed quickly. The Kalispell air was already turning cooler as Fall was coming. They had experienced one Montana winter and were not looking forward to the coming bitter cold and snow. The boys made short work of their chores and came back inside just as Uncle Jick was setting out the breakfast. It was 8 am, and they had an hour before school started.

"Kim, Bing, sit down and have some of your uncle's steamed cha siu bao."

Uncle Jick Wah was their father's older brother. They had heard the stories about Jick Wah and the railroad. Both boys were fascinated by the patch he wore over his right eye. Jick was small and energetic and could talk a mile a minute. A salesman's friendly chatter had long since replaced his initial broken English. Uncle never missed a chance to close a sale with the White folks of Kalispell.

The bao was tasty and steaming hot. Both boys devoured the meal, knowing that they likely would not eat again until supper hours from now.

"Kim, you go and open up the store before school. I'll be along soon."

Kalispell was laid out in a grid with Main Street running north and south. The numbered avenues ran north-south, and the numbered streets ran east and west. Kalispell's Chinese quarter was along Second Ave West adjacent to the Red-Light District one block to the north on 1st Ave West. Most Chinese businesses were between 1st and 2nd Streets, including the four Chinese Goods stores owned by Lung Chong, Lung Kimlee, Ling Sing, and Quong Hai. Gee Tee's Tailor shop and the Wa Tai laundry were on the same block.

The boys worked at the Bong Tong Chinese restaurant owned by Hong Kee at 136 Main. It was a rare Chinese business that made it onto Main Street. Hong Kee's restaurant was right across from the Carter Mercantile Company and the Brewery Saloon. These businesses serviced the 42 Chinese men and one woman living in Kalispell's Chinese quarter in 1900.

Uncle Jick's "store" was little more than a small room at the southern end of Main at 4th Street.

Main Street Kalispell Montana. Wilson's clothing and dry goods. Library of Congress

Kim and Bing entered through the front door with the key that Uncle kept hidden. Kim turned around the "Open" sign and inspected the shelves' merchandise lining the back and sidewalls.

"Bing, look at these underpants for ladies."

"Those are lingerie, dummy. Boys wear underpants."

Well, whatever you call them, they're silly looking. Why do they have this hole in them?"

"That's probably so the ladies can pee. Don't you know anything?" Bing said smugly.

Jick Wah's store sold typical dry goods merchandise, but his specialty was selling fancy, frilly lingerie to the ladies of the night who worked in the bordellos along the back streets and Kalispell alleys. He had the lingerie made by two Chinese dressmakers in Spokane for five dollars each and then resold them at a 30% to 40% profit. Business was good.

The local prostitutes highly prized his products, but enterprising Uncle Jick never took a sale for granted.

At every opportunity, Jick snuck into the bordellos with his suitcase full of lingerie. Dressed in Chinese clothing, no one paid any attention to him, assuming that he was one of the hired help. He walked right in like he owned the place and then headed up the stairs to the girls' rooms. Listening at each door, he knocked when he found a quiet room. By now, all the girls knew Jick and let him right in, eager to peruse his latest offerings.

"Knock! Knock!"

"What do you want? Go away unless you got business in here."

"It's Jick Wah. I have some new lingerie for you, Verna dear."

The bed squeaked, followed by hurried footsteps. The door flew open.

"Come in, Uncle Jick! Hurry up. What's in your case tonight? I hope you didn't sell everything to that fat Leilani!"

"No worries, Verna. You are always my first customer. You get to choose first."

Opening the suitcase on the bed, Jick bragged, "These new pieces are just in from

Paris. They're a bit more expensive, but the quality is very good."

Verna's eyes lit up as Jick pulled out piece after piece of the dainty and frilly white lingerie. "I want one of each! I hope you have my size,"

"Of course, Verna. And tonight, I have a sale. You can buy three pieces for $40. Usually, these new French styles go for a lot more money."

"I don't know if I have $40. Do you want to stick around and help me to try them on, Jick? You can even take them all off and sample Verna's deserts. What do you say, Jick?"

"Jick says if you don't have the money, I go to Leilani's room."

Looking a little hurt but not wanting to lose out to Leilani, Verna reached into her ample brassiere and sputtered, "Oh alright, Jick. Here's your $40. You can't blame a girl for trying. Now, I want this one, and this one, and this negligee."

Jick took the money from Verna, packed up, and was off to the next room and then the next bordello. Business was good that day, really good.

"Stop daydreaming about naked ladies, Bing. I think Uncle Jick just makes up half the stuff he tells us, anyway."

"No way! It's all true. I bet someday he'll take me with him to sell negligee to his lady customers," Bing added proudly.

"He calls them "ladies of the night," Kim corrected.

"Come on, Bing. We have to get to school. Let's walk up Main Street so we can see the new Masonic Temple they're building."

"Ok, but we have to hurry. You were too slow feeding the chickens this morning."

The boys walked up Main Street, pausing briefly at 3rd Street to inspect the new Masonic Temple's progress. The ornate brickwork was a thing of beauty.

"Let's go, Kim. I want to go check out the saloons."

"You don't drink, and Uncle told us to stay clear of those places."

Kalispell Montana Main Street 1905. Library of Congress.

"I know, but we can look."

"You just want to get an eyeful of those hurdy-gurdy girls."

"So, what if I do?"

They ran up Main Street, crossed 2nd Street, glancing at the Pastime Bar on the left, the Silver Dollar Saloon on the opposite side of Main Street, and finally Bing's favorite, the Brewery Saloon. There were no hurdy-gurdy girls this morning.

"I wish we had time to go and see the locomotives at the Great Northern Railroad Depot," Kim said hopefully.

"No way, Kim. We'll be late for school just so you can go and see those old trains. The trains are moving out of Kalispell, anyway. They moved the mainline to Whitefish. That's the new division point, not Kalispell."

"I know, but there are still some locomotives here in the Roundhouse, even if we are just a branch line. I love those huge locomotives."

"Forget about it. Let's get to school."

The boys turned right at 1st Street and ran over to Central School on 2nd Avenue East. The two-story brick building was the finest school the boys had ever seen.

"Made it! Now, get to your class before they give us a tardy slip."

Central School originally housed Kalispell's high school and grade school. The building was designed by Great Falls architect William White and constructed entirely out of local materials for $20,000. Low Family Collection.

Mr. Huntley's class was Kim's favorite time of the day. He loved math and science, and Huntley knew his stuff, or at least Kim thought he did. Most of the students were horsing around, but Kim was spellbound, absorbing every word, concept, and formula.

Kim felt someone poking his head, "Hey, China boy. You got a nice ponytail! Just like a girl!"

"Cut it out!"

"Why? What you gonna do about it, China boy?"

Ralph was the class bully and never missed a chance to pick on weaker students. He leaned forward over his desk, knocked off Kim's mandarin hat, and grabbed his queue.

"Hey, looky here. I got a horsey tail! Come on, Kim, make a horse noise. You know what a horse sounds like, don't you? Giddy-up!"

Ralph yanked on Kim's queue pulling his head and upper body backward.

"Stop it! Mr. Huntley, Ralph is being an idiot. Make him stop!"

Mr. Huntley turned around from the chalkboard, saw the class in chaos, and stormed to the back of the room.

"Both of you go to the principal's office immediately!"

"But Mr. Huntley..." Kim began.

"Not another word from either of you. You have disrupted my lesson for this morning. Now, get out of here before I personally paddle both of you!"

Bully Ralph's shoves and taunts punctuated the long walk to the principal's office. "You think you're so smart, Kim. I bet you fight like a girl, too."

Kim stopped, turned around, and confronted his tormenter with his right finger in Ralph's startled face, "You want to fight, you moron? My Uncle Jick is a Kung Fu master, and I am his best student."

"Oh, do you think I am scared of your karate moves?"

"It's Kung Fu, stupid, and yes, you should be scared. If you fight me, you will end up in the hospital wishing you had kept your big mouth shut!"

Ralph, clearly now unsure of himself, was silent as they approached the principal's office.

Both boys were given stern warnings but avoided suspension for fighting.

Outside the office, Ralph glared at Kim, "We aren't done here, China Boy. Tomorrow outback, we fight!"

That afternoon Kim ran all the way home, anxious to discuss the day's events with Uncle Jick. He'd know what to do. He was so excited that he forgot all about his plan to stop at the new Carnegie Library to check out the books on the Wright Brothers' flying machine. Kim was fascinated with flying, but that would have to wait until this Ralph business blew over.

Bursting through the front door of the store, Kim spotted Uncle behind the counter.

"Uncle, you got to teach me Kung Fu really fast! Ralph's a bully. He called me names and yanked on my queue in class, and I'm going to cut the thing off!"

"Slow down, Kim. What are you talking about?"

"I told you! I have to fight him tomorrow after school, and I have to get rid of this thing. It's a real problem in a fight. It might as well have a sign: "pull here to make Chinese boy's head spin around!"

"You know, Kim, you can't cut off your queue. If you go back to China without your queue, the Manchus will chop off your head. It's a fact!"

Without hesitating, Kim replied, "I don't care. I'm in America right now, and my problem with Ralph is in America. If I want to back to China, I'll grow another queue!"

Uncle Jick shook his head but suspected Kim would not be dissuaded from his plan. "It's 1905, Kim; you never know when you might go back to the old country. What's this about Kung Fu?"

"I told Ralph you are a Kung Fu master and that you could kick his butt! Actually, I said that I was your best student in the dojo and that I would not show him any mercy."

Uncle Jick was flabbergasted, "Kim, just because I am old and Chinese doesn't mean that I'm a martial arts master. I have never set foot in a dojo. I don't have time for that nonsense. Too much work to do,"

Kim was shocked, "But you always told us how you Chinese had to fight the White railroad boss in the mountains so they would stop whipping the Chinese workers!"

"That's right, Kim, but it was your father who did most of the physical stuff. He was big and strong and never backed down from any man. I'm the small, wiry brother. I'm fast as lightning but not much of a fighter."

Kim groaned, "What am I going to do now?"

"You don't have to fight him. You just have to sell it."

"What do you mean?"

"Well, it's just like selling anything. It's all in the presentation. You learn a few moves and act confident, and Ralph won't want anything to do with you and your Kung Fu."

"Ok. Teach me a few moves. Whatever you know will help."

"Well, I remember how your father used to practice this martial arts stuff. I'll show you what he used to do."

"Here, stand like this and wave your hands around in front of you and make a scary noise."

Kim did his best to copy Uncle's version of Kung Fu. "How's this?"

"Not bad, but squat down a little and make that fierce noise."

Kim copied the motion and let out his best Kung Fu shriek.

"Perfect!"

"But I'm still going to cut off this queue!"

"Suit yourself, Kim. But remember, no trips back to the homeland until you grow a new one."

True to his word, that night, with Bing's assistance, Kim cut off his queue.

"That's better. Now I'm ready for that bully Ralph."

The next day Uncle's plan worked like a charm. Kim did his best Kung Fu imitation, let out a fierce shriek, and made a lunge at Ralph. Ralph took one look at Kim and backed off. Like most bullies, he wanted no part of what looked like a real fight.

Four years later, in 1909 as the Chinese Revolution was gaining support, Kim went around Kalispell's Chinese quarter with a huge basket and personally cut off the queue of every single Chinese man. The emboldened Chinese were well on their way to overthrowing the 300-year-old yoke of Manchurian oppression.

As the Great Northern train rolled along through the Cascade wilderness, Kim smiled as he recalled that basket full of Kalispell queues.

That was quite a day. I wonder what happened to all those queues.

The Great Northern continued through Washington state, passing thru Steven's Pass. As they approached Wellington, the silence on the train was eerie. Each passenger held his breath and whispered a prayer, recalling with a chill the avalanche that buried a Great Northern Train this past March killing 96 passengers. The collective sigh of relief was audible as the train continued undisturbed. The Great Northern train finally pulled into the Seattle King Street station in the late afternoon. The 550-mile journey from

Seattle King Street Station

Kalispell to Seattle was a return to civilization. Remote Kalispell's population of 5500 people was dwarfed by the over 200,000 who called Seattle their home. However, Salem, Oregon, and the Hop Lee home was Kim's final destination.

Two years had passed since the family portrait with the three Hop Lee Children in Chinese costumes. Elsie, Ella, Bill, and Kay waited for Kim dressed in their everyday American play clothes. The girls sported large white bows in their hair, and all four had a jade bracelet on their right wrist, a symbol of their parent's protection and love.

"When's Kim getting her, Mama?" Elsie asked.

"We've been out here for hours," two-year-old Bill complained.

"Your father went to the train station downtown to pick up Kim. He should be here anytime."

1910 Elsie, Ella, Bill, and Kay in Salem, Oregon waiting for Kim's arrival from Kalispell Montana. Low Family Collection

Kay looked around at the front yard at their home on Church Street. The overgrown grass needed cutting.

Oh well, Kim's a boy, and he'll have his nose in a book. He'll never look at the lawn, and he wouldn't notice if he did look.

Just then, Hop's Laundry Wagon pulled up with Bessie leading the way.

"Dad! Did you bring Uncle Kim?"

"Where is he?"

"Hurry up, Dad!"

Hop laughed, "Slow down! One at a time, before you bowl over Kim and your old dad with all your questions."

Kay couldn't believe her eyes. Her 10-year-old little brother, who left their Dai Fow home six years ago dressed in a Chinese Mandarin coat and skull cap, had been completely transformed. In his place was a grown young man in an American suit and tie.

"Hey! What did you do with my little brother?" she laughed, running up to Kim with her three children in tow.

"Kay! *Nei hou*! I see you have three other little people to boss around!"

"I always have time to order you around, Kim."

"Just my luck. So, who are you? My name is…"

"We know you're Uncle Kim," Ella blurted out.

"We've been waiting a really long time," Bill added, rolling his eyes.

"Children, introduce yourselves," Kay scolded.

"I am Elsie, and I'm the oldest."

"I'm Ella, and I like to sing."

"You know me, Kim. Can you show me how to ride a bike?"

Kim laughed, "I am pleased to meet my new Salem family, and yes, Bill, I'll have you riding a bicycle in no time."

Bill's face lit up, and he grabbed Kim's hand and pulled him towards the house.

"We have lots of boy stuff to talk about," Bill called out to Kim, relieved that he was no longer the only boy in the Hop Lee family.

1910 Bill, Kay and Ah Ying in Salem Oregon. Low Family Collection

Chapter Twenty-Three

Sky Ships, Model Ts, and the American Dream – 1911

"Well, young man. What exactly are you going to do with this flying machine?"

Kim looked at the Daily Capital Journal reporter, unsure of how to answer such an obtuse question.

"I plan to demonstrate that my perfected flying machine has incorporated significant improvements over the Curtiss straight biplane."

"How long have you been interested in aviation?"

"I began studying the principles of flight and aviation while living in Kalispell, Montana. Over three years, I read every book and manuscript on aviation and aeronautical engineering that I could lay my hands on at the Carnegie Library. I even corresponded with Orville and Wilbur Wright."

"You must know Silas Christofferson, the young pilot who just moved to Portland last year."

Carnegie Library Kalispell, Montana. Post Card. Low Family Collection

"From what I hear, he is more of an aviation showman, a daredevil. I am an aeronautical engineer. It is science that gave man flight, not Barnum and Bailey."
[1]

"What's your brother-in-law have to say about having this contraption in his front yard here in Salem?"

Ignoring the reporter's question, Kim continued to extoll the virtues of his flying machine.

"While the basic steel frame and oiled cambric fabric skin are standard, there are several new design elements on this biplane. The stabilizers are hung on a pivot at the end of the biplane wings. It is possible, using these equilibrators, to make shorter radius turns and maintain the center of gravity much better than in any other flying machine today. I am certain that with a little refinement, this plane

---

1. Silas Christofferson was an early aviation pioneer and stunt man. On June 8, 1912, 50,000 people in Portland, Oregon watched Silas launch his aeroplane form a tiny strip on a downtown Portland building. He died in a 1916 aviation accident.

can turn very sharp corners." [2]

"Do you mean it can turn on a dime?"

"You heard it here first."

What kind of an engine will power this flying machine?"

"I have just sent off for an electric motor which will be fed with electricity from a fine wire coming off an ordinary incandescent bulb."

Continuing, Kim explained, "The wingspan of this prototype flying machine is 4 feet 8 inches. Once I have perfected the structural design, control surfaces, and the incorporation of the motor, then I will build a full-sized aeroplane that I intend to pilot myself."

"Well, Kim, we expect to see you piloting your new flying machine over the streets of Salem in the months to come. Good luck, young man."

"I should have my flying machine ready in time for the Salem Cherry Festival this coming July. I will fly overhead and lead the procession through the streets of Salem."

"Looks like you have quite an audience interested in your flying machine, Kim," the reporter laughed as he turned towards the crowd gathering on the sidewalk.

"Don't touch that!" Kim yelled at a little girl, reaching out for the control stick.

The five-year-old with jet black hair and almond-shaped eyes returned Kim's gaze without blinking or moving her hand.

"Is this how you fly the plane?"

"Yes, but it's delicate. Hands off!"

"I want to fly a plane someday."

"Girls aren't pilots."

---

2. The concept of wingtip control surfaces was validated in 2017 in an article by J Mills and R Ajaj in Aerospace. Flight Dynamics and Control Using Folding Wingtips: An Experimental Study.

"You want to bet? My dad says girls can drive, so why can't I fly a plane?

"Where are your parents anyway? They should be watching you!"

"My dad is Lee Hing. He grows hops with Mr. Lee. My name is Leah," she explained.

"Well, Leah, why don't you come back when you're a bit older. Then I'll teach you about aeronautical engineering," Kim offered.

"Sure thing, Mr. Kim. Don't forget my name. It's Leah Hing with two Hs'," she shouted as she ran after her father walking down Church Street. [3]

Not everything exciting that year in Salem was airborne. Hop's laundry business, while mundane and definitely earthbound, had its share of excitement. The business was booming despite the ongoing competition from the Salem Steam Laundry. Hop maintained his edge by offering personalized, high-quality service with free home deliveries of clean laundry bundles. Hop's horse-drawn laundry delivery wagon was a well-known sight for the citizens of Salem.

The white dapple mare stood by, ready for the daily laundry delivery run. Hop climbed up onto the seat of the wagon and took up the reins.

"Giddy up, there, Bessie!"

With a flick of the reins, the wagon began its leisurely roll through the streets of Salem. They passed the Oregon Statesman office and the Ladd Bush Bank at the corner of Commercial and State Streets.

---

3. Lee Hing worked with Hop Lee on his hop ranches. His daughter Leah kept her word. She became an aviation pioneer and was the first US-born Chinese American woman to earn a pilot's license in 1934.

"Hi, Mr. Hop!" called out Thomas Livesley, [4] who was coming out of the bank at that moment. "Watch out for those new-fangled cars barreling down the streets. Don't want to spook Bessie."

"Not Mr. Hop. Just call me Hop like everyone else around these parts. I'll do my best to keep Bessie under control today."

"OK, Hop! By the way, when are you going to purchase that hop farm next to mine in Mission Bottom?"

"I just need to save a little more money from this year's harvest. And then I have to catch Dr. Skiff when he's in a selling mood."

"Well, keep the faith, Hop."

"Have a good day, Thomas, and bring your laundry by anytime for a free wash and professional hand ironing job."

"Thanks, Hop."

Bessie was well-known throughout Salem as a free-spirited horse with a mind of her own. Passersby gave Bessie a wide berth when encountering Hop's laundry wagon. After his first delivery, Hop was turning the wagon around to head south on Commercial when disaster struck. He heard the clang of the bell and instinctively pulled back on the reins, but Bessie was already in full-gallop mode.

"*Aiyaah! Aiyaah*! Whoa, Bessie! Whoa!"

The streetcar rumbled by only inches from the wagon and the runaway horse!

"Clang! Clang!"

"Watch out, Hop! Get Bessie under control!" Joe, the conductor, shouted as the passengers on the streetcar held on for dear life.

Bessie and the streetcar were on a mad head-to-head race towards the Willamette River when suddenly, Bessie swerved to the left. The ending was not pretty. Hop

---

4. Thomas A. Livesley 1863-1947 was an American businessman and politician in the state of Oregon. A successful hop farmer and broker, Livesley was known as the "Hop King" of Oregon. Livesley served as mayor of Salem and as a state representative.

saw the telephone pole a split second before the collision.

"Whoa, Bessie, you stupid horse!" as he pulled the reins sharply to the right.

The glancing blow of horse and pole careened the out-of-control wagon back down Commercial street, tipping it up onto its right-sided wheels. The weight of the loaded wagon flipped the wagon over.

Hop had been thrown from the wagon and was lying in the middle of Commercial street. He looked up and groaned as he watched the wagon and horse overturn, spilling the entire load of clean laundry packages into the muddy Salem street. It was a mess!

Joe stopped his streetcar and came running back to check on Hop.

"Hop, are you OK?"

Hop looked up at the gathering crowd, "Yes, just bumped a bit, but how is Bessie?"

"Why are you worried about Bessie, Hop?"

"She's a good horse. Where is Bessie?"

Joe looked back down Commercial Street and spotted Bessie casually munching apples from the Anderson home tree.

"Looks like Bessie came loose from the harness. She's having breakfast, Hop!"

"Hop chuckled, "She is better at eating than working! Maybe it's time to spend money on one of those new horseless carriages."

Hop's friends helped him turn the wagon upright, collect the muddy laundry bundles and gingerly place Bessie back into her harness. Remarkably, Bessie completed the trip back to the Hop Lee laundry without incident. This abbreviated trip was Bessie's final laundry run through the streets of Salem. The future had arrived, and for Hop, it was horseless.

"Do you know how to drive that thing, Hop?" George Sun asked. "Personally, I wouldn't trust it. The darn thing will probably blow up and kill you!"

"This is the future, George. Besides, Bessie would rather eat apples than deliver loads of laundry."

"It's awfully red and bright. Why couldn't you get a black horseless carriage like everyone else?"

"Well, George. Red is a good luck color for Chinese, and besides, a red laundry car will get lots of attention and will be good for business."

"Do you know how to operate it?"

"Well, no, but it can't be that difficult. I'll ask Kim for a lesson because that young man loves machines. He's building that crazy flying contraption in my front yard. Have you seen it?"

"Seen it? The whole town is talking about young Kim Seung. He is quite the scientist and engineer. I hear they are running out of things to teach him at Salem High."

"I don't have much use for flying machines, but if he can teach me to operate this horseless carriage, that's all I need."

After school that afternoon, Kim stopped by the laundry, looking for some work to earn money to purchase parts for his flying machine. Financing his aviation endeavor was more challenging than he had expected.

"Have any work for me, Hop?"

"No, but you don't look like a laundryman anyway. I have another job for you, Kim. Can you teach me to operate my new horseless carriage?"

Kim's eyes lit up at the mention of a new machine. "Sure, Hop. Let me see this new machine of yours, and I will have your driving through Salem in no time at all."

"She's a beauty with a 4-cylinder 2.9 L water-cooled engine, producing 20 horse-power," Kim recited with admiration.

"To start the car, first you retard the spark, throttle barely open. Now come to the front of the carriage. Turn the crank with your left hand. One half-turn clockwise, and the engine should start. Go ahead and turn the crank, Hop"

Hop grabbed the crank with his left hand, braced himself, and gave the crank one-half turn. The beast coughed, sputtered, and then came roaring to life.

"Perfect, Hop. Now advance the spark until she smooths out and purrs like a kitten."

"What are all these pedals for?"

"The one on the right is the brake. The middle pedal is for reverse, and the pedal on the left is the clutch pedal. This is the handbrake lever."

"How do I make her go faster?"

"Use this lever on the right side of the steering wheel. Push it down to go faster and push it up to idle the engine.

"What is this lever on the left?"

"That's the spark advance. Remember how we started the motor?"

"Where do you put the fuel?"

"The fuel tank is under the seat. You check the fuel level with this wooden stick."

"This is quite the modern contraption, Kim. Let's go for a ride and deliver some laundry."

Hop's red laundry delivery Model T became a common sight on the streets of Salem. Hop's instincts were correct. The flashy red vehicle was terrific advertising for the Hop Lee Laundry. He even started home delivery of eggs to promote his Poultry and Egg business on Ferry Street. That July, Mr. R.J. Hendricks approached Hop with a proposition.

"Hop, what would you think about having your red Model T in the Salem Cherry Fair parade? The parade is July 7th this year."

"What would a Chinese laundryman be doing in your parade?"

"Well, Hop. You are the most famous and well-liked Chinese in Salem, and people recognize your Red Laundry Model T. It would be great free advertising."

"I might need young Kim Seung to steer the vehicle. I don't want to spook any horses."

"No problem, Hop. I have the perfect use for your Model T. You can drive Queen Ann along the parade route as the Royal Court's official car. We will decorate your vehicle with thousands of red roses and cherries!".

"And I will do the Queen's laundry for free," announced Hop getting into the spirit of being in the Cherry Fair parade.

On July 7th, the Chinese residents did themselves proud by turning out in full force in the parade. Dressed in native costume and led by a Chinese orchestra, the Orientals attracted much attention in the procession. The entire Hop Lee family eagerly participated in the Cherry Fair Parade. Elsie, Ella, and Willie dressed in their finest Chinese costumes and marched alongside George Sun's children. Kim Seung drove the red Model T wearing his latest acquisition, a pair of aviation goggles and a leather pilots' helmet. Hop and Kay rode upfront, and in the rear seat, Princess Ann in her royal robes, surrounded by a sea of flowers and cherries. It was a day to be remembered for Salem and the Hop Lee family.

1909 Ford Model T Touring. Creative Commons 2.0 Wikimedia Commons.

1911 ended as it began, as a year of change for all Salem residents, especially for the local Chinese. With the overthrow of the Manchurian Dynasty in China, 300 years of oppression was suddenly lifted. The celebration amongst the Salem Chinese was no less boisterous than with their brethren in the homeland.

"It's time, Hop. Let me help you do this," Kim offered.

"No, I will do the honor myself." Hop took the razor in his right hand, grabbed his queue in his left, and with one slice became a liberated man.

"At last, I am free of that cursed symbol of Manchurian rule! May they crawl back into their hole and rot. We are now free men!"

Kay smiled at her husband and his new appearance. "My hubby is a free man."

Hop kissed his wife, walked outside, and ran two flags up the mast he had been preparing for this day.

The lower flag was red with a blazing yellow sun surrounded by nine yellow stars, the symbol of the newly formed Republic of China. The flag flying high atop the pole was the one that Hop flew every day, hoping that someday it would be his own; the red, white, and blue stars and stripes of his adopted homeland, the United States of America.

A reporter for the Oregon Statesman preserved the moment, "Hop Lee, whose place of business is on the South Commercial Street, is thoroughly American in his ideas. He believes in a republican form of government and is intensely earnest in his patriotism. Over his door floats the new republic's flag, a red body with a blue field now, a blazing sun. He is only one of the thousands who have had a taste of liberty in America and appreciates it much more than most native-born Americans."

"Get the children, Kay. I want them to be a part of this celebration."

"It's picture day at school, Hop. The girls are taking photos with their classes. The boys had to wear ties to school and Lulu had a bow in her hair this morning. She refused a pretty colorful bow. Lulu insisted that black is more stylish."

"What does a nine-year-old know about style?" Hop laughed.

"Our Lulu, knows her own mind and she definitely has a flair for drama."

"I can't wait to see her photo," Hop replied now intrigued.

They are probably taking the photo about now."

"Let's go and watch," Hop suggested.

They arrived at Garfield School just in time to see Elsie's third-grade class take their photograph. The 29 students and their teacher, who only looked a bit older, were positioned on the front steps of the school with its welcoming doors opened widely.

"Look! There's Lulu in the front row," Hop whispered proudly.

Class photograph 1911 – Elsie Hop Lee is in the first row second from the right. Richard Hem Lai Sun is first row left. Low Family Collection.

"It's hard to see her bow. Isn't that George Sun's boy on the left?" Kay asked.

"This is my American Dream, Kay. Lulu is going to college and someday will be a teacher herself. Mark my word!"

"Whatever you say, dear."

Garfield School 528 Cottage Street NE– Courtesy of Virginia Green and Thomas Green.

office in a manner that shall merit entire approbation.

CHINESE LAUNDRY IS MODERNIZED

HOP LEE HAS AUTO TO KEEP ABREAST OF THE TIMES IN WASH BUSINESS.

Talk about progressiveness! Salem can boast of real written-down-in-black-and-white progressiveness even among her foreign population.

Hop Lee is the owner of a fine laundry on Commercial street. Hop Lee's son or some other Celestial who happened to be handy always pushed the freshly washed and ironed clothes in the proverbial basket to their owner. The clothes were bundled in, nicely packed in a clean white sheet, and wheeled carefully to the back steps. This process sometimes occupied the precious hours of half a day when the owner of the clothes happened to live in the suburbs of the city. Hop Lee thought, and rightly too, that these hours might be more profitably spent over the ironing board and he scratched his brain and thought and wondered—

Finally a bright idea struck him and he strolled down to a garage to look at an automobile. Hop Lee thought that would be the very thing to save him time and loss of labor so the laundry now sports a new auto delivery wagon, a beautiful new red one, and the washing and ironing contingent are kept at their work while a chauffeur drives the delivery wagon. Can you beat it?

KIM SEUNG INVENTS A SKY SHIP

YOUNG CHINAMAN FROM SAN FRANCISCO ATTENDING HIGH SCHOOL HERE, THINKS HE HAS IMPROVED THE BIPLANE.

H. Kim Seung, a Salem high school student, has been interested in aviation for three years, and has been working for a year perfecting a model of an improved flying machine. Kim has never seen an aviation meet, but hopes to fly himself one of these days. His model is nearly completed. It is made on a steel frame with oiled cambric and weighs about seven pounds. It has a spread of four feet and eight inches. The machine is an improvement on the Curtiss straight biplane. The biplane of this machine is conclaved and possesses the graceful curves of a bird's wings. The biplanes are otherwise similar to those used on most flying machines.

Another improvement that young Kim claims is on his stabilizers which are hung on a pivot at the end of the biplane. By means of these equilibrators it is possible to make shorter turns and maintain the center of gravity much better than by any machine yet made. In fact, young Kim is almost certain he can make a machine that will turn a sharp corner. He has sent for an electric motor of one-fifteenth horse power which will be fed with juice from a fine wire or an ordinary incandescent bulb and he expects to hire a hall and exhibit his flying machine as soon as he gets it fully developed and under perfect control.

This young man came to Salem from San Francisco on account of the superior educational advantages of this place and is one of the most earnest and devoted students of the Salem High School. When he has perfected his motor he expects to build a larger machine and under-take actual aerial voyages from the Capital City next summer.

January 16, 1911. Capital Journal

Chapter Twenty-Four

Kim Graduates Early – June 1913

"Hurry up, Uncle Kim. We can't be late for your big day! Elsie encouraged.

"What's the rush. We have plenty of time. I'm graduating a year early."

Ella and five-year-old Bill barged into the back bedroom.

"Come on, Kim, we want to see you with your cap and gown," Ella pleaded.

"Ok! Ok! Let me put my suit on first. Where is my mortarboard anyway?"

"And where's my yearbook?" Kim added, frantically searching the room.

"I have it!" Arthur announced, parading into the room wearing Kim's mortarboard. "The gown is too big."

"Give Kim his hat, Arthur! We have to get going to the Armory. Dad's letting Kim drive us to the graduation in the Model T, and I'm sitting up front," Elsie bragged.

<hr/>

The trip from the new home at 296 South Church Street to the Salem Armory on Liberty was less than one mile, but the family enjoyed riding in Dad's shiny red Model T. Kim drove east on Ferry Street, passing Hop's new business at 436

Ferry.

"Wave at Dad!" Ella called out. "He really misses the old laundry on Commercial, but they finally tore down that old building."

"We were all born in that laundry," Elsie added. "Lots of memories."

"Now Hop's got his chicken, ducks, and laundry business all under one roof," Kim said

"Slow down, Uncle Kim," Ella shouted.

"No! Go faster," Bill encouraged.

"This machine will top out at 45 mph!" Kim shouted gleefully.

Reluctantly, Kim slowed down as they approached Liberty Street, pulled up to the Armory, and parked Hop's car behind the Armory. It was still light in Salem with the June 6th sunset just before 9 pm.

"Let's find seats upfront so we can see. Hurry up! The program starts at 8:30 pm sharp," Elsie bossed.

"OK. But I have to go and line up with the other graduates," Kim explained, heading for the back of the auditorium.

Salem Armory at southwest corner of Ferry and Liberty Streets 1912.

The Salem High School orchestra provided musical interludes with a violin solo by Miss Mary Schultz. The room was packed with the friends and family of the 62 graduates. Suddenly, the orchestra struck up "Pomp and Circumstance," and the 62 graduates marched in adorned in their caps and gowns.

"There's Kim," Bill shouted. "Hi! Uncle Kim!"

"Shush!" the girls scolded Bill as they excitedly waved at their uncle.

From there, the program went downhill fast with a string of boring speeches. The invocation by Dr. R.N. Avison was tolerable, but the speeches were endless. Dr. E. O. Sisson of Reed College in Portland gave the commencement address, "Constructive Advances in Education."

"When's he going to finish" Bill groaned, sliding down in his seat.

"Sit up, Bill, and be quiet!" Ella scolded.

"I wonder what Uncle Kim's doing. He's looking down and not paying attention," Ella observed.

"He's probably designing another airplane or some other flying machine," Elsie laughed quietly.

"No, I think he's writing in his yearbook," Ella observed.

"Well, he better pay attention. They're starting to call out the graduates' names."

"No problem. They won't get to Hong for a bit if it's alphabetical."

The wait was shorter than they expected, with E.B. Millard calling out the graduate's name and presenting each diploma with a flourish and handshake.

"Kim S. Hong – scientific. Kim is Salem High's most advanced scholar. He completed his courses a year early with the highest marks!" Millard announced as the crowd applauded politely.

When Millard finally got to the last person, Ive O. Wechter, the entire audience let out a relieved cheer.

"Are we done? Let's go and get Uncle Kim," Bill shouted.

"Uncle Kim, what were you doing during the ceremony? Ella asked.

"I was paying attention, of course."

No, you were not. Let me see your yearbook, Elsie," demanded.

Kim handed over the yearbook to his niece, who opened it to the front page.

"I was signing my yearbook."

"It's pretty," Bill gushed. "You had more fun than I did."

As they were waiting in line for refreshments, a reporter from the Capital Journal approached Kim.

"Well, young man. You certainly burned through the Salem High School curriculum in record time. What's next for you?"

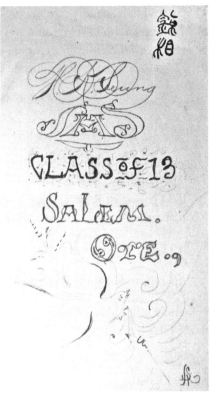

Kim S. Hong. 1913 Salem High School Yearbook.

"I'm going to UC Berkeley and then Wharton School of Finance in Philadelphia followed by a career in the diplomatic service," Kim announced.

"That a pretty long-term plan for someone so young. What about that plane you have in Hop's front yard? Will you be taking that with you?

"I think studies come first. I'll put my aeronautical career on hold for now."

"Here, Uncle Kim. We got cookies and punch for you," Bill whispered, tugging at Kim's sleeve.

"Give some to the nice reporter, Bill," Ella instructed.

Bill looked down at his plate and the dwindling supply of treats.

"I won't have any left."

The reporter laughed, "No worries, little man. You enjoy the cookies. You earned them if you sat through the same speeches I did."

"Thanks, Mister," Bill beamed, munching on the pecan cookies with his face covered in crumbs.

"Let me say goodbye to my Geometry teacher before we go," Kim requested, heading over to greet Mrs. Smith

"Hello, Mrs. Smith. I'll be leaving for CAL soon. I enjoyed your math classes."

"You were my best student, Kim. Here, I have something for you to remember us at Salem High School."

Kim smiled as he inspected the photograph.

"You've come a long way; Kim and you have a long way to go. Don't forget your friends here in Salem."

KS Hong and Salem High School geometry class. Low Family collection.

The following October, Kim wrote the Hop Lees in Salem from Oakland.

14 October 1914

Dear Sister Kay and Family,

"Classes here at CAL are going great. I study lots but have made many friends. Math and Science are my strengths, and I will probably declare for an engineering major soon. I am enclosing a photo of my surveying course. It was good to get out of the classroom and do something practical for once.

I joined the Chinese Club and met more Chinese than I ever saw in Kalispell or Salem. My best friend is Sun Fo, the son of Dr. Sun Yat-sen. He is a year ahead of me. We study together and talk about his father's struggles to lead the Revolution. Maybe someday I will meet Dr. Sun. Until then, I will keep studying. Every day, I take the cable car up Telegraph to the campus from our apartment on 6th Street in Oakland. Mom gives me a quarter, and the fare is only a nickel, so I have some money left over for lunch.

Mom says hello and that she is looking forward to visiting her Salem, Oregon grandchildren very soon.

PS. Don't let Hop chop up my airplane for firewood. I expect to finish it someday when I return to Salem.

Your Loving Brother and Uncle,

Kim S. Hong

Kim Hong in beret with hands on hips in UC Berkeley surveying class 1914. Hong Family Collection

Sun Fo and his father Dr. Sun Yat-sen. Sun Fo graduated from UC Berkeley in 1916 and was the president of the Chinese Club. Kim S. Hong was the president-elect. Public Domain. Wikimedia Commons

Chapter Twenty-Five

A Small Fortune for a Hop Farm – 1914

I n the decade since they purchased their first hop farm six miles north of Salem, the Hop Lees had acquired two more farms in the same vicinity. In February 1912, Hop purchased the 30-acre Horace Stevens farm in the South Bottom for a little less than two hundred dollars per acre and an additional 32 acres from John Z. Painter. All three farms were within a short radius of each other in the Keizer and Clear Lake areas, and all were in the name of Hung Hop Lee. The crown jewel of Hop's grand scheme, the original Alvis Smith homestead next to Claggett Cemetery, was now within his grasp. It was one of the finest farms in the Willamette Valley, in the incredibly fertile bottomlands surrounding the Willamette River. The 553-acre property was sold to Dr. Mark Skiff in 1905 for $12,000. Hop was kicking himself for not pursuing the land ten years ago because now the land value had skyrocketed. Sensing a windfall, Skiff now seemed open to unload the property for the right price.

Hop stood for a moment in front of the dentist's office. He took a deep breath and then walked through the office door.

"Hi, Hop! What brings you into my office? Do you have a toothache?"

"No, Dr. Skiff. I heard you might be interested in selling your land in Mission Bottom near the Claggett Cemetery."

Mark Skiff paused, looking at the Chinese laundryman more closely, "It's a lot of money, Hop. Are you sure you are in this league?"

"Well, Dr. Skiff...,"

"Call me Mark. We are old friends, after all, Hop."

"Well, Mark, I have a little money and some small hop farms, but it may be time to get out of hops. Those women next door to my office have the vote. They convinced Salem to go "dry," and now they want to ban drinking everywhere. That would be very bad for our hop business." [1] [2]

Mark Skiff paused. It was true he had heard rumblings of a growing Prohibition movement and had seen those Temperance Women on Commercial Street. Things were not looking great for hop farmers. It was starting to affect his dental practice as some patients disliked his affiliation with alcohol. [3]

"How much money do you have, Hop?"

"Not much, Mark. I am just a laundryman, but I can scrape together $25,000 if you can give me some time."

"The land is worth three times that much!" Dr. Skiff exploded.

"Well, that's the best I can do."

"I already turned down offers up to $35,000, Hop."

"Sorry to hear that. Maybe you should have taken that offer. Times are changing, Mark. Who made that offer? I have lots of friends around Salem. Maybe I can talk to them for you and get them to give you a little more. Hate to see you get stuck with this land."

Skiff was clearly puzzled and unsure of Hop's motivation. But he kept thinking about those Temperance Women.

---

1. Hop Lee and Hong Hop Lee in 1912 signed contract with Jos Harris for 30,000 pounds of hops at 14 cents per pound for the years of 1913-1917.

2. In November 1913 Salem voted to go "dry," banning the sale of alcohol. Governor Oswald West signed an executive order on December 4, 1914 announcing statewide alcohol prohibition following a ballot initiative. Oregon went "dry" four years before the National ban on the sale and production of alcohol with ratification of the 18th Amendment on January 16, 1919

3. Founded in 1883, the Oregon Women's Christian Temperance Union was a powerful political and social force.

"Tell you what, Mark, if I can match that offer, will you consider doing business with this laundryman?"

Skiff hesitated. "I can't promise anything, but I will always listen to a friend. My office door is open to you, Hop."

"OK, Mark. I will try to find a little more money. But we better act fast before the bottom falls out of the hop market.

The meetings went on for a couple of weeks. Hop even brought one of the Temperance Women with him, who lectured Dr. Skiff on the evils of alcohol. She had his attention and not in a good way.

On the fourth visit, Hop began, "I can borrow enough money to give you $30,000 for the land, Mark. But that's all I can do. I will be penniless, and Ah Kay will kill me if she finds out I have spent all our money and gone into debt to buy worthless hop land."

"Skiff was looking out the office door to see if the Temperance "Bonnie Brigade" had followed Hop. Returning his gaze to Hop, "Not enough. I need $50,000 for the property."

"Sorry, I guess I wasted a friend's time. Have a good day." Hop stood and turned towards the door. "Bring your laundry by, and I will do it free for a good friend. Best hand washing and ironing in Salem."

Skiff was unsure but had visions of a mob of Temperance Women picketing his office. "Wait, Hop! How about $46,000?"

Hop took his hand off the front door, turned around, and smiled at Skiff. "OK, Mark, we settle on $38,000."

$42,500, Hop, and I can carry most of it." [4]

Hop smiled broadly, extending his hand, "You drive a hard bargain, Dr. Skiff!"

"Alright, Hop. But you have to let me tell RJ Hendricks at the Oregon Statesman that I sold you the land for $42,500 cash."

---

4. $42,500 in 1914 is equivalent to over $1 million today.

"Sure, Mark. Tell you what. If you include all the farm equipment on the farm for one dollar, then you can tell the newspaper whatever you like!"

Dr. Skiff hesitated, pondering his options.

"Come on, Mark. What are you going to do with an old plow anyway!"

"OK, Hop. We have a deal," Mark Skiff extended his hand, which a smiling Hop shook vigorously.

On his walk back to his laundry on Commercial Street, Hop pondered on what he would do with the extra $10,000 he had in his pocket.

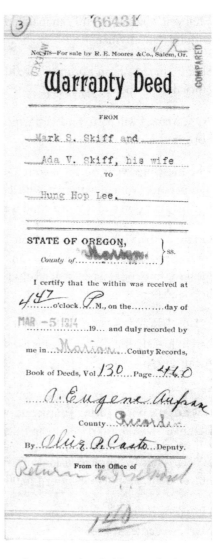

***

That evening, after dinner, Hop put the children to bed, "Good night Elsie, Ella, Willie, Arthur, and little Albert." Hop gave each of his children a kiss goodnight and tucked them into their beds.

"Good night, Papa."

Hop turned out the lights and hurried into the front room, where Kay was waiting patiently. She knew that Hop enjoyed putting the children to bed. How many times had Hop told her about being a lonely bachelor in Gum Saan and longing for a family? Hop was a good and loving father.

My precious jewel, I have a birthday gift for you and a card I picked out just for you."

Kay opened the card first and burst out laughing. "I am a bit older Hop after all these children."

You could have a **MILLION** birthdays and I'd love you anyhow !!

love again
"Hubby"

Popo Kay kept this one birthday card from her husband in her huge scrap book.

Hop kissed his wife. "You have given me a happy home and family, Kay. Thank you."

The next day Hop awoke with an inspiration.

"The family grows, and we buy a hop farm. We have another baby and buy another hop farm. Everything is changing. When I was a bachelor, nothing much changed. Now everything is constantly changing. We need to spend some money and make a Loo family portrait to preserve this moment and to celebrate our family and the new hop farm."

That afternoon, the Hop Lee family assembled at the Parker Photographic Studio on the corner of Commercial and Chemeketa.[5] Dressed in their finest American clothes, they were a model Salem family.

"OK. Everyone, look this way! Hop, stop grinning!"

"I can't help it. I am a happy father today."

Ella burst out in giggles, and baby Albert started to squirm.

Hop Lee Family 1914. Ella, Elsie, Kay, Albert, Low Sun Fook aka Hop Lee, Wille, and Arthur. Low Family Collection.

---

5. The Parker Photographic Studio owned by Waldo H. Parker was the largest photographic studio in the Pacific Northwest. WH Parker learned his craft working for Eastman Kodak. The studio was located above Barnes Cash on Commercial street and was originally the Trover - Cronise Sutdio

"You better take the photo, Waldo," Hop advised as he placed his arm around Willie.

"One, two, and three!"

The bright flash and puff of smoke froze the moment for all time. Hop had no idea how their lives were about to change forever.

Four-year-old Arthur immediately came over and jumped onto Hop's lap, taking his father's hand and placing it onto his shoulder.

"Give Dad some space to breathe, Arthur," Elsie scolded.

"No, he's my Dad and I got stuck on the end."

Hop laughed and patted Arthur's head while his beautiful son snuggled in more closely.

"*Ngo oi nei*, my son," Hop said softly, stroking Arthur's face.

At that moment, Hop knew that all of his dreams of finding roots and a family in Gum Saan had come true.

While the Hop Lees were the model of the assimilated, Westernized Chinese-American family, in April, Elsie and Ella took part in a two-act stage production entitled Carnival of Children dressed as Chinese emigrants from the old country. [6]

—*ell*—

---

6. The Carnival of Children under the direction of Mss. Beatrice Shelton features 139 little tots in a production of song and dance. The Little Chinese Emigrants were played by Else Hop Lee and Ella Hop Lee. Oregon Daily Journal Wednesday April 28, 1915.

HOP LEE BUYS

Chinaman Puts Fortune Into Land Here.

Fine Farm Changes Hands—Dr. Mark Skiff Disposes of Valuable Place—Show How Values Increase.

One of the finest farms in the Willamette valley changed hands this week when Dr. Mark Skiff, the well known dentist of this city, sold his 553 acres of rich soil located six miles notrh of Salem on Kaisers Prairie, to Hop Hung Lee, a Chinese laundryman of Salem. The deal was made for $42,500 cash.

According to Dr. Skiff the deal has been on for several weeks but only became a realty on Thursday of this week when the papers were signed. The purchaser has already made negotiations to have 50 acres set to hops and the remainder of the property will probably be used for farming purposes. Hop Lee owns three ranches within a radius of several miles of his recent purchase and his plan is to combine the four into one large hop field.

In 1905 Dr. Skiff bought the Kaiser farm for $12,000. Since that time he has made a number of necessary improvements to the property. Several years ago he was offered $20,000 for the place but refused to take it in the belief that it was worth much more. Later $35,000 was offered, which conclusively proves that the price of land in the Willamette valley is almost tripling itself in value every year.

March 8, 1914 Statesman Journal

Chapter Twenty-Six

Wheeling and Dealing

B etween 1904 and 1914, Hop fulfilled his American Dream, acquiring six hop farms in the incredibly fertile Willamette Valley. With each successive purchase, Hop learned the lessons of buying a property using someone else's money and someone else's name. The naming part was brilliant. While Hop could never purchase land as a Chinese, his wife, born in San Francisco, most certainly could. American-born, Ah Kay aka Hung Hop Lee, became the youngest landowner in the state of Oregon.

Hop's cash purchase of the 122-acre Fedit property in March 1904 was the last time he used his own money to pay the entire price up front for land. Hop's wheelings and dealings allowed him to purchase the additional farms with little or no money down, taking out mortgages and loans to cover the cost.

"I have my eye on another Hop farm in near Clear Lake, George."

"Well, how are you going to pay for another farm. You should make some money from the first farm before you stretch yourself thin," George advised.

"Well, I have a plan to take care of my cash flow problem."

"What's your get-rich scheme this time, Hop?"

"I've been in Salem for over twenty years. These people trust me with their laundry, their chickens, and, as it turns out, with their money."

"You do have a lot of friends in Salem, but how does that help you buy this farm,

Hop?"

"My friend Mr. Bush at the Bush and Ladd Bank will loan me the money on my good name."

"How are you going to pay the bank back for this loan. You have a family to think of now."

"These farms will make money growing hops. I'll hire managers and use the farm income from hop sales to pay back the bank and I'll make a tidy profit along the way."

"You know, Hop, farming requires a lot more than land. You'll need horses, wagons, and tons of farm implements. All of that costs money."

"Not a problem, George. I have that covered."

"How?"

"Remember Jim Sing? He's been struggling to make ends meet, leasing Les Brown's hop farm in Polk County."

"Yes, Jim's getting too old for farming. So, what?"

"Jim is going to sell me everything for a song."

"What do you mean by everything?"

"I get his two brown mares, Queen and Topsy, harnesses, an old wagon, harrow, burlap sacks, and tons of farm implements and tools. If it's not nailed down, I get it!"

"For how much?"

"We settled on $368. It's a fire sale!"

"Well, Hop, you always have a scheme to make money, my friend."

——— *ele* ———

In February 1907, Hop and Hung Hop Lee purchased their second property, the

80-acre MJ Crayton farm, for $3550. They paid $1000 down and $2000 carried by Crayton at 6% interest. One year later, in 1908, they purchased the Stevens Ranch of 32 acres in South Bottom for $1200. In January 1909, Charles E Lebold sold Hop 33-1/3 acres for $1,000, which Hop financed with a 5-year mortgage at 7%. In February 1913, 79-year-old Lafayette Harpole sold Hop the 34-acre farm for $2800, which Harpole carried without interest.

Most of the 1914 purchase price of the 612-acre Mark Skiff farm was carried by Dr. Skiff on a 10-year note at 6% interest. Hop borrowed the remaining $8,000 from the Ladd and Bush Bank at 7% interest.

Hop walked the one block up Commercial Street to the Ladd & Bush Bank at the corner of State and Commercial Streets. He smiled, thinking about the thick wad of cash hidden in his derby hat.

Entering the bank, he made a beeline for A.N. Bush's office, who looked up and smiled as his old friend greeted him.

"Hello, Mr. Bush. Today is a big day!"

"What's special about April 15th, Hop?"

"Today, I keep my word," Hop replied proudly.

Ladd & Bush Bank. Salem, Oregon. Low Family Collection.

Taking off his black derby, he turned it upside down, emptying its hidden contents onto the desk."

"Well, this is a special surprise, Hop. You shouldn't be walking around with all this cash."

"No problem, Mr. Bush. Everyone in Salem likes old Hop, and everyone thinks I am just a laundryman," Hop laughed.

"Now, I have paid you back in full for last year's loan!"

"I never doubted you for a second, Hop," Nes Bush replied, shuffling through the pile of money. "How much is this?"

"Ten thousand dollars," Hop replied proudly.

"I knew from the night we met at your laundry fire over 30 years ago that you are a man of your word."

"Well, I just wish the hop prices would recover. Prohibition is not good for business. I still have more loans from your bank to pay off, and things are looking like I'm not going to be able to sell enough chickens or wash enough laundry to make much difference," Hop said glumly.

Nes Bush looked at his long-time friend and paused before replying, "You know Hop, with dropping interest rates, you can consolidate all of your loans and pay them off with cheaper dollars."

The light in Hop's mind went off. "You mean I can pay you back and make money at the same time?"

"Well, you won't make a fortune, but I am here to help a friend. You will have to put up your farms as collateral."

They signed the papers two days later. Hop received $18,000 at 6% interest, which he used to pay off more expensive loans at 7% - 8%. Listing his eight properties as collateral made Hop and the Bush and Ladd Bank partners for the foreseeable future.

In Hop's way of thinking, he was using the bank's money to pay them back and was making money in the process!

This is the American way!

Family lore states that Hop purchased a new farm with the birth of each new son. The truth is much more enlightening. Hop's purchases of new farms roughly coincided with the birth of his first six children, including three daughters and three sons. Hop, after all, treated his daughters and sons equally and had similar expectations for the boys and girls.

That evening in 1914, after he purchased the 612-acre Alvis Smith homestead, Hop pulled out the Chinese fortune, scanned the calligraphy, and shook his head in disbelief. Somehow the Chinese fortune teller had known. What had seemed like an impossible dream 16 years ago was now a reality. The fortune teller's prediction that Hop would buy land in Gum Saan was correct not just once but six times over.

Willamette Valley Hop field. Post card. Low Family Collection.

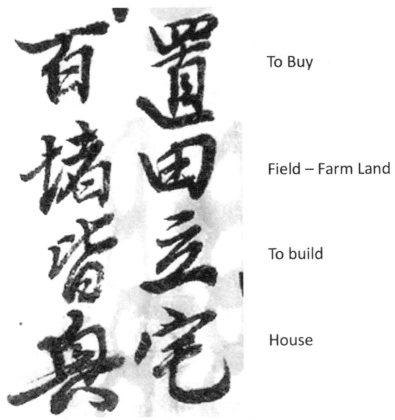

To Buy

Field – Farm Land

To build

House

Detail from Low Fortune Teller Scroll.

Hop's belief in the American Dream and the fertile Willamette Valley soil flew in the face of an unseasonable dry spell and declining hop prices. In 1914 an early heat wave was sweeping the country. By May, the pavement on State Street was already like rubber, with a 98-degree temperature recorded in the shade on the thermometer in front of Barr's jewelry store. In Oregon and the Willamette Valley, in particular, crop yields were reduced by the continued hot weather and shortage of rainfall. When a local newspaper reporter questioned Hop's faith in the hop market and asked what he would do if the drought continued, his answer was ever confident. "Then I'll grow something else that's good."

Believes in Valley Soil.

Hop Lee is having several acres of land cleared and will plant more hops. He has full faith in the profitable returns from Willamette valley soil. When asked what he will do with his four big hop yards north of Salem should the dry wave make hop growing unprofitable, this astute Chinaman replied: "Then I'll grow something else that's good."

Statesman Journal December 30, 1914

Chapter Twenty-Seven

Tragedy at the Mill Race – April 27, 1915

A s if one son weren't enough, Hop was blessed with three strong and healthy boys. Willie was already six years old, full of energy and an independent spirit. Arthur, born on April 2, 1911, was a handsome and quiet boy. Albert was the youngest son, born on January 13, 1913. Hop was very busy making entries and corrected entries in his journal. Writing the American dates was a mystery that eluded and puzzled Hop to no end. Using the Chinese calendar would have been much more straightforward, but Hop insisted on being an American, even if he couldn't vote or become a citizen. Hop was more American than any other man, woman, or child in Salem in his heart. He studied the US Constitution and flew the American flag over his place of business. The desire to be an American burned within him. [1]

The stranger that appeared in Salem's Chinese Quarter seemed to have no family, no past, and an uncertain future. George Sun tried to find out about the stranger, but the man rarely spoke, and no one in the Chinese Quarter knew anything about him.

"Hop, we need to check this man out. He has no job and lives by himself in that rundown hotel on Ferry street. I want to know what he is up to. It's not natural!"

---

1. The expensive clothing was made for each child by a German seamstress, whom Hop hired to come to the home twice a year.

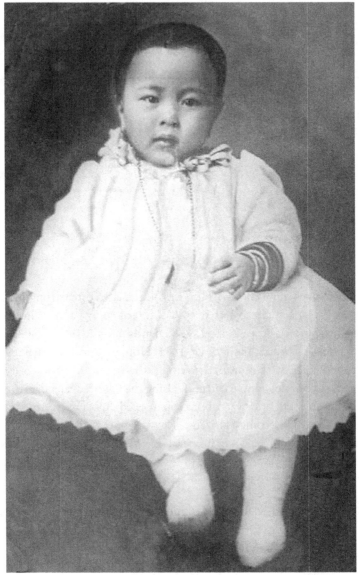

Arthur Hop Lee as a toddler in 1912. Low Family Collection.

"We should just send him packing before we find the trouble he is bringing," Hop agreed.

"Why don't you go and see if he needs a job. At least then, it will look like we want to help."

"I am everyone's friend in Salem, but I don't like the man," Hop replied.

"Alright, let's think on this a bit, but at the first sign of trouble, we show him the road out of Salem."

"Agreed!"

Hop was surprised when a few days later, the stranger showed up at his poultry store on Ferry Street.

He entered, closed the door behind him, looked directly at Hop, and blurted out, "I am Chun Lun. I want to buy your son."

Incredulous and speechless, Hop stared at the Chinese.

"You have three sons. I have none. I have money and will buy your son. Not the oldest one, Willie, and not the baby. I want the middle son, the one you call Arthur."

Hop exploded, "My children are not for sale! Who do you think you are? You cannot buy my son like a sack of rice! Now get out of here before I call the police!"

Chun Lun's face darkened as he continued, "I need to adopt your son so he can take care of me. How much money do you want?"

"I said GO AWAY!"

The stranger glared at Hop, not moving an inch. He clenched his fist into a tight ball. The veins in his neck and forehead bulged. He looked like he was about to explode. Lun then abruptly turned and walked out of the store, slamming the door behind him.

Hop immediately picked up his new hand crank phone. "Kay! Is that you? Where is Arthur? Find him quickly!"

"He's right here with me, Hop. What's going on? Why are you upset? You're scaring me."

"That strange Chinese man came into my store demanding that I sell Arthur to him! I think he's crazy. There's no telling what he'll do!"

"Don't worry so much, Hop. He probably is just rambling."

"I don't think so, Kay. He knew all about our three boys. He knew their names and ages! He wants Arthur!"

"Hop, I'll watch him like a hawk. Maybe you should come home now."

"I'll be right there. Don't let Arthur or the other children out of your sight."

The stranger disappeared, and life slowly returned to normal. Just to be safe, Hop enlisted the watchful eyes of his friends throughout Salem to let him know if Chun Lun reappeared.

A week later, on April 27th, Hop went to work at the laundry as usual. It was a brisk and sunny Spring morning in Salem. The day was uneventful. Beatrice Hundsaker brought in a basket full of dirty clothes for Hop to wash and iron. Hop supervised his employees, Loo Gon and Loo Tom, who were cousins from Hoiyin. They had both been working at the Hop Lee Laundry for over ten years.

Late in the afternoon, Willie showed up to make his usual daily delivery of clean laundry to nearby Commercial Street customers. Hop made the more remote deliveries in the new red automobile that had replaced his horse-drawn laundry wagon in April 1911. He was proud of the red "Hop Lee Laundry Car." Everyone in Salem recognized Hop's red automobile, and driving it made Hop feel important and American.

Hop loaded Willie's cart with a dozen packages of clean laundry. He smiled at his energetic young son. *It is good for Willie to learn to be independent and to appreciate the value of hard work.*

"Here, Willie, take these bundles to Mr. Hendricks at the Statesman office in the Griswold Murphy Building. These bundles are for Uncle George, and then take these bundles to the women in the Temperance office next door. Can you remember all that, Willie?"

"Sure, Dad! Mr. Hendricks, Uncle George, and those ladies who don't like your hops!"

"Well, yes, but don't talk to them about our hop farms. Just drop off the laundry and leave quickly. OK?"

"OK. I can carry more in my cart."

Hop looked around and spotted a package for Mr. Bush. "Here's another one for Mr. Bush at the Ladd and Bush Bank. Do you remember where the bank is?"

"Sure, Dad. You took me there to deposit my money in the bank."

"A penny saved is a penny earned, or something like that, Willie."

Hop opened the laundry's front door, and Willie wheeled his laundry-laden cart into the Salem afternoon sunshine. "Good-bye, Pop," Willie called out as he turned back to wave at his father.

"Be careful, Willie, and come right back here when you finish your deliveries."

Willie's first stop was at the Statesman office on Commercial Street not far from the Hop Lee Laundry.

"Hi, Willie. Thanks for bringing my laundry," R.J. Hendricks greeted his old friend's son.

"Hi, Mr. Hendricks," Willie answered, handing over the three bundles of laundry. Each bundle was wrapped in brown paper with Chinese writing, indicating its owner.

"Willie, did I ever tell you a story about how your father arrived in Salem in a Well's Fargo stagecoach? No? Well, it was quite an arrival. The whole town started calling him Hop Lee from the very first day."

"They all call him Hop, not Hop Lee, and he really hates being called Mister Hop Lee. He likes being called just plain old Hop," Willie wxplained.

"Your father has more friends in Salem than any person I know. He has been here a long time and has always been a friend with a helping hand for his neighbors."

"So long, Mr. Hendricks. I need to make my other deliveries."

"Bye, Willie. Say hello to your mother for me."

The rest of Willie's deliveries were uneventful, and he made sure not to hang around the Women's Temperance office too long. He dropped off the laundry and made a beeline for the door, just like Dad had instructed him. As he entered the laundry with his empty laundry cart, Hop was talking on the phone.

"What do you mean he's not at home? I thought he was with you. No, he's not here at the laundry."

"Pop what's the matter?"

"Not now, Willie. Your brother is missing."

"Kay, calm down. He must be hiding. No, he's not with Willie. Willie just got back from his deliveries. OK, I'll ask him."

Willie, do you know where Arthur is?"

"No, Pop. I thought he was with Mom at home. I haven't seen him all afternoon."

"Kay, Willie doesn't know where his brother is. I'll be right home."

The short walk home was a blur as Hop imagined his son being kidnapped and held by Chun Lun.

If that evil Chinaman took Arthur, I will hunt him down and kill him!

Kay was frantic and in tears by the time Hop and Willie arrived home. "Hop, he's gone. I thought he was with you all afternoon! I should have called you sooner."

"Kay, it is not your fault. I will call the police, and we will send out a search party for Arthur."

Officer Williams arrived at the home on South Church Street, and began the interrogation of Hop and Ah Kay. "When did you notice Arthur was missing? When did you last see him? Could he be at a friend's home? What was he wearing?"

The questions went on for some time, but in the end, all they knew was that Arthur was missing and no one had seen him for hours.

"We'll send out a search party and canvas the neighborhood first."

Hop was on the phone, "George, Arthur is missing. I am sure it was that Chun Lun who took him. Gather the Chinese together and begin a search of the Chinese Quarter. Go to the hotel where Chun Lun was staying. Thank you, George, but I am worried."

The search went on well into the night with the police and hundreds of Salem's residents, Chinese and Whites, desperately hunting for little Arthur.

"Arthur! Arthur! Where are you? Please come home now," Kay pleaded.

Soon her voice was overwhelmed by her sobbing. "Please, Arthur, come home to your mama."

Hop placed his arm around his wife, "My dear Ah Kay, you must rest. Go home and be with our children. They need you now. I will stay out here with the search party."

"Mrs. Hundsaker, can you take Kay home?"

"Of course, Hop," Beatrice replied as she took Kay's arm and led her back to the home on Church Street.

Hop stayed out all night going down every alley and street in Salem, searching for his four-year-old son. After several hours, hope was fading. Finally, sitting on a curb, Hop felt the weight of the entire world on his shoulders. It was too much to bear.

Several times Hop thought he heard Arthur's little voice, "Papa, I'm over here!"

But each time, he stopped and listened. There was nothing but the wind in the trees or the sounds of the creek.

As the sun rose the next morning, only Hop and a few police were left to continue the search.

"Mr. Lee, maybe you should go home and try to rest. We will continue the search and will call you as soon as we know anything," Officer Nicholson offered.

"No. I am the boy's father. I must continue to search until we find Arthur," Hop replied with a deep forlorn sadness in his voice.

The police had switched their search to Mill Creek and were slowly heading upstream towards the mill race.

"We need to turn the water out of the mill race to search the waters," Nicholson instructed the other police officer.

Arthur Hop Lee 1914. Low Family Collection

About 9:30 a.m. Officer Nicholson was wading in the shallow waters of Mill Creek near the High Street Bridge when he spotted a small shape washed up against the bridge stanchion.

At almost the exact moment, Hop also spotted the motionless shape. At first, Hop thought it was a rock or a small log, but immediately knew it was his worst fear come true.

Hop raced into the creek with water splashing all around. He was still carrying the blanket he'd brought to keep Arthur warm. At that moment, Nicholson was hovered over the shape, motioning for Hop to stay back.

Hop raced ahead in the creek and got to Nicholson as he was turning the shape over. It was little Arthur! Nicholson picked up the lifeless boy and gently placed Arthur into Hop's arms.

Arthur looked like he was sleeping. Hop tenderly wrapped his son in the blanket and began the long walk home.

The police maintained a respectful distance. Hop's friends and neighbors silently watched Hop carry his son home through the streets of Salem, holding him closely and sobbing with tears streaming down his face. It was the longest walk of Hop's life.

Beautiful and beloved Arthur was gone. The community and especially the mothers of Salem wept for little Arthur. It was a moment of grief that touched the entire community. The flowers and cards flowed like a river of tears from friends, neighbors and total strangers. The long list of those sending flowers included the George Sun Family, the Baptist Primary Sunday School, and Jane A. Chadwick, the wife of Oregon's fifth governor, Stephen F Chadwick.

The Hop Lees held a Christian service for Arthur in their home at 296 South Church Street on Thursday, April 29th. Hundreds of friends, Whites, Chinese, and African Americans crowded the 2 p.m. service. Arthur had been a member of the First Baptist Church Sunday School. Reverend H.E Marshall spoke touchingly of Arthur and Mrs. Theodore Roth and Miss Mina Giles sang the Christian hymns, "When He Cometh" and "Asleep in Jesus." Arthur's ornate wooden casket was covered with mounds of beautiful flower arrangements and wreaths. Late in the afternoon, Arthur was laid to rest in the Pioneer Cemetery with his Sunday School teachers serving as the pallbearers.

Foul play was never publicly claimed, and no charges were ever filed. But when the autopsy revealed that little Arthur did not have any water in his lungs, Hop knew that Arthur had not drowned. His death was not an accident. Hop knew what had really happened and who was to blame.

That evening alone in the parlor, Hop pulled out the fortune and stared in disbelief at the characters that foretold this tragedy.

Mrs. Jane A Chadwick send a card and flowers to the Hop Lee home.

Blasted fortune! Now your words will haunt me forever. I should have listened to your warning and protected Arthur.

The following Tuesday morning, May 3, 1915, a ray of hope shown into the Hop Lee household, cutting through the overwhelming gloom that had settled over the entire family. The cycle of life continued with the birth of a new baby girl, precisely one week after Arthur's death. Her grandmother sent her milk name, Edith, and her Chinese name, King Gew. She would be called Isabel.

The parents and children were gathered around baby Edith, sleeping peacefully on a pink satin cushion. Hop lovingly caressed the forehead of his youngest son, two-year-old Albert, and his newborn daughter, declaring, "Yesterday, he was my baby, and today she is my baby."

Hop kept the beloved photograph of Arthur in the parlor of the home above the piano. Arthur was gone but never forgotten.

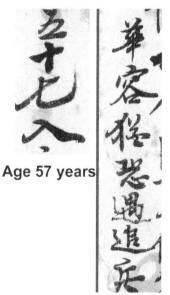

Age 57 years

Your face turned ashen
Something is very bad.

Somone is chasing after you.
You will feel scared.

This is very tragic.

You must be very careful

Detail from Low Fortune Teller Scroll. Low Family Collection

Chinese Boy Is Drowned at Salem

Salem, Or., April 28.—The body of Oscar Hop Lee, the 4-year-old son of Hop Lee, a well known and wealthy Chinese merchant and hopman of Salem, was found at the headgates of the Mill Creek millrace, near the Salem water works, this morning. The boy had been missing from his home, 296 South Church street, near Mill creek, since yesterday afternoon at 4 o'clock, although search was not begun until 8 o'clock last evening because his mother thought the lad was at the store with his father, and his father thought he was at home.

Hop Lee was on the shore when the body was found. He wrapped it tenderly in a blanket and carried it to his home.

The Oregon Daily Journal Wednesday April 28, 1915.

Shaft of Light Shines Through Thick Darkness of China Family: Child Born

A beam of light shone through the overshadowing gloom in the household of Hop Lee, whose little son was drowned in the mill race last week, when a baby daughter was born to them yesterday morning. She is a pretty, plump little girl and will take the name of Ada Hop Lee.

"Yesterday, he my baby," said the well known Chinaman as he stroked the head of his two-year-old son, caressingly, "but today, she my baby," he added as with the pretty young mother, the family gazed upon the dainty little mite who was sleeping guietly on a pink satin comforter. Both mother and baby are doing well.

Last Tuesday a four-year-old son, Oscar Hop Lee, wandered to the mill race near the Hop Lee home on South Church street and was drowned. The family was bowed in grief over the death. However the burden is somewhat lifted. The fond parents still have five children, three girls and two boys.

Statesman Journal May 4, 1915.

Chapter Twenty-Eight

Hop's Gloom and Depression

"Don't bother Father," Elsie whispered to Willie, who was peering into the darkened parlor.

"What's wrong with him? He's just sitting there in the dark. He hasn't moved all morning. I know because I've been watching him since after breakfast."

Hop's spirits darkened more with each passing day following Arthur's funeral. He refused to eat and spoke to no one. Edith's birth's initial joy was soon overwhelmed by the dark and foreboding sadness that enveloped and consumed Hop like a heavy dark blanket of grief. Hop was drowning in his despair just as his son had drowned in Mill Creek.

Little Ella heard the whispering and entered the room quietly.

"We have to do something, and we better do it soon. He's getting worse every day," she whispered.

"I know, but what should we do?"

"You're the oldest! You should know what to do!" Ella replied.

"I think we should just leave him alone and give him some time."

Albert pushed open the door, "What's going on in here?"

"Shhh!" the girls scolded their little brother. "Father's in there."

"So? I need him to come to the poultry store to help with the chickens," Albert lamented.

"Don't worry about those stupid chickens so much!" Elsie, chided.

"Dad told me to take care of the store, but I'm just a kid, and those chickens need Dad!" Albert exclaimed.

"Maybe Mom knows what to do," Willie offered.

"She's busy with the baby, and she hasn't spoken much either for days," Ella replied. "Maybe I can ask Rev Marshall at the Baptist Church to say a prayer for Dad."

"Ella, you know he doesn't really believe in that church stuff. He just pretends for us," Willie quipped.

"Well, it's worth a try, and what great ideas do you have, Willie? Just because you're the boy doesn't mean you know what's best for Dad!"

"Stop it, you two! You're not helping, and you're giving me a headache!" Elsie scolded.

"Just because you're the oldest doesn't mean you can boss us around!" Ella pouted.

"Alright. Sorry, but be quiet."

"What about the chickens?"

"Be quiet, Albert," they all replied in unison.

Sitting in the darkened parlor, Hop remembered the weight of his son's lifeless body in his arms as he carried him home along Church Street. Arthur's face was peaceful, but he was dead. Hop quietly sobbed as he sank deeper into the abyss.

What kind of a father am I? I knew that evil Lun Chu was after Arthur, and I did nothing to protect him. I don't deserve to live. Please, put an end to my worthless life.

Elsie, Albert, and Arthur Hop Lee. Low Family Collection.

Slowly, Hop descended into a restless slumber as his sobbing subsided, but the hell that surrounded him refused to take him.

The next morning, the Salem morning sun's first ray entered the parlor through a smudged pane of glass, but it did nothing to lift Hop's spirits. Hop gazed at the beam of light and followed its path out the window towards the cherry tree in the front yard. His gaze settled upon the winged monstrosity that dominated the yard. As Hop awoke, the shape came into focus, and the rage in Hop began to simmer and then boil.

Kim's worthless flying contraption! I told him to get rid of that thing! It was a foolish waste of time and money! There was no way I was going to give him hard-earned money for a motor. And now he has gone off to college and left that ugly, worthless aeroplane behind to torment me!

All of Hop's grief was instantly funneled into an all-consuming rage. His world was spinning out of control and was red with fury. Hop stiffly rose from the chair and stumbled as he headed out the back door. Outside, the cool Salem air did nothing to temper Hop's wrath.

"That blasted evil aeroplane is the problem, and I can fix it once and for all!"

Hop opened the shed's door and groped around in the semi-darkness.

I know it's in here. Where is that ax?

Rummaging around behind a work table, Hop grasped the smooth handle of the long ax. He pulled, but it was stuck under a pile of unused tools. With one final tug, the whole pile of rakes, shovels, and baskets came tumbling down on top of him.

Laying on his back on the shed floor, Hop felt the ax's smooth wooden handle still firmly in his grasp.

"Ahaa! Now I can fix this problem and make that plane into firewood kindling."

Hop sat and then stood up with the pile of tools scattered over the shed floor. He ran out the door and headed around the side of the home towards the front yard. As he came around the corner of the house, the object of his misplaced fury came into view.

"Now you are mine! I will destroy you, and I will bring Arthur back!"

Hop charged forward with the ax raised over his head, the wooden and silk airplane set firmly in his sights.

With a final lunge, he swung the ax forward, shrieking, "Arthur, come home!"

Just as he swung, Hop felt himself flying forward towards the ground with the weight of his four children on his back.

"No, Papa! Don't do it! Don't destroy Kim's dream. Please, Dad! It won't bring Arthur back."

Hop found himself flat on the ground with Willie, Albert, Ella, and Elsie sitting on his back. He looked up and spotted the ax lying on the sidewalk, far from its intended target.

He sheepishly looked at his four children as he sat up. The children silently returned his gaze.

Willie broke the silence, "We all miss Arthur, Dad. But we need you too."

"Yes, Dad. We couldn't let you wreck Uncle Kim's plane. It won't help Arthur, and besides, he made us promise to look after it when he went to college," Ella explained.

"And your chickens need you too!" Albert added, poking his head out from behind Elsie.

Hop laughed as he gave Albert's head a gentle tousle. "Let's go inside, and let's not mention this to Mother."

Chapter Twenty-Nine

A New Home in Salem – 1916

As the excitement over Kim's aeroplane faded, other worries clouded Hop's thoughts. Every day the painful walk past the Mill Creek Raceway on his way to work was more than Hop could bear. He shut his eyes when he drew near, but he could never block out the horror of that day. Hop became quiet and withdrawn as the weeks wore on, hardly looking up when customers came into the store. The man who was Salem's friend was alone with his pain.

Hop had his head buried in the ledger book at the laundry and poultry store, but his mind was back at Mill Creek with Arthur. It was dark, and he was wading into the cold waters, searching for his son. The creek waters began to rise, covering his legs and then his chest. Hop felt the swift current pulling him under, but he couldn't stop searching. As the water covered his head, Hop felt something poking him. *It must be Arthur!*

"Hop! Wake up!"

Hop looked up and saw his son, "Is that you, Arthur? Hold on to me. I can save you."

"Hop! It's me. Wake up!"

Hop squinted at the dark shape in front of him. Arthur faded away as his friend George Sun came into focus.

"What are you doing here, George? Did you see Arthur? He was right here."

"Hop, you have to stop this. Everyone is worried about you."

As his store came into focus, Hop felt the deep sadness of losing Arthur yet again.

He hung his head, "I know, George. I can't take this any longer."

George gently placed his hands upon Hop's shoulders. "Every day I see you like this, my friend. We have to change something."

"You're right, George. Every day I walk to the store and pass that blasted Mill Creek raceway, and it all comes back to haunt me. I close my eyes and hurry past, but it doesn't help."

"Yes, and then at night, you do the same thing all over again. I know. I've seen you running past the raceway with your eyes shut. It's a wonder a horse hasn't run you down!"

"I didn't know it was that obvious. I should have known, George. It was in the fortune."

"Forget the fortune teller, Hop. Kay and the children need you."

George paused, "You have to move your family, Hop. Move far away from here. Go over by Willamette University. There are lots of young people there to take your mind off this sadness. And take another path to work!"

The tinkling bell announced Hop's next customer.

"Hello, Hop. How's business?"

"Good morning, Otto," Hop greeted his old friend. "Sold any automobiles this week?"

"Hop, needs to move his family away from that blasted Mill Creek raceway. Too many bad memories about his son," George interrupted.

"We are all so sorry about Arthur, Hop. Every parent feels your sadness."

"He needs a new place to live. Hop is going crazy walking by that raceway twice a day."

"There is a house for rent over where we live on State Street, past the Capital and the University. It's at State and 13th Street."

"Perfect!" George exclaimed. "You're moving up in the world, Hop. You'll be neighbors with the governor!"

Two weeks later, all of Hop's friends and neighbors turned out to lend a hand on moving day. The new home Hop selected was at 125 North 13th Street. It was a one-story wooden house with three bedrooms, a living room and parlor in front, and a large kitchen with a walk-in pantry. It was perfect for the growing Hop Lee family. The two older girls, Elsie and Ella, had their room with Willie and Albert in the second bedroom. Hop, Kay, and Isabel slept in the main bedroom in the back of the house. Kay picked out a new couch and some expensive thick rugs to cover the wooden floors.

Hop proudly displayed his most recent acquisition, an upright Bush & Lane piano. No one played the piano but Hop reasoned that they could all take lessons. This was America, after all, and what was more American than a piano in the parlor? But all this newness could not entirely erase Hop's sadness. Hop placed Arthur's portrait directly above the piano when no one was watching.

The Hop Lee family was now far removed from the remnants of Salem's Chinatown. The walk down State Street took Hop past the Oregon State Capital to the north and Willamette University to the south. These were two of Hop's favorite Salem institutions. Hop preached the core values of education and statesmanship to his chil-

Arthur 1912

dren every night at dinner. They were living the American dream, and Hop wanted to be certain that his children did not waste their American citizenship, a prize that he was personally denied.

Several days after the move, Thomas Reynolds stopped by the home to see his old friend, Hop.

"Hello, Kay. How are you on this fine Salem day?"

"Good morning, Thomas. Hop is already at the store over on Ferry Street."

"Yes, I figured. There is no time to rest for Hop."

"What brings you to our home, Thomas? And where is your stagecoach?" Kay laughed,

Thomas smiled and paused before continuing, "The City Council asked me to stop by as Hop's friend."

"Yes, what is it, Thomas?"

"Well, Kay, you see, there have been complaints about your cow."

"Who cares about Hop's old cow?"

"Personally, I like Greta, but some of your neighbors think that a cow doesn't belong in your front yard, Kay. You do live next to the State Capital."

"Which neighbors?"

"That's not important, but let me help you move Greta to the backyard. OK?"

"Sure, Thomas. Willie, give Mr. Reynolds a hand with your father's cow!"

"Here, Willie. You lead Greta around to the back, and I'll finish cleaning up the front yard," Thomas directed, handing Willie the halter.

After completing the job, Thomas found Kay on the porch.

"Mrs. Reynolds can help you to organize a luncheon in your home to meet some of your neighbors, Kay. She knows most of the women from church and can help you plan a nice afternoon get-together."

"OK, Thomas. I don't want to trouble her, though."

"No trouble at all, Kay. My wife loves to entertain."

Martha Reynolds stopped by the following afternoon.

"Kay, we'll have fun planning a small party for the neighborhood women and their husbands. They must become your friends."

"I have another idea. Let's have a surprise party to celebrate Hop's birthday," Kay suggested.

"I had no idea it was Hop's birthday. That's perfect."

Quietly, Kay added, "He needs something to take his mind off of Arthur." Kay paused and then changed the subject abruptly, "How do we start?"

"Well, let's plan the menu and then start on the games."

"Games?"

"Yes. Parlor games to keep the guests entertained. Don't worry. I'll show you what to do. It's easy."

"Who do we invite?"

"Leave it to me. I know all the women from church."

After an hour, the two women had prepared the menu and plans for their birthday affair.

"It will be a dinner party. We will invite some of Hop's oldest friends, Mr. and Mrs. Otto Wilson, Mr. and Mrs. James Long, your neighbors Mr. and Mrs. Nelson Eley, and a special guest," Martha added mysteriously. [1]

"Who is the special guest?"

"Well, the State Legislature is in session, so there are some important politicians and staff in town. We can invite a friend of ours, Miss Elizabeth Braun. She's here from Portland for the vote in the State Senate."

"Perfect. Hop loves American politics. He says he wants to be a statesman when he's done doing laundry and dressing chickens."

---

1. Otto Wilson Sr. owned Wilson Buick and the first Salem automobile in 1903. Hiram Nelson Eley 1851-1927 was a Salem Contractor and builder for over 40 years. He arrived in Salem in 1886. They lived across the street from Hop at 1317 State Street.

Hiram Nelson and Mency Eley Hop's new neighbors at 1317 State Street.

"Kay, your husband has so many friends; he could do anything he sets his mind to."

Kay looked nervous. "What will I talk to them about?"

"It's the women you have to win over. Just ask them about their children. That will keep them all occupied for some time. They all like to talk about themselves and their families."

Elsie and Ella hand-delivered the invitations to each home and made a stop at the Capitol Building for Miss Braun's invitation.

On Saturday morning, the day of the dinner party, Elsie had all the children lined up with a list of their chores in hand. Today was Mother's big day, and everything had to be perfect.

"Isabel, you mop the floors and make sure you don't miss anything!"

"Willie take the rugs outside and give them a good beating! And don't come back until those carpets are dust-free!"

"Albert, you can dust all the furniture with this feather duster, and don't play

Oregon State Capital – University of Southern California Libraries.

around with it. This is serious."

"Stop being so bossy!" the children said in unison.

Just then. Grandma Hong walked in, overhearing the commotion, "Don't worry, children, I will help you. We'll have this place spotless in no time."

Elsie, unperturbed by the mini mutiny, continued, "Ella, you come into the kitchen and help Mrs. Hundsaker and Emma prepare the food."

"What are you doing, Miss Bossy pants?" Willie asked with a smirk.

"I am organizing. It's what I do best."

"Just because you're the oldest doesn't mean you can boss us around all day!"

"Well, get used to it because I am in charge. Mother said so,"

The children grumbled but went about their chores. In the end, they all pulled together and made the place spotless.

Ella had flowers delivered for the special occasion, choosing Dad's favorite, red carnations, set off by delicate ferns. She added candles to the table. The dining room was exquisite.

Ella, Grandma Hong – Ah Ying and Loren in Salem Oregon.
Low Family Collection.

Later that afternoon, Kay was in her bedroom preparing for dinner. Elsie, having discharged the cleaning and cooking responsibilities, came in to help her Mother get ready.

"What are you going to wear?"

"I don't have a thing to wear. I look like a hop farmer," an exasperated Kay grumbled.

"Mother, you are a very stylish lady. Everyone says so."

"Well, I did listen to Kim when he was going to Salem High School. Every day he came home and couldn't wait to tell me about the latest fashion the schoolgirls were wearing or the most recent perfume they were all raving about."

"Odd that your little brother was your fashion consultant," Elsie laughed.

"Well, I was a good student. I copied everything the girls did, their clothes and hairstyle. And I love that Jicky perfume they wear. It's very expensive, but your father doesn't mind."

Elsie helped Mother pick out a pleated skirt and a frilly white blouse. Kay wore laced high-topped shoes. Her long hair was done up high on her head, and she topped it off with a pretty picture hat. Kay loved hats and bought a new one every Easter. Once, she had to have a particular hat, so she put two dollars down and paid a dollar a week until she got her precious hat. Today, the final touch was a beaded French purse.

"Well, Mother, you look very sharp. You certainly don't look like any hop farmer I ever saw."

Jicky Perfume

Kay looked in the mirror and gave a nervous smile. "I guess I'm passable. Now, where is that Jicky perfume?"

The dinner party got off to a good start with the guests all arriving at 6 pm. Elsie and Ella were the perfect hostesses, serving the six-course meal Mrs. Hundsaker prepared along with lemonade and fresh berries. Ella entertained the guests playing the piano with a beautiful rendition of La Espinita.

After dinner, the children lined up and brought in Hop's surprise birthday cake, a special carmel crunch toffee cake with whipped cream, one of Emma's secret baking marvels.

"All right, Dad, make a wish and blow out your candles!"

With moist eyes, Hop looked at the smiling faces of his five children and whispered, "There is nothing more any person could want. My life is complete."

Isabel and Albert jumped on Hop's lap, and Elsie, Ella, and Bill gave Hop hugs and kisses, making Hop blush from all the attention.

With five children draped over him, Hop blew out the candles to the applause of his guests.

"Happy Birthday, Hop!"

"Happy Birthday, Mr. Lee," Miss Braun said. "You know, Mr. Lee, with this family and your countless friends, you could easily be a statesman or politician!"

"Hop smiled, "Only in America could a humble laundryman and hop farmer have friends and family like all of you."

Otto Wilson laughed, "Hop, now you need to come by my store on Commercial street so we can get you into a brand new All-American Buick."

The evening was perfect. Kay followed Martha Reynold's advice, asking each woman in turn about her children and her husband's business. As predicted, the women loved talking about themselves and had a memorable evening at Kay's dinner party on 13th Street. Kay became part of the White Salem social circle that day. The women became her good friends and regularly sent photos and cards to Kay. She proudly displayed the pictures on the piano and the cards she kept for decades in her treasured scrapbook.

Hiram Nelson Eley and Mency Eley and children.

316   RUSSELL N. LOW

Chapter Thirty

The Great War and Flu Come to Salem – 1917

T he United States' entry into World War I on April 6, 1917, occurred three years after the hostilities' started between Allied powers and Germany. Hop, who was in his 59th year or 60th by Chinese counting, was in no danger of being drafted. However, all three of Kay's brothers registered for the draft, and according to newspaper accounts, two of the brothers served in the war.

Before the war was over in November 1918, over 44,000 Oregonians served in the "war to end all wars." Over half of them volunteered. One thousand and thirty of Oregon's sons did not come home from the war in Europe, including 69 from Marion County and 30 from Salem. The Yanks' presence buoyed the exhausted Allies. The British and French forces, combined with the Yank's contributions of men and war supplies, turned the tide on the Western Front.

The war effort in Salem required sacrifice and contributions all around. One of the most enthusiastic workers with the Red Cross was Hop's daughter, Elsie. Although only 13 years old, Elsie recruited several children in her neighborhood and taught them how to knit. The local Red Cross gratefully received the caps, mittens, and scarfs knitted with love for the overseas Oregon soldiers.

Everyday life in Salem was affected by the war effort. As supplies and goods were redirected, shortages of goods for civilians were inevitable. The U.S. Food Administration was set up to deal with anticipated food shortages by coordinating production, transportation, and food distribution. President Wilson appointed Herbert Hoover, who grew up in Newberg, Oregon, as head of the new agency.

1917 Elsie and girlfriends knitting for the Red Cross War Effort. Low Family Collection.

Hoover, the son of a Quaker blacksmith, would be elected as the 31st President of the United States in 1929.

Campaigns with posters encouraging civilians to reduce consumption of meat, wheat, fats, and sugar were a part of everyday life. The cry for *Meatless Mondays* and *Wheatless Wednesdays* urged Americans to modify their diets for the good of our boys overseas. Despite their best efforts, a critical shortage of sugar was front-page news in Salem. Sugar became one of the first items to be rationed. In 1917 the U.S. Food Administration allotted each American family two pounds of sugar per month. Even before the announcement, rumors of rationing led to the "sugar hoarding" of 1917. Panicked men and women swarmed the stores, buying up all the sugar in a frenzy. This hoarding of sugar created the shortages that they feared.

Fundraising for the War effort arrived in the Pacific Northwest with a drive to help Belgian children affected by the war. Elsie and her friends sold Forget-Me-Not bouquets for ten cents apiece for the Belgian Baby Campaign. The nation-wide drive was timed to coincide with the birthday of Queen Elizabeth of Belgium and was in response to an anti-German propaganda campaign.

Save the Belgian Babies fundraising campaign WWI.

In the kitchen, Elsie and Ella helped Mrs. Hundsaker prepare the family dinner.

"Use plenty of local fruits and vegetables. That will fill the children's stomachs and conserve the foodstuffs the soldiers need," Elsie instructed.

"And make the portions smaller, and only cook what we can eat," Ella added.

"You girls are model citizens. All American households should be run so wisely."

At dinner that night, Bill and Albert were famished, as usual, staring at the pile of greens on their plates.

"We're not rabbits, you know!" Bill complained.

"Where's the meat and bread?" Albert asked.

"It's *Meatless Monday*, and *Wheatless Wednesday* all rolled into one!" Elsie proclaimed. "Isn't it wonderful to help our troops?"

"Why don't you just go and knit them another scarf instead?" Bill asked.

Hop, who had been observing the exchange with amusement, dug into his

Elsie Hop Lee knitting goods for the Red Cross War Effort and the overseas soldiers. Low Family Collection.

salad, proclaiming, "Remember to preach to Gospel of the Clean Plate!"

"Yeah! We know, Dad. We Chinese don't waste anything, ever!" Bill smiled.

On the Homefront, the Hop Lee family continued to grow with a new family member's biannual addition. Four months after the United States entered WWI by finally declaring war on Germany, Kay and Hop celebrated the birth of their seventh child, Wy Gwun, whose American name was Loren, on August 21, 1917.

Before coming home from work that day, Hop stopped by the Daily Capital Journal's office on Commercial street and placed a birth announcement for his new son. That evening Hop sat down with his Loo Book of Family History and recorded Wy Gwun's birth.

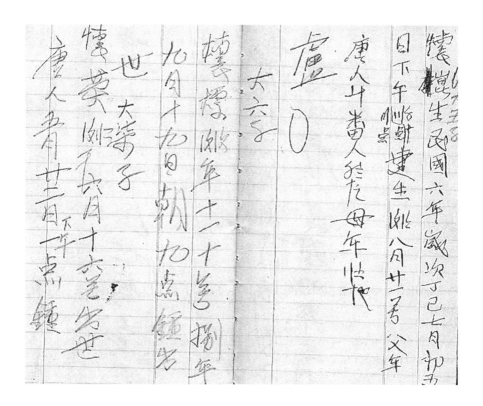

Hop's journal entry August 21, 1917. Low Family Collection. Our 5th son Wy Gwun was born July 5, 1917, at 3:50 pm. On the American calendar, this is August 21. I am in my 60th year by Chinese counting. In American, I am 58 years old, and his mother is 27 years old.

Hop then opened the evening paper and searched for his notice of Wy Gwun's arrival.

"Where is it, Kay?"

"Where is what, Hop?"

"The baby's birth announcement for Wy Gwun?"

Hop frantically flipped the pages over and over, searching for his son's name.

Finally, he turned to page 8 and quickly scanned the "All Around Town" section. Halfway down the middle column, he found it.

> **Loren Irvin Hop Lee is his name. He** was born this morning at the home of his parents, Mr. and Mrs. Hop Lee, 125 South Thirteenth street. He is the seventh child. His mother was born in San Francisco. He has two uncles, brothers of his mother who are in the service of the United States, one in the engineers corps and the other in aviation.

Daily Capital Journal August 22, 1917.

"Well, they misspelled his name, but at least Gwunde's birth is recorded in the paper."

"Which of his uncles is in the military? It says here that one is in the engineer's corps and the other in aviation."

"They must mean Kim and Bing. That's news to me. Maybe I should check with mother."

Putting down the paper, Hop pulled out a small package and handed it to Kay. "My friend, Yellow Fox, came by the store and dropped a present for the baby. Isn't it beautiful? It is a little blanket woven from sheep's wool," Hop explained.

——*ele*——

On Monday, November 11, 1918, news of the Armistice marking the end of hostilities reached Salem by wire at 1 am. Clanging fire bells at city hall followed by blaring factory whistles awakened startled Salem residents. That night, spontaneous parades in Salem's streets preceded the official parade the next afternoon as Salem and the rest of the world celebrated the end of the Great War. Three pm was the time announced for Salem's Victory Parade. The parade would start at the Salem Armory, proceeding West along Court Street. Governor Withycombe declared a holiday beginning at 1 pm, setting the stage for a spectacle of thousands of Salem celebrants. The recent lifting of Mayor Walter Keyes's October 12th Spanish Influenza ban, further assured a joyous mood at the festivities.

Isabel and Loren Hop Lee with Native American rug, a gift from Yellow Fox.

1

"Hop, put down that chicken! It's time to close up shop!" George Sun called out, rushing into the Hop Lee Poultry Store on Ferry Street.

"I have work to do, George. Mrs. Fredit needs these chickens. No time to lose."

George stood in the doorway stunned. "Hop where you been? The war's over. Governor Withycombe says it's a holiday, starting right now!"

Hop looked up, staring at his friend, "What are you talking about, George?"

"I'm saying the war in Europe is over! Done! Finished! The whole town is celebrating. We need your red Model T to ride in the parade. Hurry up! They're lining up at the Armory right now."

"Well, that explains why I haven't had any customers all morning."

Dropping the grateful chicken back into its coop, Hop took off his apron, reached for his Derby hat, and followed George out into the cool Salem November air.

1. The 1918 flu pandemic first appeared in Oregon that Fall. Eventually, the flu pandemic was more deadly than WWI, killing 3,675 Oregonians. Oregon was less affected than other states and Salem less affected than Portland. The first cluster of cases in Salem was at the Chemawa Indian School. On October 12th Mayor Keyes banned public meetings, churches, lodges theaters, dances, and places of public amusement. Improving conditions by the end of October led to the lifting of the ban on November 11th. In 1918 32 Salem citizens died from the "Spanish Flu. By December and in in the New Year 1919 the flu pandemic dramatically worsened placing a staggering burden on hospitals and medical personnel.

Hop and George drove the Model T down to the Armory and got in a very long line. They were behind the local guard, the SATC [2] company from Willamette University, and the Salem High School cadets. Next came the Grand Army of the Republic, followed by a host of veterans of every conflict. Frankly, anyone in a uniform of any type went to the front of the line.

As they were waiting, Hop sat bolt upright, exclaiming, "I need my flag!"

"Do you mean your Chinese Republic flag?"

"No. I need my red, white, and blue American flag to fly from the car. It'll be perfect. But I can't get out of line now. What..."

As Hop was pondering his dilemma, Bill walked up draped in Hop's American flag.

"Hi, Dad. Mom said to look for you and to bring your flag!"

"Your mother is brilliant!" Hop shouted, jumping down and taking the flag from Bill.

"And here's a pole to fly it from."

"Perfect!" Hop called out as he propped up the pole and flag from the back seat.

Where is everyone else?"

"The girls and Albert are walking with their classes, and Mom is coming with baby Gwunde and Isabel. Mrs. Hundsaker is helping out.

No sooner had Bill spoken than Kay appeared holding Gwunde wrapped in three blankets with three-year-old Isabel leading the way."

"Bill, go help your mother and Gwunde into the front seat. George, you, Isabel, and Bill sit in back," Hop instructed. "Hold onto the flag, Bill, and keep it waving."

---

2. SATC – Student Officer Training Corps.

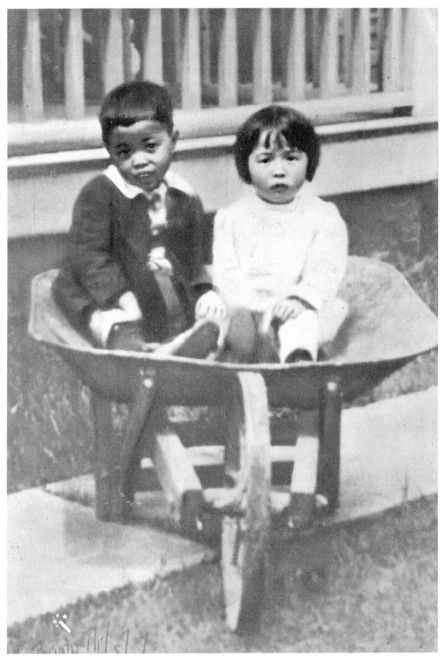

Albert and Isabel Hop Lee 1917. Low Family Collection.

Lenta Stolz Westacott. Lenta Westacott was awarded a 4th Place Ribbon for her decorated automobile in the 1912 Cherry Festival Parade.

Governor Withycombe rode in a shiny black Model T behind the bands and soldiers, waving at all Salem voters.

Hop was far back in the middle of the parade, but he was glad to participate in this grand American celebration.

Driving down State Street in his red Model T, Hop passed by the lineup of gayly decorated automobiles that stretched for blocks.

"Look Hop! There's Mrs. Lenta Westacott driving her Model T."

"Hello, Mrs. Lenta," Hop called out.

"Hello, Hop! Make way for this lady driver!" [3]

"Your car is gorgeous, Lenta," Kay admired.

"Yes, It's a whole new world for women. Today, we can drive and vote!"

"So long, Lenta," Hop waved to his old friend.

"Keep waving that flag, Bill. Today, we are red, white, and blue all the way through!"

―――*ele*―――

That next afternoon Hop made a rare surprise visit, stopping by the new home on 13th Street while delivering bundles of clean laundry to his Salem customers.

"Father's here!" shouted Albert, who spotted Hop from the front porch.

The screen door swung open as Isabel and Gwunde scrambled off the porch into the front yard.

"Dad! Why are you home so early?"

Hop smiled, admiring his three children, "Where is everyone else?"

"Bossy-pants Elsie and Ella are at the Red Cross sewing masks, and Bill is at the laundry with you," Albert replied.

"Well, then you three children come over and sit with me so Kim can try out his new camera and take my birthday portrait," Hop instructed as he picked up Gwunde, gently placing him on his lap.

---

3. Lenta Westacott lived at 575 Court Street near the Hop Lee's previous home at 296 Church Street.

Kim S. Hong with Marion and daughter, Isabel,
1919. Low Family Collection.

"Aren't you supposed to be at college?" Isabel asked.

"And where's Grandma?"

"I came to get away from the Spanish Flu and to check up on my aeroplane since you moved from the old home on Church Street."

Isabel and Albert exchanged glances but were silent.

December 1918 Hop Lee in his favorite derby hat with Albert, Gwunde, and Isabel in front of the family home in Salem, Oregon. Low Family Collection.

"Where is my aeroplane, Hop?" Kim asked with growing concern.

"Don't worry, Kim. The children stood guard over your blasted invention. It's in the backyard with Greta. Now take the picture."

"OK, one, two, and three. Now smile!"

Kim's concern about the Spanish Flu was well founded. The death and destruction of WWI ultimately was far surpassed by the effects of the Spanish flu which killed three times as many Oregonians. More than empty statistics in the news, the death from the flu was personal and struck very close to the Hop Lee home.
4

Gwunde's first birthday party, in August 1918 was touched by both WWI and the Spanish Flu. The invited guests included Mrs. Otto Wilson and her children Otto Jr. and Margaret, neighborhood children Richard Upjohn, Margaret and

---

4. 1,030 Oregonians lost their life in WWI vs. 3,675 who died from the Spanish Flu.

Elizabeth Lewis, and Mrs. Ivan Bellinger, daughter Jane, and 2-year-old Ivan Jr. Lola Bellinger arrived early with baby Jane and Ivan Jr. in tow.

"Hello, Lola," Kay greeted her neighbor. The Bellingers lived only one block away on 12th Street.

Lola smiled weakly as Kay patted her on the shoulder and showed her into the parlor where Ruth Wilson was preparing the party with Ella and Elsie.

"Here, Lola. Have a seat. How have you been?"

Lola had hoped that the birthday party would be a distraction from the sadness that followed her everywhere. But as always, no one knew what to say to her.

Dr. Ivan Bellinger and son, Ivan Jr.

The three women looked at each other in an awkward silence.

Finally, to break the ice, Lola pulled out a photograph.

"Isn't Ivan handsome in his uniform? He was so happy this day with Ivan Junior."
5

Kay and Ruth nodded in agreement.

"How are you holding up, Lola?"

"As well as can be expected. I have to take care of the children. Ivan Jr. reminds more of his father every day," Lola replied staring at the photograph of her son and her husband.

"Dr. Bellinger had such a promising medical practice. We all loved him. He was kind and patient had perfect bedside manner," Ruth said.

"Yes, Ivan was one of a kind. The army sent back his belongings from Fort Riley in Kansas. This photograph was the one he took with him. I never thought it would come back without. Him," Lola replied softly with a single tear trickling down her cheek.

"It is so ironic that a young army doctor died from the flu before even leaving our shores."

Changing the subject, Lola pulled out another photograph.

"Kay, here is the photograph of me that you requested."

"Your photograph will have a place of honor on our piano, Lola."

Here, let's take Ivan and baby Jane into the other room to play with the children," Kay offered.

---

5. 7-year-old Richard Upjohn was the son of Don Upjohn of the Capital Journal. The Upjohns lived next door at 163 N 13th Street. Eleven-year-old Margaret and eight-year-old Elizabeth Lewis were the daughters of John H Lewis the Oregon State Engineer living at 165 N 13th Street. The Otto Wilsons lived across the street at 1336 State Street.

Kay kept this photograph of Lola in her album for over half a century. Aune Family Photographic Studio, Portland, Oregon.

"Yes, and we'll keep them busy with games and birthday cake," Ella added entering the room.

The rest of the day went off without a hitch. The mood was fun and Lola did her best to join in the celebration of Gwunde's milestone, but her mind was a million miles away. Walking into the living room, she stared at the photograph of Arthur over the piano.

At least I have the children to keep me company. I hope that nothing ever happens to them.

Lola's words were prophetic as the following January 1919, Ivan Jr, became one of the 3, 675 Oregon citizens to die from the Spanish flu pneumonia. Little Ivan was 2 years and 10 months old.

Ivan Bellinger Jr. 1916 - 1919

* *

In honor of little Lorena Hop Lee's first birthday, a merry party was given at the home of her parents Mr. and Ms. Hop Lee of 125 North Thirteenth street Wednesday afternoon. During the afternoon the guests enjoyed many interesting games. After which delightful refreshments were served.

Mrs. Otto Wilson assisted the hostess in serving. Those present were: Mrs. Ivan Bellinger and children, Jane Elizabeth and Ivan, Jr., Mrs Otto Wilson and children, Otto Wilson, Jr., and Margaret, Richard Upjohn, Margaret and Elizabeth Lewis.

* *

Loren Hop Lee's first birthday August 18, 1918,

Chapter Thirty-One

A Cold Salem Winter – December 1919

T he cold snap in December 1919 produced 22 inches of snowfall and bitterly cold temperatures that dropped down to six degrees below zero. The eight Hop Lee children celebrated the winter wonderland from inside their warm home on 13th Street. Two-year-old Gwunde, in particular, was overjoyed by the snow and ice and couldn't wait to get outdoors. This morning Isabel, Albert,

Isabel, Albert, and Loren Hop Lee admiring Salem snow in 1919. Low Family Collection

Skaters on frozen Willamette River 1919

Gwunde, and their older sister Ella gazed out the living room window at the snowdrifts surrounding the home.

The mantle of snow covering the Salem streets blocked streetcar traffic, and going anywhere was hazardous for automobiles. Although the snow came early this year, it was the bitter cold that grabbed Salem residents by the throat and froze exposed ears, nose, and fingers of anyone foolish enough to go outdoors without a scarf, mittens, and head covering. The Willamette River froze over, providing a skating rink for the hearty among Salem's residents.

Hop Lee, as usual, was already at the poultry store on Ferry Street. Willie was usually helping his father, although, in truth, he would have rather been at the Boy Scout meeting or playing in the snow. Father was loving but strict and did not tolerate idle play when there was work to be done. With Hop, there was always work to be done.

As the oldest son, Willie felt the weight of his father's expectations. Once when Willie had gone to play baseball instead of working at the laundry, Hop was furious. When Willie did finally show up, Hop chased him around and around the laundry with a belt. Fortunately, Hop was getting quite round in the middle, and little Willie was much too quick and nimble to be caught by his father. Albert, who witnessed the foot race, almost died laughing when Willie, baseball glove in hand, darted out the door and down Ferry Street.

Today, however, Hop had the children stay at home, out of the freezing cold. He knew the girls would be smart enough to stay indoors.

I hope Gwunde doesn't go exploring outside. Hop worried about his two-year-old son. Even at this young age, Gwunde was a handful. When there was a puddle, he'd always stomp in it; when there was a hole, he'd jump in it. If he saw a tree, he'd have to climb to the top branch, and god forbid, if Gwunde saw danger, he'd go for it with a full head of steam.

Back home, the children had grown tired of watching the snow and had dispersed, looking for something else to occupy their time. The girls were making lunch in the kitchen.

"Where's Gwunde? I hope he's not outside in the snow," Ella worried.

"Willie, you better go and check the backyard for your brother," Elsie directed.

"I can't wait until spring and warmer weather so we can play outside," Isabel said gazing at the white snow-covered yard.

Gwunde was wandering around the house, searching for the secret passageway that Willie had promised him was hidden from view. He heard a dripping sound and headed for the bathroom.

Hop Lee Home in Salem Snow 1919. Low Family Collection

"Drip, drip, drip!"

As he entered the bathroom, Gwunde spotted the wall-mounted white porcelain sink with its two silver faucets.

Ah hah! Someone left the water running!

Gwunde climbed up on a stool, grasped the silver knobs, and turned each until the water stopped dripping.

There, that's better! No need to waste water. Father will be proud of me.

1919 Isabel and Loren Hop Lee Salem, Oregon. Low Family Collection

Hop's days were long, often not getting home from the laundry and poultry store until 9 pm. Willie and Albert usually joined Father at 3 pm right after school and continued working until they all came home at 9 pm. There wasn't too much time for the boys to play or for the usual sports that kept the White boys occupied. Today, Hop had excused the boys from work because of the bitterly cold weather, giving them a rare day off.

Hop's arrival home every evening was a joyous moment to behold. The children hid behind doors, furniture, and in closets while Hop entered a dark and silent parlor.

"Oh, my! Where is my family? They must have forgotten about their dear old father," Hop lamented, sitting down on the sofa with his head hung low as he peeked at their hiding places with a sly smile.

Just at the moment when he was about to burst out laughing, the lights came on, and on cue, all six giggling children pounced on Hop's round belly and broad shoulders.

"Surprise, Papa!"

"We got you, again!"

"You didn't see us did you, Papa?"

Elsie and Ella each kissed Father while Isabel and the boys jumped on Hop, laughing gleefully.

"I thought you forgot about me!"

"Never, Papa. We just like surprising you!" Isabel explained.

When the commotion finally died down, the children went about the task of helping Father undress.

Willie took off his shoes one at a time. Albert removed his socks, Gwunde jumped up on Hop's lap and undid his necktie, pulling on the end until it came undone. Hop leaned forward. Elsie helped Father remove his coat while Ella slipped off Father's black silk vest.

Leaning back, Hop sighed, "Now, that's more like it!" He reached into his pocket and pulled out a 25-cent piece for each of his children. The routine, however, was not quite complete.

Hop waited expectantly and smiled when Albert leaned over and kissed Father's big toe.

Hop laughed, reached down, and clutched his son, pulling him up onto his round belly exclaiming, "Here you go, Albert," as he handed him a $1 coin.

"That's not fair! I want to kiss your other toe!" Gwunde pouted.

"Sorry, Gwunde. Your poor father is out of money! Maybe tomorrow."

Just then, Kay came in holding baby Leslie. [1]

"Children, let your father get up and have his dinner."

"The children groaned, "We haven't seen Father all day. Please, just a little longer."

"Well, I have a surprise visitor for you tonight," Mother added mysteriously.

"Who is it?" Elsie asked

Kay stepped aside, revealing Grandma Hong.

"Popo!" The children shouted as they gathered around their grandmother.

"How did you get here?" Gwunde asked.

"Well, Gwunde, you and your brothers and sisters were too busy making a fortune undressing your Father. You didn't notice me entering through the kitchen."

"And Hop, you shouldn't make them kiss your big toe! That's disgusting."

Hop laughed but looked a bit sheepish.

"Children, let Grandma sit down on the couch," Kay instructed her brood.

The children first gathered around Grandma, but Gwunde was soon sitting in her lap.

"Did you bring me any grapes?"

"Not this time Gwunde."

"I like it when you peel the skin. Albert says the grapes are naked."

"I didn't say that! Well, not exactly," Albert protested.

---

1. Leslie –was born on November 10, 1919.

"You did too say it," Gwunde insisted.

"Boy's stop pestering your grandmother."

Just then, there was a sharp knocking at the front door. "Rap! Rap! Rap!"

Willie ran to the door and opened it widely. "Hi, Miss Emma! Do you want some dinner? Pop says you're always hungry."

Emma was a six-foot-tall German woman who helped Kay in the kitchen. She was renowned for her feet. They were the most enormous and flattest feet in Salem, and Emma was indeed always hungry. She often showed up in the afternoon and just waited and waited for hours until dinner time. The children loved Emma, and Kay found her help in the kitchen indispensable. She and Mrs. Hundsaker had taught Kay all of the culinary secrets that made her a cooking wizard in the kitchen.

"No, today I will help Kay to prepare a simple meal for the family and guests."

Emma, Kay, Ella, and Elsie retreated to the kitchen while the children played with Hop on the sofa.

Chinese Jook by iandeth. CCA 2.0. Generic Wikimedia Commons.

"Dinner will have to be simple and quick tonight. We are getting a late start," Kay advised.

"Let's make jook [2] from the left-over turkey carcass," Elsie suggested.

"That may take too long," Kay warned.

"Don't worry. Ella and I got a head start on the meal this afternoon. We just have to warm it up and add a few green onions and cha siu barbecued pork for flavoring."

Elsie took the lid off the large pot on the stove, revealing the steaming rice porridge made from yesterday's turkey bones.

"You girls are a marvel," Emma complimented the two girls as she admired their creation with a growling stomach.

"And I made an upside-down pineapple cake for dessert. It's your Father's favorite," Kay laughed, revealing her surprise in the cupboard.

After dinner, the children sat quietly and waited for Father to begin the lecture. They knew it was coming because it was the same every night.

"My children, you must be good and respectful. You must never do anything to harm the Loo family name. Our name and your family are all we have in this world. Never cheat. Never steal and never tell a lie. And above all else, always keep your word."

The children came to be proud of their standing in the Salem community. They were the Hop Lee family, and they carried their father's lessons with them like a mantle of pride.

Decades later, Elsie fondly recalled, "We were well taught. We had good manners. We were well behaved. The town was very proud of us. We were bright. We were clean. We did nothing wrong."

---

2. Jook is a type of rice porridge that's popular in many parts.

After the mandatory lecture, Hop tucked the younger children into bed.

"Good night, Father."

"Good night, children," Hop replied as he gave each of his children a kiss and pat on the head. "Your old dad is proud of you."

The following day Gwunde woke up early and climbed out of bed, trying not to wake up his brothers sleeping across from him. The wooden floor was icy on his bare feet. Heading to the bathroom, he paused when he came upon a most unusual sight. Hop with a pitchfork in hand was about to do battle with the bathroom ceiling.

Gwunde thought the ceiling looked odd. It was wet and bulging downward like a pregnant whale.

Hop took aim with his pitchfork, thrust the tines into the belly of the whale, and then jumped back.

"Aiyaah!" he called out as a flood of water gushed from the ceiling, drenching the bathroom with enough water to create an ankle-deep flood.

Gwunde jumped up and down in the flooded bathroom with more water dripping down from the destroyed plaster ceiling.

Hop then quietly faced the sink, turning on each faucet with a slight turn of the silver handles. "Drip! Drip Drip!"

He then turned and smiled at Gwunde.

"We need to leave the water running, so the pipes don't freeze and burst, Gwunde."

Hop suspected what had happened and who was the culprit, but you know, he never raised his voice or even showed the slightest irritation. Hop liked everyone, and he certainly enjoyed his two-year-old son. What was a little flood between a father and his son? Besides, his rambunctious Gwunde took his mind off business worries. Trying to predict the worsening hop market with no end in sight to

Isabel and Loren Hop Lee in Salem 1919. Low Family Collection

Prohibition, would give any hop grower a whopping headache. [3]

Years later, Gwunde often retold the story of that cold winter with Hop Lee's pitchfork and the burst water pipes, always marveling at his father's patience.

That evening, Hop admired the latest portrait of the growing Hop Lee family. He then rummaged around in his desk and pulled out the folded-up fortune. As he scanned the paper for its latest revelations, Hop laughed out loud.

---

3. Chinese hop contracts reflected a concern about a worsening hop's market during Prohibition. Hop Lee and Hong Hop Lee who had 96 acres in hops at the Fook Chong Ranch signed a contract with the English Firm Bird & Company for one-fourth of their 1920 and 1921 crops at a price of 30 cents per pound. The 1919 price was about 85 cents per pound. The Oregon Statesman October 30, 1919.

"I can't believe that old fortune teller knew his stuff. *Many babies! Not really trying. They just kept coming!* He had no idea!"

—ele—

They weren't thinking of having children, but no matter what, they had plenty of kids.

Many Babies – Not Really Trying –

They Kept Coming[162]

Loo Family Fortune predicting a large family - a Willow Forest. Low Family Collection

Hop Lee Family in Salem, Oregon 1919. Low Family Collection

Chapter Thirty-Two

Noodles and Poultry – 1922

The partnership of Wah Hong's Noodle Shop and Hop's Poultry and Egg business was an inspiration hatched from a casual comment over a bowl of steaming noodles three decades before. On that fateful day in 1891, Hop launched his poultry and egg business, and Hong Lem Wah, the master of the jook-sing noodles, lamented the lack of local duck eggs, a key ingredient in his creation. The partnership seemed obvious, but it took three decades to bring the businesses under one roof. Fate intervened when Hong's noodle shop lost its lease at 170 North Liberty and had to seek a new home.

"Don't worry, Lem. You can move your business into my Poultry and Egg store at 439 Ferry street," Hop reassured his long-time friend. "We have plenty of space, and you can have all the duck eggs you could possibly want."

That afternoon Lem showed up with an old truck loaded down with a gas-burning stove, pots, pans, bowls, tables, stools, and the most crucial piece of equipment: the ten-foot-long four-inch-thick bamboo pole. He immediately began the process of converting the front room into a noodle shop.

Hop entered from the back room accompanied by his four-year-old son, Gwunde, and two clucking hens who had escaped their cages. Gwunde was carrying a basket full of duck eggs.

"Here, Mister Lem. These eggs are for your noodles. Can I have some?"

Lem's friendly smile lit up the room. "Sure, Gwunde. The first bowl is on the house. After that, you will have to buy your noodles."

Loren and Isabel in Salem Oregon. Low Family Collection.

Gwunde frowned, "I don't have any money."

"Maybe we can trade. You bring me something, and I'll make you some noodles."

Gwunde considered the offer for a moment, and then his face lit up.

"I'll bring you a catfish and crawdads!"

Lem laughed and extended his hand, "Perfect! We have a deal. Noodles for a catfish."

Gwunde spent the afternoon watching Lem set up his bamboo pole in the back of the store. Lem positioned a large three-foot-high table in the center of the courtyard. He then attached the long bamboo pole to the back of the table with a flexible strap. The other end of the pole extended past the table for several feet. Lem mounted the pole and began bouncing up and down, testing the springiness.

Adjusting the strap, he tried it again, bouncing up and down on one leg.

"That's about right. Here you try it, Gwunde."

Lem reached down, picked up his young friend, and placed him on the end of the bamboo pole.

Gwunde tried to copy Lem. "My legs are too short!"

"Don't worry. I will be your legs until you get bigger," Lem laughed as he bounced Gwunde up and down on the pole.

"OK. Now, we get some dough for the noodles."

Lem returned with wheat flour and a bucket of water. Slowly mixing the water and flour, he created a doughy mound with a depression in the middle.

"Now, where are those duck eggs you brought me, Gwunde?"

Gwunde ran back into the shop and quickly returned with his basket of eggs.

"Here you are, Mister Lem."

Lem took the eggs and started cracking them on the edge of the table.

"Here, Gwunde. You try. Crack the egg and put the yolk and egg white into our dough."

In a few minutes, all dozen duck eggs were sitting in the middle of the mound of dough with their sunny yellow yolks smiling back at Gwunde.

"OK, now we wash our hands and start to mix the eggs and dough."

Standing on a chair, Gwunde leaned over and pushed the dough back and forth. The yellow dough felt delicious, squeezing out between Gwunde's little fingers.

"OK. That's enough. Now we try out our bamboo pole and make some real springy jook-sing noodles," Lem proclaimed.

Lem placed Gwunde on the end of the pole and bounced him up and down. With each bounce, they flattened and kneaded the dough.

"Now it's my turn, Gwunde," Lem said as he mounted the pole and began to rhythmically bounce up and down on the pole on one leg. Lem expertly moved the pole over the flattened dough's surface, kneading it into the perfect consistency.

Lem dismounted from the pole and came to inspect the now flattened sheet of noodle dough.

"Nice work, Gwunde. Now, where is my noodle cutting knife?"

Rummaging around in his box of utensils, Lem reappeared with a 10-inch-long knife which he expertly wielded to produce long beautiful strips of noodle dough.

"There, Gwunde. Now, we are ready to make Hong's famous jook-sing noodles," Lem announced as he escorted his young friend inside to the newly installed kitchen.

"OK. You wait upfront. I can't show you all of my secrets, or you will open your own noodle shop and put Uncle Lem out of business," he laughed.

The 20-minute wait felt like an eternity to Gwunde. He tried to imagine the steaming bowl of delicious noodles. After a while, he could smell the noodle creation. His stomach growled in anticipation.

Les and Loren aka Gwunde 1922 Salem Oregon. Low Family Collection.

Finally, the door to the kitchen opened, and Lem appeared carrying two bowls of steaming noodles. Placing a large bowl in front of Gwunde, Lem smiled, "Here you go, Gwunde. You are now my official assistant jook-sing noodle chef."

Gwunde inhaled the noodles, slurping the delicious noodles as he sucked up his jook-sing noodles one by one, leaving the broth and a few bits of pork and vegetables in the bottom of the porcelain bowl.

Gwunde jumped up from the table and ran towards the door.

"Where are you going, Gwunde? What's your rush?"

"I have to go fishing."

Lem laughed, not realizing that this was the beginning of a new specialty dish at Hong's Noodle Shop; Jook-sing Noodles with Catfish and Crawdads.

A few days later, the phone at the Hop Lee home rang, startling Elsie. Isabel jumped up from the table and ran for the candlestick phone in the parlor.

"Hello? What did you say? Hulee? There is no one named Hulee here."

Oh! Hop Lee! Of course. Why didn't you say so? Yes, this is the Hop Lee residence."

"Oh, hello, Dad. Do you need me to come down to the laundry to bring money? I have my skates by the door. I can be there in a flash!"

Western Electric Crank Phone.

"You want Elsie? Why? She doesn't even know how to skate. At least not fast like I do."

Putting down the phone receiver, "Elsie, Dad wants to speak with you," Isabel said, clearly disappointed that she had not been called into action.

"Hello, Father."

"Lulu, I need you to bring Leslie to the poultry store right away."

"I'm supposed to go to the park with my friends. We have a dance practice today."

"That can wait. Just bring Leslie and make sure he isn't wearing nice clothes, or your mom will kill us. Understand?"

"Yes. Bring Les dressed in a burlap sack, and don't tell Mother."

"A sack isn't necessary. Just don't have him in church clothes."

"OK, Dad. We'll be there in a few minutes, but then I'm going to the park with Mildred, Helen, and Abigail."

The poultry store on Ferry Street was a short walk down State Street past the State Capital Building, turning left at High Street. The store sold chickens, a few geese, and lots and lots of eggs to Hop's regular Salem customers. He kept track of purchases and payments in his little log book with a running tab for each customer. Hop extended credit to anyone in need, but it was best to keep good records.

"Thanks for bringing little Leslie. We'll have someone drop him off at the park after we're done here," Hop said.

"What are you guys up to?" Elsie asked, now intrigued with the mystery job for which her three-year-old brother had been summoned.

"Never mind. You just go and have a good time with your friends in the park, Lulu."

"OK. We'll be in the east end of the park on that bench in front of the pampas grass."

Leslie and Loren on 13th Street in Salem, Oregon 1922.

Hop looked down at Leslie, wondering if he weighed enough for this job. *I guess there's only one way to find out.*

Hop took Leslie out back behind the store. He had set up a large barrel next to the tree stump.

"OK, Les. I need you to stand on top of this barrel and keep the lid on the barrel. Can you do that?" Hop asked, lifting his son on top of the barrel.

"Sure, Dad. This is easy."

"Well, that's not everything. There's going to be a turkey moving around inside."

"No problem, Dad. Turkeys don't move very fast, and I'm pretty strong."

"OK. You wait down here, and I'll lift you on top of the barrel when the turkey are good and ready, and then you just hold the lid down. Got it?"

"I'm ready, Dad."

"Albert, bring out the turkeys."

Albert appeared from inside with a coop containing five agitated turkeys, all squawking and flapping around.

"Here you go, Dad."

"Bring them over by this stump. When I'm done with them, quickly take the turkey and throw it in the barrel and put the lid on top."

Albert nodded, smiling, understanding his father's scheme and Leslie's purpose.

Hop grabbed the first turkey out of the coop, quickly placed it on the stump. With one practiced swing of his ax, Hop chopped off the turkey's head.

"OK, Albert. Quick throw the turkey in the barrel and put the lid on before it makes a bloody mess!"

Albert grabbed the still thrashing, headless turkey, ran over to the barrel, and chucked it inside.

"Quick! Put the lid on top," Hop instructed as he lifted Leslie up and set him down on the barrel lid.

"Hold that lid down, Les."

The turkey continued to thrash around. Leslie felt the headless chicken bumping up against the sides of the barrel.

"How long do you want me to stand up here?"

"Until he quits!" Albert laughed.

"Good job, Leslie. Keep your balance. Here comes another turkey dinner."

They repeated the process until all five turkeys were in the barrel. Leslie had outstanding balance and didn't lose a single turkey.

"Nice work, boys. Five turkeys in the barrel ready for plucking and not too much turkey blood where it doesn't belong. I don't think your mom will notice the red stain on your pants."

"Let's do it again, Dad." Leslie implored.

"That's enough for today. Five plucked turkeys are what Mrs. Fredit ordered. Now, let's get to plucking the feathers and dressing our turkeys."

Les and Loren aka Gwunde 1922 Salem, Oregon. Low Family Collection.

After they completed the order, Hop had Albert take Leslie over to the park to find Elsie.

She was on the bench by the pampas grass with her three girlfriends.

"Hi, Lulu. Here's Les. Can you take him home and maybe wash his pants before mom sees him?"

"Why? What that on his pants? Oh gross! You have blood all over him!"

"It's just turkey blood, and it's not really that much."

"I don't want to know how you got all that turkey blood on your brother. Just don't let him get it on our dance costumes."

Elsie Hop Lee. Salem, Oregon. Low Family Collection.

Chapter Thirty-Three

Hop Farming for a Chinese Entrepreneur – 1922

T he family's expanding hop farms required year-round attention provided by the farm's managers, the Ging brothers Sun and Yet, and their cousin, Ging Gai. Hop still liked to keep his fingers in the business, and with five farms,

Oregon Hop vines with Fir grove in the distance. Public Domain. California Historical Society and USC Libraries

there was plenty of in-person oversight required, especially during picking season, which began at the end of August.

"Albert, bring the horse and buggy around to the front and bring Gwunde and Leslie with you," Hop instructed while lacing up his 24-inch leather boots.

"Why can't we take the Model T to the hop farm?" Albert asked.

"They need it to make laundry deliveries. Business first."

"Kay, are you ready? Those hop-pickers are lining up at the camp store with their hop tickets in hand."

Hop waited for a reply but shook his head when he heard the singing coming from the parlor. Smiling, he finished lacing up his boots and walked quietly into the front room where he found Kay cleaning and sweetly singing opera along with the gramophone record.

Kay looked up and stopped singing just long enough to explain, "It's Galli-Curci, Hop dear. Isn't it beautiful?"

"Yes, but it's time to go. Why don't you bring the gramophone with you? You can serenade the pickers at the camp store."

"I hope they like opera, Hop."

Hop packed up the gramophone and then paused. "How many of these records do you want me to bring?"

"Better bring them all, dear. I know all of Amelita's operas by heart."

Kay was a full-time mother and a part-time cashier for the camp store at the Fook Chong Ranch near Clear Lake, Hop's crown jewel, the 612-acre original Alvis Smith homestead. The harvest was in full swing, with almost 400 pickers from all over Oregon working the fields. They stayed in the campground across the creek in rustic "cabins" or tents. Providing them with needed supplies at the camp store was a full-time job and a dependable source of income.

Amelita Galli-Curci (18 November 1882 – 26 November 1963) was an Italian coloratura soprano. She was one of the most popular operatic singers of the 20th century.

"Why do you wear those boots, Hop? You're going to drive the carriage, not ride Bessie. And we're just going to the OE train station on High Street."

"I have to look the part, Kay. I can't look like a laundryman. Today, I am a hop farmer. Besides, I'm the boss, at least if it's alright with you," Hop smiled.

"Of course, you're the boss, Hubby. Don't forget your Derby hat."

At 147 N. High Street, the OE ticket office was only one and a half miles from the 13th and State Streets family home. Most of the out-of-town hop-pickers arrived at the OE Chemawa (Hopmere) station, where ranch hands met them and took them by wagon to the local hop farms.

"Giddy-up, Bessie!" Hop called out, snapping the reins as the carriage started up with a lurch, slowly rolling along State Street.

"It's a nice day for a ride along the river. Let's take Bessie for a spin and save the money for the train fares. It will be like the old days when horse-power was only for horses," Hop laughed.

Kay sat upfront, leaving Albert and squirming Gwunde in the back. Hop was correct; the late summer weather in Salem was perfect for a carriage ride. Today the weather was dependably sunny with clear blue skies, a high of 75 degrees, and a cool breeze coming off the river.

"The river is beautiful, Hop."

"It's hard to believe that it's been over 40 years since Sai Ying and I passed by here on that steamboat from Portland," Hop reminisced.

"I still have the journal that I started on the boat that day with Sai."

"How many more names are you planning on writing in that journal, Hubby? I think eight children is enough."

Hop smiled, "You never know."

The one-hour carriage-ride up the River Road was a challenging adventure for Gwunde, who never sat in the same place for more than a few minutes.

Willamette River postcard. Low Family Collection.

Bouncing up and down in the back seat, Gwunde felt the warm breeze on his face as he inhaled the smells of the countryside. Free at last.

"Aiyaah! Gwunde, sit still!" Kay gently scolded her rambunctious son. " Why can't you sit still like Leslie? Albert, control your brother!"

"Gwunde has the spirit of the dragon. Our son is not made to sit still," Hop laughed.

Gwunde was imagining flying fire-breathing dragons as the carriage turned off onto Wheatland Ferry Road. The cemetery headstones fascinated Gwunde as they passed by Claggett Cemetery and then pulled into the Fook Chong Ranch. Gwunde ignored the old wooden buildings. Things got more interesting as they proceeded over the bridge crossing Claggett Creek and descended through the groves of fir trees into the vast bottomland's hop fields.

"What's that funny building over there?" Albert asked.

"That's the hop drying house," Father replied. "We have two of them on the ranch."

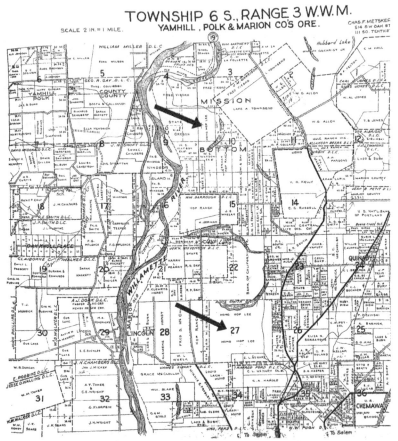

1941 Metzker Map of land plots shows two of the five the Hung Hop Lee farms (arrows). Plot 27 south of Clear Lake is the original Alvis Smith homestead purchased by Hop Lee in 1914.

"Are the hops wet?" Gwunde asked.

"After we pick the hops, we take them to the hop drying house and spread them out on the floor about 18 inches deep. Big wood-burning furnaces under the floor heat the hops and dry out the moisture. It takes a day to dry them out, and then we store them in warehouses in big 500 bound bales." Hop explained.

"Why does the hop house have two smokestacks?" Albert asked.

Hop drying house on the Fook Chong Ranch. Low Family Collection.

"Those are called cupolas. They draw the hot air up through the hops and keep the air circulating to dry out the hops. There's no smoke," Hop laughed.

"Can we go inside to see?" Albert asked.

"Not today. We need to inspect the hop picking," Father explained as the carriage made its way past row upon row of hop vines.

The carriage came to a stop, and dozens of people working the hop fields surrounded them immediately.

"Basket Full!" someone called out from inside the rows of hop vines.

"Basket Full!" came another voice.

"What's going on, Dad?" Albert asked.

"The pickers have been out working for a couple of hours. Once they fill their baskets with hops, they call out "Basket Full." Our men transfer the hops into burlap sacks, and the scale carrier weighs the hops. We punch their ticket with

Hop picking family on Fook Chong Ranch. Low Family Collection.

the weight of the hops. That ticket is how they get paid, or they can use it for supplies at the camp store."

"What if they lose the ticket?"

"No tickee, no payee!" Hop laughed with a feigned accent.

"That would be a bad day for a picker, so they are pretty careful with those tickets and keep them pinned to their shirt."

Albert and Gwunde stared in fascination at all the activity in the hop yard. The pickers were everywhere wearing gloves and long-sleeved shirts for protection from the sharp hop vines.

Hop was busy talking to one of the Ging foremen about the progress with the harvest. The Chinese foreman was huge. He was over six feet tall and must have weighed north of 250 pounds.

Gwunde and Albert had never seen a Chinese that big.

Hop pickers from the local community at Fook Chong Ranch 1920's- Low Family Collection.

"Ta?c méeywi,"   Hop greeted his old friend.

"Jo sahn," Yellow Fox replied in Cantonese, smiling.

Turning back towards his family, Hop said, "This is our foreman, Jim Yee. The Chinese call him Ging Gai. He has been my friend for many years although, he almost chopped off my head when we first met along the Snake River."

Gwunde's eyes grew large, "Tell us the story about how Jim chopped off your head, Dad."

"I said, almost chopped off my head. Maybe another time for that story."

Gwunde looked at the huge Chinese, who stared intensely at the boy with a piercing gaze. Gwunde did not look away.

"The little one has spirit, Hop. He has no fear of this Niimíipuu."

"Yes, Gwunde will travel far and will always need a long rope," Hop replied.

"Wire down!" someone called out from the rows of hops on the right.

"What's going on, Dad?"

"Well, the pickers have been working all morning on the lower hops and picked it clean. To let them reach the upper hops, we drop the wire and lower the hops so they can pick them next."

Native American Hop picker

"I like the sound of "Wire Down" because it means we are making good progress picking the hop fields."

Gwunde and Albert stared at the pickers all converging on the new vines ready for easy picking with the wire down."

"It's like a race, Dad," Albert observed.

"The faster they can fill those baskets, the more they get their tickets punched."

"Can we help?" Gwunde asked.

"Sure. Kay, find someone to show the boys how to work in the fields."

Wire Down! Picking hops on Fook Chong Ranch. Low Family Collection.

Kay looked around for the perfect hop-pick-ing teacher. Better to be a child because adults would quickly get impatient. Kay smiled when she saw the neighbor's little girl with curly blond hair struggling with her hopsack.

Approaching the girl, Kay asked, "Can you show Gwunde and Albert how to pick hops? What's your name?"

"Audrey. Sure, I can teach boys how to pick hops."

She stared at Gwunde and smiled, "What kind of name is Gwunde?"

"It's my Chinese name, but you can call me Loren."

"No, I like Gwunde. It's cute."

"It's not cute! I have the spirit of a dragon. My dad said so."

Audrey laughed, "Whatever, you say dragon boy."

Audrey proceeded to show the boys the finer points of hop picking.

Loren "Gwunde" Hop Lee 1922.
Low Family Collection

"Go fast, but pick clean. Because once we have a full basket, we can go swimming in Clear Lake."

"I don't have a swimming suit."

"Just wear your underpants," Audrey laughed,

How about you?" Gwunde asked.

"I have my bathing suit in our tent."

Oregon State University Hops. ShareAlike 2.0 Generic. Hops are the flowers (also called seed cones or strobiles) of the hop plant Humulus lupulus,[1] a member of the Cannabaceae family of flowering plants

Gwunde thought about swimming in front of a girl in his underpants and decided he didn't mind one bit. He then started to pick faster and faster, practically running back to the basket with each load of the little green cones.

"Slow down and stop showing off, Gwunde," Albert scolded.

"I just want to go swimming with Audrey."

"Basket Full!" Audrey called out. "That was fast with your help. Thanks."

The worker showed up with his scale on a wooden tripod. The boys watched, fascinated by the green spring scale.

"Sixty pounds."

Audrey handed over her ticket, which the man punched.

"Don't lose your ticket, Audrey."

Their thoughts were interrupted by the sack buck proceeding down the row. The ranch hand loaded the full hop sacks onto a sled being pulled to the end of the row.

Fook Chong Ranch. Sack buck Low Family Collection.

"Where is he going with your hops?"

"Come on. I'll show you,' Audrey called out, running after the sled.

As the trio approached the end of the row, a team of horses pulling a flat wagon pulled up and paused as they knew to wait for the next addition to their load. The sack bucks heaved the full hop sacks up onto the wagon now piled high with freshly-picked hops.

"Where are they going?"

"To the hop drying house, of course. Don't you know anything?"

"I know those horses are named Lady and Dolly," Albert sniffed.

"Let's go swimming," Audrey laughed.

The boys found their mother, who smiled at their planned adventure with Audrey."

"OK. You be careful. Keep out of trouble. I will be working at the camp store, and your father will be busy with the ranch foremen."

Fook Chong Ranch hands at hop drying house. Low Family Collection

—*ele*—

"You're a fast swimmer, Gwunde!" Audrey admired.

"Do you want to race?"

"No, but he does," Audrey replied, pointing at an older boy watching them intently.

"You want to race me, China boy?"

Ignoring the slight, Gwunde replied, "Sure, but you better be ready to lose. What's your name?"

"Ralph and I never lose," the boy, who was a head taller than Gwunde, replied.

"OK. You race one time across the lake and back when I say 'Go!'" Audrey instructed.

"Ready, Set, Go!"

Gwunde and Ralph dove into the water and swam for the far shore of Clear Lake. Ralph splashed violently but faded quickly while little Gwunde swam with sure steady strokes. When he reached the distant shore, Ralph was far behind.

When he emerged victoriously, Audrey shouted gleefully, "You won, Gwunde! You swim like a fish!"

Pulling himself out of the water, Gwunde turned around, looking for Ralph, whom he spotted struggling in the middle of the lake.

"We better give Ralph a hand. Come on, Albert."

Albert and Gwunde pulled a sputtering Ralph out of the water, "Are you OK, Ralph?"

"Yeah. I could have made it. I was just resting."

"Sure, Ralph. No problem," Albert replied.

Gwunde looked across Clear Lake and spotted Jim Yee sitting on the bank.

"Look. There's Dad's friend. Let's go and see what he's doing."

"I don't think we should," Audrey replied. "Mom said to watch out for strangers."

"We'll protect you, Audrey. Come on!" Gwunde called out, running down the path with Albert, Audrey, and Ralph trailing behind.

"Jim! What are you doing?" Gwunde asked, coming to a stop behind the man.

"Shush! Quiet, Gwunde. I'm catching dinner."

"Can I help, Jim?"

"You can call me Yellow Fox. Here, take this line and tie a hook on the end like this."

"I want to use two hooks," Gwunde replied, smiling.

"OK. Two hooks and two worms and a little rock."

"Oh, gross! Audrey called out as she and the boys cautiously approached Yellow Fox and Gwunde.

"Now throw your line in like this," Yellow Fox demonstrated.

Gwunde copied his friend's technique, casting his line into the water. The satisfaction was immediate as the line grew taught.

"Hey! You got one, Gwunde. Don't let go. Pull it in slowly," Yellow Fox instructed.

"It's slipping!"

"Wrap the line around your hand and pull it in. Not too fast. Don't let the fish break the line. That's it."

In a few minutes, Gwunde pulled his first wiggling fish out of Clear Lake.

"She's a beauty, Gwunde!"

"*Doh jeh*!" Gwunde replied, practicing the only Chinese word he knew.

"We say qeʔciyéw'yew'," Yellow Fox smiled at his young friend. "It means thank you in Nez Perce.

"That's harder than Chinese!"

"Here, take your fish for your dinner."

"So long, Yellow Fox," Gwunde called out, walking back towards camp with Audrey, Albert, and one Clear Lake trout.

"Let's get some peaches from the orchard," Audrey suggested.

The sweet tree-ripened peaches were perfect following the morning's hop-picking, the afternoon swim, and Gwunde's fishing adventure.

"These are great!" Ralph said. "You guys want to meet after dinner at the campfire?"

"Sure. There are two brothers from Tennessee in the camp that can really play the guitar and banjo. We all love to sing," Audrey replied, smiling.

"How about you two? Can you come?" Ralph asked.

"We'll check with our mom at the store."

They found Kay and Leslie at the camp store as expected. What they didn't expect was the small crowd of hop pickers and children gathered around the store listening to Kay's rendition of Galli-Cucci performing Verdi's La Traviata opera. Leslie was busy cranking up the gramophone for another round when the boys appeared.

"Mom! You have a fan club!" Albert gushed.

"They do seem to appreciate my singing," Kay blushed. "I've been too busy singing to sell many supplies. Don't tell your father."

"Can we go to the campfire with Audrey and Ralph?" Albert asked.

"Maybe, you can sing at the campfire," Gwunde suggested hopefully.

"Not tonight boys. It's best for Father to drive the carriage back to Salem in daylight. Besides, my voice is worn out."

Hop who had been watching the scene unfold, consoled his sons, "Sorry, boys. There will be other campfires. Let's take your fish home for dinner."

On the way back to Salem, Gwunde was quiet, thinking about his afternoon with Audrey and wondering if they would ever meet again.

Hop pickers Fook Chong Ranch. Low Family Collection.

Audrey and her family at the Fook Chong Ranch 1920's- Low Family Collection.

Chapter Thirty-Four

Where Have All the Chinese Gone? – 1924

B y the 1920s, there were only two other Chinese families remaining in Salem. Eventually, the George Sun and C.Y. Huie families also left Salem. Thus, the ten Hop Lee children grew up in a community, having little if any contact with Chinese. Hop's plan to have his children become American in every way, starting with Gretta the cow and moving the family home farther and farther from

1924 Isabel and girlfriends in Salem, Oregon.Mildred, Esther, Dorothy and Helen, May, Edna, Helen & Isabel.

Chinatown, had accomplished its end. Their friends, their schools, and their church were almost exclusively White. Hop's children were like shining stars in this sea of white. They were bright, well-mannered, well-dressed, and excelled in school. In short, they were model young Salem citizens who would make any Salem parent proud. [1] Elsie and Ella dedicated all their free time to their chosen sanctuary, the Salem Public Library, where they met a budding writer named Beatrice White. The three girls immersed themselves in the world of fiction, forging strong connections as they shared their passion for reading.

Kay's friends were also from Salem's White community. Kay, who had grown up in a sea of San Francisco Chinese, now was at home in a world with names like Upjohn, Bush, Pearcy, McEvoy, Bellinger, Lewis, Ayres, Painter, Pohl, and Wilson. [2] She did not miss Chinatown or even the Chinese. Her new world of beaded purses, Jicky perfume, and new Easter hats suited her just fine.

Loren, Leslie and neighborhood friend, Richard Upjohn, playing on 13th Street in Salem. Low Family Collection

---

1. The Sun family moved to Portland, Oregon and the Huie family moved to Walla Walla Washington and later to Fresno, California.

2. Lois and Don Upjohn and their children Richard, Rowena, and Florence were her next-door neighbors. Don was editor at the Statesman Journal and later at the Capital Journal. Lois was the first woman in Salem to graduate from law school.

Lois Upjohn with children Richard, Margaret, Rowena, and Florence lived across the street. Low Family Collection

Kay's new friends taught her about opera and made her a member of the Order of the Eastern Star. Kay was at home engaging with these neighbors and Hop's important friends and business associates.

The society pages of Salem's newspapers regularly announced the social events for the Hop Lee children. In February 1924, Elsie and Ella Hop Lee attended the wedding of their classmate Lillian Huie at the family home on South High Street. Her father, C.Y. Huie, was packing it in, closing his imported Chinese Bazaar, now called Kwong Fook & Co., after thirty years in Salem. It was a time of transitions, and in May 1924, Ella, seventeen-year-old and ready to take on the world, graduated from Salem High School. Hers was the only non-White face amongst the 203 graduating seniors.

Salem High School Sophomore Class. Ella Hop Lee is in the front row.

On November 24th, Miss Elsie Hop Lee celebrated her 20th birthday by entertaining Salem's finest young women at the Colonial Dames Tea Shoppe. Seasonal fruits and flowers adorned the "delightfully appointed" tables with covers for Miss Elaine Clower, Miss Josephine Bross, Miss Ruth Ross, Miss Helen Gatke, Miss Olive Tomlinson, Miss Mildred Tomlinson, Miss Frances Hodge, Miss Ella Hop Lee, Miss Helen Pettyjohn, and Miss Elsie Hop Lee. Miss Josephine Boss entertained the young women with musical numbers. [3]

Elsie was an English major at Willamette University, one block east of the family home. In Salem, almost everything was within walking distance. But this was ridiculously close. Elsie could roll out of bed, walk the one block to 12th Street and be in class within five minutes. With a flair for the dramatic, Elsie loved dancing and theater. Last year she was the producer for the University's annual May Day celebration. Elsie studied ballet and was a member of Mrs. Ralph Whites' Senior Ballet Class. Last Christmas, they entertained 60 of Salem's finest couples with an evening of dancing at Derby Hall.

---

3. Society page. Oregon Statesman, Friday November 24, 1924.

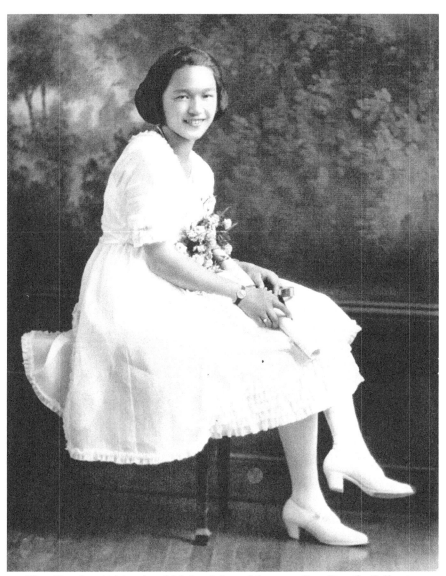

Elsie Hop Lee 1924 at her 20th birthday celebration. Low Family Collection.

Ella and Elsie Hop Lee 1924. Low Family Collection.

Yet, some ties to old customs were hard to break even for the highly Americanized and modern Hop Lee family. Trouble was brewing on 13th Street.

"I will not! I am not one of your chickens to sell! How could you?" Elsie fumed as she retreated into the safety of her bedroom, slamming the door.

Hop stood in the parlor stunned. Elsie never raised her voice and never slammed doors.

"Lulu, please come out and talk to your father," Hop pleaded using his daughter's pet name.

There was only silence.

"Elsie, open this door!"

More silence. The door opened a crack, and a beam of light from the bedroom window lit the hallway floor.

Ah, maybe there is hope.

"That's better, Lulu. Come out and talk to me."

Elsie emerged with her face still reddened. She followed Hop into the parlor and sat across from him without uttering a sound.

Hop searched for words, looking at his oldest child, remembering rolling the red egg on baby King Siu's forehead as if it were yesterday. Instinctively, he reached under the cushion where Ah Kay had found his precious red egg that morning.

Finally, Elsie broke the silence, "Father, how could you? I listened to all of your lectures every night at dinner. Work hard, study, remember the family name, become American. Those are your words. Well, I believed in your words, and I worked hard to make you and this town proud."

"Yes, Lulu. You are my pride and joy. All of Salem is proud of you. Next year you will be the first Chinese to graduate from Willamette University. My daughter!" Hop said, sitting up straight, looking into her eyes.

"Father, it broke my heart when your White friends laughed at you. You told them your daughters were going to college, and they gave you a horse laughing! But you persisted. You told them I was going to go to college and become a teacher. I knew I had to succeed so you would not be embarrassed by your own words."

"You have always made me proud, Lulu."

"Then how can you expect me to turn my back on all of my dreams and your words to marry some Chinese man I don't know and do not love?"

Hop felt his advantage slipping away.

He immediately regretted his next words, "Because I am your father, and I know best."

Isabel Hop Lee 1924. Low Family Collection.

"You are my father. You do not own me. If this is your plan, you do not know what is best for me! Who is this Chinese man anyway?"

Elsie regretted giving her father an opening. *I should have stopped and not asked about this Chinese.*

Hop seized the moment, "Wei Gin is an herbalist from the very best family. He has a good business and comes highly recommended by the matchmaker. And your birthdates are compatible. You must meet him."

"You talked to a matchmake about me?" Elsie sputtered.

"Yes, of course. That is how these things are done. We paid the matchmaker good money to search for the perfect husband for you."

"I will not meet him or any other man your matchstick lady picks out! I am a modern woman, an American woman, and I will decide for myself whom I will or will not marry!"

"Lulu, you are being unreasonable. Your mother and I had an arranged marriage. I remember that dreadful matchmaker Fong Shee...."

"See! I told you! You just admitted the matchmaker was a mistake!"

"That's not what I meant," Hop interrupted, trying to regain his advantage. *Aiyaah! I shouldn't have mentioned that old hag, Fong Shee!*

"Your mother and I never met before our wedding, but we fell in love afterward, and now she is my partner, my wife, and your mother."

"She was a child! Now she has ten children! Is that your plan for me?" Elsie fumed.

Sensing that the moment was spiraling out of control, Hop backed off, "Maybe we should go have some noodles at Lem Wah's. A bowl of jook-sing noodles sounds perfect right now."

"OK, Dad. I'll get the others. The boys are always hungry."

"No. I meant just the two of us. It will be like the old days when I used to push your stroller up and down Commercial Street to show off. I was such a proud father."

"OK. Just two bowls of noodles, but no more talk about arranged marriages and Chinese herbalists. Agreed?"

Isabel and Friends in front of the Hop Lee home on 13th Street in Salem, Oregon in 1924. Low Family Collection.

"Whatever, you say, Lulu," Hop replied, searching for his Derby hat as they went out the door and into the early morning Salem air.

They both knew this discussion wasn't over. Not even close. But a steaming bowl of Lem's house-specialty jook-sing noodles was the perfect peace offering.

As they were walking east on State Street, Hop admired the State Capital Building, a symbol of his American dream.

"I will tell you a secret, Lulu," Hop confided.

"What is it, Dad? You're not sick, are you?" Elsie replied with a worried expression.

"No. No. I am as strong as a Chinese water buffalo. My secret is my American dream," Hop replied mysteriously.

Elsie waited as they continued walking, wondering what her father was cooking up now.

"When I retire in a few years, I want to become a statesman," Hop announced proudly.

"Do you mean like an ambassador?"

"Well, yes. Something like that. I have many powerful friends who could use my help connecting to the Chinese people and government. I have more friends on both sides of the *Chinese Question* than anyone alive."

"You would be perfect for that job, Dad," Elsie encouraged. "You are the only person I know who can make money and make friends in the same breath."

Yes. But it's not about money. It's about understanding people and treating everyone like your friend."

Just as Elsie was about to reply, a gush of wind and bundle of energy came up behind them and flew past heading down State Street.

"Isabel! Slow down on those roller skates!" Elsie called out after her little sister.

Isabel slowed down, turned around, and waited.

"What's the rush, little one?" Hop asked, laughing.

"I got the call, Dad! Uncle said they have too much money at the laundry. I have to go and pick it up and bring it home."

Isabel often got the call, requiring her to either pick up or deliver money to one of Hop's businesses. She always ran to answer the phone just in case she was needed. And she kept her skates by the front door to make a quick exit onto State Street.

"You're holding me up. This is a timed pickup! I can get there in five minutes or less if no one stops me! I gotta go. Uncle's waiting with the bag of cash."

"OK. Why don't you meet us at Lem Wah's for some jook-sing noodles on the way home?" Hop suggested.

Isabel was already skating furiously down the sidewalk when she called out, "OK. Make mine extra spicy. It makes me skate faster!"

Hop laughed, relishing the joy that his family brought him.

Isabel Salem Oregon 1924 Low Family Collection.

That night, Hop opened his journal to a blank page, paused for a moment, reflecting on his life and made this entry.

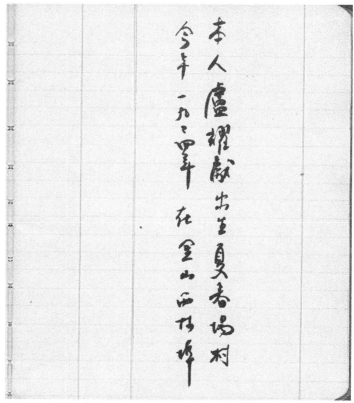

It is 1924 in Salem, Oregon in Gum Saan. I am Loo Yao Hing, one very lucky Chinese man from Ha Chun Chong Village. Low Family Collection.

Chapter Thirty-Five

Hop Keels Over – 1925

H op sat in the darkened parlor, alone and in silence, with the simple note in his hand. It was folded in half, but he knew what it said. Its words were burned into his heart. Hop's thoughts flashed back over his time in his adopted town.

I have spent over four decades in Salem. I know every businessman, politician, and chicken farmer for miles around. They are all my friends, and I am their friend. We were all equal until now. Now, they turn their back on my family.

Hop opened the note, hoping the words had magically changed.

"Dad, they said no. All of them. Not one of the schools would even interview me."

Hop felt a tear trickle down his face. He knew in his heart that his Elsie was the best, brightest, and most motivated new teacher in Salem. She would be a fine addition to any school. *Elsie is a Hop Lee, after all.*

Their lineage had always been a source of pride and inspiration. Now being Chinese was a curse. The schools would not say it out loud, but he knew it was the reason, and it crushed his spirit. Hop was no longer one of them. For the first time in this town, he felt alone and apart from the people he thought were his friends.

I talked to all my friends about Elsie - teachers, principals, politicians, businessmen, and farmers. They let me wash their clothes. They bought my eggs, and they took my credit for decades. But they will not hire my Elsie because she is Chinese. All I have to show for my friendship is this wretched note.

For the indomitable Elsie, life went on full speed ahead in a new direction, 3000 miles west, as she applied for and was immediately accepted for a teaching position in Hawaii. Graduation was quickly approaching, and the Hop Lee household was in turmoil.

"I can't believe you are graduating from college today," Ella exclaimed.

Elsie smiled as she adjusted her cap and straightened her gown. "You're next little sister."

"And then you're going to leave us in just two weeks! I've never been without you, Lulu. What am I going to do?"

"Well, at least things worked out finding a job. Hawaiians don't mind that I'm Chinese. So, Honolulu, here I come.

"Yes. Dad's pretty depressed that his friends wouldn't give you a teaching position here in Salem. He's really going to miss you."

"Well, look on the bright side. At least Dad dropped all that talk about an arranged marriage to some Chinese herbalist. Yuk!"

"Yes, but I'm next in line for Dad's cupid's arrow!"

"My advice, Ella, is to lay low or elope," Elsie laughed.

"Boy, wouldn't that make dad have a cow, and I don't mean Gretta."

Commencement at Willamette University took place on June 10, 1925. Elsie was one of 85 graduates ready to take on the world. Her English degree suited Elsie's teaching interests, but her heart was in drama and theater, if truth be told.

Events were rapidly developing as Elsie was scheduled to take the train to San Francisco on August 13th. She would set sail for Honolulu the following week.

Time was running short. There was so much to do and so many things left unsaid.

Willamette University Salem Oregon Post Card. Low Family Collection.

Elsie's friends threw her a string of bon voyage parties. On Tuesday, August 11th, Josephine Bross and Frances Hodge hosted an attractive handkerchief affair at the Bross home. The guest included Elsie Hop Lee, Mrs. Warren, Beryl Maresters, Ruth Ross, Myrtle Jensen, Mildred Tomlinson, Florence Young, Mildred Hansen, Irma Baughey, Mary Gilbert, and Carol Cheney. All the girls came dressed in their best flappers' attire and brought a hand-sewn handkerchief for their dear departing friend.

Hop awoke early on the big day he had been dreading for weeks.

It's my fault Lulu has to leave. My friends let her down. Now I will never see her again.

Hop got dressed and went into the kitchen to make Lulu's favorite breakfast when she was a child, pancakes shaped like turtles with chocolate syrup and strawberries.

"Jou sahn," Elsie greeted.

"*Nei hou*, Lulu," Hop replied, overjoyed at seeing his daughter and hearing her speak Chinese.

"Oh, Dad. You remembered my favorite turtle pancakes with chocolate syrup. I haven't had those for years."

"And fresh strawberries for my little one."

The two sat and ate breakfast, seated at the kitchen table. Both were preoccupied with millions of thoughts and emotions. Neither spoke.

"Dad, don't feel bad about my leaving. It's for the best," Elsie comforted her father, knowing it would do little good.

"Lulu, I so wanted you to get a job here in Salem. I feel like these friends of mine turned their back on us."

"Don't hold it against them, Dad. This town loves you. They just weren't ready for a school teacher with a cow in the backyard," Elsie laughed, trying to lighten the mood.

"I guess you're right. It's all Gretta's fault."

"I have something for you, Lulu," Hop continued pulling out a black silk bag from his tunic. "So, you won't forget your father."

Elsie opened the bag, revealing a jade bracelet. "Dad. It's beautiful. *Doh jeh*."

"It is to protect you on your journey, as are these."

Hop handed her three Chinese coins. "Throw these into the water from the big ship taking you to Hawaii."

"Dad. You don't believe in those superstitious tales, do you?"

"Just do it, Lulu. My mother-in-law, Ah Ying, swore by these three coins. So, who are we to argue? It can't do any harm."

"OK, Dad. Three Chinese Coins into the water it is. I miss Grandma Hong."

"Me too, Lulu. She was one strong lady with swift feet, so the legend says."

Kay and Elsie Hope Lee outside the family home on August 13, 1925 as Elsie begins her journey to Hawaii to start her new teaching job. Low Family Collection

Continuing, Hop added, "Yes, those stories about grandma were pretty incredible. But you know, she never denied they were true. She always just smiled and changed the subject."

Outside the home on 13th Street, Kay, dressed in her finest furs, was prepared to take Elsie to the Southern Pacific depot to begin her trip to San Francisco and Hawaii. Kay would accompany Elsie and then visit her brothers, Kim and Bing, in Stockton.

"Are you sure you packed enough clothes, Lulu?"

"Yes, mother. Hawaii is summertime year-round. I won't need my long johns or winter coat," Elsie laughed.

"Be sure to write and watch out for bad boys!"

"Yes, Mother," Elsie smiled. "No bad boys."

"I mean it, Lulu. You watch out, and don't be too trusting."

"Your Mother is right, Lulu. Watch out and remember the family name. Otherwise, I will drop my chickens and go over to that island and fetch you home!"

"Yes, Father. Now, both of you have got to relax. You raised me to be a smart and proper lady, and no one is going to take advantage of this Salem girl."

"I know, Lulu. They won't know what hit them once Elsie Hop Lee makes it to the Big Island," Hop laughed.

"I wish you could come to the train depot, Dad."

"Me too, but I have to open the poultry store for my customers," Hop replied glumly, certain that he was making a mistake.

As the carriage was pulling away, Hop stood and watched his daughter grow smaller and farther away. The 21 years of her life with him in Salem flashed by in an instant.

Where have all the years gone? I have so much I should have said to Lulu. Now it's too late. I'll never see Lulu again, ever!

Suddenly, realizing that he'd forgotten his most special gift, Hop spun around, looking for Bessie.

Where's that blasted horse? Ah! There you are.

Jumping up on his old friend, Hop and Bessie slowly galloped south on 13th Street towards the depot. It was only half a mile, but Bessie had seen better days and was in no rush.

"Come on, you, old horse. Get a move on!"

Bessie would not be rushed and arrived at the depot in due time without breaking a sweat.

Hop jumped off Bessie, tied her up to a railing, and ran inside, hoping that he wasn't too late.

"Lulu! I almost missed you," Hop exclaimed, panting from the short sprint.

"Dad! What are you doing now?"

"I had to give you this present," Hop explained, reaching into his pocket.

Salem, Oregon train depot built in 1918 on 13th Street. Photograph courtesy of Valfontis. Public Domain.

He opened his hand, revealing a perfect red egg.

"It is for good luck and is just like the one I rolled on baby Lulu's forehead 21 years ago."

"Dad, you are so sentimental. Thank you."

Hop then gave his daughter and hug and whispered into her ear, "I love you, Lulu."

"I love you too, Dad."

As the train pulled away from the station, Hop stood waving at his firstborn child.

"Have the red egg for your lunch, Lulu!"

Elsie smiled and settled in for her long journey to Hawaii, surrounded by the love of her family and the warm red egg in her pocket. The crinkled-up letter of reference from Dad's friend was for insurance, but she doubted she'd need it. [1]

—— *ele* ——

The following week, Friday, August 21, 1925, began like any other day at the Hop Lee home. Hop was up by 6:30 am, had breakfast, and was working at the poultry store on Ferry Street by 8:00 am. This routine had kept him young, fit, and prosperous in Salem for four decades. He saw no reason to change course just yet. Still, Hop felt the changing tide more with each passing year.

Maybe it's time to slow down and follow my dream to be an American statesman. I am not getting any younger. But there is always another flock of chickens to buy. And who would watch after my hop farms? No time to retire today. More work to do.

Hop had been having these thoughts more and more lately. Watching Lulu, who had been his pride and joy for two decades, leave so suddenly brought his life into focus. He now realized that very soon, all the children would be gone. What good would a few more dollars or chicken eggs be to him, then?

Hop was in a funk, and he figured that there was no way out except through more hard work.

What else do I know how to do?

The tinkling doorbell brought him back to the poultry store.

"Good morning, Hop," Mrs. T.A. Livesley greeted her old friend.

"Good morning, Mrs. Livesley."

"Please, I must be Edna to you by now. Kay has been my friend and neighbor for all these years."

"Yes, Edna. How is Mr. Livesley today?"

---

1. Elsie carried a letter of introduction from Mr. William S. Walton, Vice President of the Ladd & Bush Bank.

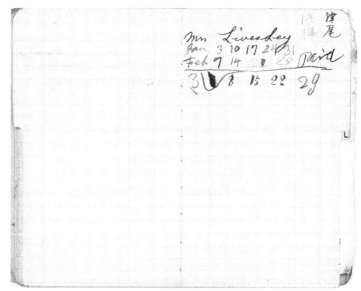

Hop Lee's record book of Poultry & Egg accounts. Low Family Collection.

"Fine, as always. Word is you have a special on chickens today, and I want to make Thomas a special dinner. Can you have two dressed chickens and three dozen eggs sent over to our home this afternoon?"

"Yes, Edna. I will add this to your tab and get right on your chickens and eggs."

"No, Hop. Today, I wish to settle up my account. How much do I owe you?"

"Well, Edna. You are a friend," Hop replied, pulling out his small ledger book and showing her the running total.

"Thanks, Hop. Give my best to Kay and the family."

Hop thumbed through the other pages in his poultry ledger book, thinking about each name and picturing the faces of his regular Salem customers TD Abbott, Joe Albert, TE Caulfield, Gilbert, Page Kane, MeEvoy, Geo Mill Hamilton, Miss Hanna, Ada Mark, Manning, VR Philips, Sara B. Savage, JA Simpson, FS Stewart, WG Tillson, Wastell, Water, Wilson, Wm Weidner, and HH Vanderwert.

The rest of the morning and the afternoon were a blur of more chicken and egg sales mixed with an unusual revenue loss.

Hop heard the squawking outside that always announced the arrival of another chicken farmer interested in selling his flock.

A minute later, the tinkling doorbell confirmed the prospective sale. Hop sold chickens on commission, so there was no risk. Any chicken was a good chicken for his business.

"Hello, Mister Hop. How are you this fine Salem summer day?"

"Please, Alvin. It's just Hop. No mister for me."

"Alright, Hop. I have my flock of chickens outside. They are fine plump birds that will sell quickly," Alvin explained.

Hop looked at his friend before responding, "Alvin, I hear you and your Mrs. are having some financial troubles. It is none of my business, but as your friend, I will tell you that they are paying more in Albany."

"Are you sending business to your competition?"

"I am taking care of a friend. If you can't get down to Albany, I will gladly take your chickens."

"Thank you, Hop. You are right. I won't forget you or your honesty."

That simple exchange and a commission sale lost became a legend around Salem for years, as Alvin told friends and the reporter, Will Carver, about Hop's business dealings that placed friendship above profit.

Albert arrived right on time, at 3:10 pm. Heading south on High Street, the short half-mile walk from Salem High School to the Poultry and Egg Store on Ferry at Liberty Street took Albert less than 10 minutes.

"Hi, Dad."

"Hello, Albert. How was school today?"

"Same old stuff. Nothing new."

"Well, you study hard. I want you to be successful and do more with your life than selling chickens and eggs."

"I like what you do, Dad. You are the most popular and successful businessman in Salem."

"There is more to life than selling and buying, Albert. Go to school and get a good education. Make money with your brains and not your hands."

"That's what you have always done, Dad."

"Well, I guess you're right. But anyway, do as I say, not as I do or something like that."

"Sure, Dad. Whatever you say," Albert laughed.

"Go gather the eggs," Hop sputtered.

Albert enjoyed this time working with his father. No one else worked at the poultry store. It was just the two of them, working and talking about everything and nothing at all. It was a special time for a father and son, and Albert knew it.

The three hours flew by with chores, egg gathering, and plucking and dressing a few chickens. At 6 pm, Albert usually headed for home and dinner.

"Time to go home now, Albert. Say hello to your mother and the family."

"Can't I stay with you tonight, Dad?"

"No. You have worked enough today."

"Please, Dad. I like it here, and you have a lot more orders to fill. We can get through the work faster with two of us here."

Hop looked around and realized that Albert was right.

"OK. Just tonight. Have Uncle Lem make us two bowls of House Specialty Jook-Sing Noodles," Hop laughed.

Albert jumped up and ran to find Uncle Lem and two bowls of noodles.

Hop and Albert found Lem hard at work in his kitchen, preparing steaming noodle bowls for his Salem customers. A bowl of Lem Wah's jook-sing noodles was as dependable as the rising sun and was guaranteed to put a smile on your face. Lem had been hard at work in his noodle shop for decades. He was the model of dependability.

"Hello, my old friend," Hop called out from the counter.

Lem looked up and grinned when he spotted his oldest friend in Salem. "Hello, Hop. How are you and Albert tonight?"

"Can't complain, Lem. What's for dinner?" Hop asked with a laugh.

"No fancy steak tartare here. Just delicious and steaming jook-sing noodles, any way you like them."

"Well, you know what we like. Two bowls, please, Lem."

As Hop and Albert were waiting for their favorite dinner, the door to the shop opened, and George Sun entered.

"Hop! How are you, my old friend?"

"Hi, George. This is like a reunion of old Chinese men looking for a free meal," Hop replied, waving for George to come over and join them.

"Hey, Lem! Look who just walked in. Make yourself a bowl and join our old timers' club for dinner."

"Sure thing, Hop. I'll be right there."

George Sun

A few minutes later, Lem came out of the kitchen carrying four bowls of House Specialty Jook-Sing Noodles.

The guys watched Lem approach with anticipation and growling stomachs.

"Lem, I've been eating your noodles for decades, and the sight of a steaming bowl still makes me drool. I can't help it!" George exclaimed.

"Well, I guess that's quite a compliment. Just don't make a mess on the floor," Lem laughed.

Jook-sing noodles

As the four enjoyed their dinner serenaded by appreciative slurping sounds, Hop looked at his two oldest friends in Salem and smiled.

"We have had a good life here in Salem. Not like the old country, but we did a lot better here."

"Do you think you'll ever go back there to live, Hop?" George asked.

"No, my life and my family are here in Salem. But times are changing. Lulu left for Hawaii last week. I am afraid she is just the first to leave us," Hop lamented.

"You know, Hop, we were bachelors like Lem for decades, and we were fine. In fact, we had a good time."

'Sure, I remember the poker parties and the police raids."

"We learned how to become hop farmers together," George reminisced.

"You were the first, George. I was a good student, though."

"Whatever happened to your cousin Sai Yee in Albany?"

"He passed on a few years ago. Sai Yee and I came over together. Except for a brief forgettable time along the Snake River, Sai Yee spent his whole life in little Albany."

"Hop, he once told me a funny story about your first job as a railroad cook. Something about burning the rice and getting run out of camp."

"Yep! That was my first and last time in the kitchen," Hop laughed, rubbing the back of his head.

"What's wrong with your bald head, Hop? You keep rubbing it," Lem observed.

"Nothing. I just have another headache. It'll go away soon."

Changing the subject, George lamented, "Well, Hop, we've been here in Salem for almost half a century. It has been a good life. I just wish we could have become American citizens. It's not fair."

"No, it isn't fair. But I will keep flying my stars and stripes every day. They can't ever take that away from me, and we can always dream."

"Let's make a toast," George said, raising his teacup.

"How about to old friends, old dreams, and Lem Wah's jook-sing noodles," Hop replied.

"Old friends, old dreams, and Lem Wah's jook-sing noodles," the four recited in unison with raised teacups.

George Sun with Maxine and Hem Lai Sun in George Sun's Salem Store 1920's
Public Domain. Oregon Historical Society.

Back at the poultry store, Hop was reviewing the next day's orders while Albert was in the basement candling the eggs. Albert liked inspecting the eggs held over a burning candle. It was like looking for a precious jewel amongst a sea of white and brown eggs, and the job was a lot more fun than plucking chickens.

Upstairs, Hop found his mind wandering as he looked over his receipts and outstanding payments. The poultry and egg business kept food on the table and was more dependable than hop farming. Prohibition was like a two-ton weight squashing the hop market and his profits.

I hope the price of hops comes back soon. I can't keep storing these crops forever.

His mind then turned to Kay, his precious jewel. Ah Kay had been his wife and business partner for over two decades. He pictured Ah Kay wearing her red wedding dress and red veil in her parents' home in Dai Fow. So much had happened since then.

With baby MeiMei, we now have ten children. I have six sons to carry on the Loo name.

1922	1915	1925	1858

Stanley Born	Arthur Dies	?	Birth

Close up of upper right section of Hop Lee's Cantonese Fortune. Low Family Collection.

Hop pulled out the fortune teller's report and reread it for the hundredth time. Its meaning was clear, and his time had come. The first year listed was his birth year in 1858. Combined with the second year listed, 1925, the fortune foretold the beginning and the ending of his journey.

As Hop stood up, his head throbbed with searing pain, and a grey curtain fell over the room. His right leg collapsed. As he fell, Hop grabbed for the edge of the table, but his right arm wouldn't move. The table with the dreaded fortune scooted across the room. Crashing to the floor, Hop could feel and smell the wooden planks pressing against his face. Struggling to open his eyes, Hop saw a shape approaching, blocking the white light.

"Dad! Dad! Are you OK? What happened? Please wake up, Dad!"

Hop smiled when he saw his little Arthur reaching out to him. Two other shapes came out of the light. Sai Wing and Yuen Shee surrounded and embraced their son. Hop felt their warmth and love and peace.

Come with us, Son. We have been waiting for you.

No! It is too soon. I have to take care of Kay and the children. We have a new baby girl.

It is time. Your family is here. Come. Leave your chickens and turtles and hops. They will be fine. Albert will......

No! I can't leave yet. I must go back.

The light receded, and Hop opened his eyes.

"Dad! Please wake up," Albert pleaded with tears streaming down his face.

Hop whispered, "It's OK, Albert. I just need to rest. I saw Arthur and your grandparents."

"Please, stay, Dad. I promise to be good and pluck all the chickens."

"Albert, you are a good son. Now, go get a piece of paper and a pen. There is something I have to do."

Albert ran to fetch the paper and pen and returned quickly, not wanting to let his father out of his sight.

"OK, Albert. You write the sign to put on the door. It will say: "No Buy Today – Hop Lee.""

With a shaking hand, Albert carefully formed the letters.

"Make the sign big, so my customers can read it."

"OK, Dad. Here is the sign - "No Buy Today – Hop Lee.""

"OK. Now go and place it outside on the front door."

That simple handwritten sign at once announced Hop's concern for his customers and that for the first time in over 40 years, Hop Lee was taking some time off from work.

"Now, what should I do, Dad?"

"Call home and have Ella..."

Hop didn't finish his whispered sentence. The grey curtain descended over the room, and the intense white light grew brighter. His family approached but kept their distance, waiting.

Albert ran to find Uncle George, who, with Lem Wah, came running to help their friend.

Hop felt someone shaking him and could hear their words, "He's still breathing."

Chapter Thirty-Six

The Final Parting Gift

George Sun and Lem Wah called Dr. W.H. Byrd, one of Marion County's oldest and most respected physicians, a former dean of the Willamette University School of Medicine. Dr. Byrd rushed over to Ferry Street to examine the man who was Salem's trusted friend. Hop was breathing shallowly but remained unconscious.

"We need to call the ambulance to take him over to the Willamette Sanitarium. Hop will be well cared for, and I will be his attending physician, but we must hurry. There's not a moment to lose."

"Will Hop recover?" George asked, worried about his longtime friend.

"We can all pray for a miracle. In the meantime, we should call Hop's family and have them meet us at the sanitarium."

Scrambling to find Hop's store phone, George turned the crank and hollered, "Yes! That's right! Connect me to 1333j! Yes, the Hop Lee residence. Hurry it's an emergency!" George stepped back as he handed the telephone to Dr. Byrd.

Dr. William H. Byrd 1888.

Willamette Sanitarium Salem Oregon.
California Historic Society & USC Libraries.

As was customary, Isabel ran to answer the telephone that evening.

"No. My mother is not at home. She is traveling in California with my sister Elsie."

"Well, you can talk to me."

"I'm ten years old!"

"I'll get my sister, Ella. Don't hang up."

"Ella! There's a phone call. It's some doctor!"

Albert met Ella, Isabel, Gwunde, and Leslie at the hospital, where they gathered around Hop's bed. Mrs. Hundsaker had rushed over to watch Stan and baby MeiMei.

"Is he going to wake up?" Isabel asked.

"He looks peaceful," Ella observed. "What happened, Albert?"

"We went out for jook-sing noodles with George Sun and Uncle Lem. Dad kept rubbing his head, but he looked OK."

"Then what happened?" Isabel asked.

"Well, we went back to work, and suddenly he stood up and keeled over."

"Did he say anything?"

"He woke up and had me make a sign to put on the door saying he wasn't buying any chickens today or tomorrow. Then he closed his eyes and hasn't spoken since then."

"I wish Mom were here," Ella said.

"You know what to do, Ella," Gwunde reassured his older sister.

"Let's just stay with him and talk to him," Leslie said.

"Yeah! I'm not leaving!" Gwunde said emphatically.

True to their word, the Hop Lee children did not leave Hop's side that night or the next day. They talked to Hop and sat on the bed with him.

When the nurses tried to get them to leave, Dr. Byrd interceded and let them remain with the man who had been a friend to Salem and a father to this family.

Around 9:00 am Saturday, after a very long but uneventful night, Albert was sitting on the bed, holding his father's right hand.

Suddenly, he jumped up. "He squeezed my hand! I swear I felt it!"

"Let me feel it!"

"No, let me!"

They took turns feeling Hop squeeze their hand. His eyes remained closed, but Hop was saying goodbye in the only way possible. It was time for him to leave the family that had brought joy to a lonely Chinese bachelor.

"Wake up, Dad! Please!" Albert pleaded.

Ella comforted her brother. "It's OK, Albert. Dad has been preparing us for this day for as long as I can remember. *Remember the family name. Make Salem proud.*"

At 1:00 pm on Saturday, August 22, 1925, Loo Sun Fook, aka Hop Lee, the Chinese merchant, hop grower, and father of ten children, passed away peacefully surrounded by his family.

Kay and Bill took the train from Stockton, arriving at the 13th Street station on Sunday. Elsie was onboard the SS Maui headed for Hakalau on Hawaii when word came of her father's death. For Kay, the reality of life without Hop and caring for nine children on her own should have overwhelmed the 35-year-old Kay. Those worries would come later. For now, burying her husband and friend and talking to lawyers and bankers kept her head spinning.

Fortunately, 19-year-old Ella took the lead, attending to the long list of details with the W.T. Rigdon & Son Mortuary, the death certificate, and the church service. There was still the question of where to bury their father, and she had to arrange for a headstone in English and Chinese.

Kay and children at 13th street home in Salem.

Gathered in the 13th Street home's living room, the children and Kay were holding a family meeting.

"Mr. Rigdon said that all of Salem, including Mr. Ashael Bush, are buried in Pioneer Cemetery, where we buried Arthur."

"I think Dad had other ideas," Kay said. "He purchased plots at Claggett Cemetery near his Fook Chong Ranch."

"Dad did love it at the ranch. I think he would have given up his laundry and poultry business in a heartbeat if he could have made any money growing hops." Ella noted.

"That's why he always wanted one of us to become a farmer," Bill said.

"How do we get a headstone for Dad's grave," Albert asked.

"The CBBA in Portland can help us with the headstone," Ella offered.

"What's a CBBA?"

"Chinese Consolidated Benevolent Association," Ella explained.

"Can we tell them what it should say? Can we have a photo of Dad on it?"

"I've seen those old Chinese stones. They're all in Chinese! We can't read them," Isabel complained.

"It has to give his Chinese name and his village name plus all the dates," Ella explained.

"We've never been to his village, and I want it to say, FATHER!" Albert replied loudly.

"OK. I'll tell them we need it to say "FATHER," Ella reassured her siblings.

"In BIG LETTERS," Gwunde added.

"OK. That's settled. Now we have to plan Dad's memorial service at the Baptist Church."

"Dad had so many friends, they won't all fit in the church," Isabel noted.

"You'd have to squeeze the whole town in there!" Leslie added.

The outpouring of sympathy from Hop's friends in Salem was overwhelming. The flood of flower arrangements, mounds of food and baked goods, and telegrams was nonstop.

"Mixed asters!" Isabel called out, returning from the front door.

"How many does that make?" Albert asked.

"I'm up to 50, and the delivery boy from the florist said he is also making deliveries to the chapel."

"Make sure you write the type of flower on each card so we can send a nice thank you card to each person who remembered Dad," Ella said. "And write neatly!"

The final tally of the flower arrangements was seventy-nine. The home and chapel were a sea of pink dahlias, pink and lavender asters, zinnias, and gladiolas.

"We can open our own florist shop," Isabel mused.

Ella sat quietly, pen in hand, in the dimly lit kitchen. Tears streamed down her face as she thought about her dad and the memorial service she was trying to plan. *I wish Lulu were here. She's always been at my side, telling me what to do. Just this once, I wish Lulu were here to boss me around.* Ella had to fill the stack of Memorial Records with her dad's name, birthdate, and age, 67 years, eight days, and ten days. It wasn't nearly long enough. *What was that hymn he liked me to sing for him? Oh yes! "Lead Kindly Light." We'll have Mom's friend, Jean Pearcy, sing the hymns.* Ella took notes in the back of the program as she planned the details of her father's service.

Hymn: Lead, Kindly Light.
Mrs. Jean Pearcy.
Scripture Lesson.
Prayer.
Address.
Hymn. The Home of Soul.
Mrs Pearcy.
Benediction

Ella's hand-written notes in the back of Hop Lee's Memorial Record.

Rev. Ernest H Shanks, Ph.D., agreed to conduct the memorial service. As Ella had planned, the service began with Mrs. Jean Pearcy singing the hymn "Lead Kindly Light," followed by the scripture lesson with a reading of Psalms 121, Psalms 90, and Psalms 103 by Rev. Shanks. Prayers and an address about Hop Lee's life followed. Mrs. Pearcy performed a second hymn, "The Home of Soul." Reverend Shanks concluded with the Benediction. As the children predicted, it was standing room only that afternoon.

The Hop Lee children, Kay, and Jean and Earl Pearcy sat in the front row, occupying the ten wooden fold-down seats. Gwunde squirmed in his seat, pulling at the neck tie, choking his seven-year old neck.

"Gwunde! Sit still!" Ella whispered.

"I can't breathe!" Gwunde gasped.

"Isabel, control your brother!" Kay said, holding baby MeiMei swaddled in a blanket.

"He can't help it Mom," Albert and Bill explained, rolling their eyes.

"Gwunde, sit still like your brother Les!" Kay scolded.

Ella stood, walking slowly to the front of the chapel. With tear-filled eyes, she spoke haltingly of her father. "You knew him as Hop or Hop Lee, but his real name was Loo Sun Fook or Loo Yao Hing. No matter what name you called him, our father loved us and each of you, his Salem friends, for over forty years." Ella paused as she caught her breath. "Every night, Dad taught us to remember the family name, to work hard, study hard, and to be respectful and honest. These were the tenets by which he lived his life." The packed room nodded in agreement. "I hope we have made him proud. We were not ready for him to go," Ella gasped, wiping away the tears now freely flowing. "Dad believed in America, and his dream was to be a statesman. He wanted more than being laundry owner or poultryman." Looking at her siblings, Ella added, "He also had dreams for each of us that we must now fulfill to honor his memory." Returning her gaze to the packed room, Ella finished, "Thank you for being Dad's friends and neighbors and for taking care of our father, the man you called Hop Lee."

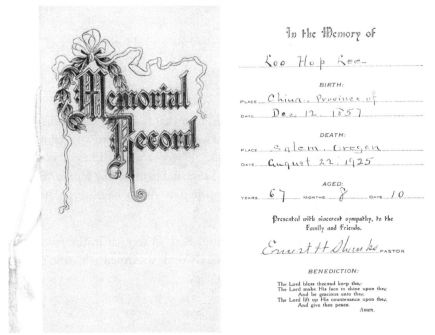

Hop Lee Memorial Record August 1925. Low Family Collection.

Rigdon Funeral Home. Salem Oregon. August 28, 1925 Low Family Collection.

At the end of the memorial service, Ella found these 15 Chinese Coins left by the few remaining Salem Chinese to protect Hop on his final journey home. According to tradition, Chinese had their bones shipped back to the ancestral village after they died. For the next half-century, Kay kept these Chinese coins in her box of little treasures along with this 1925 Lincoln penny she found in Hop's coat pocket. With his feet planted firmly on both sides of the Pacific, in the end as in the beginning, Hop's dream was to be an American. Fittingly, he chose to stay with the land and the hop fields of his adopted homeland.

Hop Lee's fifteen Chinese coins August 28, 1925. Low Family Collection

1925 Lincoln penny found in Hop's coat pocket and saved by Kay for decades.

That afternoon, standing guard over Hop's final resting spot, the single willow tree filtered the sun, casting dancing shadows on the carved red granite stone. Gwunde wrinkled his nose at the three rows of Chinese characters but smiled as he touched the bold letters written across the top, FATHER. The smell of incense lingered, but the air was still as everyone had left, taking the boiled chickens and eggs back to the Big House. Gwunde peeled one of the oranges left behind, offering his dad a slice and devouring the rest.

I'll come back to visit you, Dad.

Gwunde twirled the single eagle feather left at the grave and waited, hoping to hear his father's voice. The reply startled him.

"Come over here, boy. I need your help."

Gwunde looked up, "Dad is that you?"

Walking towards the voice, Gwunde came to the edge of Claggett Cemetery, finding Yellow Fox bent over and digging in the soft dirt.

"There's something we have to do for your father, Gwunde," Yellow Fox replied, handing him a willow sapling.

"Inspecting the tiny tree, Gwunde turned it around, admiring the delicate leaves. "It looks like a baby of Dad's tree."

"We will make Hop a willow forest," Yellow Fox explained.

An hour later, Gwunde patted the soil around the tenth willow tree.

"Now, Hop's spirit has a willow forest to guide him home."

Low Sun Fook aka Hop Lee 1892 and 1925 Low Family Collection.

Willamette sky and land that Hop loved and made his home. Bonnie Moreland Creative Commons Mark 1.0.

In the end, the Cantonese fortune teller's final prediction completed the circle, giving meaning to Hop's life in Gum Saan.

"A Willow Tree Becomes a Willow Forest"

Chapter Thirty-Seven

Epilogue – 1925

T he Oregon Statesman office at 215 S. Commercial Street was bustling with activity as reporters and editors scrambled to meet the Sunday edition's deadline. Hop Lee's death had caught everyone by surprise. The ever-dependable Hop had been a fixture in Salem for over 40 years. The editor, R.J. Hendricks, gave reporter Will Carver the assignment of paying tribute to this unlikely Salem celebrity who Carver personally knew as "Hop." The editor promised Will the front page for a well-written article.

215 S. Commercial - Oregon Statesman.

I'm missing something. There has to be more to Hop's life than the dates and facts. What else made this Chinese so beloved in Salem? [1]

His thoughts were interrupted by a tap on his shoulder. He turned to find Eloise.

"This man wants to talk to you, Will."

Carver looked the man over, clearly a farmer by his dress in overalls and work shoes covered with mud and worse.

"What can I do for you?"

"My name is Alvin. I heard you are writing a newspaper article about Hop Lee."

"Yes, that's right," Will replied, clearly irritated by the interruption. "I'm on a deadline, so make it snappy."

Alvin, more comfortable with his chickens than with newspaper reporters, cleared his throat.

"I raise chickens. You need to know Hop the way we regular people knew him."

Will's interest was piqued, "Go on."

"My business is not doing really well with the prices of chickens being low and all. It's hard for any of us chicken farmers to make a living and feed our families."

"OK. But I'm not writing about the poultry market," Will interrupted.

"I sell my hens to Hop at his poultry store on Ferry Street. Yesterday, I took my flock to Hop to sell on commission."

"Yes, I understand how chickens are sold," Will replied, looking at his watch.

---

1. In 1917 the Oregon Statesman purchased this two-story building at 215 S. Commercial Street at the Southwest corner of Ferry and Commercial. In August 1925 Will Carver wrote his article about Hop Lee in this building. What he may not have known is that until 1913 the Hop Lee Laundry was located on the left side of this very same building at 225 S. Commercial and that the competing Capital Journal was in the center of this building from 1890-1914. The two newspapers merged in 1980 to form the Statesman Journal.

"Well, Hop wouldn't buy them. Not a one."

"Why not?"

"Hop told me to take them to Albany because they are paying more for chickens. Hop gave up a commission sale to help my family," Alvin finished.

"You're telling me he sent business to his competitors rather than make a quick profit?" Will asked, looking over his piece.

There was no reply. Will Carver looked up. The chicken farmer was gone, but his story stuck with Will, who at that moment came to know the man Hop Lee as the people of Salem had known him for 40 years.

Will finished his piece and ran into his editor's office, waving the copy.

"I have it!"

The Oregon Statesman - Sunday Morning August 23, 1925

Stroke Proves Fatal to Chinese Merchant

Hop Lee Called Early Saturday Afternoon

**Reliability and Integrity Known
Throughout Entire Willamette Valley**

By Will Carver

"No Buy Today – Hop Lee

This was the last business action of Hop Lee, well known Salem Chinese who became ill yesterday and left this word to explain why for the first time in nearly 40 years, his "office" was not open.

Hop Lee will be missed by hundreds of Salem and Willamette Valley residents who had had personal knowledge of Hop Lee's reliability and integrity at various times during the two score years of his residence here.

A story of Hop Lee must be something more than a mere sketch of his life and his death. It must show something of his influence upon the Chinese population of this city when at one time, the colony numbered well over 200. With George Sun, C.Y. Huie, and Bin Sin, he was a member of his group that counseled their brethren during turmoil and peace. Did a member of his race fall foul of the white man's law or become ill or need other assistance, Hop Lee, with these other three now living, was ready to represent Chinatown's interest in the matter.

Now there is no Salem Chinatown; perhaps 30 is the total of the city's Chinese population at present.

Hop Lee's first laundry was located on South Commercial across from the present site of the Marion Hotel. After being in this location for nearly 15 years, Hop Lee moved to a building on Ferry Street. Several years ago, he was forced to move because of the erection of modern structures. The laundry Hop Lee passed from Salem a few years ago when he entered the commission business specializing in poultry and eggs.

Hop Lee (he always objected to being called "Mister") owned several hop yards and farms as well as Salem residence property. He not only enjoyed Salem's goodwill because of his commercial attainments but was respected because of the popularity of his family. Hop Lee's children attended Salem schools and, as they graduated, took their place in the business and social life of the city.

Here is an instance of the why of Hop Lee's popularity. Recently, a local farmer visited Lee and asked that the Chinese merchant purchase his flock of hens. Knowing that the farmer was in need of money, Hop Lee told him of a better market in another town, although this cost him a commission deal.

Hop Lee was affected with a stroke of apoplexy Friday night. He died at a local hospital at 1 p.m. Saturday.

He is survived by his wife and nine children. The children are Elsie, Ella, William, Albert, Isabel, Leslie, Kay, Loren, and Clifford. Mrs. Hop Lee and daughter Elsie are now in Stockton, Cal., from which point the daughter had expected to leave for Honolulu, Hawaii, where she has accepted a position in the island school system."

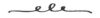

Elsie Lulu Hop Lee Low – King Siu 1904 – 2000

Elsie Hop Lee 1908 and 1930.

Elsie, the oldest of Hop Lee's ten children, taught English and Drama at Hakalau School on the island of Hawaii. She also instructed her students, as well as her nieces and nephews, in etiquette, manners, and proper speech. Elsie later taught at Farrington High School in Honolulu. Elsie remembered Hop as a good father who taught his children the importance of honor and the family name.

Ella Hop Lee Low – King Sin 1906 – 1929

Ella Hop Lee 1908 and 1929

Ella was blessed with beauty, intelligence, and a wonderful singing voice. Ella played and sang along with the Galli-Curci opera records while doing housework in Salem. Her clear, sweet soprano voice filled the family home on 13th Street and later in Stockton. Ella attended Willamette University for two years and later studied at the University of California at Berkeley. Ella was the rock that supported the family after her father died in 1925. Her tragic and untimely death in August 1929 as part of a wedding party accident left a void in the family that was never filled.

William Hop Lee Low – Wy Fay 1908 – 1983

William Hop Lee 1908 and 1947

As the oldest of Hop's six sons, Bill carried the weight of his father's expectations. Father considered playing baseball and Boy Scout activities frivolous. When he was 15 years old, Bill went to live in Stockton. Enjoying his freedom, Bill learned to bake from Uncle Bing and purportedly went to Chinese school.

Bill graduated from UOP in Stockton with a degree in chemistry. Unable to be hired locally as a Chinese chemist, Bill followed Elsie to Honolulu in 1938, where he found work and love. He married Amy Chan Young, a nursing student at Queen's Hospital. Their two children, Chris and Susan, were born in Honolulu.

Arthur Hop Lee Low – Wy Hing 1911 – 1915

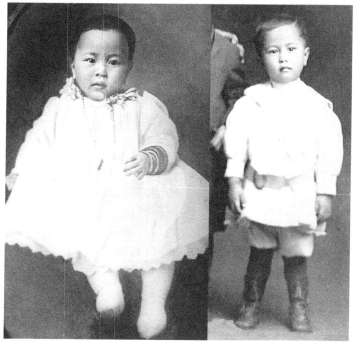

Arthur Hop Lee 1911 and 1915

Arthur may have inherited the same genes as Ella, as he was blessed with good looks. He was a favorite in the First Baptist Church Primary Sunday School. Arthur's untimely death in April 1915 left a horrendous hole in the family and in Hop's heart. His death, which Hop believed was a murder, was a tragedy from which the family never fully recovered. Hop displayed Arthur's infant photograph over the Bush and Lane piano in their Salem home. Arthur was gone but was never forgotten. In the 1920 census, the family continued to list Arthur as a son who then would have been nine years old.

Albert Hop Lee Low – Wy Sing – 1913 – 2003

Albert Hop Lee Low 1914 and 1945

Albert, Hop's third son, was the father's loyal helper in the Poultry Store. He never strayed from Hop's principles of hard work and family loyalty. Albert attended Tri-State University in Indiana, studying aeronautics in the 1930s but was unable to complete his studies due to lack of funds at the height of the Depression. Returning to Portland, Oregon, Albert found work in the shipyards and later in custodial work. In 1944, he married Margaret Wong. They had two sons, Timothy and Perry. For his entire life, Albert tended to his father's grave in Claggett Cemetery.

Isabel Hop Lee Low – King Gew – 1915 – 2001

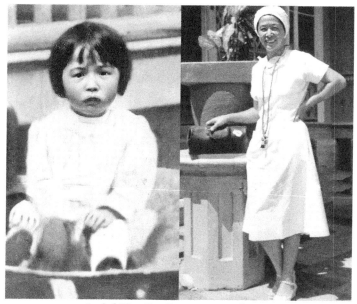

Isabel Hop Lee Low 1917 and 1960

Isabel, born the same week that Arthur drowned in 1915, was bright, studious, and a fast skater. In Stockton, Isabel was the center of attention with the Chinese boys. However, to date Isabel, you had to get past her mother, Kay, who accompanied Isabel on all of her dates. Isabel married Dr. Clarence Ing in 1935. Isabel later became one of the early Chinese American women physicians. She dedicated her life in service to others as a missionary doctor, first in British Guyana and later in Hong Kong. She and Clarence ran a boat clinic for indigent families in Aberdeen Harbor in Hong Kong. In recognition of her long career of service, Loma Linda voted Isabel Woman of the Year. Isabel had three children, Clarence Jr., Kenny, and Pamela.

Loren Hop Lee Low — Wy Gwun 1917 – 2008

Loren Hop Lee Low 1918 and 1942

Loren, tall, good-looking, and strong as an ox, possessed an independent streak that took him far from home. Gwunde loved adventure and the outdoors. Loren took his father's lectures about honor and the family name to heart when he enlisted 11 months before Pearl Harbor. It surprised no one when he came home with a Silver Star for gallantry in action. After the war, Loren worked as a carpenter and married the love of his life, Rose Fong. They had four children, Curtis, Russell, Laurel, and Alisa. Gwunde focused his boundless energy on running and cycling.

Leslie Hop Lee Low – Wy Bew – 1919 – 2011

Leslie Hop Lee Low 1921 and 1945

Leslie, intelligent, articulate, and quick to please, fulfilled his father's wish to have a family doctor. Pursuing this path during the Depression was no easy matter. Leslie read the Salem hop prices to his mother from the Capital Journal. Depressed hop prices during Prohibition combined with Depression-era poverty made advanced education a distant dream. When FDR repealed Prohibition in 1932, Leslie was able to attend college at La Sierra College and medical school at Loma Linda University. In 1948, Leslie married Cora Lee in Stockton, where their family included Randall, Cathy, Carol, and Candace

Clifford Stanley Hop Lee Low — Wy Yin — 1922 – 1943

Clifford Stanley Hop Lee Low 1923 and 1942

Stan was only three years old when his father passed away in 1925. Stan grew up with his younger sister, MeiMei. The two were closest in age and were inseparable. Stan enjoyed the freedom of visits to the hop ranch in Salem, Oregon.

Tall, slender, and quiet by nature, Stan dreamed of following his older brother, Loren, into the Army Air Corps in WWII. Underage, he needed Kay's written permission to enlist. When she relented, Stan became a nose gunner in a B-24 Liberator in New Guinea. The sequel to this novel, entitled "The All-American Crew," describes Stan and Loren's WWII adventures.

Constance MeiMei Hop Lee Low– May Gew – 1925 – 1987

Constance MeiMei Hop Lee Low 1927 and 1945.

MeiMei, which means "little sister" in Chinese, was only four months old when her father died in August 1925. As Gwunde said, MeiMei was his favorite little sister. After Kay returned to the farm in 1937, MeiMei became a very young chauffeur for her mother, driving her around Keizer. She attended the Clear Lake School, where her big brother, Gwunde, bid on and won MeiMei's basket at a basket social. When he wrote MeiMei from overseas, Gwunde reminisced that he wouldn't trade their wonderful childhood for all the rice in China. MeiMei became the lead medical technologist at White Memorial Hospital in Los Angeles. In 1946 she married Dr. Evan Fong. Their family in Sacramento included Martha, David, and Donna.

Ernst Hofer
Publisher Capital Journal

AN Bush
Ladd & Bush Bank

RJ Hendricks
Publisher Oregon Statesman

John McCourt
Supreme CT Justice

Hop Lee
Laundryman and Hop Farmer

Ed Hirsch
Landlord & State Treasurer

Dr. BL Steeves
Physician, Mayor, Banker

Thomas Livesly
Hop Grower, Politician

Charles McNary
US Senator

Hop's Unlikely Circle of Friends and Neighbors

Hop's circle of friends and neighbors was a who's who of Salem, Oregon, at the turn of the 20th century. They were an unlikely compilation of newspaper publishers, bankers, and Republican politicians. What they had in common was a friendship with the man they called the Chinese laundry magnate. It is remarkable how many of these men arrived in Salem in the 1880s at the same time Hop arrived from Albany, Oregon.

Ernst and Andy Hofer were from Iowa. Ernst was born in 1855, and Andreas in 1861. They arrived in Salem with their parents in 1884. By 1888 the Ernst brothers had taken over the Capital Journal newspaper. Their flamboyant writing became a hallmark of the Republican paper. The Hop Lee Laundry at 191 S. Commercial was just two doors south of the Capital Journal office. Many of the articles and advertisements about the Hop Lee family were written by Ernst Hofer for the Daily Capital Journal. Although they sold the newspaper in 1912, Ernst continued his friendship with Hop. He and his wife sent flowers when Hop passed away in August 1925.

R.J. Hendricks was the other newspaper publisher in Hop's circle of close friends. Hendricks arrived in Salem in 1884, the same year as Hop. The 23-year-old Hendricks immediately purchased the Oregon Statesman located two blocks from the Hop Lee Laundry at 266 Commercial Street. RJ Hendricks taught Hop about advertising and covered the events in the Hop Lee family. In 1927 when Elsie needed someone to vouch for her family and Elsie's American-born status, RJ Hendricks supplied a sworn affidavit attesting to his relationship with Hop Lee for four decades and his personal knowledge of Elsie's birth in Salem in 1904. RJ Hendricks was the owner, editor, and publisher of the Oregon Statesman from 1884 -1928.

A.N. Bush was the son of Asahel Bush II, the founder of the Oregon Statesman and the Ladd and Bush Bank. AN Bush took over the bank in 1913 when his father died. It was A.N. Bush who gave Hop the loans allowing him to purchase the multiple hop ranches. AN Bush had a personal relationship with the Hop Lee family for over 60 years. He continued to write letters to Kay thanking her for the holiday turkeys and cakes every year until his 90th birthday. For decades, Kay kept in her scrapbook yellowed newspaper clippings about her friend from the old days, AN Bush.

Ed Hirsch was Hop's landlord at his first laundry in the Rector Building on S. Commercial Street. Born in Germany in 1836, Hirsch arrived in Salem in the 1860s. Hirsch served as Oregon State Treasurer from 1878- 1887. He subsequently was on the Salem City Council and was appointed as Salem's Post Master by Presidents McKinley and Roosevelt. An autographed photograph of Ed Hirsch was proudly displayed in Kay's photo album.

John McCourt 1874-1924 was the 51st Associate Justice on the Oregon Supreme Court. Born in 1874, he moved to Salem, Oregon in 1890. He graduated from Willamette University Law School and passed the Bar Examination in 1896. In 1921 McCourt was appointed to the Oregon Supreme Court. He tragically died in office in September 1924 from septicemia and endocarditis from a dental infection. When Hop died the next year, Mrs. John McCourt sent her condolences and a bouquet of lavender asters.

B.L. Steeves, an ENT physician, who was born in 1868 in New Brunswick, Canada, came to Salem, Oregon, in 1888. He was elected Salem's Mayor in 1915 and was President of the Salem Bank & Trust Company. The Steeves family belonged to the Methodist Church, where the parents knew Elsie and Ella Hop Lee. The day following Hop's death in August 1925, Mrs. BL Steeves sent Kay her condolences and prayers in a personal letter which Kay saved for half a century.

Thomas Livesley, born in 1863 in Wisconsin, was a successful Oregon hop grower and broker known as the Hop King. Livesley moved to Salem in 1894. He was elected Salem's mayor in 1927 and to the Oregon State House of Representatives in 1936. Thomas Livesley owned the property inSenartor just north of Hop's Fook Chong Ranch and, in 1924, built the home that is the current Oregon Governor's mansion. Mrs. Livesley was one of Hop's regular customers at the 436 Ferry Street Poultry and Egg Store.

Charles McNary was one of ten children born on a farm north of Salem, Oregon, in 1874. Charles was orphaned when nine years old. McNary attended Stanford University and then Willamette University Law School. His political career as a Republican US Senator from 1917-1944 culminated in a run for the White House on the Wilke-McNary ticket in 1940. The McNary Fir Cone Farm was located immediately southeast of Hop's Fook Chong Ranch. McNary wrote reference letters for Hop's sons, Loren and Stan, to enter the Army Air Corps.

Otto J. Wilson, Sr. was a visionary and early adaptor of the automobile, bringing the first vehicle to Salem in 1903 and establishing the first automobile dealership that became Wilson Buick. The Wilsons were neighbors who lived on State Street near the 13th Street Hop Lee Family home.

Don Upjohn was a lawyer and editor for the Statesman Journal and the Capital Journal. His spouse, Lois Upjohn, was the first woman to graduate from Law School in Salem and the second in the state of Oregon. The Upjohns were next-door neighbors on N. 13th Street from 1920-25. Kay kept photographs of the Upjohn family in her treasured photo album.

Afterword – 1991

Almost seven decades later, the four met, each clutching the mysterious invitation which said simply: *It is time. Please come to remember them so others can know their story.*

The journey of researching and creating this story began 30 years ago, in 1991. As an aspiring videographer, I gathered four of Hop Lee's children around my dad's old album of early 1900s family photographs. With minimal prompting, Loren, Elise, Isabel, and Leslie described their experiences growing up in Salem's Hop Lee family.

They arrived not as two doctors, a school teacher from Honolulu, and a carpenter turned marathoner but rather as siblings with stories to share. Collectively, they had survived the Depression, a couple of wars, marriages, and the tragic deaths of siblings and spouses. But today, they met as the children of Hop Lee and Hong Hop Lee. None had seen the album of old photos of their childhood for several decades. But the images sparked memories that were at times humorous, thankful, and painful of the man that Salem knew as "Hop."

"This is Leslie," Isabel proclaims, pointing at a faded photograph.

"No, that's Loren," Les argues.

"That's up on the farm in Oregon," Loren explains, remembering the Percheron horses, Duke and Barney.

Elsie grabbing the album, asks Isabel, "Is this you?"

"Start at the beginning now. Let's make a script," Leslie directs, handing the album to my sister, Laurel. "Bring this in and say, 'I was looking through this old album. I can't recognize these people. Can you tell me....'"

Laurel willingly obliges, "Aunties and Uncle, here is a photo album I found, but I don't know who any of these people are. Can you tell us some stories about each of the pictures?"

"Who is this?" Elsie asks, picking up a photograph from 1917.

"That's my baby picture when I was a wee-wee small one," Loren laughs.

"You remember distinctly, of course!" Elsie replies.

"This a picture of Dad in 1918," Les explains, pointing.

"Tell us about grandfather, because I don't know him at all," Laurel redirects the conversation.

"He was a very handsome man," Elsie replies.

"He wore that black derby. He liked that Derby." Isabel recalled.

"He had more than one. I think mother used to save money and buy him one for Christmas," Elsie added.

Loren agreed, "He was a fan of Derby hats. He liked them so much, he wore them everyplace he went. I don't remember too much about him because he died when I was only seven and one half, but I remember him kind of round in the middle. He was a gentleman. He was easy to get along with and a good businessman."

"Didn't mother have to tie his shoes?" Rose asks from the gallery.

"Yeah, he couldn't tie his own shoes," Loren confirms. "The family had to help him there a little bit."

"Every night when he came home, you children had to take his shoes off, take his necktie, take his hat, take off his coat, take his vest, and you all got twenty-five cents for it," Elsie explains.

"He used to give us a dollar when we would kiss his big toe!" Les interrupts to uproarious laughter.

"That, I don't know," Elsie replies, shaking her head.

1991 Leslie, Isabel, Elsie, and Loren. Low Family Collection

"What was Popo like back then?"

"Popo was a stylish lady," Isabel explains, pointing at a photo. "She's wearing high-top shoes, and she has a big picture hat, and she has a gathered silk skirt with a very frilly white blouse. She has long hair done up high on her head. She looks pretty sharp."

"She bought a hat every Easter. She loved hats. We didn't have any money, but she would put two dollars down, and we would pay a dollar a week," Elsie adds. "I was still there, so it was before 1925."

Laurel takes away the album and redirects the conversation. "Tell us about your father."

Elsie replied, "Well, he was a martinet. He made you folks work. Bill and Albert had to go down to the store as soon as they got through school. Bill loved to play baseball and Boy Scouts, but his father had no use for either. Bill's job was to work, and when he didn't show up, the lickings were really something."

"Father worked hard to make money. It wasn't always easy. He was highly respected. Everybody who went by called out, 'Hi, Hop! Hi, Hop!' That was his name.

He was a good businessman. He trusted people."

"I know how to speak Chinese for one reason. If I wanted any money, I had to say it in Chinese or I didn't get it. You had to say it all in Chinese. And he never gave me fifty cents. He always gave me a dollar or two dollars. Because he said, 'Girls must always have money. Otherwise, they will go and do things to get money!' So, I never had to worry about money, actually, because he always gave me more than I ever asked for." Elsie explained.

"He was a very good father. He sent me to school, when everybody made fun of him. 'Whoever heard of girls going to college?' He replied, 'My girl's going to teach school!' They gave him a horse laugh. So, when it came time for me to graduate, I had to get a job. I had to teach school. Otherwise, my father would be embarrassed or ashamed rather."

"All the lessons, he taught us. Every night at dinner, we would have to sit and listen to a lecture about how to be good. The family name. I think we were well taught. We all had good manners. We were well-behaved, and the town was very proud of us. We were bright. We were clean, and we did nothing wrong," Elsie continued.

"I have some good ones and some bad ones," Isabel added, looking down. "I remember, whenever he wanted anything. There was that old-fashioned telephone that you had to wind. He'd ring home for either some money if they ran out of money downtown. I'd have to go down to get it and bring it home, and then when they needed it, I had to run it down again. I used to love to roller skate. I could go down there in less than five minutes on roller skates. It was about a mile from the house to the store. Oh yeah! I was fast!"

"With each boy, mother got a farm," Isabel explained.

Elsie clarified, "Father looked at mother and said she is so young. She won't have any money when I go, and she must have money. So, for the first three of us, he bought a farm. Then for the fourth or fifth, he bought the Mark Skiff farm, which was 800 acres, and he went into hock. We never recovered. He never bought another farm because we didn't have any money."

Les, who had been silent, adds, "I can't remember any of this except for one thing. I would go down to the poultry shop with dad, and when they would kill a turkey, they had a big washtub and a board. They'd cut the head off the turkey and put him in there, and I'd stand on the washtub until the turkey quit, to keep the blood from flying all around. I was about three then, I guess."

The freely flowing stories continued for the next hour.

The images, voices, and thirty-year-old video preserve a family and a slice of Salem's history that has long since passed. However, the impetus for this book arrived in the mail twenty years later when all the pieces fell into place to tell Hop's story.

The package from another time was wrapped in brown paper and tied with twine. The return address was partly written in Chinese with the address in English, "Route 2, Box 258 Salem. Oregon USA." The smudged postmark was at first hard to make out. It was from Salem, but the date gave me chills when it finally appeared on a blown-up photo – January 30, 1942.

My hands trembled as I opened the box, gently removing the twine and brown paper wrapper. Inside the box were old photos of the Hop Lee children from the early 1900s, property deeds, a journal, and a mysterious folded-up yellow parchment buried at the bottom.

The yellow parchment looked like it had been unopened for decades. I set it aside while I explored the other contents of the box. The black and white photos told stories of my father's generation, and the farm deeds held clues about Hop Lee's purchases in the name of his young American-born wife.

When I finally got around to gently unfolding the parchment, I encountered a mysterious hand-brushed scroll of Chinese calligraphy written in black ink with intriguing pink circular markings. Only much later did I realize that this was Hop Lee's treasured fortune. Having completed a journey of thousands of miles over hundreds of years, the family fortune was finally sharing its secrets and predictions with the world. Hop's willow forest still lives on today, guided in part by the predictions of a Cantonese fortune teller, who 150 years ago, foretold Hop's life's journey.

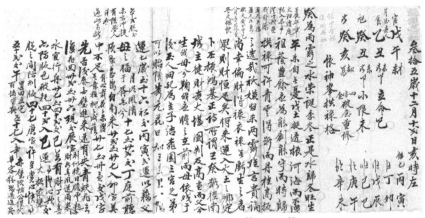

Hop Lee's Fortune Teller Scroll

Acknowledgments

Ann Lossner for her research and writings about the history of Keizer and the Fook Chong Ranch. My email communications with Ann two decades ago were an important part of the early days of my journey to uncovering the story of the Hop Lee family in Salem Oregon. Anne's books, "Looking Back People and Places in the Early Keizer Area" 1990 and "More Looking Back" 1995 describe the people and places in early Keizer history, including the Fook Chong Ranch, Hop Lee, and Claggett Cemetery.

Ann Lossner

Merrialyce Blanchard. Special Collections librarian Oregon State Librarian located the photographs of Salem Chinese and the Metzker Maps of Keizer, Oregon clearly showing land owned by Hong Hop Lee including the original Alvis Smith Homestead just south of Clear Lake.

Phil Choy for his assistance in translating Hop
Lee's book of family history. I discovered the
book of handwritten Chinese characters in
the bottom of a cardboard box containing my
grandmother's treasures that had almost been
discarded. Since Kay did not read or write, I
assumed and hoped that this little journal had
been written by Hop Lee. Phil and his friends
confirmed my suspicions with their translations
which directly connected me with the man and
grandfather I had never met.

Phillip Choy

Dr. Lilly Cheng for her expert translations of
Hop Lee's fortune teller document and the
1903 list of gifts for the bride. The ancient
form of writing on the fortune kept its secrets
locked away for over 100 years. As Lilly translated the document without any knowledge of
my grandfather or his story, she revealed in eerie
detail Hop Lee's life's journey as predicted by a
Cantonese fortune teller 150 years ago.

Dr. Lilly Cheng

Helen Chong for her expert translations of the
22 generations of the Loo Family Jiapu which I
brought back from a trip the the Loo Ancestral Village, Ha Chun Chong, in May
2016. Helen's translations of the jiapu helped to establish Low Sun Fook in the
lineage of the Loo family tree.

I am indebted to Vivien Shen of the Guangzhou Office of Overseas Chinese Affairs for helping me in May 2016 to visit Hop Lee's ancestral village, Ha Chun Chong, in Hoiyin, China. During this visit, I stood in my grandfather's now abandoned home, which he left in 1877 to begin his journey to America. The village on the seashore of southern Toishan is likely much the same as it was 140 years ago. Vivien translated as the village elders shared stories of the Loo family, and in return, I gave them a copy of the 1919 photograph of the Loo Family in Salem, Oregon. In the end, this visit to learn about my grandfather connected me to these people and this village.

Vivien Shen

Thomas Gregory / tátlo, Nez Perce Language Team Leader, Nez Perce Language Program for the Nez Perce Tribe for his invaluable assistance in bringing to life the Nez Perce language and culture. The connections between Hop Lee and the Nez Perce tribe over decades was kept alive by the stories of his son, Gwunde, who described in vivid detail Yellow Fox the Chinese hop man who reappeared every planting season and who visited Hop's grave with him in Claggett Cemetery. Some clues, including the painting of a Nez Perce warrior on his Appaloosa horse in the Hop Lee parlor and the Native American rugs shown in family photos are tantalizing pieces of this story.

tátlo Thomas Gregory

The Hop Lee children, Leslie, Elsie, Isabel, Albert, and Loren who in 1991 began this journey of discovery by telling me stories of growing up in Salem, Oregon. In a videotaped interview while reminiscing over an album of old family photographs from the early 1900s, each of them had an important part of the story to tell. Their shared memories sparked a rare and lively conversation about their father, Hop Lee, mother, Kay, their experiences growing up in Salem and on the hop farms near Keizer, Oregon.

Loren Low

Photographer Bonnie Moreland for the use of her gorgeous photographs of Oregon scenery including the Willamette Valley, Columbia River Gorge, and Hells Canyon along the Snake River in Eastern Oregon.

Bonnie Moreland

Family members generously contributed photographs, heirlooms, and stories that formed the foundation for this novel. The main characters of the story Low Sun Fook, aka Hop Lee, his wife Kay and their ten children shared their journals, and photo albums that span 120 years. Kay's brother Kim Seung Hong was an early photographer who recorded life in Salem in the early 20th century. Isabel Low Ing was the family archivist who painstakingly preserved these photographs in albums for each of her siblings and her mother.

Kim S. Hong

Later generations were equally generous in sharing photographs and records. This work would not have been possible without the contributions of Laurel Low Depolo, Christopher Low and Patricia Gowan, Candace and Randall Tom, Catherine Low Doo, Alisa Koo, Arabella Hong Young, Dorothy Yim, Susan Ito, and Edith Au.

Isabel Low Ing

Kay Low, who for decades preserved Hop's fortune teller document, the 1903 Chinese list of wedding gifts, countless letters, cards and photographs that tell the story of Salem's Hop Lee family in rich detail. Many of these documents she could not read. Somehow, she knew that almost half a century after her death, Hop's grandson would need them to tell their remarkable story. Finally, we all should thank Hop Lee for living a life so full of rich and colorful events and for having dreams that inspire all of us to celebrate and cherish our immigrant roots.

Kay Low

Kylie Pine, curator of the Willamette Heritage Center, generously assisted me in locating photographs of Salem, Oregon in the 1800s, including those of the Salem Fire Brigade and Tiger Fire Company #2 in Chapter 6. Kylie's enthusiasm, encouragement, and assistance with the research was very much appreciated.

Kylie Pine

Finally, I wish to thank all of the readers of my first books, "Three Coins" and "The All-American Crew" for your generous and heartfelt appreciation of the stories which preserve our rich immigrant history in Gum Saan. All Americans come from bold and resilient ancestors who overcame hardship to make a life for their families and descendants in America. We are stronger as individuals and a nation because of this immigrant spirit born from the diversity which is at the heart of our nation.

Apendix

Nez Perce Words and Phrases

Niimíipuu –   Nez Perce

Nimipuutímt –   Nez Perce language

ʾehé Russell, –   Yes or what's up Russell

qeʾciyéw'yew' – Thank you

taʾc méeywi –   Good morning

Qo'c 'ee hexnu' – Goodbye

Nazóg –   Chinook salmon

Cantonese Words and Phrases

zhuī zhú   *to chase*

Sin saan   *mister*

Jo sahn   *good morning*

Do jeh   *thank you*

Neih hou   *hello*

Saig fahn mah?   have you eaten

Gum Saan   gold mountain

Fai dee lah   hurry up

Dai Fow   First City or San Francisco

Ngoihmóu   *mother-in-law*

jeuhngfu   *husband*

Fon Gwei Low.   *American or Western food*

cha siu bao   barbecued pork bun

tai soeng lou   fortune teller in Cantonese.

1895 Sanborn Fire Insurance Map – Hop Lee Laundry on South Commercial Street

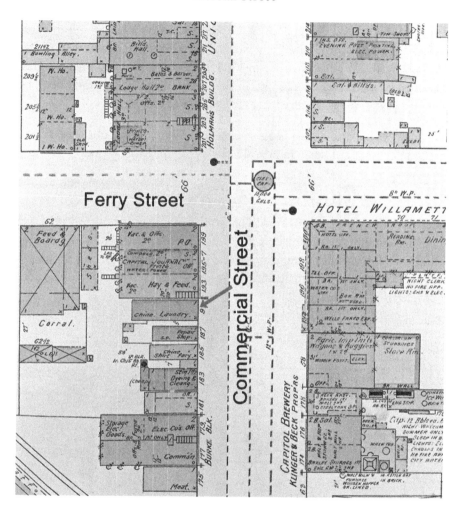

Between 1885 and 1913, the Hop Lee laundry occupied various locations in the block at the southwest corner of South Commercial and Ferry Streets. In 1895 the laundry was at 191 S. Commercial in a wood building south of the Smith Brick building that was home to the Capital Journal newspaper and the Post Office. The next year the laundry moved to 189 S Commercial and then to 187 S Commercial. After Hop married in 1903 the Hop Lee home is listed as 191 S. Commercial Street two doors south of the Capital Journal. To make room, he temporarily moved his laundry to 213 S. Commercial Street.

Hop also entered into raising hogs, chickens, and ducks with a hog yard located at 181 S. Commercial street, indicated in yellow on the Sanborn Map.

In 1910 the streets were renumbered and the laundry at 191 S Commercial Street is listed as 225 S. Commercial. In 1913 the wooden building where Hop laundry was located was torn down. That year he moved the laundry to 436 Ferry street between Liberty and High streets. This became a joint laundry and poultry store until Hop closed the laundry business in 1921 after almost four decades in Salem. He then continued to operate the Poultry Business on Ferry Street and the multiple Hop Ranches.

1903 Lists of Bride Gifts from Low Sun Fook

This list of gifts for Kay was prepared in China by Low Sun Fook aka Hop Lee's family. The items in this list are a treasure trove of riches that would have cost a small fortune in 1903. Gold, jade, porcelain, and special mud silk garments represents the finest and most elegant gifts for this young bride. The date on the cover is July 1903, indicating that Hop purchased these elegant items before he met Kay and her family in San Francisco. He likely took this list with him to impress her parents with his wealth and generosity.

The following translation of the list was provided by Dr. Lilly Cheng. There are 20 items listed at the top and 20 items at the bottom with the quantity indicated below each item.

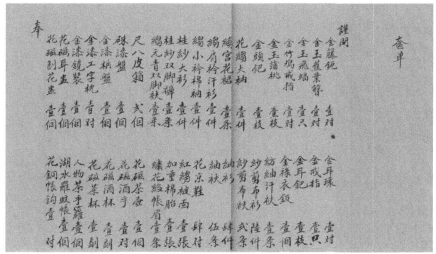

1903 List of gifts for the bride shipped from China.

Top – quantity 1 for all items except for 7th item which has two

Left to Right

1. Porcelain flower pot with flowers, used for make flower pot -1

2. Beautiful porcelain soup bowel with two handles

3. Lacquer with gold in a frame

4. Lacquer pillow – so special – gold with words on it, shape of a word, very special pillow worth a lot of money

5. Gold lacquer special display tray, beautiful Wow!

6. Lacquer made with a special red paint

7. One foot plus 8 inches of a leather suitcase. (quantity 2)

8. Pants – one for inside liner the other for outside. One of special mud silk, the other of wrinkled silk, very special kind of silk, mud silk only from Canton. Mud Silk - Ancient Process

9. Special mud silk made into a large women's top, wide top, very nice

10. Small vest with cotton material,

11. Wool sweater knitted,

12. Palatial design, flowery skirt, embroidered

13. Embroidery top, beautiful.

14. Special decoration for hair made of gold, beautiful

15. Gold and jade pin

16. Ring gold with small little good luck chicken

17. Gold Jade special design of a flying bat pin (bats are good luck)

18. Gold and jade special hair pin with banana leaf design

19. Golden vine

20. Two Characters on Right slightly higher: "We respectfully show you these beautiful gifts."

Bottom

Left to Right

1. Flowery hooks made of copper for bed screen.

Cantonese use beautifully designed hooks for the screen.

2. Same hooks but made in the shape of a watery lake waay

3. Special tea tray with people design

4. Tea cup, porcelain with beautiful design

5. Wine goblet made of porcelain china

6. Wine vessel

7. Tea pot beautiful

8. Screen totally embroidered - very fancy

9. Heavy duty cotton for Chinese quilt, double duty quilt

10. Red cover for quilt

11. Handmade embroidered shoes with flowers.

12. Short sleeves Long Sleeves-

13. Short and Long sleeves – just embroidered sleeves, border 5 sets

14. Pants made of special silk, 2 pairs

15. 6 tops

16. Sleeveless summer top 1

17. Gold pin for clothes 1

18. Gold earring 1 set

19. Gold ring 1

20. Gold earring 1 set

462   RUSSELL N. LOW

Letters from Salem Businessmen

```
STATE OF OREGON  )
                 )  ss.
COUNTY OF MARION )
```

        I, the undersigned being first duly sworn, depose

and say that I was well and personally acquainted with

Mr. Hop Lee, now deceased, and his wife Hong Hop Lee.

That Mr. Hop Lee during the year 1904 was engaged in the

laundary business in the City of Salem, Oregon. His place

of business being very close to mine. And I do positively

know that ELSIE HOP LEE was born on the 25th day of

November 1904.

        That the said Elsie Hop Lee was the first born child

of Hop Lee and Hong Hop Lee.

R J Hendricks

Publisher Oregon Statesman
since 1884

Subscribed and sworn to before me this 12th day of August,1927.

Notary Public for Oregon

My commission expires May 10, 1931.

Robert J. Hendricks affidavit is support of Elsie Hop Lee.

Robert J. Hendricks was the owner, managing editor, and publisher of the Oregon Statesman from 1884-1928. Both Hop and RJ Hendricks were in there 20s when they arrived in Salem in the early 1880s. The newspaperman and the laundry magnate-hop grower had a friendship that lasted for four decades.

—*ele*—

The relationship with the Bush and Ladd Bank facilitated Hop's purchase of the six hop farms between 1904 and 1914. Vice President Walton and A.N. Bush became good family friends and business associates.

Even after Hop died in 1925, Kay continued his relationships with the business community of Salem, Oregon. Hop's long-standing dealings with the Ladd & Bush Bank and with the Bush family continued. Kay sent Vice President Mr. Walton and A.N. Bush and his family Thanksgiving, Christmas, and Birthday gifts, including turkeys, chickens & eggs, fruit cakes, fruit cakes, cream, and cakes. A.N. Bush sent handwritten thank you letters to Kay until his 87th birthday. After that year, he dictated the letters but always signed them himself.

From
A. N. BUSH
Salem, Oregon

1942
Jan. 27th

Dear Mrs Stop Lee:-

I learn at the house that your jar of Cream was very fine and used to Make me a cake and my dessert at dinner the night of the 25th = They are sorry that they did not tell me where it came from. I thank you very much for the gift. The cake and dessert were good. I hope that some time I may be able to return the favor.

Yours truly

A. N. Bush

A. N. BUSH
PIONEER TRUST BUILDING
SALEM, OREGON

SALEM, ORE.
JAN 6
Wd—3.0
1945

CENTENARY
OF THE
TELEGRAPH
3¢
UNITED STATES POSTAGE

Mrs K. Hop Lee Low.
236 West Euclid Avenue,
                Stockton,
                    California.

PIONEER TRUST COMPANY
        SALEM, OREGON   Jan. 5- 45

A. N. BUSH

Dear mrs Hop Lee Low:- We Thank you for your
fine cake. we had it on our table Christmas
day and it was Enjoyed by our guests. among
them was miss Sally Bush todo remembers you
She had Some finer to say about it- We sent
you today some boxes of candy which we
hope will please you. Salem is larger
than it was your day, here, but many of
The old people are gone-
    I hope all goes well with you.
            Yours Truly
                A. N. Bush.

A. N. BUSH
PIONEER TRUST BUILDING
SALEM, OREGON

SALEM, OREG
JAN 19
7-PM
1948

UNITED STATES POSTAGE
3 CENTS

1022½ "P" St.
Sacramento   4632 Pleasant Ave.,
Calif.   Los Angeles 33,
                       California

Mrs Jay Hop Lee,

PIONEER TRUST COMPANY
SALEM, OREGON—Jan. 19. 48

A. N. BUSH

Dear Mrs Hop Lee:

I received to-day a fruit
cake from you, for a birthday present.
I thank you. It is a fine gift.
And I will cut it on my ninety-
th birthday next Sunday when
I am to have a birthday dinner.
It is nice of you to remember
me and thus bring up memories
of our days of the past.

Yours truly,

A. N. Bush

List of Salem Friends Who Sent Flowers to the Hop Lee Family August 1925

Mr. and Mrs. Jos H Albert	Albert	Capital National Bank Cashier
Mr. and Mrs. JH Baker	Baker	Dairy Farmer
Mrs. G Baptec & Jeanie	Baptec	
Mrs. Theodore M Barr	Barr	Plumbing and Heating Bus 50 years
Marie Bolinger	Bolinger	Soprano
June and Wilson Breithaupt	Breithaupt	CF Breithaupt – Largest Salem Florist
Mr & Mrs Hew & Josephine Bross	Bross	Josephine Willamette Glee Club
Mr. and Mrs. AL Brown	Brown	
Clifford W. Brown	Brown	Broker Capitalist Hops & Wool
M Wm Brown & Company	Brown	Boots, shoes, and leather goods
Mrs. Bruner	Bruner	
Mr. & Mrs. SJ and Iris H Butler	Butler	Executor
June A Chadwick	Chadwick	Widow Stephen A Chadwick 5th Governor of Oregon
Miss Margaret Cosper	Cosper	50 years Salem Public Schools
Mr. and Mrs. JC Clearwater	Clearwater	Liveryman – Brother AL Clearwater
Mrs. Al "Lon" Clearwater	Clearwater	Livestock buyer, livery stables
Mr. & Mrs. Frank Geo Deckebach	Deckebach	Marion Creamery Produce Co.
Mr. & Mrs. Walter A Denton	Denton	Prominent Salem Businessman
Mistress HN Eley	Eley	Hiram N Eley Const & Building 40 yrs.
Mrs. Nathan B Elliott	Elliott	Printer
Mrs. Emma G Engdahl	Engdahl	Born Sweden 1862
Mrs. CE Figmond	Figmond	
Mr. & Mrs. Thomas K Ford	Ford	Loan Broker – Bert and Loretta Ford
Mr. & Mrs. Frazier	Frazier	
Helen and Ed Gatke	Gatke	
Esther Gibbard	Gibbard	Father- Arthur E Post Office Super of Mail
Mrs. Gow	Gow	FG Gow Onion Grower Lake Labish
Mr. & Mrs. Ralph Glover	Glover	Oregon Statesman cashier
Miss Annette Graber	Graber	Graber Brothers Plumbing
Mrs. JS Graham	Graham	First Baptist Church
Lee Hing – Wing Gin and Adams	Hing	Chinese Hop man
Mr. & Mrs David & Francis Hodge	Hodge	1862 Canada. Logging Farming
Mr. and Mrs. Ernst Hofer	Hofer	Publisher Capital Journal
Mr. and Mrs. Walter T. Jenks	Jenks	Willamette Prune Association

Hop's Friends who sent flowers in August 1925.

Mrs. Jentenbein	Jentenbein	Prune Grower
Mr. HA Johnson	Johnson	Lawyer
Mr. and Mrs. Paul D Johnson	Johnson	Clothing merchant
Mr. and Mrs. EH Kennedy	Kennedy	196 W Washington
Ladd & Bush Bank	Ladd & Bush	Bank
Loo Ying	Loo	Hop's Loo relative
Saun Lee Louie	Louie	Lunch stand / Hop grower
Mrs. Gustav Maag	Maag	Pastor German ME Church
Mr. & Mrs. Jam Mc Evoy	Mc Evoy	Mc Evoy Brothers Store
Mrs. AW McConnell	McConnell	
Mrs. John McCourt	McCourt	John McCourt Assoc Justice Supreme Court
Mr. & Mrs Robert McKinnie Hofer	Hofer	Capital Journal
Mr. and Mrs JA Mills	Mills	481 N Winter
Mrs. B. Mundigen	Mundigen	
Jung Oie	Oie	
Jean & Earl Pearcy	Pearcy	Earl Marion County Fruit Inspector, Hortic Soc Pres
Miss Alma Pohle	Pohle	School teacher
Rigdons	Rigdons	Rigdon Mortuary
Miss Alice Ritter	Ritter	
Mrs. Charles Roth	Roth	Policemen – Classical musician
Mr. & Mrs Mark H Savage	Savage	Dairy farmer
Mrs. Frank Elmer Shafer	Shafer	Fire Dept Chief / Harness Shop 170 S Commercial
Mrs. E Sigmund	Sigmund	
Mr. and Mrs. George F Smith	Smith	St Elmo Restaurant on Commercial
Mrs. G. Steiner	Steiner	Tinware Steiner & Blosser/Berger
Mrs. William H Steinhoff	Steinhoff	
Suey Sing Tong	Suey Sing Tong	Chinese Tong
SL Sun and Family	Sun	Suey Lai Sun 1894-1983
George Sun and Family	Sun	"Mayor of Chinatown"
Mr. and Mrs. Don H Upjohn	Upjohn	Gladiolus bulbs, Capital Journal, 1st Woman Lawyer
Mr. and Mrs. HH Vanderwert	Vanderwert	Pacific Fruit & Canning Co. Stock Buyer
Mr. and Mrs. BF West & Family	West	Stockbroker 435 N Winter
Mrs. Lenta Westacott	Westacott	Lenta Stolz – Strong's Restaurant
Mr. and Mrs. H Wie	Wie	
Mr. and Mrs. Otto J Wilson	Wilson	Wilson Buick
Miss Otto Wilson	Wilson	Daughter of Otto Wilson
Dr. Yick	Yick	Chinese herbalist

Hop's Friends who sent flowers in August 1925.

Ha Chun Chong Village

Nineteen-year-old Hop Lee left the Low ancestral home in 1877. Located on the southern coast of Toishan in Guangdong Province, *Ha Chun Chong* was the home of seafaring people comprised of fishermen and explorers. The Chinese character *hoi*, meaning ocean or sea, repeatedly appears in the names of relatives in the family tree or jiapu, a clear indication of their affinity with the sea. Since these ancestors were seafaring, they likely gave offerings to *Mazu*, the Chinese sea goddess and a protector of fishermen and sailors.

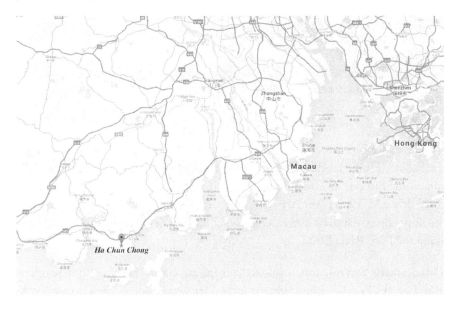

The Loo family jiapu traces 22 generations of the Loo clan. Until the eighth generation, the Loo family originally lived in Zhu Ji Lane, Nanxiong 500 km to the north. In 1272, the eighth generation moved to Ha Chun Chong village in Toishan as part of a mass exodus of the entire population of Nanxiong. The invading Mongols had conquered China, destroying cities and killing tens of thousands of Chinese with the ruling Southern Song Court, administering the

Coastal waters near Ha Chun Chong Village. Low Family Collection.

conquered regions. According to local history, the Song Court's favored beautiful concubine, Hui Fei, offended the Song Prime Minister. Fleeing the court, the concubine hid out in Zhu Ji Lane. Upon discovering her whereabouts, the angered Prime Minister planned to kill the entire population in retaliation. To avoid the impending massacre, all 97 families of Zhu Ji Lane fled south to Guangzhou along the Pearl River Delta

This dramatic and romantic story is the inspiration for a famous Chinese opera. Hop Lee, aka Loo Yao Hing, was from the 15th generation of the Loo family. As he wrote in his journal in 1877, he was Loo Sai Wing's son and Loo Man Bing's grandson.

Migration of Loo Family from Zhu Ji Lane to Ha Chun Chong Village in 1272.

In May 2016. I visited *Ha Chun Chong* village, bringing photographs of the Salem, Oregon, Low family back to the village that Low Sun Fook left in 1877. This trip was a homecoming for my grandfather, who chose to remain on his farmland rather than have his bones shipped back to China. Ultimately, the journey also connected me to a place and people I had never known. While the tour guides in Guangzhou insisted that I could not possibly be Chinese, the faces in that village looked like my father and me. I closely resembled my seafaring ancestors and modern-day relatives in that Loo village. Over a thousand years, these seafaring explorers' mixing of genes, cultures, and cuisine has created the unique blend that is who we are.

Low Ancestral Shrine Ha Chun Chong Village 2016. Low Family Collection.

About the Author

Our connections to the past are not always obvious. Yet, those connections define where we come from, who we are, and where we may be going.

Russell Low was born into a family intimately associated with the history of the American West. However, growing up in Central California, his life was more connected to hamburgers and sports than Chinese American history. His connection to the past was born out of a fascination with a treasure trove of old family photos. Many were from the

Russ Low. Photograph by Ken Fong

early days of black and white photography. Uncovering the stories behind these photographs became a decades-long passion whose fruits became the series of Three Coins novels.

Russell used skills he had honed as a physician, researcher, and educator in the search for these stories. Applying these skills to historical research uncovered previously unknown dramas involving human trafficking, kidnappings, romance, hop farmers, laundrymen, and war heroes.

Low's storytelling takes us on a journey beginning with a nine-year-old slave girl who struggled to find freedom and romance. The three Chinese coins she threw into the water on her trip to Gum Saan in 1880 touched off a string of events that changed her life. Across decades and multiple generations, these ripples continue to change the world in ways she could never have imagined.

The "All American Crew" tells the story of Ah Ying's grandsons, Stanley and Loren, in the Pacific during WWII. The saga begins by reconnecting Stanley to his family's beginnings in America at the Presbyterian Mission Home in San Francisco. His transformation from a Chinese American boy, not yet old enough to vote or drink beer, to a B-24 Liberator nose gunner is set against the lives of the other nine American men, who are his crew members. Along the way, Stanley experiences loneliness, his first beer, his first romance, and the horrors of war. His older brother, Loren, joins the Aviation Engineers and builds the runways that the Liberators and fighters will need to win the war in the Pacific. The connections between these brothers and the events and people of WWII form the foundation of this third novel in the Three Coins series.

Avengers, Wildcats, and Crickets expands the World War II saga through the vivid memories of a man who lived through the battles in the Pacific Air War. Andy Winnegar's views of the war from a TBM Avenger torpedo bomber provide a rare personal perspective that assures unmatched accuracy.

The research and writing now continues with a return to the Chinese American communities of San Francisco and Salem, Oregon, in the 1800s. There are so many more stories to explore and preserve for future generations.

Russell lives in La Jolla, California, with his wife, artist Carolyn Hesse-Low. Their family celebrates art, creativity, and exploration of things past and present. You may learn more about the author of "Three Coins," "The All-American Crew," "Avengers, Wildcats, and Crickets," and "A Willow Tree Becomes a Willow Forest" at https://www.russlow.com/.

Bibliography

1.Branting, Steven D. Lost Lewiston, Idaho: Elegies and Bygone Places. The History Press 2014.

2. Chang, Iris. The Chinese in America. A Narrative History. Viking 2003.

3. Corbett, P., & Corbett, N. The Chinese in Oregon, c. 1870-1880. *Oregon Historical Quarterly, 78* (1), 73-85. 1977.

3. Farkas-Ah, Tye Lani. Bury my Bones in America. Carl Mauitz Publishing 1998.

4. Fitzgerald, K, Straus K, and Pine K. Searching or Salem's Early Chinese Community. (2021) Oregon Historical Society;122(4):456-484.

5. Frankin, Phillip L. STAGECOACH. Book one. Wells Fargo and the American West. Simon & Schuster Source 2002.

6. Hsu, Madeline Y. Dreaming of Gold, Dreaming of Home: Transnationalism and Migration Between the United States and South China, 1882-1943. Stanford University Press 2000.

7. Landeen, Dan and Pinkham Allen. Salmon and His People: Fish & Fishing in Nez Perce Culture. Confluence Printing 1st edition 1999.

8. Lee, Erika. At America's Gates. The University of North Carolina Press 2005.

9. Liestman, D. Nineteenth-Century Chinese and the Environment of the Pacific Northwest. *The Pacific Northwest Quarterly, 90 (1), 17-29. 1988*

10. Lossner, Ann. Looking Back. People and Places in the Early Keizer Area. 1990.

11. Lossner, Ann. More Looking Back at People and Places in Keizer and its Vicinity.1995.

12. Low, RN. Three Coins: A Young Girls Story of Kidnappings, Slavery and Romance in 19th Century America. 2019.

13. McKeown,, Martha Ferguson. Come to Our Salmon Feast. Portland: Binford & Mort Publishing 1959.

14.McKeown, Martha Ferguson. Linda's Indian Home. Portland: Binford & Mort Publishing, 1956.

15. McNary of Fir Cone. Life Magazine August 12, 1940. P 83.

16. McWhorter, Lucullus Vsirgil. Yellow Wolf: His Own Story. Caxton Press. 2008 First printing 1940.

17. Minnick, Sun Sylvia. Samfow: The San Joaquin Chinese Legacy. Panorama West Publishing 1988.

18. Nokes, R Gregory. Massacred for Gold. The Chinese in Hells Canyon. Oregon State University Press 2009.

19. Pfaelze,r Jean. Driven Out: The Forgotten War Against the Chinese Americans. Random House 2007.

20. Renag, Putsata. Bitter Harvest. Chinese farm workers helped Oregon establish its reputation as an international beer capital. Oregon Humanities. The Harvest. https://www.oregonhumanities.org/this-land/stories/bitter-harvest/.

21. Siu, Paul CP. The Chinese Laundries: A Study of Social Isolation. New York University Press 1987.

22. West, Elliott. The Last Indian War. The Nez Perce Story. Oxford University Press 2009.

23. Wong, Kristin and Wong Kathryn. Fierce Compassion. The Life of Abolitionist Donaldina Cameron. New Earth Enterprises 2012.

24. National Archive Immigration Interviews Kay Low, Elise Hop Lee Low, Bill Hop Lee Low, and Isabel Hop Lee Low, 1925-1939.

25. Tracy, C. Race, Crime and Social Policy: The Chinese in Oregon, 1871 – 1885. *Crime and Social Justice, (14), 11-25. 1980.*

26. Wong, M. R. *Sweet Cakes, Long Journey: The Chinatowns of Portland, Oregon.* 2004.

Also By Russ Low

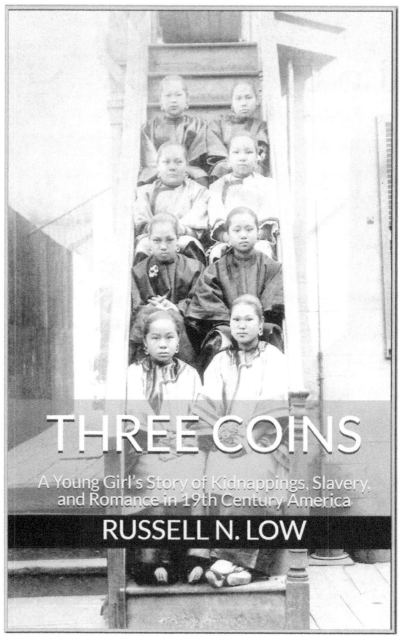

Three Coins - A Young Girl's Story of Kidnappings, Slavery, and Romance in 19th Century America.

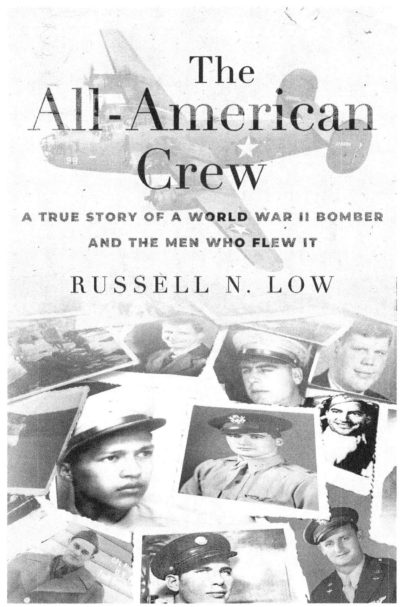

The All-American Crew: A True Story of a World War II Bomber and the Men Who Flew It.

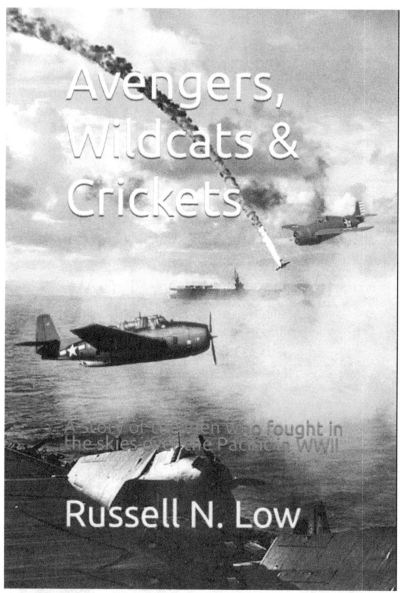

Avengers, Wildcats, & Crickets - A Story of the Men Who Flew in the Skies Over the Pacific in WWII.

Made in the USA
Las Vegas, NV
13 October 2023

79038617R00272